"Did you forget so [...] asked.

"No, I just figured I'd see a lady to her door," Daniel replied.

"I'm not a lady, I'm your boss," she retorted with a smile.

"I have a terrible confession to make," he said as they reached her small front porch.

She pulled her house key from her purse and looked at him cautiously. "A confession?"

He nodded. "I have to confess that from the moment my new boss showed up I've wanted to kiss her."

"You kissed me last night on the forehead." Warmth filled her cheeks as she thought of that tender kiss.

"That's not the kind of kiss I'm thinking about," he replied, and took a step closer to her.

She was playing with fire and she knew it but was unable to help herself. "Then what kind of kiss have you been thinking about?" she asked, her heartbeat speeding up.

"[...] and sla [...]"

"Did you tell him something?" Olivia asked.

"No, I just squeezed it to get rid of the crick," Hazel replied.

There it is, Olivia thought, and smiled with relief.

"I have a terrible toothache though. It's still as bad as the first time I felt it."

She pulled the house's thin blue door with her hand, and it opened while groaning.

He smiled as he approached, and that made the woman in the shop looking up to check the time.

You lifted your chin again on the wet bed. I'm sure that was all. Let me see them there ...

"Poor me, I feel old too," Olivia thinks aloud, and regains calm at the touch of his hand.

She was leaning in, watching the screw turn as she tried to fix herself. "Peace of mind ... Maybe ... I'm finding your blood, I told you, but now ... I'm here waiting for an answer."

"... this, kind." He pulled her into his arms and tilted his lips down to hers.

SCENE OF THE CRIME: WHO KILLED SHELLY SINCLAIR?

BY
CARLA CASSIDY

First Published in Great Britain 2016
By Mills & Boon, an imprint of HarperCollins*Publishers*
1 London Bridge Street, London, SE1 9GF

© 2016 Carla Bracale

ISBN: 978-0-263-91894-6

46-0216

Our policy is to use papers that are natural, renewable and recyclable products and made from wood grown in sustainable forests. The logging and manufacturing processes conform to the legal environmental regulations of the country of origin.

Printed and bound in Spain
by CPI, Barcelona

Carla Cassidy is a *New York Times* bestselling author who has written more than one hundred books for Mills & Boon. Carla believes the only thing better than curling up with a good book to read is sitting down at the computer with a good story to write. She's looking forward to writing many more books and bringing hours of pleasure to readers.

Chapter One

Daniel Carson sat at the small desk in the Lost Lagoon sheriff station. The blinds at the windows were pulled shut, giving the office complete privacy. Outside the small glass-enclosed room, the sound of the other men in the squad room created a low buzz of constant conversation.

They would all be discussing the arrival of the new sheriff, one appointed by the state attorney to take over and root out any corruption in the department until new elections could be held in the small town.

It had been almost a month since the former sheriff, Trey Walker, and Mayor Jim Burns had been arrested for drug trafficking and attempted murder. They had been moving their product from the swamp lagoon through underground tunnels to Trey's house where it was trucked out of the state. The scandal had rocked the tiny Mississippi swamp town.

As deputy sheriff, Daniel had stepped into the position of interim acting sheriff, a job he'd never wanted and couldn't wait to end.

She should be arriving at any moment. Sheriff Olivia

Bradford, sent here from Natchez. Daniel knew nothing about her, but he expected a pit bull, a woman who not only had the ability to fire anyone at will, but who also had the power of the bigwigs of the state behind her.

It was no wonder the men were anxious to meet their new boss—anxious and more than a little bit apprehensive. Heads would roll if she found anything or anyone she didn't deem appropriate for the department. Everyone was concerned about their jobs.

Daniel checked his watch. Ten minutes after ten. He'd been told she would arrive around ten. He was probably the only one in the building who couldn't wait for her to arrive.

He leaned forward in the chair, unfastened the sheriff badge from his shirt and placed it on the top of the desk. He whirled it like a top. The spinning motion mirrored the dizzying chaos the drug scandal and the near murder of Savannah Sinclair and Daniel's best friend, Deputy Josh Griffin, had unleashed inside his head for the past month.

The newly discovered tunnels that ran beneath the entire town were still being mapped and explored by a team of volunteers under the supervision of Frank Kean, a former mayor who had stepped back into the official position when Jim Burns had been arrested. Eventually a special election would vote in a new mayor and sheriff, but not until Sheriff Olivia Bradford conducted a full investigation.

Daniel stared down at the sheriff badge. He'd be glad to give up his position of authority and return to the squad room as just another deputy. He much preferred being in the field rather than stuck behind a desk.

He became aware of the absence of conversation through the closed office door. The men in the squad room had apparently fallen silent and that could only mean one thing. Sheriff Olivia Bradford had arrived.

A firm knock fell on the office door and then it opened and she stepped in. His mind refused to work properly as he got his first look at the woman.

Lily. His head exploded with memories of a woman he'd met five years ago at a crime conference in New Orleans, a woman he'd wound up in bed with for a single night of explosive sex.

Her dark chocolate eyes widened as she gazed at him. She froze, as still as a sleeping gator on a log. It was obvious she recognized him, too.

She cleared her throat, turned and closed the door behind her and when she faced him again, her pretty features were schooled in a business-like coolness. "Sheriff Daniel Carson?" she asked.

"Former sheriff now that you've arrived," he replied and got up from the desk. Okay, so they were going to pretend that they didn't know each other. They were going to act as if that night five years ago hadn't happened.

"I'm Sheriff Olivia Bradford," she replied, a statement that was unnecessary.

"And you're here to take over for me." He pointed to the badge on the desk. He walked around the desk and she made her way behind it and sank down.

She hadn't changed much in the time since he'd last seen her. Her dark brown eyes were still pools of mystery and her long black hair was caught in a low ponytail at the nape of her neck.

That night it had been loose and silky in his fingers and her eyes had glowed with desire. The khaki uniform she wore couldn't hide the thrust of her breasts, her slender waist or her long shapely legs.

Tangled sheets, soft skin against his and low, husky moans, the memories tumbled over themselves in his brain and he desperately tried to shove them away.

She sat down and motioned him into one of the two straight-backed chairs in front of the desk. As he sat, she grabbed the badge from the top of the desk and pinned it onto her breast pocket.

When she looked at him once again her eyes were flat and cool. She appeared the consummate professional. "I've been filled in about the issues with the former sheriff and mayor. I'm sure you have heard that my job here is to clean up any further corruption that might linger in the department. I also would like to go through any crime records for the past five years or so, since Trey Walker was sheriff."

"I'll see to it that you get whatever you need," he replied. It was as if he was having a little bit of an out-of-body experience as he tried to process the woman he'd known intimately and briefly before and the woman who now sat across from him.

"I hope my taking over doesn't stir up any resentment with you."

He laughed drily. "Trust me, I couldn't wait to get rid of this position. I never had any desire to be sheriff. It was just something that got thrust on me due to unforeseen circumstances."

"Good, although my job here isn't to make friends with anyone." She spoke the words with a slight upthrust of her chin. "I don't know how long I'll be here, but my basic job is an internal investigation into both the way crimes were handled under Sheriff Walker and to look at the current employees and see if there are more bad players in the department."

"I'm sure you'll find that most of us are all working on the same page," he replied. Throughout the years, had she ever thought about that night with him? He'd certainly been haunted off and on with memories and wondering whatever happened to the passionate woman he'd met in a bar.

He noticed the gold wedding band on her finger. So, she was married. A faint disappointment winged through him, surprising him. He had no interest in marriage, and certainly that single night they had shared hadn't grown into any kind of a relationship with her.

She was his boss now, and both the wedding ring on her finger and the coolness in her eyes let him know the brief encounter he'd shared with her wouldn't absolve him from intense scrutiny in her investigation. Not that he would ever mess around with a married woman and not that he expected to be treated any differently from any of the other men.

They'd had a one-night hookup years ago and hadn't

seen each other again. Hell, he hadn't even known her real full name. He'd only known her as Lily.

"I'd like to have a meeting with all the deputies at two this afternoon. Could you arrange that for me?" she asked, breaking into his wayward thoughts.

"Yes, I'll see to it that all of the men are here at that time. We have a nineteen-man work force. In the meantime, do you want me to start gathering the crime files? I'm assuming the employment records are in there." He gestured to a nearby file cabinet.

"Yes, please get me the files. I don't want to waste any time." She stood and walked to the file cabinet and Daniel took that as a dismissal.

He left the office and closed the door behind him. Half a dozen pairs of eyes were staring at him. He ignored them all and walked over to the desk where he had sat a month ago as a deputy.

As he eased down in his chair, several of the other deputies surrounded him. "What's she like?" Deputy Josh Griffin asked.

"She looked like a mean witch when she walked in," Ray McClure exclaimed. "A great-looking mean witch," he added with a smirk.

Daniel held up a hand to silence any further questioning from any of them. "If you thought she was going to be a soft touch because she's a woman, get that thought right out of your head. I suggest you all be on your toes and conduct yourselves as professionals. My gut feeling is that she's going to be tough as nails and none of us are secure in our jobs."

It was a sober group of men who returned to their desks. Daniel stared down at his blotter, still trying to process that Olivia Bradford was the young woman he'd known for a night as hot, sexy Lily.

He pulled his cell phone out of his pocket. He had calls to make to the men who weren't in to let them know a full staff meeting had been called for two that afternoon.

After that he would be busy pulling files from the small room dedicated to files and evidence in the back of the building.

While he was completing these tasks, he had to figure out a way to forget that he'd ever known, even briefly, a sexy, passionate woman named Lily.

OLIVIA GRABBED THE employment files for the men on the force and then sank back down at the desk. She'd nearly lost it when she'd walked into the office and seen that man again.

Daniel. She'd never expected to run into him after all these years. Shock still washed over her as she thought of the handsome dark-haired, green-eyed man.

That night in New Orleans she'd been a twenty-five-year-old deputy who had lost her partner and good friend in a shoot-out the week before. She hadn't wanted to attend the conference but her boss had insisted that it would be good for her to get away from Natchez and her grief.

She'd kept to herself during the four-day event, venturing out to a bar near the hotel only on the final night in town. She hadn't been looking for company. She'd wanted only to drown her grief in margaritas and then return to the hotel to pack and prepare to leave early the next morning.

She hadn't expected Daniel to sit next to her, and she certainly hadn't anticipated finding succor for her grief in his arms. It had been a foolish, impulsive night, and hopefully he had no idea how the unexpected sight of him had shaken her to her very core.

She shoved away thoughts of Daniel and instead spent the next hour focused on the employment records for the eighteen men and one woman who comprised the law enforcement in Lost Lagoon, Mississippi.

Most of the deputies had been born and raised in Lost Lagoon, although there were a few who had been hired in from other towns. There were no disciplinary notes, nothing to indicate that Trey Walker had endured any issues with any of them.

But Trey Walker had proven himself to be a crook and a lowlife, and she didn't trust his record keeping. At noon she pulled out a chicken salad sandwich that her mother had made for her before she'd left their rental home that morning.

Although Olivia had arrived in town two days earlier, she'd spent those days turning a renovated shanty on the swamp side of town into a livable space for the duration of her stay.

The place had come partially furnished, but Olivia had pulled a trailer behind her car, which had carried the extra furnishing and personal items to make their stay here as comfortable as possible.

She'd just finished her sandwich when a knock sounded on the door. She called for the person to come in and Daniel entered carrying a box. He set it on her desk.

"That's the files on all the crimes that have occurred for the last five years," he said.

She eyed the box dubiously. "That's it?"

He cast her a smile that instantly shot a spark of heat in her. She'd forgotten about that sexy smile of his. "We're a small town. Except for the last couple of months, there's been very little crime in Lost Lagoon."

She looked back at the box, unwilling to hold eye contact with him while that smile still lingered on his features. "That would be a daily box for Natchez."

"You aren't in Natchez anymore. I got hold of all the officers and they will be here at two for a meeting."

She finally glanced back up at him. "Thank you, I appreciate the cooperation."

He nodded and then left the office. She stared at the box and then set it down next to the desk. She'd take it home with her to look at thoroughly that evening. In the meantime, she had to gather her thoughts for the meeting that was to take place in a little more than an hour.

The responsibility that had been placed on her shoulders was heavy, and she was aware that many eyes would be on her work here. She wasn't afraid of hard work and she didn't worry about the scrutiny.

She had worked long and hard to climb the ranks in

the Natchez Sheriff Department. She'd taken on cases nobody else wanted, worked harder and longer than anyone one else and had garnered not only a stellar reputation, but also dozens of honors and awards.

She wasn't about to let this temporary stint in Lost Lagoon ruin her reputation. She would do her job here and do it well.

It was exactly two o'clock when she stood in the front of a conference room where nineteen deputies sat in chairs before her. She wasn't nervous—rather, she was determined that all of the men would not only respect her, but also fear her just a little bit.

There was only one female deputy and she sat in the front row. According to the employment records she was forty-three-year-old Emma Carpenter and had worked as a deputy for the past ten years.

"Good afternoon," Olivia began briskly. "As all of you probably know by now, I'm Sheriff Olivia Bradford and I'm here to ferret out any further corruption that might be in this department. Consider yourself on notice that I'll be looking not only at your work performance here but potentially investigating your personal lives, as well."

Her words were met with a grumble of discontent. She ignored it. As she had told Daniel earlier, she wasn't here to make friends.

"Over the next couple of days, I'll be meeting with each of you individually," she continued.

"Looking for snitches," a voice in the back muttered.

She identified the man who had spoken as a small,

wiry officer with ferret-like features. She stared at him for a long, uncomfortable moment, until he broke eye contact with her and looked down at the floor.

"I'm not looking for snitches. I'll be getting input from each of you on how to make this department run more efficiently and I'll also be looking for anyone who isn't working in the best interest of law enforcement." She was aware of the warning in her voice and she also knew her tough words wouldn't make her the most popular person in the room.

Her gaze fell on Daniel in the second row. As deputy sheriff he would have worked closely with Trey Walker. Was he the upright, moral man she'd like him to be, or did he hide secrets that would put them at odds?

Time would tell. She'd already identified ferret-face as a potential troublemaker, and she had a feeling by reading Emma Carpenter's body language that the woman was potentially a suck-up, probably assuming since they were both women they'd share some kind of special relationship.

When Olivia put on her badge, she was neither male nor female, she was simply an officer of the law. She didn't like suck-ups and she definitely didn't like troublemakers.

She finished the meeting by instructing everyone to go about their business as usual and then returned to her office and closed the door.

For the next couple of hours, Olivia continued to study the background checks and any other pertinent information that was in the files about the men and the one woman who would be working for her.

It was her task to find out if any of those lawmen had also been involved in the drug-trafficking scheme. It was hard to believe that Trey Walker and Jim Burns had acted all alone, but it was possible nobody in the sheriff's department had known anything about it. She hoped that was the case. There was nothing she hated worse than a dirty deputy.

Even as she tried to stay focused on the paperwork in front of her, visions of Daniel intruded again and again, breaking her concentration.

She was still stunned that fate had brought them together again. Thankfully, he hadn't mentioned the night in New Orleans when they'd sat in the bar and talked about jazz music and Mardi Gras. She'd seen him before at the conference, so she knew he was a lawman somewhere, but neither of them had talked about where they worked or where they were from.

They'd had drink after drink and hadn't mentioned crime or their work. Their conversation had been superficial and flirtatious, just what she'd needed to escape the grip of nearly overwhelming grief.

What happened after they'd left the bar and gone to his hotel room had been crazy and wild and wonderful, but she'd left town early the next morning never dreaming that she'd ever see him again.

It was just after five when she decided to call it a day. She wanted to spend most of the evening going through the box of files that should hold not only information about the recent arrests of Trey Walker and Jim Burns, but also any crime investigations that had occurred under Walker's watch.

She grabbed her purse and the box and headed out of the office. She had only taken a couple of steps into the squad room when Daniel jumped up from his desk and took the box from her. "I'll carry it to your car," he said.

"Thanks," she replied. Tension filled her. Did he intend to mention that night once they stepped out of the station and were all alone? She didn't want to talk about it. She didn't even want it mentioned. It had been an anomaly and had nothing to do with who she was or had been.

He led her to the back door of the building that would open up on the parking lot. "Have you gotten settled in okay here in town?" he asked as they stepped outside and into the late August heat.

"I've rented one of the renovated places along the swamp, and, yes, I'm settled in just fine." She walked briskly toward her car.

"Have you had a chance to look around town?"

"Not really, although I did meet with Mayor Frank Kean yesterday and he assured me his full cooperation while I'm here. I'm hoping to do some sightseeing in the next day or two." They reached her car and she opened the passenger door to allow him to set the box inside.

"The Lost Lagoon Café is a great place to eat, but I'd stay away from the diner. George's Diner is actually just a hamburger joint, but if you want really good food then I'd recommend Jimmy's Place. It's a bar and grill that serves great food."

"Thanks for the information, but I will probably eat at home most of the time."

He placed the box in the passenger seat and she closed the door and hurried around to the driver door. "I'll see you in the morning," she said and before he could say anything else she slid into the seat and closed the door.

As she pulled away, she glanced in her rearview mirror. He stood in the same place, a tall, ridiculously handsome man watching her leave.

She'd been instantly attracted to him when they'd met in the bar and she was surprised to realize that after all this time she was still attracted to him.

She squeezed the steering wheel more tightly. No matter how attracted she was to Daniel and he to her, nothing would come of it. There was too much to lose.

Her tension eased the moment she pulled into the short driveway in front of the small bungalow-type house. It was painted a bright yellow, not only setting it off from the green of the swamp land behind it, but also making for a bit of cheer among the row of ramshackle and deserted shanties that lined the street. Only a few of the shanties had been renovated and appeared like gems among the others.

She got out of the car and went around and grabbed the box from the passenger seat. She hadn't even made it to the door when it opened and her mother smiled at her.

Rose Christie had been a godsend over the last couple of years. Olivia had always been close to her mother, but their relationship had deepened when Olivia's father had died of an unexpected heart attack seven years ago.

Rose opened the door wider to allow Olivia to walk into the tiny living room that held the futon where Olivia slept, an upholstered rocking chair and a small television.

The kitchen area was little more than a row of the necessary appliances with room for a small round table and chairs.

Olivia had just set the box of files on the top of the table and taken off her gun belt, which went on the top of one of the kitchen cabinets, when a squeal came from one of the two bedrooms. Olivia crouched down and braced herself as a dark-haired, green-eyed four-year-old came barreling toward her.

"Mommy, you're home!" She threw herself into Olivia's awaiting arms.

Olivia pulled her daughter close enough that she could nuzzle her sweet little neck. "Ah, nothing smells better than my Lily flower."

Lily giggled and hugged Olivia tight. "Silly Mommy, Nanny's sugar cookies smell better than a flower."

"Not better than my Lily flower," Olivia said as the two broke apart. "Come sit and tell me what you did today."

Olivia and Lily sat side by side on the futon while Rose bustled in the kitchen to prepare dinner. "I played dolls and then Nanny and I watched a movie."

As Olivia watched and listened to her beautiful

daughter relay the events of her day, her heart swelled with love.

Unexpected and unplanned, Lily had added a richness, a joy in Olivia's life that she'd never expected to have. She was bright and more than a little precocious, and now Olivia couldn't imagine her life without Lily.

By eight thirty dinner had been eaten, Lily's bath was complete and she was in bed in one of the two bedrooms. Olivia's mother had retired to the other bedroom, leaving Olivia alone with a box of files and conflicting thoughts she'd never believed she'd have to entertain.

She'd never thought the day would come when she'd meet the man who had fathered Lily. She'd never considered what she might do if she did run into him again.

Daniel.

She was his boss and he was the father of her child. Should she tell him about Lily or should she keep the secret to herself? What was the right thing to do for everyone involved?

She didn't know the answer.

Hoping the right answer would eventually present itself to her, she opened the box of files and pulled out the first one.

Chapter Two

Daniel had spent a restless night plagued by dreams of New Orleans and the passionate woman who'd come with him back to his hotel room from the bar. He'd finally awakened before dawn and after a shower and two cups of coffee, he thought he was prepared to face the woman who was now his boss.

Lily had only been a dream, but Olivia Bradford had already shown herself to be a formidable figure. Daniel wasn't afraid of her digging into his professional or personal life. He'd never even taken a free cup of coffee from the café in his position as deputy and as temporary sheriff. He had nothing to hide, but there were several deputies he knew who didn't hold themselves to the same standards.

Olivia appeared to be the type who would leave no stone unturned both in her internal investigation and any others that might present themselves, due to Trey Walker's dictatorial style and lack of real investigations during his reign as sheriff.

Daniel arrived at the station at six forty-five ready for roll call at seven o'clock. He was unsurprised that

Olivia was already in the office. He had a feeling that she was the type of woman who wouldn't abide anything but strict punctuality.

Apparently, the men knew that, too. Even the deputies who had often been stragglers to roll call were all present, uniforms neat and eyes clear.

Five deputies worked the day shift and then five worked the evening shift until midnight, then five more were on duty from midnight until eight in the morning. The extra four worked shifts when the others had days off.

Daniel had worked the night shift until he'd become sheriff and then had changed to the day shift. He assumed he would continue his day shift even now that Olivia was here.

At precisely seven the five men working the day shift were in the conference room and Olivia walked in. Today she was clad in a pair of black slacks, a crisp white short-sleeved blouse with her badge pinned to the blouse's pocket and her gun belt around her waist.

Her hair was pulled back and her makeup minimal. She held a file in her hand. "Good morning," she said. "The first thing I'd like for you to do is stand up one at a time and state your name."

Daniel stood up first, followed by Josh Griffin, Wes Stiller, Ray McClure and Malcolm Appleton. Daniel and Josh were particularly close, having been friends for years, and they had worked together to bring down Trey and Jim.

Once they had all introduced themselves, Olivia held

up the file in her hand into the air. "I spent most of the night going through criminal file records for the last five years and one in particular captured my attention."

Daniel knew immediately which file she held in her hand. It was woefully thin and unsolved. Guilt immediately pooled in his gut as he and Josh exchanged a quick glance.

"Who killed Shelly Sinclair?" Olivia's question hung in the air for a long, pregnant moment before she continued. "This is a two-year-old unsolved murder case and as far as I can tell, very little was done at the time of her murder in the way of an investigation." She placed the file down on the table in front of her.

"That's because at the time of the murder we knew who had committed it," Ray said. "Bo McBride killed Shelly. He was her boyfriend at the time."

Olivia frowned. "Then why isn't the case closed?"

"We couldn't find the evidence necessary to make the arrest," Wes said.

"Is there another file someplace? What I have here surely doesn't contain all of the interviews and statements of people who might have been involved in the case." Olivia's dark eyes radiated confusion as she looked at each of the men.

"A good solid investigation was never done," Daniel said as the guilt knot in his gut twisted tighter.

"I don't understand," Olivia replied.

"That's because you weren't working for Trey Walker," Josh added. Daniel knew Josh had suffered just as much guilt as Daniel had with the way the case had been shunted aside. "Trey had made up his mind that Bo was guilty and he made it clear that any of us who wanted to investigate further did so at the risk of our jobs."

Olivia's lush lips pressed together in a sign of obvious disapproval. "You have an unsolved murder that's now become a cold case and a shoddy investigation at best at the time the murder occurred. We're going to reopen this case and get it solved. Daniel, I'd like to see you in my office and the rest of you get back to your usual duties."

"What a waste of time," Ray grumbled when Olivia had left the room. "Everyone knows that Bo did it. It's not our fault that we couldn't prove it."

"Not everyone is so certain that Bo was responsible," Josh replied.

That's the last of the conversation Daniel heard as he left the room to head to Olivia's office. He was glad that she was being proactive in the case of Shelly's murder. The unsolved case had been like a stain on Daniel's soul for far too long.

He knocked on the door and then entered the office where she gestured him into one of the chairs in front of her desk.

"I read what little was in the file, but I want you to tell me about Shelly Sinclair and her death," she said.

Daniel nodded and tried to school his thoughts. The scent of a lilac-based perfume filled the air. He hadn't noticed it yesterday, but he remembered it from the night they had hooked up in New Orleans. He had found it dizzyingly intoxicating then and it still affected him on some primal level.

"Daniel?"

Her voice yanked him out of the past and to the present.

"Sorry…yes, about Shelly. She was found floating in the lagoon at the south end of town. She'd been strangled. The area has a bench and some bushes, and from the scene it appeared some kind of a struggle had ensued. Her purse and phone was found on the bench, but her engagement ring was missing and has never been found."

"Now tell me about Bo McBride."

Daniel shifted positions in his chair, oddly disappointed that her eyes held nothing but professional curiosity about a crime. Of course, that was how it should be. A married woman shouldn't be interested in the five years that had passed since a hot hookup had occurred.

"At the time of the murder, Bo owned the place that is now Jimmy's Place. Bo and Shelly had been a couple since junior high school and it was just assumed that eventually they'd get married. They often met at the bench by the lagoon late at night before Shelly started her night shift working as the clerk in The Pirate's Inn. When Shelly wound up dead it was only natural that Bo would be one of the prime suspects."

"And from what I read in the file, his alibi was that he was at home sick with the flu on the night that Shelly was murdered."

"And the last text message on Shelly's phone was

from Bo telling her he was ill and couldn't meet her that night," Daniel replied.

Olivia shuffled through the few papers that were in the file. "And no other suspects were pursued? All I see in here are interviews of Shelly's sister, Savannah, her brother, Mac, their parents and a couple of Shelly's friends. Is there anything more you can tell me that isn't in this file?"

"Several things have come to light in the last couple of months. Shelly told some of her friends that she was in a sticky situation, but we never managed to figure out what that meant. While we were investigating the attacks on Shelly's sister, Savannah, we discovered that Eric Baptiste had become friendly with Shelly right before her death, a detail we never knew during the initial investigation."

Olivia held up her hand to stop him. "I'm already confused by names and incidents I know nothing about. Obviously you can't completely update me in a brief talk right now." She frowned thoughtfully. "What I'd like you to do is head up a four-man task force and focus efforts on starting this investigation all over again from the very beginning."

"I'd be glad to do that. I always felt like Bo was an easy scapegoat and the crime wasn't investigated right from the start. Is there anyone in particular you want on the task force?" he asked.

She shook her head, her dark hair shining richly in the light flooding in from the windows behind her desk. "You know the men better than I do and you know who you'll work best with. I just want go-getters, men who want to work hard and close this case with a killer behind bars."

She narrowed her eyes. "I want this cleaned up before I leave here."

There was nothing of Lily in the hard-eyed woman seated across from him. "We'll get it cleaned up," he said, hoping his words of confidence would somehow soften her features.

They didn't. Instead, in an effort to get a small glimpse of the woman he'd briefly known, he changed the subject. "I couldn't help but notice the wedding ring on your finger. I'm glad that you found somebody important in your life."

She stared down at the band for a long moment and then looked back at him, her eyes shuttered and unreadable. "I got married to a wonderful man, had a daughter and then last year he died. It's just my mother, my daughter and me now."

"Oh, I'm so sorry." That's what you get for trying to take the conversation to a personal level, he thought.

She frowned. "I'm not the first young widow and I won't be the last. What's important to me now is my family's well-being and my work. And now, don't you have a task force to pull together?" She raised a perfectly arched eyebrow and glanced toward the door.

Daniel beat feet to the door and it was only when he was back at his desk that he processed what he'd just learned about her. She wasn't married. She was a widow.

Although he was sorry that she'd lost her husband, he wasn't sorry that she was single. Right now the night they had spent together was like a white elephant in the room whenever they were alone together.

Sooner or later he was going to bring it up. He was going to have to talk about it. Sooner or later, as crazy as he might be, he hoped that just maybe there might be a repeat of that night in their future.

OVER THE NEXT two days, the task force was pulled together and assigned to work from a small conference room in the back of the building.

Daniel had chosen Josh Griffin, Wes Stiller and Derrick Bream as his team. It was obvious the men had a good relationship and equally obvious, as Olivia had observed the deputies over the last two days, that Daniel was a natural-born leader. All of the men respected and looked up to him.

Olivia had spent most of the two days interviewing the deputies who worked for her and finishing up going through case files of crimes that had been handled by Trey Walker.

Daniel had been right; for the most part other than during the last couple of months, Lost Lagoon had been relatively free of any serious crimes. Oh, there had been the usual domestic calls and shoplifting… Petty crimes that had been resolved immediately.

She'd arrived in her official capacity on Monday morning and by Wednesday evening she had learned that everyone in Lost Lagoon seemed to move at a slower pace than anywhere else in the world. She'd discovered that the town was rich in pirate lore and that a new amusement park being built on a ridge just above the town had the business owners excited about new commerce.

It was after seven when she packed up to leave to go home. She'd already called her mother to tell her to go ahead and feed Lily and get her ready for bed.

She was surprised to leave the office and see Daniel at his desk. She'd assumed he'd gone home at four when he was off duty.

"I thought you'd have left by now. Don't you have a family to get home to?" she asked.

He reared back in his chair, looking as fresh and alert as he had that morning. "No wife, no family and no desire for either. I'm a confirmed bachelor," he said. "I assume you're headed home?"

"Eventually, but before that I want to go to the scene of Shelly's murder. I haven't really gotten out and about town much and I just want to get a feel for where the crime took place."

Daniel frowned. "I'd rather you not go there by yourself. How about I drive there and you follow me? I can give you a better idea of what things looked like on that night."

"I can't ask you to do that," she protested.

"You didn't. I offered. Besides, it's my job to assist you." He stood as if it were settled. "I was ready to knock off for the night anyway."

Minutes later Olivia followed behind Daniel's patrol car toward the south end of town. They traveled on Main Street, and as she drove she glanced at the various businesses that lined the streets.

So far she'd only gone from the station to her home on the west side of town. She hadn't ventured into the heart of Lost Lagoon. On one side of the street she noticed an ice cream parlor and made a note to be sure and visit it with her mother and Lily. Lily loved ice cream.

Lily. If she'd been conflicted at all about telling Daniel that their night of passion had resulted in a daughter for him, her conflict had been resolved when he'd said he had no desire for a wife or a family and that he was a confirmed bachelor.

She focused back on her surroundings. On one corner a shop held a large sign that indicated it was Mama Baptiste's Apothecary and Gift Shop and further down the road was a two-story hotel named The Pirate's Inn. In between were shops catering to tourists, a dress boutique and Jimmy's Place where the parking spaces in front of the three-story building were filled with various makes and models of vehicles.

Olivia's stomach rumbled as she thought of all the people inside enjoying a meal. She'd skipped lunch that day and although she knew Rose would have kept something for her to zap in the microwave for dinner, her stomach was ready to be fed as soon as possible.

While they continued on, the buildings ended and Main Street joined an outer road that she knew circled around the entire town.

Olivia followed him onto the outer road and then

when he stopped and pulled to the curb, she did the same. On the opposite side of the road in the near distance was a row of bushes broken only by a stone bench.

Daniel got out of his car and she followed suit. Here the smell of the swamp was thick in the humid air. The scent of tangled musty foliage battled with a fishy smell, and the humidity was thick enough to cut with a knife.

Daniel joined her by the side of her car. "Bo worked the night shift at Bo's Place and Shelly worked the night shift at The Pirate's Inn. Before she went into work, Bo often sneaked away and the two of them would meet here for a few minutes before they each returned to work."

"So Shelly showed up that night, but according to the message that she got from Bo, he didn't come." Olivia stared at the bench where a young, beautiful woman had spent the last minutes of her life. Who had met Shelly here in the middle of the night and strangled her to death then threw her body in the nearby lagoon?

They crossed the street. Beyond the bushes and the stone bench was a grassy area that ran from one edge of the swampy growth to the other side, and beyond that the lagoon water sparkled darkly in the waning sunlight.

"No evidence was found?" Olivia asked.

"The bushes on the left side of the bench were trampled down, indicating that the struggle occurred there, but we didn't find anything in the way of evidence." His voice held a wealth of frustration.

"From the minute I read this file, I've been haunted by her," Olivia said softly.

"You aren't the only one. I've spent two years with her ghost haunting my dreams, begging for justice. In the last year, Shelly's sister, Savannah, kept her sister relevant by dressing up like a ghost and walking on the grassy area just in front of the lagoon."

Olivia looked at him in surprise. "Really?"

"On Friday nights teenagers would gather and hide behind the bushes, waiting for the ghost of Shelly to appear. Savannah used a tunnel that runs from her backyard to the base of a tree." He pointed to the right of the grassy area where a cypress tree rose up. "She'd wear some gauzy white dress with a flashlight tied to her waist beneath to give her a ghostly glow. She'd walk across to the other side where a cave led back to the tunnel that would take her home."

"Why would she do such a thing?" Olivia asked, wanting to know all the ins and outs of this case.

Daniel shoved his hands in his pockets and stared at the dark lagoon water. He appeared haunted, his eyes fixed in the distance and his posture one of faint defeat.

"When Shelly was buried, Savannah's parents moved away and left her and her brother, Mac, the family house. Mac married and moved out soon after that. According to Shelly, she wasn't allowed to speak of her sister, either to her parents or to her brother. She did her ghostly walks to hear the teenagers behind the bushes gasp and shout out Shelly's name. It was her way of keeping her sister alive."

He pulled his hands from his pockets and turned back to gaze at Olivia. "Thankfully, Josh caught on to what she was doing and with his love she's healing. But she needs closure. She needs her sister's killer behind bars to fully embrace the life she's building with Josh."

"Tomorrow I'd like you to go with me to interview Bo McBride. I know small towns and that often people are hostile or suspicious of strangers. I think I'll get more answers if you're with me."

Daniel nodded. "Just tell me when and I'll be glad to go with you."

Olivia walked forward and sat on the bench, as if she could somehow pick up something from the horror of the crime that had happened so long ago.

It was darker here, the sinking sun unable to penetrate the shadows formed by the swamp vegetation and the trees with thick Spanish moss dripping from their branches.

Daniel sat next to her. His spicy cologne was familiar as it wafted to her. It wasn't just a familiar scent she'd noticed over the last couple of days, but one she remembered from a night that shouldn't have happened. It was a night that should have been erased from her memory bank long ago.

"Tell me about Bo McBride," she said in an effort to keep away memories that had no place in her head.

"Bo was one of the golden boys in town. He was liked and respected by everyone. He was handsome and had a beautiful girlfriend. His business was extremely successful and at least on the surface it appeared he had the world by the tail."

"Do you think he killed Shelly?"

His features were dappled by shadows and his eyes glowed silvery green in the falling of twilight. They had glowed like that when he'd taken possession of her body. Darn it, she had to stop remembering him naked and filled with desire for her.

He raked a hand through his thick short hair and leaned back against the bench. "Do I think Bo killed Shelly? My gut instinct is that he didn't."

"And how good is your gut instinct?"

He grinned at her, his perfect white teeth flashing bright. "Better than most, but in this case I guess time and more investigation will tell us if it's on the money."

"Who found her body? I didn't see anything in the report."

"An early morning jogger named Tom Dempsey. Tom is sixty-seven years old and jogs at odd times of the day and night. It was four in the morning when he saw Shelly floating in the swamp and called it in. Thankfully, we managed to retrieve her before any gators or other wildlife got to her."

Olivia had been involved in many homicide cases in Natchez, but for some reason the case of Shelly Sinclair was hitting her hard. She rose from the bench, not wanting to sit another minute in this place of death.

Daniel stood, as well. "I have a favor to ask you," she said as they walked back to their cars. She paused and gazed up at him. "I've been watching the way you interact among the men and it's obvious they look up to you. What I need to know is if I can trust you completely?"

She held his gaze steadily. She might be making a mistake, but she needed somebody on the inside, somebody who had worked closely with the other men in the department.

She had no real reason to trust Daniel. A single night in bed certainly wasn't the basis to build trust on, but her gut instinct told her he was the one man in the department who was an upright, by-the-book lawman.

"Of course you can trust me completely," he replied. The earnestness in his eyes comforted her.

"Then what I'd like to do is meet you for coffee one evening soon at the café and have a talk about some of your fellow officers," she said.

He frowned. "I'd really rather not do that at the café where people can see us together or might overhear the conversation. I don't want the men to think I'm being a snitch."

"Of course, I didn't think about that."

"Why don't you follow me to my place now and we can talk privately there?"

Olivia thought about all the questions she had about some of the deputies. "Okay," she agreed a bit reluctantly.

It was only when she was back in her car and following him to his place that she thought this might be a bad idea. First and foremost she was running only on a gut instinct and his word that he was trustworthy.

More important, she feared that in the privacy of his

home he might bring up that night they'd shared five years ago, a night she'd spent the last five years trying desperately to forget.

Chapter Three

He'd been vaguely surprised when Olivia had agreed to come to his home to talk, but as he pulled into the driveway he punched the garage door opener that would open both sides of the double garage and she apparently understood that he intended for her to pull in next to him.

No need for anyone to see her car parked outside his house. It was one thing for them to be seen together in an official capacity, but another altogether for them to be together in their off-duty hours.

The last thing she would want was any kind of gossip to start up about her, and there was no reason to invite it by being careless at this point in time.

When she was parked inside and out of her car, he punched the button to close the doors behind them. "Call me paranoid," he said when they were both out of the cars. "I just think it best if people don't know we have any kind of a relationship outside of work hours."

"I appreciate it and I agree."

When he opened the door that led from the garage into the kitchen, he was grateful that by nature he was a neat and tidy man. He didn't have to worry about errant boxers dangling off light fixtures or beer bottles lined up like soldiers awaiting a trip to the trash. He gestured her to the round oak kitchen table and then moved to the counter to make a pot of coffee.

"Nice house," she said as she sat. "Big for a man who told me he has no desire for a wife or a family."

"Thanks, it really is more than I need but it was a foreclosure and I couldn't resist the great price. It needed a little cosmetic TLC, and I've managed to finish it all up."

The coffee began to brew and he turned and leaned against the cabinet to face her. "Don't worry, I didn't buy it with ill-gotten gains."

"That never crossed my mind. From reading the records, I know that you and Josh Griffin were instrumental in the arrest of Trey Walker and Jim Burns."

"It was mostly Josh. Savannah had been attacked and Josh hunted through the underground tunnels to see if he could find any evidence. What he found was an entrance that led up to Walker's garage filled with meth."

"So you trust Josh."

"With my life," he replied easily. "He and I are not only fellow deputies, we're also close friends." He had the ridiculous impulse to walk over to her and pull off the clasp from the nape of her neck that held her beautiful long hair captive.

He turned back to the cabinet and pulled out two cups. "Cream or sugar or both?" he asked.

"Just black is fine," she replied. "What about Emma Carpenter? Is she a good deputy?"

It was obvious this private meeting was just as she'd indicated it would be, an opportunity for her to pick his brains about his coworkers. He poured their coffee and then joined her at the table.

"Emma is a hard worker. She's thoughtful and meticulous and I'd trust her under any circumstances."

Olivia cupped her hands around her coffee mug. "I'm just trying to get an idea of the people who work here for the department. The employment files were relatively inadequate as far as any notes of discipline or commendations anyone might have received."

"For the most part we're a good team," he said.

"For the most part..." she echoed with a raise of a dark brow.

Daniel sighed. "I don't want to believe that any of the other officers had anything to do with the drug-trafficking issue."

"I sense a *but* on the end of that sentence."

He smiled ruefully. "But there are a couple of men I don't completely trust."

She leaned forward and he caught a whiff of that lilac fresh spring scent that had once driven him half-mad with desire for her. It still affected him on a visceral level, evoking unwanted memories of the night they'd shared.

"Who don't you trust?" she asked.

He watched her lips move and remembered the fiery kisses they'd shared. He mentally shook himself and focused on the topic at hand. "I don't want you to think that I'm some kind of snitch, but you do have a right to know potential problems within the department."

She took a sip of her coffee, her eyes dark and unfathomable over the rim of the cup. "Give me names," she said as she lowered her cup back to the table.

"Ray McClure. He was very close to Walker, but insists he had no idea what was going on when it came to the drugs flowing in and out of town. He also seemed particularly eager to point a finger at Bo for the murder of Shelly."

"I'd already identified him as an issue," she admitted. "He's lazy and borders on insubordination. Do you think he might have had something to do with Shelly's murder?"

"I doubt it. I think he was just following Trey's lead in proclaiming Bo guilty in order to please Trey and to not have to do the work of a real investigation."

"Who else?"

Daniel thought of all the men he worked with on a daily basis. "Randy Fowler isn't somebody I'd trust to have my back. He works the night shift and he recently moved his mother into a fairly pricey nursing home in Jackson. He'd bitched about the cost for months before he moved her, but now suddenly he's not complaining anymore."

"Was he particularly close to Walker?"

Daniel shook his head. "Not that any of us noticed, but he and his wife were friendly with Jim Burns."

"Is there anyone else that you can think of?"

"Not really. I've worked with these men for years,

and in most cases I grew up with them. Ray McClure is a local. He was a surly and lazy kid who never changed. As far as Randy Fowler goes, he isn't a local, but was hired in from Tupelo about six years ago. He keeps himself a bit distant from the other men."

He took a drink of his coffee and eyed her intently. "Are we ever going to talk about that night in New Orleans?"

She froze and a faint pink color filled her cheeks. "I was hoping we wouldn't."

"I think we need to. I feel like there's a snapping gator between us in the room every time we're together," he replied.

She took another sip from her cup and carefully set it back down on the table. "That night in New Orleans was completely out of character for me. I had recently lost my partner to a domestic altercation gone bad. I didn't want to be at the conference in the first place. I went to the bar to be alone and drown my grief in booze."

"And then I showed up."

For the first time since the day she'd arrived at the station in her official capacity, she smiled. The beauty, the memory of that smile punched him in the stomach.

"Yes, and then you showed up and you were charming and easy to talk to and suddenly you looked better than the booze." Her cheeks flamed a deeper pink. "It was a wild, crazy night that shouldn't have happened."

"Why did you use the name Lily?" he asked.

"My mother called me Lily from the time I was a little girl. Mom's name is Rose and she always told my father he had two beautiful flowers in the family. But it didn't take me long working in law enforcement to realize that people took me far more seriously as Olivia, which is my legal name. So I stopped being Lily and became Olivia and I named my daughter Lily."

"I have to admit I thought about you over the years. I wondered what had happened to you, if your career had taken off and if you'd found love."

Her eyes radiated surprise that was quickly masked. "It was only a month after that conference that I married and then got pregnant immediately. Phil was a great husband and father."

"Tell me more about him." Daniel said, wanting to know what kind of a man had captured her heart.

She leaned back in her chair and her features softened. An irrational stab of jealousy raced through Daniel. "Phil owned a small but successful restaurant. He had a huge heart and he loved me beyond reason. Even after my daughter, Lily, was born, he encouraged me to pursue my career. Along with my mother's help, we made a good team, me working law enforcement and him running his restaurant, and then he had a heart attack and died."

"Are you hoping to marry again?"

"I'm open to the possibility. I had a great husband and I know how good marriage can be, but if it doesn't happen I'm good alone with my mother helping me raise Lily and my career that consumes me."

"How old is your daughter?"

"She just turned four."

"I'm still attracted to you." The words fell from his mouth before his brain had fully formed them.

She cast her gaze away from him and out the nearby window where darkness had fallen. "I'm only here temporarily and I'm your boss. Any kind of a personal relationship between us would be completely out of line."

She looked at her wristwatch and then grabbed her purse. "Speaking of my mother and my daughter, I need to get home." She stood and looked toward the garage door. Daniel had a feeling she was escaping from the conversation rather than simply deciding it was time to go home.

Daniel got up to walk her to the door. "If it's any comfort, nobody knows about that night. I never mentioned it to anyone and have no intention of ever talking about it." He opened the door and punched the button inside to raise the garage door on the side where she had parked.

"I appreciate that. I'm here to do my job, Daniel, and nothing more." She stepped down the stairs to the garage floor and hurried to her car.

When she'd driven out and away, Daniel closed the door and returned to his chair at the table to finish his coffee. At least they'd talked about it, he thought.

However, she'd said nothing to tamp down a simmering desire that had grown inside him from the moment he'd seen her again.

More importantly, she'd told him all the reasons why they couldn't and shouldn't get involved again, but she hadn't said the one thing that would have shut him down permanently.

She hadn't said she wasn't attracted to him and in the omission of those words, he held on to just a little bit of hope that he would have her in his bed once again.

OLIVIA HAD A restless night. Both Lily and her mother had been asleep when she'd finally gotten in. She'd gone into Lily's room and kissed her sweet, sleeping daughter on the cheek and then had zapped a plate of leftover meat loaf that her mother had made for dinner.

By ten thirty she was on the futon, but sleep remained elusive as she played and replayed her conversation with Daniel in her head.

She hadn't wanted to talk about that night. She hadn't even wanted to think about it. She had spent far too many nights while married to Phil thinking about that single night of madness with Daniel.

Phil had been in love with her and she had loved Phil, but she hadn't been in love with him. He was a good, solid man and she'd been the best wife she could possibly be to him during their marriage. But it had been the one-night stand with Daniel that had haunted her dreams.

She was awakened the next morning to kisses being rained on her face and the scent of bacon filling the air. "Mommy, you didn't kiss me good-night last night and so you have to kiss me a zillion times this morning," Lily said. She was a vision of little-girl innocence in her pink cotton nightgown and with her dark hair sleep tousled around her head.

"I think I can manage that," Olivia replied. She grabbed Lily and pulled her onto the futon with her and then proceeded to deliver kisses all over her daughter's face and neck.

Lily's giggles rang out, sweet music to Olivia's ears.

"Okay you two…breakfast in fifteen minutes," Rose said. "Lily, you can help me set the table while your mother gets ready for work."

Olivia took a fast shower, dressed in a pair of tailored black slacks and a white blouse and then joined her mother and daughter at the table for bacon and pancakes.

Breakfast was always a joy when the three of them shared it together. Rose had been a loving, nurturing mother to Olivia and once Lily was born, she'd become beloved Nanny and had watched Lily whenever Olivia and Phil were at work.

Rose was a wonderful mix of common sense and naïveté. She had a good sense of humor and a fierce love of her little family. She believed the world was a good and happy place, and Olivia never brought the evil she worked with home to share with her mother.

Many times over the years Olivia had downplayed the danger she'd faced at work in an effort to protect her mother from worry.

"As usual, a great breakfast, Mom," Olivia said.

"It's always good if it's got syrup," Lily quipped and

used her tongue to capture an errant dollop of the sweet goo that had escaped onto her lower lip.

"Are you going to be late tonight?" Rose asked.

"You'd better be here to kiss me good-night," Lily exclaimed.

"I kissed you while you were sleeping last night. Besides, you know how it works. If I'm not here to kiss you good-night, then Nanny gives you double kisses," Olivia replied.

"And I think I gave her triple kisses last night," Rose exclaimed.

Minutes later Olivia left the house and headed for the station. She hoped the issue of her and Daniel's previous encounter had been laid to rest, for she was depending on him to accompany her as she interviewed some of the key players in the two-year-old murder case of Shelly Sinclair.

So he'd thought about her over the years. His words had surprised her. She'd always figured she'd been nothing more than a slight blip on his radar. A sexy guy like him had to have had plenty of hookups before and after that night they'd shared.

Of course it didn't matter if he'd thought about her or her about him. It didn't matter if he was still attracted to her and she was attracted to him. Nothing would ever come of it.

She wasn't a young, vulnerable woman anymore. In fact, she rarely thought of herself as a woman. She was a mother, but she was also a law enforcement official. She wore those titles much more easily than that of simply a woman.

It was nine o'clock when she and Daniel left the station and got into her car to drive to Claire Silver's small house on the swamp side of town where she lived with her new husband, Bo.

"Bo moved in with Claire when his family home was burned down by the high school coach who had become Claire's frightening stalker. They got married a couple of weeks ago," Daniel said.

"I read the file on Claire's stalker, Roger Cantor," Olivia replied. She'd been grateful that there was no awkwardness between her and Daniel. It was as if their conversation the night before had never happened, and that was the way she wanted it. In fact, the tension between them that had been apparent since they'd first seen each other had dissipated.

Daniel guided her to a renovated shanty much like where Olivia was staying. "They're my neighbors," she said as she pulled her car to a halt in front of the house. "I'm staying five houses down in the bright yellow place."

Daniel had called ahead to let Bo and Claire know they were coming, and Bo opened the door before they reached it. "Daniel," he said in greeting and then held out a hand to Olivia. "Sheriff Bradford, it's nice to meet you."

Bo McBride had a firm handshake and clear blue eyes that appeared as if they wouldn't know how to hide a secret. His dark hair was long and slightly shaggy and his features were well-defined and handsome. "Please, come in," he said and gestured them into a small living room where a petite curly-haired blonde woman stood at their appearance.

Further introductions were made and then the four of them sat at the kitchen table where Claire offered them something to drink and they declined.

"I'm glad you're reopening the case into Shelly's murder," Bo said.

"News travels fast around here," Olivia replied drily.

"The small town gossip mill is alive and well," Bo replied and then frowned. "I was basically run out of town on a rail in the weeks after her death because of nothing but gossip. Sheriff Walker made it clear that I was guilty and it was only because they couldn't find evidence that I was still walking around free. It destroyed the life I'd had here."

Claire placed a hand on Bo's arm. "Bo couldn't kill anyone, especially not Shelly, who he loved with all his heart."

Olivia pulled out a small pad and pen from her purse. "I need you to tell me everything you can about that time. I want names of the people Shelly was close to, ideas you might have as to who might have wanted her dead…anything that will guide us as we dig into this case."

For the next hour, Bo talked about his long-term relationship with Shelly. He was honest about the fact that he wasn't sure if Shelly ever would have married him, that she had longed for a life away from Lost Lagoon.

But, Bo's successful business was here, along with his mother, and he had no desire to leave the small town.

Both Olivia and Daniel asked questions and not once did Olivia get the feeling that Bo was hiding anything from them. He confessed to them that he still owned Jimmy's Place, that at the time of the murder many of his customers had turned away and that was when he suggested to his best friend, Jimmy Tambor, that he take over as manager and rename the place.

For almost two years following Shelly's murder, Bo had built a new life for himself in Jackson, coming back to Lost Lagoon only in the dead of night on the weekends to visit his mother, whose house Jimmy had moved into to help care take of her.

"I came back a couple of months ago when my mother passed away and while I was here I met Claire." He covered her petite hand with his and smiled at her lovingly. "She convinced me to stay in town and fight for my innocence, but then her life was in danger and my sole concern became keeping her safe."

"So, you haven't done much investigating on your own into Shelly's murder," Olivia said.

"If you're asking me if I know who killed Shelly, then the answer is no. I'm no closer to knowing today than I was on the night she was murdered," he replied. "All I know is I didn't do it and I'm as eager as anyone to get the killer arrested." His eyes blazed fervently.

"So, what did you think?" Daniel asked Olivia once they were back in her car.

"I'm mostly a facts-only kind of person, but my gut instinct says that he's being truthful," she replied.

"How about we grab a hamburger at George's Diner before we head back to the station?" he suggested. "It's not too far down the road from here."

Olivia glanced at her watch. It was just after eleven. "All right," she agreed. She'd eat a quick lunch and be back in her office by noon to check in on things there and to write up a complete report on the interview with Bo and Claire.

Daniel pointed the way, and before long she was parked in front of the small building with a huge sign on top that read George's Diner.

"It doesn't look big enough to be a diner," she said as they got out of the car.

"I told you it's really just a glorified hamburger joint. Most people order and take out. There are only five stools at a counter inside. George has everything from fried gator to shrimp scampi on his menu, but most people come here for the burgers. It's a dive but he makes the best burgers you'll ever wrap your mouth around."

The interior of the small establishment was empty and held the gamy odor of the swamp and hot grease. "We'll eat in the car," Olivia whispered, finding the variety of cooking smells unpleasant.

At that moment a big man lumbered out of what she assumed was the kitchen. Jowls bounced as he greeted them with a smile and slapped two menus in front of them.

"I heard there was a new sheriff in town." His deep

voice resembled that of a croaking bullfrog. "George King," he said. He swiped a hand on his dirty white apron and held it across the counter to her.

Olivia shook his hand and mentally thought of the small bottle of hand sanitizer she kept in her purse. "Sheriff Bradford," she replied as she shook his thick, meaty hand.

"So, what can I get for you two? I got some fresh gator meat in this morning," George said.

"No gator," Daniel replied. "We'll take two of your special burgers and a couple of sodas to go."

"Got it." George disappeared back into the kitchen area.

"Did he know Shelly?" Olivia asked.

Daniel smiled. "Everyone knew Shelly. Why?"

"George is a big man with big hands. It would have been easy for him to strangle a young woman and then toss her into the lagoon."

Daniel's grin widened. "Once a lawman, always a lawman."

"Exactly," she replied, wishing his smile didn't create a ball of heat in the pit of her stomach.

Minutes later they were back in her car. She used her hand sanitizer, placed a couple of napkins on her lap and then took the gigantic burger wrapped in foil from Daniel. Daniel, too, had placed a napkin across his lap.

Two beef patties, two kinds of cheeses, tomato and lettuce, bacon and barbecue sauce, the first bite created an explosion of flavor in her mouth.

"Tell the truth, it's the best you've ever tasted," Daniel said with a knowing smile.

She finished chewing and swallowed. "Okay, I admit it."

They ate in silence and when they were finished, Daniel took their trash to a nearby bin and disposed of it and then they were back on the road headed back to the station.

"Still listen to blues music?" he asked.

It had been part of their conversation at the bar, the fact that they both loved old blues classics. "These days my music list mostly exists of 'Itsy Bitsy Spider,' 'The Wheels on the Bus' and any songs from kids' shows. What about you?"

"Still love my Billie Holiday and of course B.B. King," he replied.

They spent the rest of the ride talking about the old masters of blues music. Once they returned to the station, Olivia headed to her office and Daniel returned to his desk.

It sat in the middle of her desk, a brown-wrapped package addressed to her. It didn't belong there and she had no idea how it had gotten there.

She opened her office door and saw Daniel and Josh talking together. "Josh… Daniel, could you come in here?" She hoped her voice didn't betray a faint whisper of fear the presence of the unexpected package had wrought inside her.

Both men got up and when they entered her office she pointed to a brown-wrapped box on her desk.

"That was here when I came in. I didn't touch it, but it doesn't have any postage and it's addressed to me."

Daniel frowned in obvious concern. "How did it get here?"

"I don't know. It was just here," she replied.

"I'll go get Betsy," Josh said. He left the office. Betsy Rogers was the dispatcher/receptionist.

"You weren't expecting any deliveries of any kind?" Daniel asked.

She gave a curt shake of her head. "No, nothing."

"I'll grab my fingerprint kit," Daniel said.

By the time he returned to the office, Josh and Betsy were also there. "It was left just outside of the front entrance," Betsy said. "I don't know how long it was there. Ray noticed it when he came back from lunch and gave it to me and I brought it in here."

"Then you didn't see who left it or how it was delivered?" Josh asked.

"I don't even know how long it was out there," Betsy replied.

Daniel pulled on a pair of gloves and approached the box. It looked fairly benign other than the fact that there was no return mailing address or official mail markings.

Josh and Olivia stood in the office doorway. Was it a bomb? Had she already made enemies she didn't know about? Or maybe it was a welcoming gift from somebody in town. She didn't want to jump to conclusions, but she definitely didn't like surprises.

"It's light," Daniel said. "I don't think it's a bomb or anything like that."

He opened his fingerprinting kit and got to work. Olivia watched as he carefully brushed the top of the box. "Got one here," he said and transferred the print to a piece of tape and then placed it on a card where he wrote where it had been found.

It was a tedious process and Olivia found herself holding her breath. She wanted any fingerprints from the package, but more important, she wanted to know what was inside.

Although it could be something nice, like home-baked cookies or a handmade knickknack with a note inside saying who it was from, she still couldn't shake a bad feeling.

It took nearly twenty minutes for Daniel to finish fingerprinting the entire package. He pulled two different sets of prints from it. "I imagine the prints belong to Ray and Betsy. Their prints are on file so I can easily compare them," he said.

"But the fact that you found no other prints means whoever left it probably wore gloves," Josh said, his words only increasing Olivia's nervous tension. "Open it."

"I'll open it," Olivia said. If there was anything inside that might be harmful, then it was her job to shield her deputies.

Daniel looked as if he wanted to argue with her, but she gave him a stern look and he stepped aside. She tried to keep her fingers from trembling as she carefully removed the brown outer wrapping to reveal a plain white box with a fitted lid.

She removed the lid and sighed in relief as nothing exploded or shot out. Inside was a wad of tissue paper. She pulled it out and stared at the contents, her brain momentarily unable to make sense of it.

A stuffed dark brown dog was in the bottom, its throat slashed and white stuffing spilling out. A folded piece of paper was nestled next to the mutilated toy.

"Let me," Daniel said tersely. He still wore his gloves and he plucked the paper from the box and opened it. In bright red lettering it read: Let Sleeping Dogs Lie.

"I think we can assume from this that Shelly's killer is still here in town," Josh finally said.

"And reopening the case has him shaken up," Daniel added.

Olivia stared down at the note and then at the ripped little dog. She tried, without success, to stop the icy chill that crept up her spine.

Chapter Four

Daniel was ticked off and worried. He'd hated to see the fear that had momentarily filled Olivia's eyes. He also hated the fact that somebody was warning them off the case, for the package contents could only be taken as a warning.

Somebody had moved damn fast, since they'd only officially reopened Shelly's case the day before.

He'd moved the package into the evidence room and Olivia had insisted she was fine and needed to write reports. He'd left her alone in her office and spent the next couple of hours checking out the fingerprints he'd pulled. Just as he suspected, they'd matched both Ray and Betsy.

He'd also talked to Ray, who had spent his lunch hour at the Lost Lagoon Café and had spied the package against the building near the front door when he'd returned.

Part of the problem was that he doesn't know how seriously to take the warning. Was it a direct threat against Olivia? Or was it just some fool thinking it would be funny to shake up the new sheriff?

He definitely intended to err on the side of caution. Apparently, Olivia was on the same page. It was almost four in the afternoon when she called him into her office.

"You doing okay?" he asked as he closed the door behind him.

Her eyes were dark, but her features were more relaxed than they had been before. "I'm fine, but I'm not sure if I should be. I'm not particularly concerned about my own safety, but I am a little worried for my mother and Lily."

"Why don't I follow you to your place after work and I can check things out there for you?" The last thing he wanted was for her to worry about her family.

"Oh, that's not necessary," she protested with a vehemence that wasn't warranted by the situation.

"Humor me," he replied. "I'd feel better if I took a look around."

She didn't appear particularly pleased, but she finally nodded her head. "Okay, I should be leaving here in about an hour."

"I'll be ready," he said and then once again left her alone in the office.

"You worried?" Josh asked as he scooted his chair closer to Daniel's.

"I'm concerned. I don't know whether to be really worried or not," Daniel admitted.

"It could have been just some sort of sick prank," Josh said, but his tone of voice indicated he didn't believe his own words.

"Maybe, but just to be on the safe side I'm heading over to Olivia's place after work to check out the locks she has on her doors and windows. She's not so afraid for herself, but she's concerned about her mother and daughter being safe."

"She has a mother and a kid?" Josh looked at Daniel in surprise. "I figured she was hatched from a bad-ass badge and I definitely didn't figure her for the maternal type."

Daniel smiled inwardly. Although Olivia had only shown herself to be tough and strictly professional while in this building and in Lost Lagoon, he had memories of a much softer, much hotter Olivia in his mind.

"She wasn't hatched and she does have a mother and a little girl here with her," Daniel said.

"Divorced?"

"Widowed," Daniel replied.

"I'm sure she wore the pants in that family," Ray quipped from his desk.

Daniel looked at him with irritation. "Don't you have something better to do than eavesdrop on private conversations?"

"As a matter of fact, I do." Ray got up from his desk. "I'm outta here. I'm meeting a couple of buddies at Jimmy's Place for a few drinks."

"I'd eat my hat if that man ever stayed to the end of his shift," Josh said drily once Ray had left the squad room. "You think he's dirty?"

"Hard to tell." Daniel reared back in his chair. "He was definitely close to Walker, but it's possible Ray really didn't know about the drug trafficking. I mean, let's be honest here—Ray isn't the brightest color in the box, and Trey probably didn't trust him to keep their dirty little secret. If he is dirty, Sheriff Bradford will figure it out."

"Anyone else she looking at closely?" Josh asked.

"Maybe Fowler," Daniel replied, knowing he could trust his friend not to take the information any further. "And that's just between the two of us," he added anyway.

"Randy definitely came into some money from somewhere."

"If there's any dirt in the department, the sheriff will sweep it out. That's what she's here for, but she definitely wants to close out Shelly's case, as well."

"That ripped-up dog was creepy. I hope it was somebody's idea of a sick joke."

A knot of tension formed in Daniel's chest. "Yeah, so do I."

The men got back to work and twenty minutes later, Olivia appeared in the office doorway. "I'm ready to head home."

Daniel stood and together they left the building by the back door and stepped out into the parking area. Olivia always drove her private car to work, but used her official patrol car during the day.

She now headed to her private car, a four-door navy sedan with a child's car seat buckled into the backseat. "I'm sure this isn't necessary," she said. "There are locks on the doors and windows. I just panicked for a minute when I saw that dog and the note."

"Panic isn't a bad thing," he replied easily. "I'd just like to check things out to assure myself that your family is safe and sound when you aren't home."

He realized he didn't intend to take no for an answer. Not only did he want to check the security of the house, he wanted to meet her mother and daughter, see Olivia in the setting of her home and family.

"Knock yourself out," she finally said. She got into her car and Daniel hurried toward his.

Minutes later he pulled up in front of the small bright yellow place where Olivia was living during her time in Lost Lagoon. He jumped out of his car and caught up with her on the front porch.

They scarcely cleared the door when she was attacked by a little dark-haired girl who threw herself at Olivia. Olivia crouched down and grabbed her daughter close, her features soft and loving as she nuzzled little Lily's neck. Her laughter mingled with Lily's.

This was a side to Sheriff Bradford that none of the other men would see—the soft, maternal side that Daniel was surprised to discover he found crazy attractive.

A woman, presumably Olivia's mother, stood at the stove and smiled at Daniel. She was an attractive woman with dark hair and eyes like Olivia's. "Just give them a minute and then we'll introduce ourselves," she said loud enough to be heard over the giggles.

Olivia released her daughter and stood. "Mom, this

is Deputy Carson, and this is my mother, Rose. And this little munchkin is Lily."

"Hey Deputy, you want to see my room?" Lily asked, her green eyes bright with friendliness.

"Maybe in a little while," Olivia replied. "Right now Deputy Carson is going to check out the doors and windows in the house."

Rose's expression turned to one of simmering panic. "Has something happened? Is something wrong?"

"Not at all," Daniel replied smoothly. "Whenever somebody moves into one of these renovated shanties, somebody from the sheriff's department does a sort of well check on the place. You'd be surprised how sloppy and cheap some people are when they renovate."

"How nice," Rose said. She relaxed and Olivia smiled at him gratefully. Her smile, so rare and so beautiful, filled him with warmth.

"I'm just finishing up a big pot of jambalaya and a pan of corn bread," Rose said. "After you do your check, you'll eat with us." Daniel started to protest, but Rose raised a hand to stop him. "It's no extra work and I insist."

"You can put honey on your corn bread, Deputy, and it's really, really good," Lily said.

Daniel smiled at the cute child who looked so much like her mother. "How can I turn down corn bread with honey? And why don't you show me your room? I'd love to see it."

Lily nodded eagerly and grabbed his hand. A new, different kind of warmth swept through him at the feel of her tiny hand grasping his. "Come on," she said. "It's mostly pink."

It was definitely pink—pink bedspread and pink curtains at the window. Lily showed him her princess shoes and her fashion dollhouse. Olivia stood in the doorway, her smile one of bemusement as Lily insisted he sit on her twin bed to see how comfy it was.

Lily was chatty and cute and obviously bright as she continued to give him a tour of everything in the room. He finally walked over to the window and opened it. He then closed it, turned the lock and tried to open it again. It didn't budge.

"Why did you do that?" Lily asked.

"Uh, to make sure when it rains it can't rain inside," he replied. "And now I need to check all the windows in all the rooms."

"I'll help you, Deputy," Lily said eagerly.

Olivia shadowed them as they went into Rose's room where a double bed was neatly made up with a yellow-flowered spread and white gauzy curtains were opened to allow in the late afternoon sunshine.

"Nanny won't get wet," Lily said once they'd tested her window. "If the window let in rain she could always wear a raincoat to sleep in, but that would be silly."

"That would be silly, but now we know she won't have to do that," Daniel replied.

With Lily's help they finished checking every window in the house. All of them locked firmly and the only issue Daniel saw was the locks on the doors.

"You need dead bolts on the doors," Daniel said once

they were all back in the small living room and standing in front of the black futon where he realized Olivia must spend her nights. "I'll head out now to the hardware store and grab a couple and install them."

"Oh, no, I can't let you do that," Olivia protested.

He smiled at her. "You can't stop me from doing that," he replied.

"By the time you get back, supper will be ready to serve and I'm not letting you get out of here without eating a good meal for all of your trouble," Rose said.

Daniel left the house and got back into his car. Although he'd wanted to check the general safety of the house, he was almost sorry he'd come.

Seeing Olivia interact with her mother and daughter had shown him a new dimension to her. He admired and respected Sheriff Olivia Bradford. He'd once lusted over a woman named Lily. But seeing Olivia soft and maternal had reignited a desire for her that wasn't just based in lust.

It was confusing, and he'd never been confused about a woman before in his life.

"He seems like a nice man," Rose said and checked the pan of corn bread in the oven.

"I like Deputy," Lily said. "I think you should marry him and let him be my daddy."

"Honey, his name isn't Deputy. You should call him Mr. Carson," Olivia replied.

Lily shook her head and raised her chin with a hint

of stubbornness. "I like Deputy and he likes me to call him that, too."

Olivia decided it wasn't worth arguing about. "Okay, but I'm not marrying Deputy and he isn't father material."

"He still seems like a nice young man," Rose said.

"He is," Olivia agreed.

"And what a nice thing for the department to do, a sort of well check on these shanties to make sure they're all safe," Rose said.

It was Rose's naïveté that allowed her to even believe such a thing. "I'm going to change clothes," Olivia said, eager to get out of her work clothing and into something more comfortable.

She went into her mother's room where her clothes were stored in drawers and hanging in the closet along with Rose's, but instead of immediately grabbing something to change into she sank down on the edge of the bed and drew a deep breath.

Seeing Daniel with Lily had twisted her heart in ways it had never been twisted before. He'd been so easy, so natural with her. Many nights she had dreamed of what it might be like if the two of them ever met, if they ever knew each other.

But he was a confirmed bachelor and had no desire for children. Nothing could be served by telling him the truth about Lily now. And oddly that broke her heart more than just a little bit.

Lily would never know about her real father. When she got old enough to ask questions, Olivia would tell her about Phil Bradford and how much he had loved his family, how much he had adored Lily.

She got up from the bed and grabbed a pair of denim shorts and a chocolate-colored T-shirt. While she dressed, she thought of that moment when Lily had said that she wanted Olivia to marry "Deputy" and he'd become her daddy.

Olivia had worked with plenty of men in the past, men who Lily had met and spent time with, but she'd never indicated that she was interested in any of them becoming her daddy.

Was it some sort of nebulous blood tie that had made Lily take so easily to Daniel? In the year since Phil had died, she'd occasionally thought about the possibility of remarrying eventually. In an ideal world, she would like Lily to have a strong male presence in her life as she grew up.

But that man wasn't Daniel. And despite the desire she had for a repeat of what they had shared in New Orleans, he would never be her husband and Lily's father.

She dressed and then went into the bathroom and removed the clasp from the back of her neck, allowing her hair to flow free beyond her shoulders. She breathed a sigh of relief as she brushed the long strands. By the end of the day she always had a tiny headache from having her hair so tightly bound.

By the time she left the bathroom, Daniel had returned, sporting two dead bolts, one for each door. They were simple but sturdy slide locks that mounted to the door and frame. He'd brought with him the tools he needed and set to work with Lily watching him and keeping up a running conversation.

Olivia set the table for four while Rose pulled the corn bread from the oven. Within twenty minutes they were all seated at the table with bowls of the southern stew in front of them and big slabs of corn bread sliced and served.

Lily grabbed the bottle of honey and looked at Daniel. "You have to drizzle it, not glob it. That's the best way," she instructed. She drizzled her piece of corn bread and then handed the honey bottle to Daniel. "Now you drizzle, Deputy."

Daniel grinned at Olivia and did as Lily had told him. The scene was so domestic and shot a pang of longing through Olivia. She steeled herself against the warm, fuzzy feeling. This was a moment of fantasy and had nothing to do with reality.

Daniel not only charmed Lily, but Rose, as well, praising her for the tasty food and talking to her about the garden she had back in Natchez. He even encouraged her to share stories about Olivia's childhood, which made Daniel and Lily laugh and Olivia cringe.

She was both slightly disappointed and equally relieved when the meal was finished, and Daniel was ready to leave after insisting he help with the cleanup.

"Thank you for the best meal I've had in months," he said to Rose and then crouched down in front of Lily. "And thank you for showing me your room and especially your princess shoes. They were beautiful."

Lily grabbed him around the neck and then kissed

him on the cheek. Olivia didn't know who was more stunned, her or Daniel. "We like you, Deputy. We hope you come back again," Lily said as she released him.

Daniel straightened up, a stunned expression still on his face. The expression slowly faded and he looked at Rose. "Now that I've installed those dead bolts, you need to use them anytime you and Lily are here alone. This area sometimes has some drunks wandering around." He looked back at Olivia. "Walk me out?"

She nodded and after final goodbyes, she followed him to his car parked along the side of the street. "You have a charming family," he said as they reached his car.

"Thanks, I'm pretty partial to them," she replied.

He frowned. "Olivia, those dead bolts I put on your doors are only temporary stop locks. If somebody really wanted into your house badly enough they could use enough force to get through those locks. I recommend you contact Buck Ranier. He owns a personal security company and could guarantee you a safer environment here."

"I don't want to overreact to what's happened," she replied. "So far all we have is an anonymous warning that I'm assuming is because of reopening the Sinclair case."

"I certainly don't want to scare you, but I also don't want to underreact to that package you got today," he replied, his eyes the deep green of the dark swamp.

"I appreciate you putting in the dead bolts, but I'm not ready to have a full alarm system installed. I don't want to frighten my mother if it isn't absolutely necessary. I just want to get more information about the package and who might have sent it and definitely why. We don't know for sure that it had anything to do with reopening the Sinclair case."

"I'd say it's a good guess that it's concerning the Sinclair case. Besides, we might not get any more information about the package," he replied. "We asked around. Nobody saw it placed where it was found. We've got no fingerprints or postage stamp to work with."

He broke off and reached out and touched a strand of her hair that had fallen forward over her shoulder. "I just don't want to see anything bad happen to you or your family." He grimaced and dropped his hand to his side and stepped back from her. "I'll see you in the morning," he said curtly.

She stood and watched him get into his car and remained watching until the vehicle was out of her sight. That simple, yet inappropriate touch to her hair had stirred her as had his obvious concern for their safety.

She turned to walk back to the house. Daniel had been a deputy here in Lost Lagoon for a long time and he was worried about her and her family. Was she underplaying the danger to herself…to her family?

It had just been a stupid stuffed animal and a note, the act of a coward, she told herself. She wished this assignment was over already.

She wished Shelly's murder was solved and she'd rooted out any dirty officers who might still be working in the department. As much as anything, she wished she hadn't seen Daniel and Lily together.

At least he hadn't asked too many questions about her quick marriage and pregnancy. It obviously hadn't entered his mind that he could possibly be Lily's father.

Still, she now felt threatened not just on a physical level, but on an emotional one, as well.

Chapter Five

"How about lunch at Jimmy's Place?" Daniel asked Olivia the next day at noon. He knew that Olivia had spent the morning combing through old files, looking for errors and checking evidence reports on Walker's reports.

Daniel had been in the small room that the task force had been assigned to work out of for the Sinclair case. If the note and the stuffed animal were, indeed, about this case, then he had a renewed determination to get it solved as quickly as possible.

"That man should have been shot," Olivia said minutes later when she was in the passenger side of Daniel's car and they were headed to Jimmy's Place down the street.

"I'm assuming you're talking about Walker," he replied.

"His files are a mess with half-written or missing reports." She drew in a deep breath as if to neutralize her irritation. "Anything new with the task force?"

"Nothing. Derrick and Wes have interviewed all of Shelly's girlfriends at the time of her murder, but nothing new has come up. Josh has been asking around to see if anyone saw somebody leave the package in front of the building. I suggested Jimmy's Place for lunch because I think it's important that you be seen around town and it's possible we'll run into some suspects there."

"And it will show the creep who sent me that stuffed dog that I'm not backing off." Her voice was firm and strong. There was no hint of the soft woman he'd seen the night before at her place. If he thought about it too long, his fingers would tingle with the memory of her silky hair from his brief touch of it the night before.

He found an empty parking space around the back of the building and together they got out and walked around to the front door.

Jimmy Tambor, Bo's best friend, greeted them. "Sheriff Bradford, it's good to finally meet you in person," he said. "Bo has told me he has a lot of faith that you'll finally be able to put Shelly's case to rest."

"That's the plan," Olivia replied.

"As you can see, we've got a pretty full house, but I've got either a table or a booth still open," Jimmy said as he grabbed two menus off a small hostess table.

"A booth would be good," Daniel said. He much preferred the intimacy of a booth.

"Just follow me." Jimmy led them to an empty booth midway down one wall. He had no sooner moved away when Daniel saw acting mayor Frank Kean, city councilman Neil Sampson and amusement park owner Rod Nixon making their way toward them.

"Incoming," he said to Olivia, who straightened in the seat.

"Sheriff, good to see you," Frank said as the three men stood by the booth. "I wanted to introduce you to two important men in town. City councilman Neil Sampson has been my right-hand man since I was thrust back into office, and Rod Nixon owns the amusement park being built on the ridge."

Olivia greeted each of them and a bit of small talk ensued. "So, how are things coming in the Sinclair case?" Neil asked. "Are you going to catch the bad guy?"

"That's what we all want," Olivia replied.

"Hopefully long before the amusement park opens," Rod said. "We're highlighting a pirate theme, but we wouldn't want people coming here to hear about an unsolved murder case of a young woman."

"We're hoping to capitalize on the underground tunnels in coordination with the amusement park," Neil said. "Paid tours through pirate paths…of course, we'll add some special effects to make it more exciting for the tourists. But, we all want Shelly's case solved. It's been unresolved for too long."

"We're pursuing several leads," Daniel said curtly. The waitress appeared at the booth. "And now if you'll excuse us, we're about to order lunch."

The men moved away and Olivia and Daniel placed their orders with the waitress, then Olivia eyed Daniel with speculation. "Okay, tell me who of those three men you don't like."

He looked at her in surprise. "What? Can you read my mind now?"

She smiled. "I'm beginning to identify your tones and facial expressions."

"That's a little bit scary," he replied with a small laugh and then sobered. "I'm not a big fan of Neil Sampson. He's ambitious to a fault and arrogant and thinks he's God's gift to all females."

"He is a nice-looking man," Olivia said.

"He's a pompous ass," Daniel returned, surprised by the twinge of jealousy that rose up inside him by her words.

They stopped talking as the waitress appeared with their orders. Olivia had ordered mozzarella sticks and a Cobb salad while Daniel had opted for a meatball sandwich and seasoned fries.

"Hmm, I'm going to have to order some of these to take home some evening for Lily," Olivia said after taking a bite of one of the cheese sticks. "Lily would eat mozzarella sticks for every meal if I'd let her."

"She's quite a little charmer, and your mother is also very nice. I enjoyed meeting them both."

"They enjoyed meeting you, too." She grabbed another mozzarella stick. "And now, let's talk about who we need to interview next in an effort to solve Shelly's murder."

The last thing Olivia wanted to talk about was Daniel's visit the night before. Lily had chattered about "Deputy" until she'd fallen asleep, and even Rose had been quite taken with Daniel.

Olivia didn't want him spending any more time with her family. She didn't want to see father and daughter together. The sight of them interacting created a deep ache in her heart that would never be eased.

"I think the next person we should interview is Eric Baptiste. He apparently had developed a friendship with Shelly just before her death. If Shelly wanted a ticket out of town, Eric would have been a good bet. He's got a degree in botany and could probably get a job teaching at some college anywhere."

"And we still need to talk with Mac Sinclair. It's hard to believe a brother might kill a sister, but we both know anything is possible when it comes to murder," Olivia replied.

"Savannah mentioned to Josh that she's secretly been afraid that Mac might be responsible. Apparently, Mac hated Bo and didn't want Shelly with him. Savannah wonders if maybe Mac met Shelly that night and they argued about Bo, and if things got heated and in a rage Mac strangled Shelly."

Olivia took a bite of her salad and considered the theory. "That might explain the missing engagement ring. Even in death he removed the one thing that tied her to Bo."

"Makes a horrible kind of sense," Daniel said. He took a huge bite of his sandwich and washed it down with a gulp of sweet tea. "So, who do you want to talk to after lunch? Eric would probably be the easiest because he should be working at the apothecary shop."

"Then Eric it is," she agreed. "We can plan on talking to Mac tomorrow."

"Sounds like a plan."

They fell silent as they continued with their lunch. Olivia found herself gazing around at the patrons, wondering if a murderer was dining here right now.

They had a handful of suspects, but no real evidence to even know if any one of their suspects should be on a short list. Supposition and conjecture, that's all they had at the moment and it was definitely frustrating.

It's only been a couple of days, she reminded herself. She shouldn't expect results so quickly. She glanced at Daniel, who was also dividing his attention between his food and the other diners.

Every time she looked at him, a memory of the passionate night they'd shared exploded in her head and a ball of simmering desire to repeat that night burned in the pit of her stomach and that was as frustrating as the unsolved crime.

After they ate, they drove down the street to Mama Baptiste's Apothecary and Gift Shop. The minute they entered, Oliva's nose filled with the scent of mysterious herbs and her attention was captured by the plants and strange-looking roots that hung from the ceiling.

Mama Baptiste was a large woman with long dark hair shot through with shiny silver strands. Clad in a bright pink peasant-style blouse and a swirling long floral skirt, she looked free-spirited.

She greeted them with a bright smile, and Daniel made the introductions between the two women. "You know he's one of my favorite deputies," Mama said and grinned.

"She says that about all of us," Daniel replied in a teasing tone. "I'll bet I won't be one of your favorites when you know why we're here. We need to talk to Eric."

Mama's smile immediately fell. "What's this about?" She looked at Olivia. "Every time anything goes wrong in this town, my boy is the first one looked at. It isn't fair. He minds his own business and doesn't look for trouble."

"We're just trying to tie up some loose ends," Olivia said.

Mama heaved a deep sigh and pointed toward the back of the store. "He's in the storeroom."

When they walked toward the back, Olivia saw that Mama didn't just sell whatever concoctions she made from her roots and herbs, but the store also held silly voodoo kits and a variety of crystals and some pirate hats and plastic swords obviously intended for tourists.

Eric Baptiste was a dark-haired, dark-eyed man around thirty. Attractive in a bad-boy, mysterious kind of way, he winced at the sight of them. "What now?" he asked.

"I'm Sheriff Bradford," Olivia said. "I'm sure you've heard that we've reopened the case of Shelly Sinclair's death, and we'd like to do a follow-up interview with you."

Eric raked a hand through his thick, shaggy hair. "Does this mean I need to come down to the station with you?"

"I don't see any reason why we can't just talk here," Olivia replied. She knew from experience that it was easier to get information from somebody who was comfortable in their own surroundings.

Eric shrugged. "Whatever." He grabbed two folding chairs leaning against the wall and opened them, then sat on the top of a large box and gestured her and Daniel to the chairs.

Olivia sat and pulled out her pad and pen from her purse. Daniel also sat and leaned back against the wall, as if content to let her conduct the interview. That was fine with her. She had no preconceived impressions where Eric was concerned.

"I've read the notes from when you were previously interviewed following Shelly's murder. I understand that at the time of her murder you were in your house alone and nobody could substantiate your whereabouts."

Eric's eyes narrowed. "If I'd known that night that Shelly was going to be killed and I'd need an alibi, I would have made sure to have somebody in my bed with me."

Olivia straightened in the chair, not liking the sarcastic tone of his voice. "It's come to light recently that you and Shelly had become quite friendly before her death," she said. She studied Eric intently and saw a brief wash of grief sweep over his features. It was there only a moment and then gone.

"We'd gotten friendly," he admitted. "Sometimes at night when she was working at The Pirate's Inn, I'd visit her to pass some of the night. It wasn't anything romantic or anything like that. We were friends, that's all."

"She never talked to you about the two of you skipping town and heading for big city lights?"

"She talked about moving to a big city, but it was just talk and it never included me. I have no desire to leave Lost Lagoon. My mother is here alone and she isn't getting any younger."

His eyes softened and any sarcasm he might have had before was gone. "I don't have many friends and I enjoyed Shelly's company on occasion. I would never hurt her. I definitely had no reason to kill her."

"Did Shelly know about the tunnels underground?" Daniel asked.

"Not that I know of. I think she would have mentioned them to me if she had known about them."

"Do you have any idea who murdered Shelly?" Olivia asked.

Eric shook his head and his eyes once again went flat and dark. "No, but I wish I did. There's very little kindness in this town, and Shelly was kind and good." He stood. "And now if we're finished here, I've got work to do."

Olivia and Daniel also stood. "Thank you for your time, Eric," Olivia said. "Please let me know if you think of anything that might help in the investigation."

Eric cast her a rueful smile. "I've had two years to think about it. If I knew anything worthwhile I would have already told somebody. She deserves justice."

Olivia asked another handful of questions, but got nothing of substance.

"What do you think?" Daniel asked when they were back in the car and headed down the street to the station.

"I'm not sure," she replied. "I think it's possible he's telling the truth, but I also believe it's equally possible that he and Shelly might have stepped over the line of friendship. He seemed pretty intense about her."

"Shelly mentioned to several of her friends that she had a sticky situation on her hands, but didn't go into any detail with anyone. Maybe the sticky situation was that she found herself in love with two men, Bo and Eric."

"Even if that's the case, we still aren't any closer to knowing who killed Shelly. Eric didn't seem inclined to admit if his friendship with Shelly had developed into something more." She was aware of the frustration in her voice.

"We'll figure it out," Daniel replied, his voice soft, yet filled with determination.

The skies had begun to darken with thick clouds, portending the early evening rainstorm the forecasters had predicted that morning. The dark clouds mirrored Olivia's mood.

She'd hoped Eric would visibly show signs of lying, that he'd slip up and say something self-incriminating, but that hadn't happened.

Now she'd spend the rest of the afternoon working on the internal investigation of the officers in the department, and Daniel and the rest of the small task force would convene to talk about how little they had learned so far.

Once she was in her private office, she found concentration difficult. She could only hope that in Shelly's case things would become clearer after they'd interviewed several more people.

It didn't help that she was spending so much time with Daniel. His very nearness enticed her to throw caution to the wind, to jump into bed with him. She knew he'd be more than willing, that he desired her. She'd seen it in his gazes, felt it like a simmering cauldron between them.

But the last thing she needed was another one-night stand with a man who had no interest in a real relationship. Besides, doing something so foolish would only undermine her authority here.

With grim determination she pulled out several files of the men who worked for her in her search for somebody who had abused their position and potentially committed criminal acts.

It was just after six when she finally pulled her head from her work and glanced out the window, shocked to see that the black clouds had created an early, false night-like semidarkness.

She put away the files and grabbed her purse, hoping to get home before the clouds released a deluge of rain. Daniel was at his desk when she stepped out of the office.

"Calling it a day?" he asked.

"I want to stop by Jimmy's Place and get an order of

mozzarella sticks for Lily and then hopefully get home before the rain starts."

"I'm heading out pretty quickly, too," he replied. "Other than Josh, most of the other day-shift people went home a little while ago."

"Then I'll see you in the morning." She headed toward the back door. She carried no work with her. Tonight she would not think about murder or Daniel.

Lily would be thrilled by the special treat and Olivia planned to spend the rest of the evening just enjoying her daughter and her mother's company.

She stepped outside the door and into the soupy, humid air. The parking lot was in semidarkness, but the few street lights she could see had come on despite the earliness of the evening.

Her car was parked toward the back of the lot. She usually left the parking spaces closer to the building for the deputies. She hurried toward the car, eager to make the stop at Jimmy's Place and then get home.

She had just reached her car's back bumper when she felt a stir of the otherwise still air. She heard the hurried slap of shoes on the pavement, but before she could turn around, something slammed over her head.

Explosive pain…a shower of stars and then she slumped to the ground in complete darkness.

Chapter Six

"At least Savannah will have a home-cooked meal ready for you," Daniel said to Josh as the two walked out the back door. "I'll have to zap something in the microwave and pretend it's home cooked."

"That's the life of a confirmed bachelor," Josh replied with a laugh.

Daniel thought about sharing dinner with Olivia, her mother and her daughter. It had been far too pleasant and had unsettled him a bit. He'd never thought about how quiet and tasteless most of his evening meals were before.

He wasn't sure now if it had been Rose's cooking or the company that had made the meal so entertaining and wonderful.

He frowned as he saw Olivia's car in the distance. Although she had only preceded them out of the building by a minute or two, she should be pulling out of the lot by now.

"I wonder if Sheriff Bradford is having car problems," he said to Josh. "She should have been on her way by now."

"Maybe we should check it out," Josh replied.

Daniel was grateful that the black clouds overhead had yet to weep a single drop of rain. He and Josh drew closer to Olivia's car and that was when he heard the moan, saw her lying prone on the pavement near her back bumper.

"Olivia!" Daniel's heartbeat went wild in his chest as he hurried to her. By the time he and Josh reached her, she sat up, but appeared dazed.

Daniel crouched down next to her. "What happened? Did you fall?"

"No…no. I was hit over the head." She raised a hand to the top of her head and when she dropped it back to her lap it was bloody. Daniel's heartbeat double-timed in rhythm at the sight of the red stain of blood on her fingers.

"I'll go get some other men to scour the area," Josh exclaimed and quickly turned and ran back toward the building.

Daniel pulled his gun and remained crouched by her side. "We need to get you to the hospital," he said urgently.

"No, that isn't necessary. I'm fine. I was only unconscious for a minute. I don't feel sick and I'm not confused. My head hurts, but I'm okay," she said.

"Are you sure?" Daniel split his attention between her and the dark parking lot, his gun ready if more danger came at them from any direction.

"Really, I'm okay."

By that time half a dozen men had burst out of the

sheriff's station, guns drawn and ready to do whatever necessary to protect their boss.

"Split up and check the area," Daniel instructed as Olivia struggled to her feet.

Daniel took her by the elbow and led her away from her car and to his patrol car. He opened the passenger door and insisted she sit. She did so without argument, and that worried him as much as anything.

"Did you see who it was?" he asked.

"No. I only heard the approach of somebody right before I got whacked. I didn't get a chance to turn around to see who was behind me." She reached up and touched the top of her head again and winced.

In the car light she appeared too pale and still stunned. Daniel wanted to kill whoever was responsible. Flashlight beams filled the lot as the men searched the parking lot and surrounding area.

She stared down at her bloody hand. "I can't go home like this. It will totally freak out my mother and Lily."

"Are you sure you shouldn't go to the hospital?" Daniel asked worriedly.

"No, I don't need a doctor," she replied firmly. "Thank goodness I'm hardheaded."

"You can come to my place and clean up," Daniel suggested and ignored her attempt at humor. He found nothing remotely funny about any of this.

"In fact, I think I should take you there now." He gestured toward the men working in the parking lot. "I'll see that Josh stays here and oversees the sweep of the area." He wanted to get her out of here and some-place safe.

She leaned back against the seat as if relieved to have somebody else momentarily in charge.

Daniel reholstered his gun and walked over to Josh. "Can you take care of things here? I'm going to get her away from here and to my place for the time being."

Josh's features were grim in the faint light. "I can't believe anyone would be so brazen as to attack her here at the station." He looked at the men and nodded. "I'll see to it that every inch of this parking lot and beyond is thoroughly searched for anything that might be evidence."

"I knew I could count on you," Daniel replied.

"Always," Josh replied. "Now get her out of here. If we find anything at all I'll call you and let you know."

"Thanks." Daniel headed back to his patrol car, knowing that Josh would do a thorough job. When he reached his car, Olivia had already closed the passenger door and buckled herself in.

Daniel got in behind the steering wheel and looked at her intently. "I'm going to ask you one last time. Do you need to go to the hospital and have your head checked out?"

"And I'm going to answer that question one final time. I'm shaken up and my head hurts, but I don't need a doctor. Trust me, if I was worried about it I would insist you take me to the hospital."

"Then it's off to my place," he said and started the car. She was silent on the drive and Daniel found himself gazing at her again and again, needing to assure himself that she was really okay.

The vision of her lying on the pavement would stay with him for a long time. His heartbeat still hadn't returned to a normal rhythm. They should have taken the stuffed-dog threat more seriously. Dammit, he should have done something differently so this would have never happened.

Seeing her blood on her hand after she'd touched her head had emphasized the fact that by sheer luck alone she hadn't been hit hard enough to be killed.

Daniel gripped the steering wheel more tightly as a burning rage lit up inside him. Had the perpetrator been Shelly's killer afraid of what the reinvestigation might find? Or, even more chilling, had it been a fellow deputy who was threatened by the internal investigation she was conducting?

All he knew for sure was that he would do everything in his power to see that no more harm came to her. When he reached his house, he pulled into the garage and closed the door behind him.

He got out of the car and hurried around to the passenger side to help her out. She still appeared shaken up, and he took her by the elbow to lead her into the house.

Once inside he guided her down the hallway, through his bedroom and into the master bath. He pointed her to sit on the commode while he grabbed a first aid kit from the nearby linen closet.

He opened it on the edge of the sink and grabbed a bottle of hydrogen peroxide and cotton balls. "I want to take a look at your wound. It's bled quite a bit and it's possible you might need stitches."

"Head injuries always bleed a lot," she replied. She closed her eyes. "Go ahead and do your thing, Dr. Daniel."

He was pleased to hear the touch of lightness in her voice but hated how she winced and released a small moan as he carefully parted her thick dark hair to reveal the area of injury.

He used the peroxide to dab away the excess blood as she sat perfectly still, not making another sound. "The good news is the cut isn't that big," he said when he had removed as much of the blood as possible. "The bad news is you have a nice bird's-egg lump."

"At least it's a bird's egg and not a dinosaur egg," she replied.

He stood too close to her, was able to feel the heat from her body warming his, the scent that managed to muddy his senses if he allowed it to. She'd just been attacked, and he felt as if he was under a sensual assault.

He stumbled back from her at the same time her eyes widened slightly and she stood. "Thank you for cleaning me up," she said as he busied himself returning the first aid kit to the closet.

"All in a day's work for Dr. Daniel. Now, how about a beer?" he asked as they left the bathroom and walked back down the hall toward the kitchen.

"Do you have anything stronger?" she asked. She sank down at a chair at the kitchen table.

He looked at her in surprise. "I have bourbon. Are

you sure that's a good idea? Now that I think about it, maybe a beer isn't a good idea, either."

"A shot of bourbon is a wonderful idea," she replied.

He pulled the bottle of bourbon from the cabinet and then grabbed two glasses and joined her at the table. He poured about an inch of the liquor in each glass and she drank the shot in one swallow. She then gestured for him to pour her another. He hesitated only a moment before pouring her a refill.

This time she wrapped her fingers around the glass and released a deep sigh. Her face was still pale, and more than anything Daniel wanted to draw her into his arms and tell her everything was going to be okay.

But he couldn't tell her that. The attack had come out of nowhere and he had no idea if the intent had been to wound or to kill her.

"Somebody definitely doesn't like me," she finally said.

Daniel offered her a sympathetic smile. "You shouldn't take it personally. I'm pretty sure it's not about you, but rather what you've stirred up here in reopening the murder case."

"Or it was somebody who doesn't like the internal investigation I'm conducting within the department."

"I already thought about that," he admitted. "I know that you've been looking at Ray McClure and Randy Fowler. Ray left the building about a half an hour before you did, and since Randy works the overnight shift, who knows where he was at the time you were attacked." Daniel downed his bourbon. "We'll make sure we know in quick order exactly where they were and what they were doing when you left the building."

He poured himself another shot of the smooth bourbon. "Is there anyone else you're looking at closely within the department?"

She hesitated and took a sip of her drink. "Malcolm Appleton." Daniel raised an eyebrow and she continued. "He recently bought an expensive sports car and has moved into a bigger house. There are definitely some red flags there that I'm looking into."

"Then we check his alibi, too," Daniel replied. He was both surprised and disappointed that in such a small department three of the men were under suspicion. He wasn't surprised that Ray was under scrutiny. He and Trey Walker had been close. But he was surprised by circumstantial evidence that had Randy Fowler and Malcolm Appleton potentially in her sights as dirty cops who might have participated in the drug-trafficking scheme and profited financially.

Olivia had just finished her second drink when Daniel's cell phone rang. Josh's name showed up and he answered. Daniel listened to what his friend had to say and a chill danced up his spine.

"Bag and tag and put it in the evidence room and I'll look at it tomorrow," he said to Josh.

"Bag and tag what?" Olivia asked when Daniel had hung up.

Her eyes were slightly widened and darker than he'd ever seen them. Her body was tensed, as if prepared to take a blow, and he hated that he was about to deliver a definite blow.

"Close to where we found you the men found a piece of evidence," he began.

She leaned forward. "What kind of evidence?"

"A knife. It's possible that the attacker intended to knock you unconscious and then stab you, but when Josh and I came out of the building we interrupted his plans."

A knife. Olivia tried to process Daniel's words in her overworked brain.

She motioned for more bourbon, even though she was already feeling a buzz from the first two drinks. She preferred the buzz to the utter horror that blew an arctic blast of air through her body.

"So it wasn't just an attack, it was an attempted murder," she said. "Thank God you and Josh left the building when you did. If you'd come out just three or four minutes later, you probably would have found me dead."

Daniel reached across the table and took her hand in his. Under no other circumstances would she welcome his touch, but she did so now, curling her fingers with his in an attempt to warm the icy chill that had taken up residency inside her.

"I'm not going to let anything happen to you," he said, his green eyes narrowed with steely determination. "When we got the package with the note and the stuffed animal, none of us knew how serious the threat was. We know now that a threat is real and present and

I'll make sure that nothing like this or anything else happens again to you."

She finally untwined her fingers from his and drew her hand back. She took a drink of the heat of the bourbon and then gazed at him thoughtfully.

"What I don't understand is how killing me would stop anything. Whoever is sent to take my place will continue an investigation into Shelly's death and the internal issues within the department," she said.

Daniel shrugged. "Your murder would certainly take precedence over any other ongoing investigation. Maybe the perp thinks that by hurting or killing you it will buy him some time."

"Time for what? To run? Whoever killed Shelly has had two years to run. Time to cover their tracks? We haven't found any tracks to start to follow," she replied in frustration.

She took another sip of her bourbon and realized she was passing from buzzed to more than slightly inebriated. "Jeez, I can't go home tonight. I'm wounded and I'm just a little bit drunk."

"Then you can stay here tonight," he said without hesitation. "I have an extra room and you can call your mother and tell her you're pulling an all-nighter."

What sounded even better was staying here and sleeping in the warmth and security of Daniel's arms, but she wasn't drunk enough to make that mistake again.

"Are you sure you wouldn't mind?" she asked.

"To be honest, I'd feel better if you stayed. You've

been through a trauma and you don't want to take that home to your mother and daughter."

She nodded, grabbed her purse and reached inside to fumble for her cell phone. Once she had it in hand, she called her mother and told her she'd be working through the night and would be home sometime the next morning.

When she hung up, she stared at the phone for a long moment and then looked at Daniel. "I was going to take Lily mozzarella sticks tonight."

"I can take care of that," Daniel replied, his voice so deep, so soft she wanted to lean her head against his shoulder and just let him take care of everything.

He pulled out his cell phone and within minutes he had called Jimmy's Place for a double order of mozzarella sticks to be delivered to Olivia's house.

"Jimmy has a teenager who works deliveries for him in the evenings," Daniel explained.

Olivia picked up her phone once again. "I'll text Mom to let Lily know a special treat is coming since I won't be home to tuck her in tonight."

She texted the message and then dropped her phone back into her purse. "Let's talk about something other than attacks and murder," she said. Her head ached but she wasn't quite ready to go to bed.

"What do you want to talk about?"

"I don't know…tell me about your family. Are your parents still alive?"

"Yeah, they're alive but I don't have any relationship with them. I haven't had anything to do with them since I turned eighteen." A faint hint of resentment colored his tone.

"Why is that?" she asked curiously.

He swallowed the last of his second glass of bourbon and then leaned back in his chair, tension riding his features. "My parents divorced when I was thirteen, and I became the tool they used to hurt each other for the next five years. It was dirty, it was messy and I swore then that I'd never marry and have children who could be used as pawns if things went bad."

His eyes had gone the moss green of swampy depths. "By the time they finished with me, I didn't like either one of them and I definitely didn't like myself."

"Where are they now?"

"Last I heard my father had moved to California and my mother is in Florida. Neither of them had much use for me when I became legal age and I'd definitely lost all respect for both of them."

"I'm so sorry," Olivia said. She had no idea what it was like growing up with that kind of family dynamics. It was an explanation as to why he was a bachelor and intended to remain so.

"What about you? I know you don't have your father anymore, but did you have a good life growing up?" he asked and some of the shadows lifted from his eyes.

"I had a wonderful family life," she said. "My parents were loving and supportive and I was spoiled to distraction. The worst day of my life was when my father died. He was standing in the kitchen on a Saturday morning making pancakes when he just dropped dead from a massive heart attack. He was gone before anyone could do anything for him."

She ran a finger over the rim of her empty glass. "My mother and I were devastated, and that's when my mother became such a worry wart about me."

"She must hate your job."

Olivia smiled, the gesture renewing the ache in the top of her head. "She does, but she also knows it's not only what I do but who I am. Actually for the most part my mother is almost as innocent as Lily. She believes in the goodness of people and that's part of her charm and why I try to protect her from knowing too much about what I do."

It had been a long monologue and when she finished, she gazed out the window where raindrops had begun to slide down the glass.

Between the trauma that the night had brought and the booze she had consumed, she was suddenly achingly exhausted.

"I think I'd like that spare room now," she said.

Daniel jumped out of his chair and was immediately at her side. He grasped her by an elbow and helped her up and then led her down the hallway into a guest bedroom decorated in shades of blue. He seemed to be holding her by the elbow a lot, guiding her one place or another. But the warmth of his hand on her skin was welcome and made her feel not quite so all alone.

He dropped his hand, and she stood in the doorway as he walked over and lowered a shade at the window and then turned down the bed. "Sit," he said and pointed to the edge of the bed. She obeyed, too exhausted to do anything else. "I'll go get you a T-shirt to sleep in," he said and then disappeared from the bedroom.

She fought the impulse to curl up into a fetal ball. Although she was bone weary and her head throbbed with a dull ache, her brain spun a thousand miles a minute.

She'd been in town just a little over a week and already she'd been threatened by a mutilated stuffed animal and a note and somebody had tried to kill her.

If Josh and Daniel had waited another minute before leaving the station tonight, there was no doubt in her mind that she would have been dead. The perp would have used that knife to stab her to death.

Who had been behind the attack? Had it been somebody they had already interviewed? Somebody still on their list to be interviewed? Or had it been one of the officers she was scrutinizing?

Daniel returned to the room, a folded white T-shirt in his hand. "Thanks," she said as she took it from him.

"The guest bathroom is just across the hall. Everything you need should be there, but if you can't find something let me know."

"I don't know how to thank you for everything you're doing for me."

He smiled softly. "It's all in a day's work. Now, get into bed. You should feel better in the morning, and by then maybe some of the men will have more answers for us."

He left the room and Olivia pulled herself up wearily from the bed and went across the hall to the bathroom.

There was no way she was going to shower tonight, not with her head hurting and the slight wooziness of too much bourbon.

She found a clean washcloth and washed off her face and neck, the warm soapy water doing little to alleviate the cold chill that had been inside her since she came to on the pavement in the parking lot and realized what had happened.

She stripped off her clothes and pulled on the T-shirt that smelled of fresh-air fabric softener and the faint hint of Daniel's cologne.

When she scurried from the bathroom back to the bedroom, she heard Daniel talking softly on the phone in the living room. At the moment she didn't care what he might learn or who he was probably speaking to. She was out of order for the night, and there would be time enough in the morning to deal with whatever needed to be done.

She laid her clothing on a nearby chair, placed her gun on the nightstand within easy reach and then turned off the overhead light. She crawled beneath crisp white sheets and released a deep sigh. Her body relaxed into the unfamiliar mattress, so much more comfortable than the futon at her home where she slept every night.

A soft knock sounded and Daniel opened the door. "All settled in?" he asked and walked to the side of the bed. The light from the hallway spilled into the room, making it easy for her to see his handsome features.

"Just waiting for the Sandman to come and take me

to sleep land," she replied. "Is there any more news? I heard you on the phone a few minutes ago."

"I was just checking in with Josh, and no, there isn't anything new. But you don't have to think about that now." He reached out and pulled the sheet up closer around her neck.

It had been years since Olivia had been tucked into bed by anyone, but what Daniel was doing felt like that. "On a scale of one to ten, ten being the worst day of my life, I'd say this day is hovering around twelve."

Daniel stroked a strand of her hair off her forehead and away from her face and then to her surprise he leaned down and gently kissed her forehead. "Try to get some sleep, Olivia. I swear to you that I'm not going to let anything else happen to you again while you're here in Lost Lagoon."

He turned and left the room, obviously not expecting a reply from her. She couldn't have replied anyway, for a large lump of emotion had jumped into the back of her throat the minute his lips had touched her.

She had a killer after her and a department to clean up, but at the moment equally concerning was the fact that she feared she was falling in love with Lily's "Deputy."

Chapter Seven

It was just after seven the next morning when Daniel heard the water running in the guest bathroom. Olivia was up. He'd been awake, showered and dressed for an hour.

He'd spent that time drinking coffee, making lists of alibis that needed to be checked out for the time of the attack on Olivia and chomping at the bit to get into the office and take a look at the knife that had been found at the scene.

He'd specifically told Josh he didn't want anyone else processing the knife. Daniel knew the odds weren't good that he'd find any fingerprints on it, but items sometimes gave up other evidence.

He'd also made a list of who had been interviewed in the Sinclair murder case and who they had yet to talk to. The other task force members had focused on people who had been on the periphery of Shelly's life, specifically her girlfriends at the time of her death.

He and Olivia had decided early on that the two of them would take on the potential major players in the murder, but they hadn't had enough time yet to talk to anyone except Eric Baptiste.

Things had moved too fast, had spiraled out of control without any real warning. The attack on Olivia now had given a new urgency to everything.

He took a drink of his hot coffee, the liquid adding to the burn that already existed in the pit of his stomach. It was a burn of rage that had begun the moment he'd realized Olivia had been assaulted and might have been killed.

He looked up from his notes as she appeared in the kitchen doorway. Thankfully she looked rested, clear-eyed and determined. "Good morning," he said. "How did you sleep?"

"Like a baby," she replied. She walked over to the counter where a clean cup sat next to the coffeemaker. She helped herself to a cup and then joined him at the table.

"Looks like you've been busy," she said and gestured toward the notes in front of him.

"Just writing down names and thoughts."

"Anything new come up while I slept?" She took a sip of her coffee.

"No, nothing as far as evidence or suspects, but I've come up with a new plan," he replied.

She raised an eyebrow. "A new plan? Sounds interesting."

He gave her a rueful smile. "We'll see how interesting you find it once it's implemented. My plan is that from now on you go no place without me. That means

I follow you to and from the station every day and you aren't out of my sight unless you're safe in your home."

He reached under the papers and pulled out a business card. "This is the rest of the new plan. It's Buck Ranier's card, and I want you to get a security system installed at your house today. Charge it to the department and tell your mother it's standard practice for the sheriffs in Lost Lagoon."

She held the card and stared at it and then slowly nodded her head. "Okay, consider it done."

The fact that she'd acquiesced so easily let him know that she was still frightened, although hiding it very well. "Then I'll go home this morning and get the security system installed. Hopefully it can be done this morning and I can be back at the station by noon," she added.

"And I think the next person we need to interview is Mac Sinclair. He works out of a home office and is some kind of computer tech guru. It's probably a good thing he's his own boss, because rumor is he has a bad temper."

"And we know he didn't like Shelly dating Bo, so he definitely sounds like somebody we need to talk to," she agreed. She took another drink of her coffee. "We need to step up our pace." A faint tension rode her voice, belying the calm of her expression.

"We're going to work as long and as hard as possible to find out who attacked you," Daniel replied in fierce resolve.

"I can't lose track of the reason I'm here. I still need

to find out who is dirty and who isn't in the department and solve Shelly's case," she replied.

"If we find out who attempted to kill you last night, then I believe we'll either know who murdered Shelly or we'll have the identification of a dirty cop. Unless you brought a killer with you from Natchez, then I'm sure the attack on you last night was tied to one of the other two issues."

"So, we continue to work the Sinclair case and I continue the internal investigation and hopefully by solving one of those we'll know who came after me."

"Exactly," Daniel replied.

Olivia finished her coffee and then stood and carried the cup to the sink. "I need to get home and get this security system done so we can get back to the real work."

Daniel got up from the table. "I'll take you back to the station to get your car and then I'll follow you home. When you're ready to return to the station, then call me and I'll tail you from your house back to the station."

She frowned. She obviously wasn't thrilled with his new plan, but he didn't intend to back down. She was his boss, but she was also a woman he cared about and boss or no boss, she was doing this his way.

It was just after nine when Daniel walked into the squad room after following Olivia home. She'd confirmed with Buck to get the security system installed by noon and she was to call Daniel when she was ready to return to work.

Daniel headed directly toward the small evidence

room and found the plastic bag with the knife that had been found by Olivia's body the night before.

He set it in the center of his desk and then sat and stared at it. He instantly identified it. He'd used one dozens of times when eating at Jimmy's Place.

It was a wooden-handled wickedly sharp steak knife with the familiar JP engraved in the handle. Josh pulled up his chair next to Daniel's.

"Not much help," he said. "Anyone who has ever eaten or worked at Jimmy's Place could have taken one of those without anyone being the wiser."

Daniel looked at his friend wryly. "Are you trying to put me in a happy mood as I start a new day?"

"Just sayin'," Josh replied. "I'll be shocked if you get any prints off it."

"Yeah, so will I," Daniel agreed. "But I'll print it anyway and see if the blade holds anything that might tell us something about who was carrying it last night."

"Before you get all involved with that, I need to talk to you about something."

A discordant tone in Josh's voice forced Daniel to give him his undivided attention. Josh's features were troubled. "What, Josh? What's going on?" Daniel hoped to hell Josh wasn't about to confess to having something to do with the drug-trafficking scheme or anything else illegal.

Josh drew in a deep breath and then released it slowly. "I don't know if this has anything to do with anything, but up until last night Savannah had made me promise not to tell anyone."

"Tell anyone about what?" Daniel asked curiously.

Josh stared at the wall just behind Daniel's head. "I don't know, maybe I should have said something before now, but Savannah just wanted to forget the whole thing."

"Forget what?" Daniel asked with a hint of impatience.

Josh focused on Daniel once again. "About a year before Shelly was murdered, Savannah dated Neil Sampson a couple of times. He coerced her into having sex with him before she was ready."

Daniel straightened up. "You mean he raped her?"

"Yes. She didn't want to do anything, but he forced it on her. Savannah thinks it wasn't really rape, though, because she didn't specifically tell him no but 'finally just let it happen' and then never dated him again."

"Oh man, I'm sorry," Daniel said.

"I think she's afraid to come to terms with it." Josh nodded and smiled weakly. "But her telling me is a sign she might be ready to start." His smile faded into a thoughtful frown. "Then last night I got to thinking. Shelly and Savannah looked almost exactly alike, and right before her murder Shelly told her friends that she had a sticky situation on her hands."

"And you're wondering if maybe that sticky situation might have been that Neil Sampson forced himself on her, too?"

"The thought kept me up most of last night," Josh admitted.

"Savannah had already proven that she wasn't going to tell anyone, but Shelly had more friends and was bolder. Neil probably knew that Savannah would be too embarrassed to tell anyone, but Shelly was a wild card."

Daniel rolled the new information over in his brain several times. Was it possible that the handsome, slick city councilman had a secret worth killing for? Was it possible he'd raped Shelly and had been afraid she'd tell somebody?

"I think this just moved Neil up the food chain," he finally said.

"I didn't know anything about the attack on Savannah until we got together, and she wanted me to keep it to myself. I probably should have said something sooner," Josh repeated regretfully.

"You said something now," Daniel replied.

"I'll let you get back to your work on the knife," Josh said and scooted back to his own desk.

It was just after noon when Olivia came through the door. Daniel immediately jumped to his feet and followed her into the office.

He closed the door behind him as she sat behind her desk. "What in the hell do you think you're doing?" he demanded.

"Getting to work," she said briskly.

"You were supposed to call me when you were ready to come in." He was angry with her and the surge of anger inside him surprised him.

"I figured there wouldn't be a problem with me driving from my house to here."

"You figured there wouldn't be a problem walking to your car in the parking lot last night," he countered. He took off his badge and slammed it down on her desk. "I won't stick around and watch you make mistakes that put you in potential danger. You either do this my way or I'm taking the highway." He was somewhat stunned to realize it wasn't an idle threat.

She leaned back in her chair, her brown eyes shining with a hint of amusement. "Are you overly dramatic often?"

Some of the steam left him. "Only when people I care about are involved and are being pigheaded when it comes to their own safety."

She held his gaze for a long moment and in the very depths of her eyes he thought he saw a longing, and desire for her punched him in the gut.

"Put your badge back on, Deputy Carson," she said. "I promise from now on we'll do things your way when it comes to my safety."

"And that's a real promise?"

She leaned forward and raised her right hand. "That's a real promise."

He grabbed his badge and pinned it back on and then sat in the chair across from her desk. "Did you get the security system installed?"

"Buck wired every window and door. I told Mom that the owner of the property wanted it done to protect his investment."

"And she bought it?"

"Hook, line and sinker. Have you had a chance to look at the knife that was found last night?"

Whatever emotion he thought he'd seen in her eyes

was gone and the cool, professional Sheriff Bradford was back in control.

He told her about the knife being from Jimmy's Place and that he'd found no fingerprints or any evidence that it had ever been used for anything. The blade and handle had come up clean and appeared new.

He then told her about the information Josh had shared with him about Neil Sampson. "But it doesn't make sense that he'd kill Shelly because he was afraid of her telling somebody and yet he didn't try to kill Savannah," Olivia said thoughtfully.

"You'd have to know the two sisters. Savannah was always shy and quiet. She didn't have many friends of her own. Neil might have known human nature enough to recognize that Savannah would rather keep it a secret than make any kind of a scene. Shelly, on the other hand, was a much bigger personality. She was a wild card and he might have worried about her...if something happened between them at all."

"There are a lot of ifs in this whole investigation. Maybe we can work in two interviews this afternoon and talk to both Mac and the councilman."

"I'm ready to get started whenever you are," he replied.

"Then let's do it," she said and grabbed her purse.

Oh, he'd love to do it. He'd love to take her home to the bed where she'd slept the night before and have her naked and willing. He'd love to sweep everything off her desk and do it right now.

Instead, they'd spend the afternoon talking to a man

with a bad temper and another man whose ambition might have led to murder.

Mac Sinclair lived in a modest ranch house on the east side of town. His wife, Sheila, opened the door when Olivia knocked. "Sheriff… Daniel…what are you doing here?" Sheila was a small woman with mousy brown hair and shoulders that appeared to be permanently slumped in defeat. Her pale blue eyes held a wealth of anxiety.

"We need to talk to Mac," Daniel said.

Sheila's eyes widened. "He's working right now. Can you come back at another time? He really doesn't like to be disturbed when he's working." She wrung her hands and turned to glance behind her, as if afraid her husband might suddenly appear.

"Working or not, we need to talk to him now," Olivia said firmly.

"He's in the garage. That's his workshop." With obvious reluctance, Sheila opened the door to allow them into a spotlessly clean living room.

They followed her into an equally clean kitchen and she pointed to a door. "He's out there," she said, but didn't open the door to announce them.

Mac must have one hell of a temper, Olivia thought. It was obvious Sheila was fearful of him. There was definitely no accounting for love that would keep a woman with the man she feared. Although in her years of working, Olivia had seen plenty of domestic abuse and women who, far too often, chose to stay with their abusers.

She glanced over at Daniel and thought of their initial conversation when he'd come barreling into the office. She hadn't expected his anger, an anger born in the fact that he cared about her.

But caring wasn't loving and loving wasn't commitment, she reminded herself. She needed to finish her job here and then escape from Daniel before he got any more deeply into her heart.

Thankfully, he hadn't questioned her story about her marriage and immediate pregnancy. Blessedly, he hadn't asked Lily for her precise birth date. She needed to finish up here before she made a mistake that could give away the truth about Lily's parentage.

With that notion in her head, she knocked on the garage door and then opened it. "Mac Sinclair, it's Sheriff Bradford and Deputy Carson," she said.

She and Daniel stepped down to the garage floor. Mac sat at a huge industrial desk surrounded by shelving units that held computer parts and equipment. He frowned as he looked up from a laptop that sat on the desk before him.

He shoved back from the desk, a frown furrowing his brow. "I'd ask what this is about, but I know you're re-investigating Shelly's murder. I don't know why you're wasting your time here to talk to me—we all know who is responsible. We've finally started to heal from this, and here you are to pick the scabs off old wounds."

Mac obviously didn't have a problem speaking his mind. "The investigation at the time of Shelly's murder was done by a dirty cop who rushed to judgment and did a shoddy job," Olivia said. "That's not the way I run things."

Olivia had pegged Mac as a bully, and she wanted him to know without question that she was the new sheriff in town and he wasn't about to bully her. "Now, do you have a couple of chairs where we can sit and talk to you or would you prefer to come down to the station?"

Nobody ever chose to go to the station. She and Daniel stood patiently as Mac got up from his chair, grabbed a couple of folding chairs that leaned against a wall and then opened them.

He was a big man with broad shoulders and hands. It would be easy for him to strangle his sister in a fit of rage and then carry her body to toss it into the nearby lagoon.

"I hear you aren't a big fan of Bo McBride," Olivia said as she and Daniel sat in the chairs and Mac returned to his spot behind the desk.

"Never was. Shelly was too good for him. I told her over and over again that she'd hooked her star to a loser," Mac said. He raked a hand through his thick black hair. "Shelly was smart enough she could have gotten out of this crappy town and made something of herself, but Bo killed her before she got a chance."

"Why would he kill her?" Olivia asked.

Mac shrugged. "Maybe that was the night she finally decided to take my advice and break up with him, and he went nuts."

"Where were you on the night of your sister's murder?" Olivia asked.

Mac stared at her as if she'd lost her mind. "Am I a suspect? Seriously?" His eyes simmered with a barely suppressed anger.

"At this point everyone is a suspect," Daniel said. "So, where were you?"

"I was at home…in bed. I mean at my parents' home."

"The one you and Savannah just sold," Daniel said.

"That's right."

"You were pretty old to still be living at home with your parents," Olivia observed.

"So were Shelly and Savannah," he retorted. "We all were trying to save up money and our parents supported us in the decision to live at home and sock away money. I was trying to get my computer repair business off the ground, Savannah was saving up to open a fine dining restaurant and Shelly was just hoarding her money for whatever she decided to do in the future."

"Did you know that on most nights Shelly and Bo met at the bench by the lagoon to spend a little time together before Shelly worked her night shift at The Pirate's Inn?" Daniel asked.

"Everyone in town knew that. You can't really believe I killed my own sister." Mac's hand on the top of the desk clenched into a fist. "I only wanted what was best for her and that wasn't Bo."

"Maybe it was an accident. Maybe you met her down by the bench to try to get her to break up with Bo and she refused and your anger got the best of you," Daniel said.

"I've heard you have anger control issues," Olivia added, aware that she was baiting the bear.

Mac slammed his fist down on the desk. "You're right, and stupid makes me angry and it's stupid that you are even here talking to me about this. If you believe I killed Shelly, then arrest me, otherwise get the hell out of here and leave me alone. I've got more important things to do with my time."

"He's some piece of work," Olivia said once they were back in her car. "He probably beats his wife every Saturday night just for the fun of it."

"He is a mean bastard," Daniel agreed. "He's always been a bully and possessed a hair-trigger temper, but that doesn't mean he killed Shelly."

"But nothing has taken him off the list of suspects, either." Olivia fought against a wave of frustration. "I guess it's time to talk to the illustrious Neil Sampson and see what he has to offer."

Nothing. Neil was arrogant and openly talked about his brief dating of Savannah, but indicated she had wanted to have sex with him as much as he had with her. He denied having anything to do with Shelly and didn't remember what he had been doing or who he might have been with on the night that Shelly was killed.

It was just after four when they returned to the station. Daniel went to check in with the task force team while Olivia closed herself off in her office to write up reports.

She was determined that even if they didn't solve Shelly's murder before her time in Lost Lagoon ended, the next sheriff would find the files as complete and detailed as possible.

Besides, working on reports kept her mind off Daniel. He'd been so kind to her the night before. He'd tucked her into bed and the gentle kiss he'd delivered to her forehead had made her want to pull him into the bed with her.

Shock and trauma, that was all it had been. She'd been frightened and it was only natural that she'd want somebody to hold her.

The problem was she didn't just want anyone to hold her, she'd wanted Daniel, specifically. If she were smart she'd completely distance herself from him, but he'd now appointed himself her personal bodyguard and the truth was he was the only person in the department she trusted implicitly.

After five, he knocked on her door and came into the office. "Time for all good sheriffs to go home for the day and spend their evening with their family," he said. "By the way, you never told me if Lily enjoyed her mozzarella sticks last night."

Olivia laughed. "She definitely enjoyed them. She asked me when I got home this morning when I'd have to work at night again and she could have more mozzarella sticks." She grabbed her purse and stood. "And, yes, you're right. It's time for me to go home and for you to knock off work for the night."

They walked out of the building together. Daniel

dropped his hand to the butt of his gun, letting her know he was taking his bodyguard duty very seriously.

She was definitely comforted knowing somebody had her back. Even though she hadn't come into the station until noon and it was only a little after five now, she was eager to get home and kiss her mom, hug her daughter and forget about men with bad tempers and a case with no leading suspects.

She didn't want to think about steak knives or an attack in the parking lot. Tomorrow she would be Sheriff Bradford again, but tonight she just wanted to be Olivia, Rose's loving daughter and mother to beautiful little Lily.

She was vaguely surprised when she pulled into the driveway at her house and Daniel parked just behind her and got out of his car. She exited her car and stood by the driver door until he joined her.

"Did you forget something?" she asked.

"No, I just figured I'd see a lady to her door," he replied.

"I'm not a lady, I'm your boss," she retorted with a smile.

"I have a terrible confession to make," he said as they reached her small front porch.

She pulled her house key from her purse and looked at him cautiously. "A confession?"

He nodded. "I have to confess that from the moment my new boss showed up, I've wanted to kiss her."

"You kissed me last night on the forehead." Warmth filled her cheeks as she thought of that tender kiss.

"That's not the kind of kiss I'm thinking about," he replied and took a step closer to her.

She was playing with fire and she knew it but was unable to help herself. "Then what kind of kiss have you been thinking about?" she asked, her heartbeat speeding up.

"This kind." He pulled her into his arms and slanted his lips down to hers.

Memories cascaded through her head as she parted her lips to allow him to deepen the kiss. Laughter as they'd nearly tripped over each other in their eagerness to undress. White hot desire had stolen the laughter as they'd fallen onto the hotel bed.

Those memories fell away as the here and now intruded and the fiery heat she tasted in his lips snapped her back to the present. His tongue twirled with hers, creating a flame of want in the pit of her stomach.

She wanted to fall against him, meld her body with his until she didn't know where she began and he ended. Her overwhelming desire for him and the fact that they were out in the open on her porch was what forced her to break the kiss and step back from him.

She turned quickly and put her key in the door lock. "Good night, Daniel," she said without turning around.

"Good night, Olivia."

She escaped into the house and immediately punched the code into the keypad to unarm the alarm. Then, with fingers shaking, she reset the alarm.

"Mommy, you're home," Lily came rushing toward her, and Olivia picked her daughter up in her arms and squeezed her tight, a wealth of emotion rising up the back of her throat.

"Is everything all right, dear?" Rose asked as she eyed her daughter.

"Fine, everything is just fine," Olivia assured her with a forced smile. "I'm just glad to be home and I'm ready to spend the evening with the two most important people in my life."

But everything wasn't fine. She had a killer after her and she was head over heels for the man who was Lily's father, a man who didn't even know he had a daughter.

She recognized now that she would walk away from Lost Lagoon with a broken heart…if the killer didn't succeed and she was able to walk away at all.

Chapter Eight

For the last week things had gotten weird. Daniel sat at his desk and stared toward the closed office door. He and Olivia had continued to work together each day and he'd followed her to and from the station, but she'd definitely been distant and a different kind of tension had sprung up between them.

It had been the kiss. It had been hot and sweet and had left him wanting so much more. It had also obviously been a big mistake, creating an awkwardness between them that he now both hated and regretted.

The problem wasn't that she hadn't responded to the kiss. She had. She'd responded with a fiery desire to match his. They just hadn't talked about it the next day or any day since.

They'd spent the week talking to people, checking out alibis and interviewing Jimmy Tambor about the knife that had been found. Jimmy had nothing to offer them. The knives were not only served with a variety of meals, but also kept in a silverware container where the diners could just grab one if needed.

Dead ends. Daniel stared down at the list of names

on his desk. It was a short list of potential suspects. At the top was Eric Baptiste, who had become friends with Shelly just before her death. Second on the list was Mac Sinclair. Shelly wouldn't have been afraid to meet her brother at the bench by the swamp in the middle of the night.

Last on the list was Neil Sampson, a long shot but given his brief relationship with Savannah Sinclair and the fact that Shelly had mentioned she had a sticky situation on her hands, he had made the list. Bo wasn't listed as a suspect, but he wasn't completely cleared, either. It was just a gut instinct that both Daniel and Olivia shared that he was innocent.

Frustration welled up inside Daniel. It was possible the person who had murdered Shelly wasn't even on the damned list. To further the insult of the stymied investigation into Shelly's death was the fact that they had not gotten any closer to finding the person who had delivered the trashed dog or had attacked Olivia.

He looked up to see Deputy Emma Carpenter knocking on Olivia's door. She entered and closed the door behind her. For the past six mornings, Olivia had been calling in the deputies one by one for interviews.

Daniel had no idea what kind of timeline Olivia had here in Lost Lagoon. He did know that when she finished her internal investigation into any corruption left in the department, then a special election would be held for a new sheriff and she would return to her home in Natchez.

It was as if for the past week she'd been working

especially hard on the internal investigation and not as much on the Sinclair case. It was as if she was suddenly eager to put Lost Lagoon…and him behind her.

He shouldn't have kissed her. But she'd looked so darned kissable, and he'd been unable to stop himself from following through on his need to taste her sweet lips again.

He stared back down at his desk, surprised to realize how much he would miss her. He'd grown accustomed to her face being the first one he saw each morning and most evenings the last one he saw before heading home.

Josh rolled his chair over to Daniel's desk. "You know, I've been thinking," he began.

"There's a novel thing," Daniel replied.

"Very funny. Actually, I've been thinking about our suspects in the Sinclair case and the missing engagement ring."

"What about it?" Daniel looked at his friend and fellow worker curiously.

"I'm just trying to figure out who would have a motive to take the ring off her finger. I don't see Neil Sampson having any motive. Mac definitely jumps to the top of the list. He hated Bo and he hated his sister's relationship with him. As far as Eric, maybe it's possible he was in love with Shelly and tried to get her to break up with Bo and when she refused, he killed her and took the ring."

"Sheriff Bradford and I have had the same kind of thoughts," Daniel agreed. "Taking the ring was definitely personal. I suppose it's also possible that Shelly broke up with Bo that night and gave him back the ring."

"I know that Bo had that kind of bad-boy aura going on for him, but he'd never gotten into any trouble. He'd never shown any kind of anger issues. I don't believe he was capable under any circumstances of killing Shelly," Josh replied.

"But we still have to consider him a possibility. We're basically just chasing our tails and running around in circles," Daniel replied with irritation. "Maybe what we need to do is put out the word that we're getting close to making an arrest."

"And hope the perp gets nervous enough to make a mistake? It might work," Josh agreed thoughtfully.

"I'll need to run the idea by Sheriff Bradford," Daniel said.

It was just before five when Daniel knocked on Olivia's door. At her beckoning, he entered and closed the door behind him. "It's almost time to head home, but I wanted to talk to you about a couple of things before we leave."

"What's up?" she asked briskly.

He first told her about his idea to hopefully ferret out the killer. "We can just mention to a couple of people that some new evidence has come to light and we're about to make an arrest. The active rumor mill in town will do the rest for us. Within hours of us putting out the word, everyone in town will hear the news."

"It might work," she said slowly…thoughtfully. "Why don't we have lunch at Jimmy's Place tomorrow? That seems to be the heart of the rumor mill here in town."

"Sounds like a plan," he agreed. "And now let's talk about the kiss."

Her dark eyes widened and she busied herself straightening file folders on her desk. "There's nothing to talk about."

"I disagree. It's created awkwardness between us. You've been distant and different with me since then."

She stopped her busy work, clasped her hands together on top of her desk and gazed at him. "You're right. It has been awkward and I have been trying to distance myself from you."

"Then I'm sorry I kissed you," he replied.

"Don't be… I mean, it wasn't just you, I did kiss you back." Her cheeks flushed pink. "It just brought up memories of being with you in New Orleans and we know we can't go there again."

He wanted to go there again, but he also didn't want to pressure her in any way. "Olivia, I promise I won't kiss you again unless you want me to. I don't want this barrier between us anymore. I want you to be able to trust me on all levels."

She offered him a small smile. "Okay then, we're good."

It took only fifteen minutes for Daniel to follow her home and then walk her to her front porch. The door flew open. "Deputy!" Lily said in obvious excitement. She stepped out of the door and grabbed Daniel's hand and pulled him into the house.

Olivia quickly went to the keypad to deal with the

alarm as Daniel looked down at the little girl whose hand was so warm, so trusting in his.

"I been wondering when you'd come to visit again," Lily exclaimed. "You can eat dinner with us, right, Nanny?"

Rose smiled a hello to him. "There's always plenty for another plate on the table."

"Oh, no, I couldn't," Daniel protested, despite the fact that the scent of tomatoes and garlic had his stomach rumbling.

"But you can, Nanny said it was okay and Mommy wants you to stay, too," Lily exclaimed. "Right, Mommy?"

Daniel looked at Olivia helplessly. She shrugged, took off her gun belt and placed it on top of the cabinet and then sat down on the futon. "You're here now, you might as well stay for dinner." She looked at her daughter. "And where is my greeting? Am I just chopped liver when Deputy Carson is around?"

"Ewww, liver. Yuck." Lily dropped Daniel's hand and rushed to her mother, laughing as she barreled into Olivia and toppled her over to her side. "You aren't chopped liver. I hate liver, but I love, love you!" Lily exclaimed.

Daniel's heart squeezed as mother and daughter laughed together and the heat of Lily's hand remained like a lingering tiny ghost touch in his hand.

He cleared his throat and turned to Rose. "What can I do to help?" he asked. Since he was an unplanned guest, he could at least make himself useful.

Rose pointed to a nearby cabinet. "You can get down

another plate and add it to the table. I hope you like spaghetti, because that's what's on the menu for the night."

"Homemade sauce?" he ventured.

She grinned at him. "Is there any other kind?"

"Excellent." Daniel got down the extra plate and added silverware as Olivia and Lily disappeared into Rose's bedroom, presumably for Olivia to change from her work clothes into something more comfortable.

As Daniel filled glasses with ice and water, he and Rose talked about their mutual love of Italian food, the knitted hats she made and donated for cancer victims and how much she loved her daughter and granddaughter.

By the time Olivia and Lily had returned to the living room, Olivia clad in a pair of pink capris and a white T-shirt with a pink design on the front.

Lily danced right to Daniel's side and once again slipped her hand into his. "You have to come and see the new baby doll Nanny bought for me." She pulled Daniel down so that she could whisper in his ear. "She pees her pants when I give her a bottle of water."

"Five minutes and this will all be on the table," Rose called as Lily led Daniel into her bedroom.

For the next five minutes, Lily enchanted Daniel. He saw the peeing doll and a new dress Olivia had ordered for her, and she talked about everything she had done since the last time he'd seen her.

It was impossible to think about murders and dirty cops when in Lily's world, where fairies danced and pixies played and all things were possible. It was a world of innocence and light that Daniel was almost reluctant to leave when Rose called them to the table.

The light mood continued through dinner. There was a crisp green salad, thick slices of garlic bread and a huge pot of spaghetti.

The spaghetti sauce was the best Daniel had ever tasted. He tried to get the recipe from Rose, who remained smiling but tight-lipped as she insisted it was an old family secret.

There was plenty of laughter as Lily showed Daniel how to slurp spaghetti noodles, her mouth quickly becoming covered in the red sauce. Olivia showed her playful side by challenging her daughter to a slurping contest.

Rose looked on with mock sternness and mumbled about bad manners while Daniel laughed at the antics of mother and daughter.

This was the way family was supposed to be. Meals shared in laughter, happy greetings at the front door after time away from one another. A warmth of caring in the room with everyone together.

Daniel could scarcely remember a meal with his mother and father where one or the other of them hadn't stormed away from the table in anger. The happiness and love in this house was normal. What he had experienced in his childhood had definitely been abnormal. But it had shaped him into the man he'd become.

After dinner Daniel insisted he help with the cleanup, and then it was time for him to leave. He was surprised to realize he didn't want to go back to his silent home where there was no laughter, no whisper of another person's voice.

He'd always been fine alone, but tonight the thought of going back to his quiet house wasn't as appealing as it had always been.

Olivia unarmed the security system and walked out on the front porch with him. "Thanks for dinner," he said.

"Not a problem. As far as Mom is concerned, the more the merrier when it comes to meals. Besides, it was fun and now I have to go inside and tell Lily that it really isn't proper to slurp spaghetti," she said ruefully.

He laughed. "Good luck with that."

She smiled and then sobered, her eyes unusually dark as she gazed up at him. "So tomorrow we try our new strategy," she said.

Just that quickly the pleasant evening faded, replaced by the grimness of murder and the attack on her. He nodded. "Tomorrow we bait a killer and see if he comes out to play."

It was just after noon when Olivia and Daniel entered Jimmy's Place the next day. Olivia had spent a restless night tossing and turning as she'd played and replayed the time Daniel had spent with Lily.

He would make a wonderful father, and once again she'd found herself wrestling with the idea of telling him the truth about Lily. Still, she'd awakened this morning once again strong in her resolve to keep his fatherhood a secret.

One night of him eating dinner with them, laughing with Lily and enjoying her company did not a father make, she told herself firmly. This was one secret she had to keep to herself.

She had interviewed nearly all the men in the department and had yet to find direct evidence that any of them had been involved in corruption of any kind.

Malcolm Appleton had explained his new financial situation by showing her a copy of a check that had come from his late father's estate. Richard Appleton had been a wealthy man who had passed away from cancer and left everything to his only son, Malcolm.

The only one who seemed to have come into a recent inexplicable windfall was Randy Fowler, who had not only managed to move his ailing mother into a nice nursing home facility, but had also bought a new house for himself and his wife and two children. When questioned about his uptick in finances, he'd been vague and hadn't really given her a real answer.

His bank records showed three six-figure deposits in the last six months from an account under the name of Jesse Leachman and Associates, but so far Olivia hadn't been able to find out anything about just who or what Jesse Leachman and Associates were and why they would be paying Randy anything.

Jimmy Tambor's cheerful smile pulled her from her thoughts of the morning and to the present. "A booth?" he asked.

"Or a table, either is fine," Daniel replied.

They were seated at a table just to the left of the center of the bar and grill, a place where they would easily be seen and overheard if they spoke loud enough.

Nerves bounced in her stomach as they placed their drink orders. What they were going to do wasn't without its dangers. A killer who believed himself safe was much less lethal than one who believed he might possibly be cornered.

If it was Shelly's killer who had attacked her in the parking lot, then he had acted precipitously, driven by the reopening of the case. Now he would be acting out of fear, and that always made people more dangerous.

"Don't look so nervous," Daniel said softly.

"Does it show?"

He smiled. "Probably only to me, but we're going nowhere in the investigation and I think this is our best next move."

"It's his next move that worries me," she replied.

"I've got your back, Olivia."

"I know, but I also don't want you to get in any cross fire." She took a sip of iced water. "If I had my way, it would be just the killer and me and I wouldn't hesitate to pull my trigger."

Daniel's jaw tightened. "This crime has haunted this town for too long. With the amusement park about to breathe new life here, we need to clean up this murder case."

Olivia leaned back in her chair and eyed him wryly. "If anyone was to look at us now and read our expressions, they would assume we're both frustrated and angry at our lack of progress."

"You're right," he agreed. "Maybe we should have ordered a bottle of champagne to make it look like a real celebration."

Olivia laughed. "You know I'm a lightweight when it comes to alcohol. I think we're better off toasting with sweet tea."

The waitress appeared to take their food orders and when she left, Daniel slumped into a position of complete relaxation, a pleasant smile on his face. "So, did you manage to give Lily spaghetti etiquette last night after I left?"

"I didn't have to. Once I got back into the house she told me that she knew that wasn't really the way to eat spaghetti when we were out in public. Apparently, my mother had already had a little discussion with her."

He smiled. "And did your mother have a little discussion with you, because as I remember it you were in on the hijinks, as well."

"Guilty as charged. I told Lily that Nanny didn't need to have a talk with me. I knew both of us had shown bad manners."

"She's a bright kid."

"Oh I don't know, she seems to have taken quite a shine to you," Olivia said teasingly.

"I love a woman with good taste," he replied.

The conversation halted as the waitress arrived with their food orders. While they ate they focused on laughing a lot, appearing confident and at ease. She hoped that it appeared to everyone in the place as if they had the world, or in this instance the case, by the tail.

They were halfway through the meal when Jimmy stopped by their table. "Hi, Sheriff Bradford… Daniel. I just thought I'd stop by to see how you're enjoying your meals. Everything all right here?"

"As usual, the food is excellent and everything is better than okay," Daniel replied. He leaned toward Jimmy. "We caught a big break on Shelly's murder case. It's just a matter of time before we make an arrest."

Jimmy's boyish features radiated surprise and he leaned closer to Daniel. "Is it Eric Baptiste?"

"We can't say anything right now," Olivia said coyly.

"It's Eric, I know it is. He's always been kind of strange and so intense. The only friend he ever had was Shelly and he knew about the tunnels that ran from the Sinclair house to the lagoon." Jimmy straightened. "Don't worry, I won't say anything to anyone."

"And so begins the rumor mill," Daniel said as Jimmy moved away from their table.

"And hopefully the beginning of the end where Shelly's case is concerned," she replied.

"How is the internal investigation going?"

"I'm waiting for confirmation on a couple of things and then I should be able to wrap things up pretty quickly."

"I already miss you."

She averted her gaze from his. "Daniel, you shouldn't say things like that."

"I know I shouldn't, but it's the truth. I've enjoyed

getting to know you better and getting to know your family. I've enjoyed working with you."

She looked back at him and tried not to fall into the lush green depths of his eyes, the evocative warmth of his smile. "I'm not gone yet," she replied.

She focused on the half of a club sandwich left on the plate in front of her. It was nice that he liked spending time with her. It was ridiculous how hot she knew he was to sleep with her again. It was wonderful that he thought Lily was beautiful and charming and that her mother was warm and caring.

None of that changed the truth, and the truth was he could never be a part of her life. He had no desire to be a real part of her life. He was a temporary man and she was working a temporary position in a town that wasn't her home. She was doomed to his being nothing more than a passing ship in the night just as she thought he'd been years ago.

It had been a cruel twist of fate to bring him back into her life now with Lily hungry for a daddy and her ready to move on from the heartbreak of losing one of the most caring men she'd ever known.

They were back at the station just after one, Olivia in her office and Daniel holed up in the small conference room with the rest of the task force.

Would their ruse work? Would the killer now do something that would bring him out into the open? There was no question that she was concerned about what might happen next. She couldn't foresee what consequences she and Daniel had put into motion, but she knew one of the outcomes would be a target directly on her back.

She'd already been attacked once. She just hoped that she and Daniel saw the next one coming if and when it did. From the moment Lily had been born and Olivia had returned to her work in law enforcement, she'd done everything she could to be careful, to be wary. Lily was her reason to stay alive. Olivia wanted to do her job well, but she also wanted to go home each night to her daughter and mother.

At around three o'clock, Mayor Frank Kean entered her office. Olivia greeted him and he sat in the chair opposite her desk, his features wreathed in a smile. "I hear you're close to an arrest in the Sinclair case."

Daniel had been right—the grapevine was alive and well in Lost Lagoon. "We're definitely close," she replied. She hated to lie to the mayor, but she didn't know him well enough to be sure she could trust him with the truth of what they were doing.

"Want to give me the details?"

In Olivia's special capacity here in Lost Lagoon, she didn't have to answer to the mayor as she normally would as an elected sheriff.

"At this point I'd rather not get specific. However, I promise you that if it's possible you'll know before anyone else when we make the arrest."

"I'd appreciate it," he replied. "When the special elections come up, I'm thinking about running for mayor again. I served this town in that capacity for eight years before Jim Burns beat me, and everyone knows how that turned out. My heart is in this town."

Olivia smiled at the older man. "I'm sure you'd be a fine mayor again."

"Have you heard of anyone who plans to run for sheriff after you leave?"

"No, although it's possible Deputy Carson might be interested since he served as interim sheriff before I arrived," she replied.

Frank nodded in approval. "Daniel is a good man. He would make a good sheriff, and I know he has the best interest of Lost Lagoon at heart. Has he mentioned wanting to run?"

"No, we haven't discussed it," she replied. "We've been so busy with the investigation into Shelly's murder."

He leaned forward and gave her a charming smile. "Sure you don't want to give me a hint about who the murderer is?"

Olivia laughed and shook her head. "No matter how much you attempt to charm me, my lips are sealed until we have the culprit under arrest."

"Then I guess I should let you get back to work," he said and stood.

"I promise, I'll keep you informed," she said as he opened the office door to leave. She breathed a sigh of relief the second he stepped out and closed the door behind him.

She had no idea what this newest plan of theirs might

stir up. She couldn't begin to guess whether it would be successful or not.

She was aware that if it was successful, then something bad was probably going to happen very soon.

Chapter Nine

It had been another long day. Daniel and Olivia had spent most of the morning out on the streets, drifting in and out of shops, listening to the gossip on the street and waiting…waiting for something to happen.

They'd eaten lunch at Jimmy's Place and then had returned to the station where Olivia had holed up in her office and Daniel had sat at his desk studying again and again the files and information they'd gathered about Shelly's murder to see if anything or anyone had been overlooked.

He'd gathered everyone's alibis for the night that Olivia had been attacked in the parking lot from the other members of the task force and needed to share the information with Olivia. She wouldn't be pleased by the fact that several of the men had unsubstantiated alibis.

After five, he knocked on her office door. He entered the office to find her staring out the window. She turned when he called her name.

"Sorry," she said, a faint flush of color filling her cheeks. "I was lost in my own head for a few minutes." She looked at her wristwatch. "And it's time to go home."

"I have another offer for you," he said. "I've got cold beer in my refrigerator and a frozen pizza. Why don't we go to my place and do a little brainstorming?"

She hesitated.

"I've finally gotten all the alibis from the suspects we had concerning your attack in the parking lot," he continued as an added incentive.

"Okay," she relented. "Pizza and beer and brainstorming and then I go home."

"Of course," he agreed. "I'll follow you to my place."

It wasn't long before he drove behind her car toward his house. He hadn't realized how much he'd wanted her to come over until the moment he'd asked her. He hadn't realized how lonely his evenings now seemed since he'd shared dinner with her and Lily and Rose a couple of times.

Maybe before this was all finished and before she left town, he'd throw a big pizza party with Rose and Lily included. He'd go all out and order the pizza from Jimmy's Place. An inward smile lit his heart as he thought of Lily stringing cheese down her chin, her green eyes twinkling with happiness while she enjoyed a piece of Jimmy's pizza or a big order of mozzarella sticks just for her.

Olivia was lucky to come home to a loving child and mother each evening. This thought surprised him. He'd never yearned for a family before. He'd always been comfortable in his aloneness. He didn't have to answer to anyone else and had always relished the quiet and peace of being alone after a day at work.

Something had changed. The silence in the evenings now felt a bit stifling. Maybe this new attitude had begun when Josh had hooked up with Savannah Sinclair.

He'd seen his friend and partner happier than ever in love with Savannah. Josh rushed home in the evenings to share dinner with her, to spend time with her. It was obvious he believed he'd met his soul mate and he and Savannah were making plans not only for a wedding, but also for a family.

Daniel had never thought about finding a soul mate, a woman who could fill his life with love and laughter, with shared secrets and passion.

Something about Olivia and her little family definitely had him rethinking his confirmed bachelorhood. Or was it that he was just feeling the loss of Josh in his life? The two had often spent dinner together at Jimmy's or hung out for drinks after work, shortening the time of silence Daniel would have to face when he came home each evening.

He shoved all these thoughts out of his head as he opened both garage doors and Olivia pulled into the garage on the right and he drove into his place on the left.

When they were both out of their cars, he closed the doors and together they went into the kitchen. He turned on the overhead light and motioned her to the table. "Sit and relax and I'll set the oven to preheat."

She removed her gun belt and placed it on the floor

and then sat at the table in the same chair she had when she'd last been there. She placed her purse on the floor next to her gun and holster and then smiled at him. "I hope this isn't one of those cheap, cardboard pizzas. I'm not that kind of girl."

"Of course not," he replied with mock indignation. "It has a rising crust and a trio of meat toppings." He grabbed a couple of beer bottles from the refrigerator and carried them over to the table.

She unscrewed the top and took a drink, then set the bottle back on the table and released a deep sigh. "I expected something to happen by now."

He took the top off his bottle and tossed it into the nearby trash can. "I have to admit, I did, too." He set his beer bottle on the table and grabbed a pizza stone from under the cabinet and then walked back to the refrigerator and took a boxed pizza out of the freezer.

It took him only a minute to pull the pizza from its wrapping and set it on the pizza stone. He turned to look at her. "To be honest, I don't know if I'm disappointed or relieved that nothing has happened so far."

"I'm on pins and needles," she confessed. "The waiting to see what happens is driving me half-crazy. I'm jumping at shadows. You said you had alibis for the time I was attacked in the parking lot?"

He sat across from her at the table, took a sip of his beer and nodded. "Eric Baptiste was at the swamp gathering herbs and roots for his mother. Unfortunately, nobody saw him there. Mac's wife swore that he was home with her at the time in question. Bo and Claire were having dinner at Jimmy's Place and were seen there by several people. The last person I had checked out was Ray McClure."

Olivia raised an eyebrow and at the same time the oven dinged to announce that it had reached the appropriate temperature. Daniel got up from the table.

"I had Ray checked out just because something about him has always rubbed me the wrong way. He's the one person in the department I've never really trusted."

"Besides, he's the one who found the package with the dog inside," Olivia said.

"A package he could have easily put together and brought to your office," Daniel replied. "We only have his word that he just happened to see it in front of the building."

"So, what was his alibi?" she asked.

Daniel shoved the pizza stone into the oven and then returned to the table. "He left the station approximately thirty minutes before you did. He says he went directly home, drank a few beers and didn't have any interaction with anyone that night."

"So the only person who has a definite, solid alibi is Bo."

"That's about the size of it," Daniel agreed.

"If Bo wasn't the one who attacked me, then I definitely don't believe he killed Shelly," she said thoughtfully and took another sip of her beer.

"I always doubted that Bo was responsible," Daniel agreed.

She frowned and reached up to the clip that held her

long dark hair in a tight ponytail at the nape of her neck. "If you don't mind…" She took the clasp off with a sigh of relief. "By this time of the day having my hair held so tight always gives me a bit of a headache."

Did he mind? He reveled in the sight of her lush dark hair falling around her shoulders and his fingers itched with the desire to touch those strands, to feel them wrapped around his hands.

He jumped up from the table and went to the oven to check on the pizza. The heat of the oven had nothing to do with the heat that burned in his belly, a heat of want to take her to bed.

Pizza, beer and a little shoptalk—that's all she signed up for, he reminded himself. "Just another couple of minutes or so and this should be done," he said. He leaned against the cabinet next to the oven.

"How's the investigation into the deputies going?" he asked, desperate to get his mind on anything other than the very hot images of the two of them together in his bed that was shooting off like fireworks in his head.

"Thankfully, I've pretty well cleared everyone of any wrongdoing. My last challenge was Randy Fowler, who finally came clean to me this afternoon when I spoke with him. He'd received several large direct deposit payments into his bank account over the past couple of months from a company called Jesse Leachman and Associates. When I first questioned him about them, Randy was vague and mysterious."

"Hold that thought." Daniel pulled the pizza from the oven, set it on a hot pad on the nearby countertop and then used a pizza slicer to cut it into eight pieces. He then carried it to the table, got plates and napkins and finally sat back down.

"Okay, now tell me the mystery about Randy's money," he said.

"It's a structured settlement from a drug company. He was embarrassed to talk about it because apparently he had been on a drug that was pulled off the market because the side effects messed up…uh…male performance."

Daniel stared at her. "For real?"

"For real. He'll receive checks for the next year and by then he hopes the side effects will wear off. I checked it out. I finally managed to speak to several lawyers at Jesse Leachman and Associates, who faxed me over court documents confirming what Randy had told me."

Daniel gestured for her to take a piece of the pizza. "Well, it's a relief to know it isn't dirty money."

"You can't tell anyone about it." Olivia pulled a piece of the pie onto her plate. "He was mortified to have to tell me about it."

"I can imagine. Men don't like to talk about their sex lives unless they're bragging or lying," Daniel said jokingly.

For the next couple of minutes they ate and stayed silent. Daniel tried everything in his power not to think about his sex life with the woman sitting across from him.

"Maybe one evening we could take Lily and your

mother to the ice cream parlor," he said in an attempt to get inappropriate thoughts out of his head.

She smiled, that warm, open smile of a sexy woman that had nothing to do with Sheriff Bradford. "I'd like that. I was planning on taking them before the attack in the parking lot, but that changed everything and of course I haven't been allowed to leave the house without my deputy escort."

"Maybe your deputy escort could arrange for an ice cream date tomorrow night after work," he replied.

"That would be nice," she replied and then frowned. "As long as you think it's okay for all of us to be out and about."

"I don't think our man will try anything in a public setting. Besides, trust me, nobody is going to hurt you or anyone you love as long as I'm with you."

Unable to stop himself, he reached across the table and grabbed one of her hands with his. He half expected her to pull away, but instead she curled her fingers with his. Their gazes remained locked for several heart-stopping seconds, and then she finally pulled her hand away from his.

"You know I really don't need your bodyguard detail." Her eyes had grown dark and she straightened her back against the chair. "I'm not a poor damsel in distress. I'm a trained officer of the law and I know how to take care of myself. I've faced a lot of bad actors in my career and I'm still here. I'm good at my job."

Sheriff Bradford was definitely present and in the room, Daniel thought. "Olivia, I'm quite aware that you aren't a damsel in distress. I'm not shadowing you because I think you're not capable. We've been working as partners and knowing that somebody has a target on you, I'm acting as any partner would. I've got your back and I would do the same thing for any of the men I was partnered with."

She studied his features for a long moment and then relaxed her shoulders and the darkness in her eyes lightened. "All right then, just so that we're clear."

"We're clear, now eat another piece of pizza and I'll grab us each another beer." He got up from the table and grabbed two more beers from the fridge.

Every word he'd told her was the absolute truth. He'd do the same thing for any man in the department who found himself at the heart of a dangerous investigation.

What he hadn't mentioned was that part of the reason he had insinuated himself into her life as much as he had was because he liked her and he liked her family.

There had been women in his past, but none had ever stirred such a fierce need to protect like she did inside him. He didn't remember ever feeling this way about any other woman, and it confused him.

He told himself it was because he couldn't forget the passion-filled night he'd experienced with her five years ago.

He couldn't ignore how much he wanted that same experience again. It was easier to chalk it up to lust, and that thought made it okay for him to want her once again.

OLIVIA GRABBED A second piece of pizza and tried to ignore the overwhelming pull she experienced whenever she was around Daniel.

Five years ago he'd been a sexy man in a bar offering her a night of sex, a night of temporary forgetfulness of her grief over her partner's death. He'd been a one-dimensional man who had unexpectedly wound up being the father of her daughter due to their carelessness.

He was so much more now. She admired his intelligence. He was a man of honor and committed to his job and the town he served. He respected her as his boss, but also saw and respected the woman behind the badge.

She wanted him again. Not as a husband, not as a committed boyfriend—she knew better than to wish for such things from him. But, she definitely wanted him again.

And she knew without a doubt that he desired her, too. He'd done little to hide it. It was in his eyes when he gazed at her, in the heat of his hands when he touched her in even the most simple way. It had definitely been in the kiss they had shared. It would be just a one-night stand, just like it had been years ago. Only this time she was aware that her heart would be involved.

Still, she had no illusions. If they did make love again, it would only be a memory she'd take back to Natchez with her. It wouldn't be the beginning of anything between them.

"You've gotten very quiet," Daniel said, pulling her from her thoughts.

She stared at him for a long moment. If she said what

she wanted to say, then there would be no going back. She needed to be sure of what she wanted to happen. She was sure.

"I was just thinking about us making love again," she said.

The piece of pizza he'd been about to bite into hung midair between his plate and his mouth. His eyes widened and then narrowed. "And what, exactly, were you thinking about it?"

"That it would be wrong on all kinds of levels, but I still want it to happen."

He slowly lowered his slice of pizza to his plate, his gaze locked with hers. "Do you have a specific time in mind for this to happen?"

Her heart suddenly thundered with the anticipation of what she was about to set into motion. "I was thinking maybe after we finish eating."

He shoved his plate away. "I'm full."

Olivia fought the impulse to laugh, but his actions and words fired a heat of want through her, a want she had battled since the moment she'd walked into the sheriff's office and seen him again.

"I'm finished eating, too," she replied, surprised that her voice was half-breathless.

"Then why are we still sitting here at the table?" He got out of his chair and walked around to her. He pulled her up and into his arms.

She wrapped her arms around his neck as he bent his head to meet her lips. He tasted of pepperoni, beer and a sweet hot fire that spread heat from her head to her toes.

In the back of her mind she knew this was all wrong, but her body and her response to him screamed that it was all right. One more time, that was all she needed from him.

One more chance to feel his body against hers, one more time to revel in the pleasure she knew he'd give to her. One more time it would be enough because it would have to be enough.

The kiss lasted only moments and then he stepped back from her, took her by the hand and led her down the hallway to the master bedroom.

On the night he'd cleaned up the wound on her head, she'd noticed the black-and-gray spread on the king-size bed, the matching black lamps on the cherry wood end tables and a large dresser.

This time he gave her no opportunity to notice anything as he pulled her back into his arms for a searing kiss. He pulled her so tightly against him that she could feel that he was already fully aroused and that only increased her own desire.

This kiss lingered, was more intimate than the last. Their tongues met and swirled in frantic fervor. His hands stroked up and down her back, as if eager to get beneath the blouse she wore and feel her naked skin.

She ended the kiss and stepped away from him. Evening light filtered through the curtains and lit the room with a romantic golden glow. Her fingers trembled as she began to unbutton her blouse.

By the time she shrugged it off her shoulders, Daniel had already placed his gun belt and cell phone on the nightstand and had his shirt and slacks off. He peeled off his socks, leaving him clad only in a pair of navy boxers.

As Olivia kicked off her shoes and took off her slacks, Daniel pulled the bedspread down, revealing black-and-gray striped sheets.

He got beneath the sheets and watched as she took off her hose, leaving her only in a pair of pale pink panties and a matching lacy bra.

"I can't tell you how many times I've replayed in my mind that night with you in New Orleans," he said, his voice husky and unusually deep.

"I've thought about it, too," she admitted. She got into the bed and he instantly pulled her into his arms. His bare skin was warm against hers and his hands moved to her back and her bra fastening. He had it undone in a mere second. He pulled it off her shoulders and tossed it to the floor as his mouth found hers once again.

His broad chest against her naked breasts provided an exquisite sensation and when his hands moved to cover them, a gasp of pleasure escaped her.

This couldn't be wrong when it felt so right. This couldn't be wrong because she had both eyes open and knew not to expect anything more from him than these moments in his bed.

Another gasp escaped from her as his lips left her mouth and trailed down her neck and then captured the tip of one of her breasts.

She moved her hands to the back of his head, keeping him there as he kissed and sucked. He moved his head just enough to give attention to her other breast, teasing and licking as electric tingles shot through her center and spread to encompass her entire body.

It didn't take long before she wanted them both completely naked. She needed to touch him, to taste him. She wanted him to remember this time with her as she knew she'd always remember it.

She took the lead, breaking away from him and tugging on his boxers. His eyes glowed a silvery green as she finished removing his boxers.

"My turn," he whispered. He slipped his thumbs between the sides of her panties and her bare skin. With agonizing slowness he pulled her panties down her thighs, below her knees and finally off her body.

He slid his hands back up her legs, as if memorizing their shape by touch alone. She ran her hands down his chest, loving the play of his muscles beneath the warm flesh.

He moaned as she wrapped her fingers around his hardness. She moved her hand up and down, stroking him to a higher fever of passion. He tangled his fingers in her hair and moaned her name as she continued to caress him intimately. She leaned down and took him in her mouth, and his fingers tightened their tangle in her tresses.

"You're driving me crazy," he said, his voice distorted with his desire.

She stopped and looked at him. "I want you crazy. I want you insane for me." Once again she began to lick and suck his velvety hardness until he finally pushed her away.

"No more," he panted. "If you don't stop now I'll be done, and I don't want this to be done yet."

"I don't want this done yet, either," she replied.

She hadn't had enough of him yet. The scent of his cologne dizzied her head and she wished she could capture it to have it in her senses forever.

He rolled her over on her back and began to love her body, starting at her lips and then slowly moving downward. It was as if he'd made love to her a hundred times before and knew just where to touch, exactly where to kiss to bring her the most pleasure.

Once again he latched on to one of her swollen nipples and teased and tormented. While his mouth gave special attention to her breasts, one of his hands stroked down her stomach and to the place she most wanted… needed his touch.

She arched her hips to meet him, surprised to find herself close to an explosive release. He knew just the right amount of pressure, just the right speed of finger movement to bring her quickly to the edge where she cascaded over with a violent intensity that left her breathless and weak.

"Again," she managed to gasp as her hands clutched tightly to his shoulders.

He laughed, a low sexy rumble and once again moved his fingers to touch her intimately. This time her climax was less intense but no less pleasurable.

"Now I want you inside me."

"I love a woman who knows exactly what she wants." He moved between her thighs and slowly eased into her. She closed her eyes and gripped him firmly by the shoulders, loving the way they fit so perfectly together.

They moved together in a rhythm her body remembered despite the years that had gone by. They started slow and then increased their pace, and despite the fact that he'd already given her two exquisite climaxes, the crashing waves of yet another one approached.

As if he sensed how close she was, he increased the depth and quickness of his strokes inside her. She once again gasped his name as the waves threatened to drown her and she shuddered uncontrollably.

He thrust a final time into her, moaning her name and finding his own release. He collapsed halfway on top of her, the bulk of his weight held on his elbows. His face was mere inches from hers and he used his hands to brush her hair away from her face. He then kissed her so tenderly it was as if he reached inside her and caressed her heart.

At least she knew tonight wouldn't produce any unintended consequences. She'd been on the pill since after Lily's birth. Thinking about Lily made her realize it was time for her to get home.

"I've got to go," she said.

"Stay," he replied, his voice filled with a soft yearning that tugged at her heart. "Spend tonight with me, Olivia. Just this one night, stay and wake up in my arms in the morning."

She could think of a million reasons why she shouldn't,

one of the biggest because she wanted to so badly. "I really should get home," she replied, and still she didn't make a move to get out of the bed.

"I can get mozzarella sticks delivered to Lily if you'll let her share her mommy with me tonight."

She smiled up at him. "You realize that's blatant manipulation."

"If it works then I'm not apologizing."

Her head said to get up and leave, to go home where she belonged. But for just tonight she wanted to pretend that she belonged here with him.

"Order the cheese sticks. I'm not going anywhere," she said, unaware that she had made up her mind before the words fell out of her mouth.

He rolled over to the side of the bed and picked up his cell phone. While he made the call to Jimmy's Place, she scooted out of bed, grabbed her blouse and pulled it around her. She went down the hallway first to the bathroom and then to the kitchen to retrieve her purse and her own cell phone.

She quickly texted her mother that she was pulling another overnighter and fought the wave of guilt that swept over her. She didn't like to lie to her mother, but what was she supposed to do? Text her that she'd just had hot sex with Daniel and wanted to spend the rest of the night in his arms?

She dropped her phone back into her purse and picked up her gun belt from the floor and carried them both back to the bedroom.

"Mozzarella sticks ordered and will be delivered within fifteen minutes or so," Daniel said.

"And I just texted Mom to let her know I wouldn't be home until morning." She dropped her purse on the floor and placed her gun belt on the nightstand. She then removed her blouse and got back into the bed with him.

He immediately pulled her back into his arms and she placed her head on his chest, where she could hear his steady heartbeat in her ear.

He stroked up and down her back with one hand and a relaxation she hadn't felt since first arriving in Lost Lagoon swept over her.

She'd deal with recriminations and potential regrets tomorrow. Tonight she just wanted to feel like a woman who was loved and cherished. Tonight she just wanted to pretend that she was snuggled against the man who was meant to be in her life forever.

It was a wonderful fantasy that she knew would be shattered by the morning light.

Chapter Ten

There was no question that waking with Olivia in his arms had been wonderful. Throughout the next day, Daniel could think of little else except what they'd shared the night before and then waking to the early morning dawn with her warm naked curves cuddled next to him.

He'd expected the morning to be awkward, and it had been. Olivia had been eager to get back home and shower and change and then get back to the office. She'd been distant but not completely closed off. As they drank coffee they'd made plans for him to eat dinner at her place that evening and then surprise Lily with a trip to the ice cream parlor.

He'd followed her to her house and waited in the driveway while she showered and dressed and then got into her car. He'd then followed her to the station where she'd disappeared into her office.

He knew her time here was running out with just a couple of weeks or so left. She'd been sent here to check the department for any further corruption, and he knew from her conversations with him that she'd pretty well completed her internal investigation.

Solving Shelly's murder had not been the reason she'd been sent here to take over as sheriff. It was very possible, despite the rumor they'd begun of an imminent arrest, that the case would fall on the next sheriff's desk.

It surprised him how much he would miss her when she left. He'd known all along she was only here temporarily, and he'd thought having her in his life, in his bed temporarily would be fine, that it would be enough for him.

But he wasn't ready to tell her goodbye yet. At least he had the evening to look forward to, sharing dinner with Olivia, Rose and Lily, and then surprising Lily with the trip to the ice cream parlor.

"One day at a time," he muttered to himself.

Josh looked up from his desk nearby. "Did you say something?"

"Nothing worthwhile," Daniel replied. He leaned back in his chair and released a deep sigh. "I just thought that something would have happened by now to break the Sinclair case wide open."

"It hasn't been that long since you and Sheriff Bradford put out the word that an arrest was about to happen," Josh replied.

"Yeah, but I thought once word got out, the murderer would panic and do something stupid or at least do something that would bring him into our awareness. So far all of our suspects are going about their lives as usual."

"Which begs the question of do we even have the perp on our list of suspects?" Josh replied.

"Bite your tongue," Daniel said. "I don't even want to think about the possibility that there's somebody out there we don't know about, somebody who has managed to stay out of our radar for all this time."

"If you think about it, Shelly could have been murdered by almost any man in town," Josh continued. "I mean, she was a pretty young woman sitting on a bench in an isolated part of town in the middle of the night."

"All the people we have on our suspect list have potential motive in her murder. Why would a man who just happened upon her murder her?" Daniel's frustration grew by the minute.

"I'm just throwing out suppositions. Her diamond ring was stolen. Maybe it was nothing more than somebody needing the money to pawn the ring. Or, maybe it was a potential sexual assault gone bad."

"Her purse was left on the bench and she had both cash and a credit card inside that wasn't stolen. It wasn't a robbery and you're really going out of your way to ruin my day," Daniel replied.

Josh grinned at him. "That's what good friends are for."

Daniel returned his attention to the file in front of him. He'd already considered all the scenarios Josh had brought up. It was possible the guilty person wasn't on their suspect list, but his gut instinct told him he was.

Shelly's engagement ring had been pretty, but certainly not a large diamond that could be pawned for any sizable amount of money. Besides, they'd contacted every pawn shop in the state to let them know about the stolen ring.

To the best of everyone's knowledge, the ring hadn't been pawned. Also Shelly's clothing hadn't shown any indication of a sexual attack. No rips or tears, nothing to point to a potential molestation.

At noon he stuck his head into Olivia's office to see if she wanted to go out for a bite to eat, but she declined, telling him that she intended to work through lunch.

Instead of eating out, Josh drove through George's Diner and picked up burgers and fries and the two deputies went into the small break room to eat lunch.

"I don't want to eat too much," Josh said as he unwrapped one of the smaller burgers George offered on his menu. "Savannah is making beef Wellington for dinner tonight."

"When are you going to marry that girl?"

Josh smiled and his eyes softened. "Actually, we're planning a small ceremony and a reception in two months. Savannah has had her head in bridal magazines and she's planning on doing most of the work herself. I'm actually glad you brought it up because I've been meaning to ask you if you'd be my best man."

Daniel swallowed his bite of burger and chased it with a quick sip of his soda, surprised and touched by Josh's question. "I'd be honored to be your best man," he replied.

"Good, I was hoping you'd agree."

"I know Savannah had always wanted to open a fine-dining restaurant here in town. Has she given up on that idea?"

"Not at all," Josh said. "She gave up on the idea when Shelly was murdered. She gave up on pretty much everything then, but she now intends to follow through on that dream after our wedding."

"And what do you think about that?"

Josh smiled, again a softness creeping into his eyes. "I want her to fulfill every dream she'll ever have. I totally support the idea of her opening a restaurant. Besides, it would be great if she got it up and running at around the same time that the theme park opens. Tourists will flock to a nice restaurant while they're on vacation."

"Sounds like a good plan," Daniel agreed and then frowned. "And now if only we had a good plan to get this murder case solved and filed away forever."

Daniel spent the rest of the afternoon reading through all of the interviews they had conducted, trying to glean a new name, another piece of information that might move their investigation forward.

By five o'clock he was more than ready to call it a day and enjoy dinner with Olivia and her family. "It's a perfect ice cream evening," he said as he and Olivia left by the back door and stepped into the humid, hot air.

"Lily is going to be so excited. She and my mom have been cooped up in that house since the day we arrived in town."

He was pleased that the distance he'd felt radiating

from her that morning was gone and everything appeared normal between them.

"I'll see you at your house," he said as they reached her car. He waited for her to get inside her vehicle and then hurried to his own so that he could follow her.

As he drove he tried to empty his mind of all thoughts about murder and about Olivia's assignment here being over soon. He just wanted to enjoy every minute of time with her that he could before it was time for her to move on.

It didn't take long for the two of them to park in front of the bright yellow shanty she called home for now. Lily's pixie face was pressed against the front window and lit with joy at the sight of them approaching the door.

"Nanny, they're here!" Her voice drifted out and Daniel couldn't help the smile that curved his lips at the sound of her excitement. Somehow the little minx had managed to capture a little piece of his heart.

Olivia opened the door and immediately moved to the pad on the wall to deal with the alarm. Meanwhile Lily grabbed Daniel's hand and smiled up at him.

"Nanny told me you were eating with us again tonight and I was so happy," she exclaimed.

"I was happy, too. I'd much rather eat Nanny's cooking than my own," Daniel replied.

"Do you cook bad?" Lily asked.

"I don't cook very good," Daniel replied.

"We're having my favorite, meat loaf and Nanny's homemade mac and cheese," Lily said.

"How about a hello for your mother?" Olivia asked as she unfastened her gun belt and placed it in its usual spot on the top of one of the kitchen cabinets.

"Hello, Mommy." Lily dropped Daniel's hand and rushed toward her mother for a round of kisses and hugs.

"Good evening, Deputy Carson," Rose said with a warm smile.

"Same to you and please make it Daniel."

"Then Daniel it is," she replied with a pleased expression.

"Now, what can I do to help?"

Olivia and Lily had disappeared into Rose's bedroom where he knew Olivia would be changing clothes.

"Absolutely nothing. Just sit and relax. How about a tall glass of lemonade?"

"That sounds great," he agreed and sat at the table in the chair where he had sat each time he'd shared a meal with them.

Rose poured him a glass of the cold beverage and while they waited for Olivia and Lily to return from the bedroom, he and Rose chatted about the pirate theme park that would eventually open.

"It will definitely change things around here," he said. "With all the tourists they're hoping to attract the town will benefit both financially and socially."

"We haven't had a chance to really see any of the town," Rose said as she pulled a large meat loaf from the lower rack of the oven. "Olivia has insisted we stay inside and don't go exploring. I even have groceries delivered here."

"Maybe we can change that a little bit this evening," Olivia said as she and Lily returned to the room. She looked positively stunning with her hair loose around her shoulders and clad in white shorts and a sleeveless hot-pink blouse. Lily was like a mini-me in pink shorts and a pink-and-white checked top. Daniel got back to his feet at the sight of them.

"Change it how?" Rose asked curiously.

"Daniel and I have a little surprise planned for after dinner," Olivia replied.

"A surprise? Tell me, Mommy. Tell me the surprise." Lily jumped up and down.

Olivia laughed and shook her head. "Nope. My lips are sealed. It won't be a surprise if I tell you now."

Lily immediately turned her attention to Daniel. She sidled up next to him and gazed up at him with innocent green eyes that could melt the hardest of hearts.

"Deputy, you can tell me the secret," she said in the sweetest of voices. "It's okay. You can whisper it in my ear."

He laughed and also shook his head. "No way, my little peanut. Your mother would kill me. Besides, if you just be patient and eat a good dinner, then it will be time for the secret and you'll know it."

Lily heaved a dramatic sigh. "Nanny, is it time to eat? We have to eat fast tonight."

"I'll have it on the table in just a jiffy," Rose replied. "Everyone go ahead and sit while I finish things up."

The three of them sat as Rose sliced the meat loaf and set a platter in the center of the table. She added a big bowl of green beans and a large crock dish of creamy-looking mac and cheese.

The food was delicious, but it was the company that filled Daniel's soul and made him realize just how much he was going to miss not only Olivia, but her family as well when they all returned to their life in Natchez.

"I'll tell you the secret once the kitchen is all cleaned," Olivia said as they finished eating.

Rose had never had so much help clearing dishes from the table and loading the dishwasher. Both Lily and Daniel scrambled to finish the cleanup in record time.

Olivia fought a burst of giggles as the two of them bumped into each other several times in their haste to finish up. Finally the work was done and Lily climbed up on Olivia's lap and placed her hands on either side of her mother's face.

"It's time for the secret," she said.

"Okay. Daniel and I thought it would be nice if we'd all take a trip into town to an ice cream parlor," Olivia said.

Lily's eyes widened and she clapped her hands together and quickly scampered off Olivia's lap. "That's a great surprise. So, let's go!"

It took several minutes for them to actually get out the door. Rose went into her bedroom to freshen up and grab her purse, and Olivia grabbed her gun belt and pulled her gun from her holster and placed it in her purse.

It was a grim reminder that this wasn't just a simple social outing without the potential for danger. Danger could come at them wearing any face, cloaked in any body shape and size. She only hoped she wasn't putting her two most precious people in her life at risk. She hoped Daniel was right when he'd doubted that the perp would make a move on her in a public place. Surely he wouldn't want any witnesses around.

Besides, between her and Daniel they could manage to have an ice cream parlor experience without trouble. She didn't even want to think about last night, when she'd slept in his arms and wished on a star that things could be different.

She didn't want to focus on how neatly he fit into her little family without any ripples. Rose and Lily both adored him, and he appeared to be as taken with them. Fantasy. She couldn't dwell in fantasies.

Daniel drove with Olivia riding shotgun and Rose and Lily in the backseat. As he hit Main Street, he pointed out stores and other places he thought would interest Rose and Lily.

Rose was particularly interested in Mama Baptiste's shop when Daniel told her Mama sold all kinds of herbs and spices in addition to her secret rubs and potions for ailments.

He also pointed out The Pirate's Inn, but instead of talking about ghosts and hauntings that might have scared Lily, he talked about the pirates who had once used Lost Lagoon as a land base.

Charlie's Ice Cream Parlor was located across the

street from Jimmy's Place and was a throwback to the past with pink-and-white umbrella tables dotting a patio area in front and a matching awning.

Several couples were seated at the tables as Olivia, Daniel, Rose and Lily went inside to get their cold goodies. Charlie Berk, proud owner of the place, introduced himself. He stood behind a refrigerated counter that appeared to stretch forever.

Round barrels of various flavors of ice cream were tucked inside the glass-topped counter, and on top of the counter were a variety of syrups, sprinkles and other candies to add to the sinfulness of the ice cream. The syrups were controlled by Charlie, but the sprinkles and candy containers held scoopers for customers to help themselves.

"Sprinkles!" Lily exclaimed in delight. "I love sprinkles!"

"I'm thinking a banana split sounds good," Daniel said.

"And I'm thinking a waffle cone of peanut butter ice cream with chocolate chips on top," Olivia said.

"And I'm still thinking," Rose replied as she walked up and down the counter as if overwhelmed by the many choices.

"What about you, munchkin?" Daniel asked Lily. Olivia already knew what her daughter's answer would be.

"A waffle cone with chocolate ice cream and lots and lots of sprinkles," Lily replied.

Rose finally decided on a bowl of strawberry shortcake ice cream with fresh strawberries and whipped cream topping. Orders were placed and delivered and then the four of them moved outside to one of the empty umbrella tables.

Once again Olivia was struck by the fact that they looked like the perfect family. She and Daniel had made sweet love the night before and shared dinner together and now they had their daughter and Olivia's mother out for ice cream.

What would happen if she told Daniel the truth? He talked the talk of a confirmed bachelor, but his actions said otherwise. It was obvious he was quite charmed by Lily. Would he really be so horrified to discover that he was Lily's father? Would he be angry that she hadn't told him before?

Despite the fact that she'd lain in his arms the night before and he was laughing at Lily's antics as she tried to capture the drips of her quickly melting cone, he had given her no indication that he wanted anything with her expect what they now shared…a temporary relationship while she was here.

He hadn't awakened this morning after making such passionate love with her last night and suddenly spouted words of everlasting love for her.

Nothing had really changed to make her believe he would welcome the news that he had a daughter. In the end, it was a secret she knew she wouldn't divulge to him.

For all intents and purposes, her husband, Phil, had been Lily's father. He had changed her diapers and walked the floors with her when she'd been colicky in the middle of the night. He was the man who had celebrated her first step and her first word.

Unfortunately, Lily had few memories of the big man with the big heart who had married Olivia because he'd loved her desperately and wanted to take care of her and her unborn child.

They were almost finished with their treats when she saw Jimmy Tambor approaching from across the street. "Hey, guys," he said with a friendly smile as he spied them at their table and paused.

"Hi, Jimmy. Aren't you in the middle of dinner rush?" Daniel asked.

Jimmy waved a hand dismissively. "Yeah, but they can handle if for a while without me. I had a craving for Charlie's raspberry chocolate chip ice cream and decided to sneak away for a few minutes. I've got great staff and things run pretty much on their own, so nobody really misses me when I'm gone."

He crouched down next to Lily. "And you must be the little girl who likes my mozzarella sticks."

Lily's eyes widened. "You make them?"

"I sure do," Jimmy replied.

"I love them, almost as much as ice cream," Lily replied.

Jimmy laughed and straightened up. "I haven't heard any more about the investigation. Things still on track for an arrest?"

"We're just crossing our t's and dotting our i's," Olivia replied. How she wished that was the case. She was beginning to believe that the murder wouldn't be solved before she'd be called back to Natchez. She'd spent most of the day putting her last touches on the report she would send to the attorney general about her internal investigation.

"Well, enjoy the last of your ice cream," Jimmy said and then with another of his friendly smiles he left their table and disappeared into the shop.

Olivia watched him go, her brain suddenly firing off in all directions. Jimmy Tambor hadn't made the list of suspects and yet he'd been here at the time of the murder. He had probably had a close relationship to Shelly because of his close friendship with Bo.

The steak knife that had been found next to her when she'd been attacked in the station parking lot had come from the restaurant he pretended to own, and he seemed particularly interested in keeping track of where they were in the investigation.

"Earth to Olivia." Daniel's deep voice brought her back to the here and now.

Lily giggled. "Earth to Mommy," she repeated.

"I'm here. Sorry, I just got lost in my head for a minute," she replied. Surely, she was just grasping at desperate straws in even considering Jimmy as a suspect.

"I asked if we were ready to go," Daniel said.

"Ready," she replied. They got up from the table and she made sure all the napkins were placed in the nearby trash receptacle and then they were back in Daniel's car and headed back to the house.

"We should have surprises more often," Lily said. "Like maybe every day."

Daniel laughed and Olivia watched him shoot an affectionate glance into his rearview mirror. "If you had a surprise every day then they wouldn't be special anymore. Personally, I think this surprise was very special."

"Me, too," Lily replied. "And I'm 'specially happy that you got to eat ice cream with us, Deputy."

By that time they were home. As Rose and Lily headed inside, Olivia touched Daniel's arm and lingered on the front porch. "Thanks for the great idea. It's been fun."

"It has been fun," he agreed. "But you seemed a bit distracted there for a few minutes."

"Jimmy distracted me. I found myself wondering why he isn't a serious suspect on our list."

Daniel frowned. "I guess he didn't make the short list because he and Bo have always been so close. It's hard to believe he'd have anything to do with killing his best friend's girlfriend."

"Do you remember where he was on the night of Shelly's murder?" she asked.

"I'd have to look back in the files to be sure, but I think he was working at Bo's Place that night," he replied.

"I'd like to double-check that again and maybe have another chat with Bo tomorrow," she said thoughtfully. "I don't know, maybe I'm crazy, but no stone left unturned, right?"

"Okay, whatever you want," he agreed. He held her

gaze for a long moment. "Do we need to talk about last night?"

Heat instantly fired in her cheeks. "The only thing to talk about is the fact that it shouldn't happen again. It won't happen again," she corrected herself.

"But I already want it to." He reached out and ran his fingers through a strand of her hair, then caressed his fingers down the side of her face.

She stepped away from him. Damn him. His very touch set off a yearning inside her that she had to ignore, that she somehow had to cast out.

"Daniel, I can't make love to you again because I refuse to leave here with my heart broken. We don't want the same things from life. We're wrong for each other on so many levels, and yet I've allowed myself to get emotionally involved with you and it has to stop now."

A hint of surprise shone from his eyes and then was gone. He released a deep sigh and raked a hand through his hair. "You're almost finished here, aren't you?"

She nodded. "I finished the report on the internal investigation today. Once I send it in, it should just be a matter of days before a special election is set and once a new sheriff is elected, I'll for sure be gone."

A hollowness filled her at her own words. If things were different she wouldn't have minded calling Lost Lagoon home. If Daniel loved her, if he wanted a family… but that was her fantasy and not his.

"The most important thing now is that we close out the Sinclair case before I leave," she continued, desperately needing to get the conversation back on a professional level.

"Then we go to talk to Bo in the morning and see what he can tell us about his friend, Jimmy." His green eyes were darker than usual and impossible to read.

"Good. I'll be ready to get to the office by seven," she said.

He nodded. "Then I'll be out here around that time to follow you in."

She placed a hand on his arm, unable to stop herself. "Thank you for tonight and for everything you've done to support and protect me." She dropped her arm back to her side. "But we need to keep things strictly professional from here on out." Her heart clenched. "I don't want you getting any closer to my family, especially Lily. It will just make it harder for her, for all of us, when we leave here."

"Olivia, it sounds like you're telling me goodbye and you aren't leaving yet."

"I just wanted you to understand that last night was a one-time thing that won't be repeated."

"Message received," he replied, his eyes still darker than usual. "And on that note I'll just say good-night and I'll see you in the morning."

She watched from the porch as he walked to his car, got inside and then finally disappeared from her sight. What he didn't realize was that she had been saying goodbye…goodbye to any fantasy she might have entertained about them all becoming a family. A farewell to any dreams she might have entertained about him becoming more than just the biological father to Lily.

She was in love with him and more than anything, she had to say goodbye to that particular emotion.

Chapter Eleven

The ice cream session definitely hadn't ended the way Daniel had imagined. He wasn't sure what he'd expected, but it hadn't been her confessing to him that she'd become emotionally involved with him and giving him a premature goodbye.

The next morning as he sat outside her house waiting for her to emerge, he played and replayed their conversation in his head.

She'd said she didn't want to leave here with a broken heart, which implied she was falling in love with him. It was probably good that she'd put a brake on things, because he was getting way too into her and the company of her family.

Footloose and fancy-free, that was how he'd always envisioned himself. He'd never wanted to make the same mistakes his parents had made. He had never wanted the ugliness he'd lived through when they had divorced.

But he had become increasingly aware in the last couple of months of how love had added richness to the lives of those around him and that what he'd gone through in his childhood was caused by two selfish, dysfunctional people.

For the past couple of days he'd been at war with himself, discovering that his attraction to Olivia was far deeper than mere lust and yet afraid of changing his chosen solitary path through life.

He was thirty-three years old and since the time that he was eighteen, he'd opted for comfort and ease. He didn't need or want anyone in his life on a permanent basis. He was happy being alone, he told himself.

He breathed a sigh of relief as she appeared on the porch and pulled him from his troubling thoughts. She was all business today, with her hair pulled back in a grim bun and clad in the khaki uniform of her station.

She gave him a small wave and then got into her car. He followed her to the station where they both parked and he fell into step next to her as they headed for the building.

"Sleep well?" he asked.

"To be honest, I didn't sleep well," she replied.

"That futon can't be the most comfortable place to sleep."

"It's not, but I couldn't find a three-bedroom place to rent when we needed to be here. Besides, it wasn't the futon that kept me tossing and turning all night. Shelly's murder has a hold on me like few cases I've ever worked in the past."

"Trust me, it's been a stab in my heart every time it's crossed my mind. I just wish we could have done a complete investigation when it happened."

"Your hands were tied by your boss."

"Yeah, but I should have done more." He opened the back door that led into the building and followed behind her inside.

"You're doing the best you can now, and hopefully Bo will give us some information about Jimmy Tambor to get him out of my head as a potential suspect." She frowned. "I know my job here wasn't to solve murder cases, but I'd really like to close this one out before I'm called back to Natchez."

They entered the squad room where several of the other deputies sat at their desks. "What time are we going to talk to Bo?"

"I'm going to call him and see if he's available around ten. I'll let you know what I set up with him." With a curt nod of dismissal, she entered her office and closed the door behind her.

Cool and professional, she was definitely setting a new tone between them. He'd follow her lead because he didn't want to make things difficult for her. He cared about her too much to pursue a deeper relationship with her that would only create pain and heartache for her and for sweet Lily when they left.

He sat at his desk and checked the notes left by James Rockfield, the deputy who worked the shift before him. Just because he and the small task force had been focused on solving Shelly's murder didn't mean that all other crime in town had stopped.

There had been a smash and grab at the liquor store on Main Street. The culprit had gotten away with several bottles of booze and three cartons of cigarettes. The owner had called a glass company to replace the broken front window and the security camera had captured old man Clyde Dorfman in the act. Unfortunately, James and the night crew had been unable to locate Clyde to make an arrest.

Daniel picked up the report and carried it to Ray McClure's desk. Ray sat sipping coffee and reading a sports magazine. "Take care of this," Daniel said. "I've got interviews to conduct with the sheriff."

Ray read over the report and then frowned. "How in the hell am I supposed to find Clyde if the night crew couldn't find him? They say right here he wasn't at home when they checked."

"My guess would be that he's probably drunk as a skunk and hiding out in one of the abandoned shanties. Eventually he'll sober up and head home, but in the meantime you might catch him in one of the shanties."

"How could he be so stupid? He had to have known there was a security camera."

"Clyde has never been the brightest bulb in the pack and he was probably already half-drunk when he committed the crime," Daniel replied.

Ray pulled himself out of his chair. "That man spends more time in jail sobering up than he does in that dive where he lives."

"This time if charges are pressed, he'll spend a lot more time in jail," Daniel replied. "This isn't going to be a simple drunk-and-disorderly charge."

He waited until Ray had disappeared out of the back door before he returned to his desk. Although he knew he should be thinking about the interview they would soon be conducting with Bo, his thoughts wandered back to Olivia and how much fun it had been sharing ice cream with her family the night before, how much he enjoyed eating dinner with them and how easily he'd fit into her personal life.

She was no longer simply Lily, the striking woman he'd picked up in a bar and had shared a fantasy night of lovemaking. She was Olivia, intelligent and strong and a loving mother and daughter.

It was just before nine when she stuck her head out the door and told him she'd set up to meet Bo and Claire at their house at ten.

Personally, Daniel thought the whole thing was just a wild-goose chase. The idea of Jimmy Tambor being a murderer seemed as far-fetched as alcoholic Clyde ever putting down the bottle.

At nine forty-five he and Olivia left the station to head to Bo and Claire's place. Olivia was quiet as they got into his car.

"Are you still going to be my friend?" he asked only half-seriously as he started the car.

She turned and looked at him first in surprise, and then smiled when she realized he was teasing her. "I have to keep you as a friend. You're the only one I have in town. I just can't be your friend with benefits."

"And I'll respect that," he replied. He didn't want to respect it. He didn't have to like it. He wanted her again…and again. But he knew, in the depths of his heart, she was right in her decision.

She was a woman looking for something different in

her life. Having a short affair with him wouldn't give her what she wanted…what she needed. She had told him she wanted to marry again and give Lily a father to love. He just wasn't that man.

When they reached Bo and Claire's place, Bo greeted them at the front door and ushered them inside where the four of them sat at the table.

"I've heard through the grapevine that you're rebuilding on your mother's property where the house burned down," Daniel said. Bo's childhood home had been burned down by Claire's stalker, who was now in jail.

"The contractor is just getting started, but we're hoping that within about three months or so we'll have a new home to move into," Bo said. He glanced at Claire and the love in his eyes was unmistakable. "This house has been great, but it's way too little for a family and we're both ready to start having children."

Claire smiled. "And we both want at least a couple of kids."

"You won't regret it," Olivia said. "Having my daughter was the best thing I ever did in my life."

"But I'm sure you aren't here to talk about new houses and parenthood," Bo said.

"We want to ask you some questions about Jimmy Tambor," Olivia said.

"Jimmy?" Bo looked at her in surprise. "What about him?"

"I understand you two have been friends for a long time," Olivia said.

"Jimmy and I have been like brothers since we were in grade school. He had a brutal, abusive father and an absent mother and we sort of took him in. Most nights Jimmy ate dinner with us, and during the summers he spent most of his time at our house. He was always a bit smaller than me so my mother gave him my hand-me-down clothes and treated him like a son."

"And your friendship remained strong as you grew older?" Olivia asked.

Bo nodded. "Definitely. When I opened Bo's Place, I gave Jimmy a job there and he moved into an upstairs apartment with me."

"How did he get along with Shelly?" Daniel asked.

Bo's eyes narrowed slightly. "Where are you going with this? Surely you don't believe Jimmy had anything to do with Shelly's death? He cared about Shelly. The three of us got along great. Besides, from what I heard you had a suspect ready to arrest."

"We're just tying up some loose ends, and we realized Jimmy hadn't really been investigated at the time of the murder."

Bo released a dry, slightly irritated laugh. "That's because there was no real investigation at the time of the murder. Trey Walker pointed a finger of blame squarely on me and never did anything to find anyone else who might have been responsible."

"And we're trying to rectify that," Olivia said.

"If you're seriously looking at Jimmy as a suspect, then you're dredging the bottom of the swamp. When I left town under the weight of all the suspicion, Jimmy moved in with my mother to help take care of her. He took over my business to keep it running. He's always been there when I needed him. He would never do anything to hurt me, and he knew more than anyone how much I loved Shelly."

Bo paused and released a ragged sigh as he looked first at Daniel and then at Olivia. "You're no closer to finding out who killed Shelly than Trey Walker was." It wasn't a question. It was a statement that shot a new pang of guilt through Daniel.

Olivia's features reflected not only the guilt Daniel felt, but also the painful knowledge that Bo was right.

"Surely, if there was something strange going on between Jimmy and Shelly, Bo would have sensed it," Olivia said a few minutes later when they were back in Daniel's car.

"He seemed adamant that Jimmy didn't have anything to do with Shelly's death," Daniel replied. "Bo knows Jimmy better than anyone in town."

"Does Jimmy have a girlfriend? Did he have one when Shelly was murdered?"

Daniel cast her a quick glance and frowned as he focused back on the road. "You know, now that I think about it, I can't remember any woman that Jimmy has ever dated, although that doesn't mean he hasn't had girlfriends. I never paid much attention to him, except to meet and greet when I go to Jimmy's Place for a meal."

Olivia frowned and stared out the passenger window. Who had killed Shelly Sinclair? They had no concrete evidence to point to anyone specifically. Their ruse of putting out the word that an arrest was about to happen hadn't done anything.

She didn't know what else to do to solve the crime. Bo was right, they were no closer to catching the killer than Trey Walker had been when he'd been sheriff.

"Your frustration is alive and well and filling the car," Daniel said, breaking into her troubled thoughts.

"Sorry, I can't help it. I really hoped to clear this case."

"We still have some time," he replied.

"Some time, but we don't have any more leads."

"Something will pop," he said confidently as he pulled into a parking space behind the sheriff's building. He shut off the car and turned to look at her. "We have to stay positive, Olivia. That's what makes us good lawmen—we don't stop. We don't give up."

She gazed at his handsome countenance and almost regretted her decision to halt all physical contact between them. She didn't just lust after him. Being in his arms had made her feel safe and completely feminine. He'd tapped into the woman inside her, beyond the tough cloak she wore as a strong and competent sheriff.

"Are you planning on running for sheriff when they hold the special election?" she asked, trying to forget that she'd ever experienced the wonder of being held in his arms, of being kissed so passionately.

He laughed and shook his head. "No way. In fact, I've been offered another job that I'm seriously considering. Rod Nixon called me a couple of days ago and asked if I'd be interested in heading up the security team for the amusement park."

She looked at him in surprise. "You could just walk away from your badge?"

"I don't know," he admitted. "That's why I told Rod I'd need some time to consider it. To be honest, working with a man like Trey kind of soured me for the job."

"You're good at what you do," she replied, still stunned by what he'd said about walking away from law enforcement.

"I'd be just as good at running security at the park," he countered. "Come on, let's get inside. I feel like I'm baking out here."

A few minutes later, Olivia was back in her office and Daniel was at his desk. Her blinds were open so she could see into the squad room.

Again and again her gaze was drawn to Daniel, who was on his laptop probably working up a report of their conversation with Bo.

She loved him. She was in love with him and there was nothing she could do about it. She would leave Lost Lagoon with a wounded heart that would eventually scar, but she'd never be able to forget Deputy Daniel Carson.

Each time she looked into Lily's green eyes, she would remember the man who was the girl's father. She would mourn the fact that he had no desire to have a wife or children. He simply wasn't a family man.

It was particularly cruel of fate to bring her here with him, knowing that he could never be the man in her life. It had been particularly stupid of her to allow him so far into her heart, to allow him to be a part of her family for even a brief moment.

It was noon when Daniel opened her door and asked her if she wanted to go someplace for lunch. She declined and told him she would just order in something from Jimmy's Place.

A half an hour later, a teenager delivered a chicken Caesar salad to her and as she ate she tried to keep her mind empty.

She needed a little mental break from the Sinclair case and from thoughts of Daniel. Instead she allowed her mind to dwell on Lily and her mother. Despite the fact that Lily had been unplanned, she'd been a gift from God, completing Olivia's life in a way she'd never dreamed possible.

Rose's support had also been a godsend. Only she knew that Lily hadn't been Phil's child, but rather the result of a one-night stand. Of course Rose had no idea that the one-night stand had been with Daniel.

Even though Rose hadn't approved of her daughter's risky behavior that night so long ago, she'd stood by Olivia throughout her pregnancy and after.

Sooner than later, the three of them would return to their apartment in Natchez and resume the life they had led before coming to Lost Lagoon.

They had been fine without Daniel before and they would continue to be fine when they got back home. Nothing had really changed.

After lunch she called Ray McClure into her office. He updated her on the liquor store break-in, reporting that Clyde still hadn't made an appearance anywhere to make an arrest.

"Then what are you doing sitting in the squad room?" Olivia asked. "Why aren't you out on the streets still looking for him?"

"I got hot and decided to come in for a little while," Ray replied, his voice half-whiny.

"We sometimes have to work in uncomfortable situations. It's part of your job." Olivia straightened in her chair and stared hard at Ray, who finally broke the gaze and looked down at the floor.

"Ray, I've finished up my internal investigation here," she continued. He looked at her again, appearing to hold his breath. "Don't worry. I don't believe you had anything to do with the corruption that took place here with the drug operation. But I do believe that you're lazy and a weak link in the department. I'm recommending that you be placed on probation for six months, and if you don't step up by then you won't have a job here any longer. If you do step up, then the probation will be washed clean from your record."

She expected a protest. She fully anticipated a fit of anger from Ray. Instead he released a deep sigh and frowned thoughtfully. "It was easy to be lazy when Trey was in charge. I followed him around and laughed at his stupid jokes and told him how great he was. That was all he expected from me."

"Trey is in jail and things have changed," Olivia replied.

Ray nodded. There was no surly expression, no hint

of insubordination as he straightened in his chair. "All of my life I wanted to work in law enforcement. I lost my drive, gave up my ambition to Trey. It *is* time for a change. I need to get back to the man I was before Trey was boss, and I promise you'll see a different man from now on."

Olivia nodded and noticed that as Ray left the office there was a new confidence in his gait, a determination in the set of his shoulders.

She was pleased with the way things had gone with the deputy. Her instinct was that he'd just been waiting for somebody to call him on the rug, to give him a reason to step up. He'd been allowed to fall into bad habits, but she believed he'd taken her words to heart.

She spent most of the rest of the afternoon rereading the report she intended to email to the attorney general. It had been ready to go for a couple of days, but she'd put off actually sending it, knowing that it would signal the beginning of the end of her time here.

By four o'clock she realized dark clouds had moved in, portending another storm brought on by the heat and humidity of the day and hurricane Dennis that was spinning its strength along the coast.

She'd called a meeting of the task force at four thirty and by the time she made it to the small conference room, all of the lights in the building had been turned on to ward off the darkness outside.

She was disappointed, but not surprised, that none of the task force team members had anything new to add on the Sinclair case.

She was about to dismiss them all when her cell phone rang and she saw from the caller ID that it was Bo McBride. "Bo?"

"It's Jimmy," he said, his voice frantic. "He killed Shelly. After our talk this morning, I decided to go to the bar and I searched his apartment. I found Shelly's ring stuffed in a sock in his drawer." The words tumbled over themselves, fast and furious. "He walked in and I confronted him."

"Where is he now?" Olivia asked urgently.

"He ran down the stairs and just took off in his car, a blue Camry."

"We'll take it from here," Olivia said and disconnected the call. "Jimmy Tambor is Shelly's killer and he just left Jimmy's Place in a blue Camry. Josh, get men and roadblocks set up on every road coming in and out of town. Get everyone out there looking for him. I don't want him getting out of Lost Lagoon."

The men jumped to their feet and left the room. Daniel looked at Olivia. "Come on, you can ride with me," he said.

"If he had Shelly's ring, he has to be the killer," she said. "I wonder why he'd kill her?"

"We don't need to know the why right now. We just have to find him before he gets out of town," Daniel replied as they hurried toward the exit to the parking lot.

They had just gotten into Daniel's car when Olivia's cell phone rang again. It was Deputy Wes Stiller. She punched it on speaker to answer.

"Sheriff Bradford, I found Jimmy's car," he said.

"Where?" Olivia asked, her heart pounding with adrenaline.

"It's parked in front of your house. Luckily, I spotted it while out on patrol in your area. The car is vacant. I think he's inside."

Olivia's breath whooshed out of her as if she'd been sucker punched. Terror ripped through her as Daniel tore out of the parking lot and headed for her house where a killer was now holed up inside with her mother and her daughter.

Chapter Twelve

Daniel drove like a bat out of hell, his heart beating a thousand miles an hour. Still, he knew his heartbeat couldn't be as fast, as frantic as Olivia's.

She sat straight in the seat, her lovely features taut and ashen with the fear he knew must be tearing through her. There was nothing more dangerous than a trapped killer, especially one who had two hostages in his grasp.

"Why would my mother let him inside? She's never met Jimmy before. Why would she unarm the alarm to let him in?" Her voice was soft, and he knew she didn't expect him to have the answers. He wasn't even sure she was aware that she was talking out loud.

They didn't know if he'd gone in armed. Did he have a gun? Or had he left the restaurant with one of his wickedly sharp steak knives? Even if he hadn't, there were plenty of knives inside the house that he could use to hurt either Rose or Lily.

Daniel's heart clenched tight as he thought of the little girl with the bright green eyes and loving nature. And what about sweet, naïve Rose? She certainly had no tools to know how to deal with a desperate man.

Jimmy couldn't have chosen better if he wanted vulnerable hostages.

Lightning flashed and thunder boomed in the distance as they pulled along the side of the road two houses away from Olivia's house. Jimmy's car was parked in front of her place and several patrol cars were parked on either side of the road some distance back.

It was obvious nobody had approached the house and everyone was awaiting Olivia's orders. Her fingers trembled as she unfastened her seat belt. He worried that her legs might not hold her when she opened the door to get out of the car.

She surprised him, getting out and standing tall, none of the fear he'd seen on her face in the car now present as Deputy Wes Stiller approached.

"We need to establish contact," Olivia said. "And I need to know that the two hostages are okay." Her voice broke slightly.

Daniel moved closer to her, fighting the impulse to pull her against his chest, to hold her tight and tell her that everything was going to be all right.

However, he couldn't tell her that everything was going to be okay, nor did he want to undermine her authority in front of the other men. She was the boss and she would call the shots.

"I'll try my mother's cell phone," she said. She punched in the numbers and waited. Daniel stood close enough to her that he could hear it ring over and over again until an answering machine came on. Olivia waited for the beep, and then spoke. "Jimmy, we need to talk. Answer the phone." There was no reply and the call disconnected.

By that time Bo had arrived on scene. He hurried over to Olivia and Daniel as the dark of the storm grew deeper and the lightning got closer.

"I've tried to call him, but he isn't answering any of my calls," Bo said. "I can't believe this is happening. I don't understand any of it. Why would Jimmy do something like this?"

"I don't give a damn why," Olivia snapped. "We just need to get him out of that house and away from my family." Tears filled her eyes and she looked desperately at Daniel. "I need to think like a cop, but right now all I can do is think like a mother."

Daniel looked at Wes. "Get a perimeter of men surrounding the house, but don't get close enough that Jimmy feels more threatened. Just make sure he doesn't escape out the back door."

"Got it," Wes replied and hurried toward the gathering group of officers who had arrived on scene.

Olivia called her mother again, quickly hitting speaker as the call was answered by Rose. "Olivia. He fooled me." Rose's voice trembled with suppressed terror and then she began to cry. "He said he was delivering mozzarella sticks and he had a bag from Jimmy's Place and so I let him in. I'm sorry. I'm so sorry."

"Mom, none of that matters now. I know you're scared. Is Lily okay? Are you both unharmed?" Olivia asked. Her fingers around her cell phone were bone white with tension.

"We're fine, but…" Rose's voice cut out and instead Jimmy's filled the line.

"They're fine for now, but I can't promise you it's going to stay that way," he said.

"Tell me what you want, Jimmy." Olivia's voice was once again strong and controlled. "Tell me how we can resolve this so that nobody gets hurt."

"I'll let you know what I want later." With those words, Jimmy cut the line off. Olivia immediately called back but the phone rang once and then was hung up.

"Let me try again," Bo said. He dialed Jimmy's cell phone number and punched his phone on speaker. To everyone's surprise, Jimmy answered.

"I've got nothing to say to you," Jimmy said.

"Jimmy, just give yourself up. Come out of the house and nobody will get hurt," Bo said.

"I'll go to prison. That bitch of a girlfriend of yours double-crossed me." A wealth of venom deepened Jimmy's voice.

"What are you talking about?" Bo asked in obvious confusion. "Jimmy, I'm begging you as a friend to come out and end this."

"You aren't my friend," Jimmy yelled. "You never were my friend. I was your charity case. You were the golden boy and I got your leftovers. People were only friends with me because of you. The best thing that ever happened to me was when you left town and I got to live your life. I got to live with your mother and run your business."

"What did you do to Shelly?" Bo asked.

"I took her from you. I courted her, and we had plans to leave town together, but on the night it was supposed to happen, she decided she couldn't leave you. You always won. That night I made sure you didn't win. I took her away from you forever."

Jimmy hung up and Bo stared at Daniel in confused horror. "All this time I thought we were friends, and he's hated me."

"I think we just got to the bottom of Shelly's sticky situation," Daniel said. "Shelly was torn between leaving town with Jimmy and staying here with you. She chose you and something inside Jimmy snapped."

"Does Jimmy have a gun?" Olivia asked.

"To be honest, I don't know. When I was running Bo's Place, I always kept a handgun under the counter near the cash register. I took that gun with me when I left town since it was registered to me. I don't know whether Jimmy got one or not," Bo said.

"Wes, get on your laptop and see if you can find out if Jimmy owns a gun," Olivia said.

It didn't matter, Daniel thought. Jimmy could easily kill Rose and Lily without a gun being fired. He suspected Olivia was aware of that, but her command to Wes was an effort to do something, anything.

Lightning once again slashed the sky, closer this time and followed within seconds by a round of rumbling thunder. "What happens now?" Bo asked.

"We wait." Olivia's voice was hollow. "Right now Jimmy holds all the cards. We wait to see what his next move is and then we react."

Daniel knew she was right. There was no way they could act, not with Lily and Rose at risk. At the moment, Jimmy had all the control and until he did something to lose that control, they were in a stalemate.

"No more phone calls," she said as Bo started to use his cell phone again. "We don't contact him. We wait until he contacts one of us."

Daniel gazed at Olivia. Her features were taut, her shoulders back and she appeared in complete command of the situation until he looked into her eyes. There, all of her fear simmered like a bubbling cauldron about to boil over.

Overhead the storm was nearly upon them, the lightning and thunder coming closer and with more frequency. The tempest was reflected in Olivia's eyes, and Daniel feared she'd break before this all came to some kind of an end.

And Daniel couldn't begin to guess how it might end. Jimmy had sounded like a piece of dry tinder about to explode into flames when he'd spoken with Bo.

The minutes ticked by in agonizing increments. Each time Daniel thought of the hostages inside the house, his heart ached with a fear he'd never known before. Although he cared about Rose's well-being, it was the thought of little Lily being terrorized or hurt that made him sick to his stomach.

He couldn't imagine the dark thoughts Olivia must be entertaining as they waited for Jimmy to make some kind of contact.

Although white shades were pulled shut at the front

windows, silhouettes occasionally passed in front of them, letting Daniel know that at least Jimmy hadn't already killed the hostages and then committed suicide as a final end to the standoff.

Wes left his patrol car and returned to where Olivia, Daniel and Bo stood. "Jimmy registered a handgun six months ago, but I called Jimmy's Place and talked to the bartender, who said the gun is under the counter."

"He didn't have time to grab it," Bo said thoughtfully. "Once I confronted him with Shelly's ring, he ran. I chased him down the stairs and he ran right out the back door. It's good that he doesn't have a gun, right?" He looked at Daniel and then Olivia.

"He didn't need a gun to kill Shelly," Olivia replied. Her voice held a tremble that spoke of how close to the edge of a breakdown she was.

Again Daniel wanted to take her into his arms, hold her tight against him and take away her pain. Unfortunately, he knew he wasn't what she needed most at the moment. What she needed was to have her daughter in her arms, safe and sound. What she wanted was her mother out of that house and standing next to her.

He hated that he didn't know what to do, that he didn't know how to resolve this without taking a risk, and he wasn't willing to do anything that might risk Rose and Lily.

The ring of Olivia's phone jarred all of them. She answered and put it on speaker. "Jimmy, you need to tell me how we can solve this so that nobody gets hurt."

"This is what I want." His voice was harsh and it was

difficult to realize this was the same man who greeted them at the bar and grill with a boyish smile and oozing charm.

"I want all of you to pull out, and that includes anyone you have covering the back of the house. I want everyone far enough away that I can get to my car safely," he said.

"We can do that," Olivia agreed. Daniel assumed she was willing to let him drive away from here because she could put out a bulletin to law enforcement outside of Lost Lagoon. He might leave their little town, but he wouldn't get far.

"And for assurance purposes I'm taking Lily with me. When I know I'm safe I'll drop her off somewhere and let you know where she is," Jimmy added.

"No. No way are you leaving that house with my daughter," Olivia replied frantically, and tears began to well up in her eyes.

"That's the only way this will end," Jimmy replied. "I'll give you fifteen minutes to agree to my plan. If you don't, then things are going to go bad in here very quickly." He disconnected and Olivia might have fallen to the ground if Daniel hadn't caught her.

He held her close as she wept—no longer Sheriff Bradford, but simply a terrified mother. Lightning crackled and thunder boomed overhead.

The skies had yet to unleash a torrent of rain, but the rain was on Olivia's face as she wept uncontrollably in his arms. She finally looked up at him. "We have to get them out of there. You have to get Lily out. She's your daughter, Daniel. You have to save her."

He froze and dropped his arms from around her. "What did you say?"

She swiped at her cheeks, and as he stared at her it was as if everything else around them disappeared. "That night in New Orleans...we made Lily. She's your daughter." Olivia choked on another sob. "And now she needs her daddy to save her."

Her daddy. Her age...her bright green eyes so like his own. God, why hadn't he realized it before now? Lily was his child, his own flesh and blood.

He couldn't think about that right now. If he did, he'd fall into a miasma of emotions that would mess with his head. Jimmy had given them fifteen minutes to agree to his demands.

The clock was ticking and somehow, someway he needed to bring this all to an end. Thunder boomed overhead once again, and with it an idea sprang to life in his mind.

"Move all the men back," he said to Olivia. "Call in the men surrounding the house."

"Surely you aren't agreeing to his demands," Olivia asked, her eyes wide with horror.

"No, but I want him to think we're complying with him. Get everyone moved out of the area. Trust me, Olivia. I have a plan but we need to move fast."

It took four minutes to have all of the men leave. They moved to the next street over to wait for further commands. Once they were gone, Daniel looked at Olivia.

"Call Jimmy and tell him you want to see Rose and Lily in the front window, that you won't agree to anything else until you see them with your own eyes."

"And what are you going to do?"

"Hopefully, I'm going to save my daughter," he replied grimly. With these words he raced for the side of the house. With his heart pounding near heart attack speed, he slowly moved around the back of the house and to the other side.

He crouched down beneath the window that he knew was located in Lily's bedroom. He peeked inside to find the room dark. Good. The darkness was his friend.

The unlit bedroom and the storm raging overhead were advantages. But the alarm system was a definite disadvantage. If it had been rearmed after Jimmy had entered the house, then Daniel's plan wouldn't work and the results could be catastrophic.

If he tried to open or break the window and the alarm sounded, then Jimmy would know immediately that somebody was attempting to enter the house.

Jimmy was already agitated and desperate, a dangerous combination. Daniel had no way to guess what his reaction might be. He hoped that Olivia had made the call and if Jimmy complied with her request then all three of them would be in the living room.

With the stealth of a jewel thief, he carefully removed the window screen and placed it against the side of the house next to him.

Lily was his daughter. The words whirled around in his head. Why hadn't Olivia told him when she'd first arrived here? Why had it taken this life-and-death drama for her to spill the secret?

He couldn't think of that right now. He needed to stay focused on the here and now and what he needed to do. With his heart beating a desperate rhythm, he waited for the lightning that would be followed by thunder.

He held his gun in his hand, the butt of it ready to hit the window. As lightning slashed the sky, a crackle of electricity shot through him. The thunder boomed, and at the same time Daniel used the butt of his gun to break the window just above the turn lock.

He held his breath and then shuddered in relief as no alarm sounded. Apparently in the chaos that must have occurred when Jimmy had first entered the house, nobody had thought to reset the alarm.

The clap of thunder had provided the right cover for the sound of the breaking glass. Daniel held his breath and reached in and unlocked the window and then slowly eased it up.

It was only when he'd entered the window and stood in the center of Lily's bedroom that he began to breathe again. He steadied his gun in his hand and moved toward the doorway, which would give him a direct line of vision to the living room.

Once again his breath caught in his chest as he stood just inside the bedroom doorway. If Jimmy caught sight of him, then he knew that all bets were off concerning the safety of the hostages.

He peeked his head around the doorway and saw Rose seated on the sofa, sobbing softly. Jimmy stood at the front window, the shade up, and he held Lily up under her armpits as a shield in front of him.

There was no way Jimmy could have a knife or any other weapon in his hand at that particular moment. It was now or never. Daniel burst out of the bedroom. "Jimmy. It's over."

Jimmy whirled around and Daniel didn't hesitate. He shot the man in his right lower leg. Jimmy screamed in pain and went down and Daniel holstered his gun and rushed to grab a sobbing Lily from the floor.

She hugged him around his neck and wrapped her legs around his waist, clinging to him as she cried. His child. His daughter. His heart clenched tight.

"I knew you'd come to save us, Deputy," she finally said loud enough to be heard above Jimmy's cries for help. Rose jumped off the sofa and embraced both of them.

"Let's get you out of here," Daniel said. He went to the front door, opened it wide enough to slip his hand outside and called, "We're coming out." Taking hold of Rose's hand, he led her and carried Lily to safety.

Olivia stood at the end of the driveway as raindrops were finally beginning to fall. At the sight of Daniel with Lily in his arms, she ran toward them. "Thank God," she sobbed as she took Lily from him. Daniel ushered all of them onto the lawn farther away from the house, away from danger, then used his cell phone to call in the men.

Bo entered the house with several of the other deputies. He looked down at the man who he'd believed had been his friend for so long. "I did everything I could to help you," he said.

"And I resented every handout you ever gave me," Jimmy replied. "I was glad when everyone thought you killed Shelly. I was elated when you decided to leave town. I destroyed you."

Bo smiled grimly and shook his head. "I have a wife who loves me and who I love. I'm taking back the business I built and own. You didn't destroy me, Jimmy. You destroyed yourself."

By that time an ambulance had arrived. Jimmy was whisked away under guard. The doctors would deal with his gunshot wound, and once he was well enough he would stand trial for the murder of Shelly Sinclair.

It was finally over. The crime had been solved. And Daniel had a daughter. Overwhelmed by myriad emotions, he left the scene and got into his car. He sat for a long moment and then started the engine and pulled away.

He needed to think. He needed to process everything. He felt raw and oddly vulnerable. What he needed more than anything was some time alone to figure out what he wanted and what he needed to do as a man with a precious child.

Chapter Thirteen

The cat was out of the bag. That was Olivia's first thought when she awakened on the futon just after dawn. And her timing and delivery couldn't have been worse.

She was self-aware enough to know that part of the reason she'd blurted out the information had been a little bit of manipulation. She needed him to know that Lily wasn't just a child in danger, but rather was *his* child. She'd hoped that would be the incentive for him to go to the ends of the earth to get Lily to safety.

She turned over on her side to face the front window where the sun was just starting to peek over the horizon. The storms from the night before were gone and it looked as if it was going to be a clear, sunny day.

What was Daniel thinking? What was he feeling? Did he hate her for getting pregnant, for telling him about Lily or for not telling him about his daughter the first day she had arrived here?

There was no way of guessing what might be going on in his head, because he had left last night without speaking a single word to her.

There would be no reason for him to follow her into work today. While Jimmy had been loaded into the ambulance, he'd confessed that he had been the person who had attacked her in the parking lot.

He'd believed that if he killed her then, the two-year-old murder investigation would once again become a cold case as everyone scrambled to find out who killed the sheriff. He apparently hadn't been rational enough to know that an investigation into her murder might eventually lead to him.

There was no longer any reason for Daniel to act as her bodyguard. There was no longer any reason for them to spend any time together again. The danger was now gone.

She stumbled up from the futon and over to the counter to put on a pot of coffee. As it brewed she stood at the front window and stared out, her thoughts still on Daniel.

She expected nothing from him. She never had. He could choose to be an active parent in Lily's life and they'd figure things out for custody, or he could walk away and decide to be an absent parent.

At least Lily didn't know. If he did decide not to be a father, then Lily wouldn't live with the sting of that rejection. She had poured herself a cup of coffee and was seated at the table when her mother made her morning appearance.

Clad in a pink flowered duster and with her dark hair neatly brushed, she looked no worse for the wear of the trauma of the night before.

"You're up unusually early," Rose said as she poured herself a cup of coffee and then joined Olivia at the table.

"I just woke up and decided to go ahead and get up." Olivia wrapped her fingers around the warmth of her cup. "I guess I've got a lot on my mind."

Rose looked at her in surprise. "I would think your mind would be wonderfully clear this morning. You've cleared the department from any corruption issues and you solved a crime that has haunted the town for two years."

Olivia smiled at her mother. "We didn't exactly solve the crime. It pretty much solved itself." She took a sip of her coffee and eyed her mother over the rim of her cup. She carefully set the cup back down and leaned back in her chair. "I also told Daniel last night that he was Lily's biological father."

Rose stared at her in surprise. "And is that the truth?"

Olivia nodded. "He was the man at the conference five years ago that I met in the bar and then spent a night with and wound up pregnant."

Rose spooned a bit of sugar into her coffee and stirred, obviously taking the time to gather her thoughts. "Why didn't you tell him when we first arrived here and you recognized him as that man?"

"Because in one of the first conversations we shared he told me he was a confirmed bachelor who didn't want a wife or any children. I knew we were here temporarily, so I figured there was no point in telling him," Olivia explained.

Rose studied Olivia's features for a long moment. "You're in love with him, aren't you?"

Olivia sighed miserably. "I am."

"I've seen it in your eyes when the two of you are together. I know you loved Phil, and he was there for you when you needed somebody, but I also know you didn't feel that breathless kind of passion of true love and that's what I see in you when you talk about Daniel."

"It doesn't matter how I feel about him. He just isn't cut out to be a family man." Olivia sucked in a sigh of misery.

"Pshaw, I've never seen a man more ready for a family than him," Rose replied. "He looks at you the same way you look at him. And a confirmed bachelor wouldn't have taken so many opportunities to eat dinner with an old woman and a little girl. He wouldn't have taken us to that ice cream parlor. He might not know it, but he's definitely a family man."

"None of that matters now," Olivia replied. "I'm sure he hates me now."

Rose frowned. "Why?"

"I don't know, maybe because I was stupid enough to get pregnant."

"There were two of you in the bed that night," Rose reminded her. "If you were careless, then so was he."

"But after I told him and after everything was over last night, he didn't even stick around to talk to me. He just left without saying a word."

"I'm sure everything will be just fine, dear." Rose took a drink of her coffee and then got to her feet. "How about I make French toast for breakfast this morning? I think we all deserve a little treat after the night we had last night."

"Sure, that sounds great," Olivia replied. Leave it to Rose to believe that a favorite breakfast food would magically make everything okay. Lily would be happy to have syrup on the menu for the morning.

Lily. Olivia's heart squeezed tight, making it difficult for her to breathe as she thought of how close she'd come to losing her precious daughter and her mother the night before.

Things could have gone so terribly wrong if Daniel hadn't taken the risk to break into the window and take Jimmy down.

Olivia finished her coffee and then headed for the bathroom to shower and dress for the day. By the time she had finished, Lily was awake and helping Rose with the French toast.

When she saw Olivia, she ran to her arms, and Olivia sat on the sofa for a morning snuggle. "How is my favorite girl this morning?" Olivia asked.

Olivia had spent some time the night before talking to Lily about what had happened. She'd explained that there were some bad people in the world and unfortunately one of them had gotten into the house. Lily had told her mother she'd tried to be brave but she had cried. She'd also told Olivia that she'd known in her heart that Deputy would get inside and take the bad man away.

"I'm good," Lily replied and then smiled impishly.

"I couldn't be bad with French toast and lots of syrup for breakfast."

Like Nanny, like granddaughter, Olivia thought an hour later as she drove toward the station. A little syrup for breakfast made the whole world sweet and wonderful and cast out all the evil in the world.

The closer she got to work, the more her stomach twisted into nervous knots as she tried to anticipate what to expect from Daniel.

Really, all she had to tell him was that nothing had changed. Within a couple of weeks at the most, she and her family would go back to Natchez and he never had to think about them again. Despite knowing the truth about Lily, there was no reason his life had to change at all.

He wasn't at his desk in the squad room when she walked in. She headed for her office amid cheers and congratulations from the men who were present.

Everyone was in high spirits with the closure of Shelly Sinclair's murder case, with the knowledge that the murdered young woman could finally now rest in peace.

She bowed with forced playfulness to the men and then quickly escaped into her office and closed the door. She sank down at her desk and wondered how long it would be before Daniel came in, before there was some sort of a confrontation between them.

It was ten o'clock when she saw, through the blinds, Daniel enter the squad room. He didn't speak to anyone but walked directly to her door and knocked.

He entered the office and immediately closed all the blinds that would allow anyone to see inside the private office. She watched him closely, trying to gauge his mood, but it was impossible.

He finally sat in the chair in front of her desk, his green eyes as mysterious and unfathomable as the depths of the swamps that half surrounded the small town.

"Was there ever really a Phil who was your husband?" he asked.

"There was. He was the kindest man you'd ever want to know. Although I wasn't in love with him, he was crazy about me. I married him when I was five months pregnant with Lily. He promised to love her like his own and he did so until the day he died."

"I understand why you didn't contact me when you first discovered you were pregnant. We didn't exactly take the time to get full names or addresses that night in New Orleans, but why didn't you tell me about Lily when you first arrived here?"

Olivia held his gaze steadily. "Because you wouldn't have wanted to know, because you told me you were a confirmed bachelor and had no desire for marriage or children. I didn't want to burden you with the truth."

He shook his head and raked a hand through his hair, and for the first time she noticed the deepened lines that radiated out from his eyes, indicating a night of little sleep.

"I went home last night and tried to wrap my brain around everything that had happened. I was shocked by Jimmy's actions and the fact that he'd hidden how much he hated Bo and that he'd killed Shelly. But I was completely stunned by you telling me that Lily was my daughter."

"I shouldn't have told you, at least not the way I did. But, Daniel, nothing has to change. I mean, I don't want child support or anything like that. You can just pretend I didn't tell you and go on about your merry way," she said, although each word ached in her heart.

He stared at her as if she'd lost her mind. "Everything has changed. I went home last night and sat in my living room and listened to the silence that lived there. I've always liked the quiet. But, lately, the silence hasn't felt good. In fact, it's been lonely. I've been lonely and questioning the path I'd chosen for myself." He leaned forward in the chair. "I want to be a part of Lily's life."

Olivia's heart swelled. She'd wanted this for her daughter. Daniel was a good man and he would make a wonderful father. "Then I guess what we need to do is talk about custody for when I have to return to Natchez."

"I want full custody," he said and leaned back in his chair. His eyes simmered with a wealth of emotions, but his words caused Olivia's breath to whoosh out of her. The last thing she'd ever expected was a custody battle with him.

"I… You can't…" Hot tears sprang to her eyes.

Daniel leaned forward once again. "Olivia, you didn't let me finish. I want full custody of Lily, but I also want full custody of you and Rose."

"What?" She stared at him, afraid to guess what he meant, afraid to embrace any hope of dreams coming true.

He got up from his chair and walked around her desk. He took one of her hands and pulled her to her feet. "Olivia, I was awake all night long, fighting who I believed I was and what I've become, what you've made me become."

"I don't understand." She gazed up at him, loving him so much it hurt and afraid of misunderstanding exactly what he wanted from her.

"I realized last night that I was a confirmed bachelor because I'd never met a woman who made me want to be anything else. I didn't want children because I didn't care enough about any woman to want to go there with her. What I realized last night was that I wasn't that man anymore, that I had met the woman who made me desire marriage and children and a mother-in-law who is sweet and kind."

She began to shiver as his words sank into her brain and then downward to fill her heart. "I love you, Daniel." The words escaped her.

He cupped her face with his hands. "And I love you. I love you more than I ever dreamed it was possible to love. I want you in my life, Olivia. I want you and our daughter and Rose to build a life together forever."

He stopped talking and instead took her mouth with his, kissing her with a sweet tenderness overlaying a simmer of desire that stirred her in her very soul.

When the kiss finally ended, he kept her in his

arms. "We'll need to figure out how this is all going to work," he said. "I'll quit my job here to move to Natchez. Sooner or later I'll find some kind of work there. I can sell the house and pick up stakes."

She looked up at him. "Or maybe we could just stay here. I could talk to my boss and see about getting transferred here. In fact, I hear through the grapevine that there's going to be a new sheriff elected eventually. What do you think my chances are in getting elected?"

"I think with the right man backing you, your chances are very good," he replied, his eyes shining with the happy confidence of a man who knew what he wanted and where he was going.

"I think if we work together we can accomplish anything, Olivia. But, are you sure this is where you want to be?" A frown appeared across his forehead.

"There's really nothing for me in Natchez, and with the new amusement park going in, things should be jumping here in Lost Lagoon. But, the truth is, I'll be happy anywhere as long as you're by my side."

He kissed her again, and Olivia realized all of her dreams were really coming true. This time when the kiss ended, he grabbed her by the hand and led her toward the office door.

"What are you doing?" she asked.

"We need to hit the road."

"Where are we going?" she asked.

"To your place. We need to tell Lily that she can't call me Deputy anymore. I can't wait to hear her call me Daddy." His eyes glowed with an inner happiness that matched the glow that lit her up inside.

Olivia laughed as they left the office and headed for the back door. As they left the building and stepped outside into the bright sunshine, she knew she was taking the first steps into her future…a future with a man she loved, the father of her child, and it was all going to be magnificent.

Epilogue

Late October was a good time for a barbecue in Lost Lagoon. The intense heat of summer had eased along with some of the heavy humidity. However, the fire of love hadn't stopped burning for Olivia and Daniel.

Olivia now stood at the kitchen window in his house…in their home and watched as Daniel pushed Lily in a swing on a set he'd bought the day Olivia and Lily had moved in with him.

They had tried to get Rose to move in with them, but she'd insisted she wanted to remain in the cheerful little yellow house where she could start a garden in the yard and turn what had been Lily's room into a crafting space.

Over the last month, Rose had made friends with several women, including Mama Baptiste, and the two often met for tea in the evenings and talked about herbs and cooking.

She was still available at all hours of the day and night to babysit Lily, and each Sunday Olivia, Daniel and Lily went back to the little yellow house for dinner.

OLIVIA SMILED AS she heard Lily's laughter. "Higher, Daddy. Push me higher!" Daniel's laughter mingled with Lily's, and Olivia's heart swelled with a love she had never dreamed possible.

A knock on the door pulled Olivia from the window and to the front door. Her mother entered carrying a bowl of potato salad big enough to feed an army.

"Mom, let me help you with that," Olivia exclaimed and grabbed the bowl to carry it to the kitchen, where the table already held burgers and hot dogs ready to be placed on the grill, thick-sliced tomatoes and onions and squeeze bottles of mustard and ketchup.

At that moment, Daniel came in from the backyard, his smile carefree and loving as he looked first at Olivia, then at Rose. "If it isn't my favorite soon-to-be mother-in-law," he said and kissed Rose on her cheek.

"And look, she brought enough potato salad to feed the entire neighborhood even though there are just going to be eight of us," Olivia said.

"But today is a celebration on so many different levels," Rose replied. "And besides, potato salad is always good leftover." She looked toward the window where Lily was still on the swing. "And now I'm going outside to spend some time with my favorite little girl before the others arrive."

The minute she stepped out of the back door, Daniel grabbed Olivia around the waist and pulled her into his arms. "And I'm going to spend a little time with my favorite woman before the others arrive."

As always when he kissed her she tasted his love,

his desire for her and she knew she'd never tire of his kisses. He owned her heart and soul, and each day they spent together only deepened their love for one another.

"Hmm, you taste better than anything that's going to be served today," he said when he ended the kiss.

"That's funny, I was just thinking the same thing about you," she replied.

The doorbell rang, and Daniel sighed as he dropped his arms from around her. "Darn, I was hoping to get another kiss from you, but it appears some of our other guests have arrived."

"You get the door. I still have a few things to finish putting out on the table," Olivia said with a laugh.

Daniel disappeared and returned a moment later followed by Bo and Claire. Bo carried a Crock-Pot of baked beans, and Claire guided him to the table where she plugged it into a nearby wall socket.

"It's a perfect day for a picnic," Bo said.

Olivia smiled. "It's a perfect day to celebrate."

"What can I do to help?" Claire asked as Bo followed Daniel out the back door, where they both hovered over the barbecue pit.

"Absolutely nothing. Just sit and relax. How about a cold beer or something else to drink? I've also got lemonade, sweet tea and soda."

"A glass of sweet tea sounds good," Claire replied. She looked cute as a button with her short curly blond hair framing her face, clad in a pair of denim shorts and a blue sleeveless blouse.

Olivia delivered the tea to Claire just as the doorbell

rang once again. "That will be Josh and Savannah. I'll be right back."

Olivia hurried to the front door to welcome the last of the guests. Savannah carried with her a chocolate cake and as she walked into the kitchen, Josh disappeared out the back door to join the other men at the barbecue.

Olivia looked out the window and then turned to grin at the other two women. "How many men does it take to start a fire?"

"As many as can gather around," Claire replied. "It's a man thing. Wait until they start cooking the meat. It will be utter chaos."

"I don't think Josh will fight anyone over cooking. That man is utterly hopeless when it comes to anything to do in the kitchen," Savannah replied.

Olivia had grown close to the woman who had lost her sister to murder. Since the closure of the crime, Savannah's dark eyes sparkled with happiness and she laughed more often. Olivia was glad that she'd been a part of bringing Savannah the closure she'd needed.

"Before any cooking happens, I want to get everyone together for a round of toasts," Olivia said. She moved to the back door and called for everyone to gather in the kitchen.

It took several minutes for all of them to gather and have drinks in hand. The men all had beer and the women had sweet tea. Even Lily had a glass of grape juice to raise for the toasts Olivia wanted to make.

For a moment as Olivia looked around at the people, her heart swelled with peace and contentment that had ruled her life since Daniel had proclaimed his love for her.

Since Jimmy's arrest, she had formed friendships with Claire and Savannah and had developed admiration and affection for both Bo and Josh.

"Daddy, can we drink now?" Lily asked Daniel.

"Not yet, your mother is apparently gathering her thoughts," Daniel replied.

"I hope she hurries 'cause I'm hungry," Lily replied.

"Okay," Olivia said with a smile. "I just wanted to take a moment and celebrate the fact that Bo no longer lives beneath a shadow of guilt and has reopened Bo's Place."

"Do we drink now?" Lily asked.

Daniel shook his head and Olivia continued. "And I want to celebrate Josh and Savannah's recent marriage and that she's rented space on Main Street to finally open her restaurant."

"Now?" Lily asked with a hint of impatience.

Olivia shook her head. "I'd also like to mention how happy I am to have been elected sheriff of Lost Lagoon last week." Olivia paused a moment, remembering how honored she'd been that the town wanted her to stay, that they trusted her to be the head of their law enforcement and that the powers that be had allowed her to transfer to Lost Lagoon.

"And I took the job at the amusement park and handed in my resignation at the sheriff's department," Daniel added in an obvious attempt to hurry things along. "And Olivia and I have set a wedding date for

December twelfth and I think that's everything. And yes, Lily, now you can drink."

Everyone laughed and raised their glasses and bottles to each other. Love and laughter continued throughout the barbecue. It was nearly bedtime when everyone finally left, Lily had gone to spend the night with Nanny and Olivia and Daniel were alone.

Olivia was at the sink washing up the last of the dishes that wouldn't go into the dishwasher when Daniel came up behind her and wrapped his arms around her as he nuzzled the back of her neck.

"It was a great day," he said.

"It was a wonderful day," she replied and pulled her hands out of the soapy water and reached for a towel.

"It's going to be a wonderful night, too," he whispered.

She turned in his arms and smiled up at him. "I was hoping for a nightcap of some kind."

He kissed the tip of her nose. "When you were making all your toasts you didn't mention the other thing we have to celebrate."

One of her hands fell onto her stomach. "It's early and I still want to savor this particular secret just between us for a little while longer."

She rubbed her hand over her tummy. She was a month pregnant. This time it was planned and wanted and Daniel was by her side.

"Lily will be over the moon when we tell her she's going to get a little brother or sister."

"Just imagine a trip to the ice cream parlor times one million on a chart of excitement," Olivia replied.

"Like father, like daughter," he replied. "This time I won't miss a minute of being a father."

"I love you, Daniel." Her heart was filled with her love for him. He was a kind, patient and loving father to Lily. He'd taken to fatherhood naturally.

"And I love you. I love our life together and the fact that you made me realize the man I was meant to be," he replied.

"Now…about that nightcap?"

His eyes fired with hot desire and he grinned at her. "Far be it for me to keep the new sheriff in town waiting." He took her by the hand and led her out of the kitchen and down the hallway.

The hot, sexy uncommitted man she'd met in a bar five years ago was gone, transformed into a man who embraced love of his daughter, his soon-to-be mother-in-law and her. It was no longer a fantasy she entertained, it was a reality she lived…and loved.

* * * * *

"You're not like any man I've ever tried to seduce, Dallas Cole."

"Is that good or bad?"

She cocked her head, a smile flirting with her kiss-stung lips. "Both."

"In case it's not clear, I do want you."

She stepped closer until she pressed against him. "I know."

She was damn near impossible to resist, but he made himself ease her away. "We have to trust each other."

"Yes," she agreed.

"And sex complicates things."

"It does."

"It would be easy to let myself get caught up in you, as a way of forgetting…"

"Comfort sex."

"Yes." He stole a look at her. "I don't want there to be any doubts between us. I don't want you to ever feel used."

"A little late for that," she said in a wry tone, and he realized she was revealing more about her past than perhaps she meant to.

BLUE RIDGE
RICOCHET

BY
PAULA GRAVES

First Published in Great Britain 2016
By Mills & Boon, an imprint of HarperCollins*Publishers*
1 London Bridge Street, London, SE1 9GF

© 2016 Paula Graves

ISBN: 978-0-263-91894-6

46-0216

Our policy is to use papers that are natural, renewable and recyclable products and made from wood grown in sustainable forests. The logging and manufacturing processes conform to the legal environmental regulations of the country of origin.

Printed and bound in Spain
by CPI, Barcelona

Paula Graves, an Alabama native, wrote her first book at the age of six. A voracious reader, Paula loves books that pair tantalizing mystery with compelling romance. When she's not reading or writing, she works as a creative director for a Birmingham advertising agency and spends time with her family and friends. Paula invites readers to visit her website www.paulagraves.com.

For my readers. Thank you for all your support.
I couldn't live this dream without you.

Chapter One

Sleet rattled against the windshield, a staccato counterpoint to the rhythmic *swish-swish* of the windshield wipers. Outside, night had fallen in inky finality, as if it planned to stay awhile, the Jeep's headlights the only illumination as far as the eye could see.

Nicolette Jamison forced herself out of a weary slouch behind the steering wheel and concentrated on the curving mountain road revealed in her headlights, well aware of the treachery that lay ahead for a careless driver. The switchbacks and drop-offs in the Blue Ridge Mountains could be deadly if you weren't paying attention. Not to mention the occasional reckless deer or coyote—

"Son of a—!"

The man loomed in the Jeep's headlights as suddenly as if the swirling mist had conjured him up, a tall, lean phantom of a man who turned slowly to face the headlights as she hit the brakes and prayed she wouldn't go into a skid this dangerously close to a steep drop-off.

The Jeep's wheels grabbed the blacktop and hung on, the vehicle shimmying to a stop just a yard away from the apparition gazing back at her through the windshield. For a second, she had a strange sense of recognition, as if she knew him, though she was pretty sure she didn't.

Then his eyes fluttered closed and he dropped out of sight.

Nicki's heart stuttered like a snare drum against her rib cage as she stared at the misty void where, seconds earlier, she'd seen the staring man.

Ghost, her inner twelve-year-old intoned, sending her heart rate soaring steeply for a few seconds before her grown-up side took charge. She checked the rearview mirror for coming traffic, saw only the faint red glow of her own taillights, and put the car in Reverse, backing up carefully until she could see what the front of the Jeep had concealed—a man lying in a crumpled heap in the center of the narrow two-lane road.

She pulled the Jeep to the shoulder on the mountain side of the road and parked, engaging her hazard lights and trying to calm her rattled nerves. The man could be hurt.

Or it could be a trick. Maybe she should call the sheriff's department and let them handle things.

Except…

Buck up, Nicki. This is the life you chose.

Her weapons of choice these days were pepper spray and sheer nerve, and so far, she'd survived on their one-two punch. But something about the man lying crumpled on the road in front of her made her nerve waver. There was still something eerily familiar about him, a memory tugging at the back of her mind, trying to make itself known.

Holding the pepper-spray canister out in front of her, she approached the man, easing into a crouch just beyond reach. She shifted position so that the glow from the Jeep's headlights fell across the man's face.

He was younger than she'd thought, in his midthirties at most. His pallor, combined with the sunken cheeks and shadowed eyes that came with illness, had made him look older. He was still breathing, she saw with relief.

"Mister?"

He stirred at the sound of her voice, his eyelids flickering open to half-mast, then drifting shut again. He muttered something that sounded like a string of numbers, but she couldn't quite make them out.

Gingerly, she reached out to check his pulse. Fast but steady and stronger than she'd anticipated. "Where are you hurt?"

He murmured numbers again. She made out a two and a four before he stopped.

She pulled her cell phone from the pocket of her jeans and tried to dial 911, then realized she didn't have any reception. "Damn it." She pocketed the phone and stared at him for a second, considering her options. Leaving him here in the road wasn't an option. And without cell phone reception, calling for help wasn't an option, either. The temperature was right at the freezing mark, and his skin was cold to the touch, which suggested he might already be suffering from exposure.

He was breathing. He was at least semiconscious. His heart rate was a little fast but steady as a rock, so he didn't seem likely to go into cardiac arrest anytime soon. And he'd definitely been mobile before he collapsed in front of her vehicle, so he didn't seem to have any spinal issues.

She had to get him warm, and the Jeep was the best bet. The old Wrangler had seen better days, but its heater still worked.

But how was she supposed to haul this man into her Jeep?

"Mister, think you can stay with me long enough for me to get you to my car?"

He opened his eyes, looking straight at her, and that niggle of recognition returned. "Who're you?"

"My name's Nicki. What's yours?"

"Dallas."

For a brief second, she wondered if he'd misunderstood her question. Then the memory that had been flickering in and out of the back of her mind popped to the front, and she sat back on her heels, almost toppling over.

Dallas. As in Dallas Cole, missing for almost three weeks now and presumed by most people as either dead and buried somewhere in the Blue Ridge Mountains or wintering somewhere on the coast of Mexico, a cerveza in hand and a pretty girl by his side.

The last place she'd figured on running into the missing FBI employee was on Bellwether Road in the middle of Dudley County, Virginia.

Now she could see the resemblance between the man lying in the road in front of her and the missing man whose disappearance had caused a stir all the way from Washington, DC, to the little town of Purgatory, Tennessee, where a man named Alexander Quinn ran a security agency called The Gates.

"Oh, hell," she murmured.

A frown furrowed his brow. "Where am I?"

"Ever heard of River's End, Virginia?"

His voice rasped as he answered. "No."

"Not surprising."

He struggled to sit up. Not quite sure she could trust him yet, she let him do so without her help, her gaze sweeping over him in search of injuries. She spotted healing bruises dotting his jawline and the evidence of old blood spotting the front of his grimy gray shirt, but no sign of recent injuries.

Mostly, he looked exhausted and cold, and while she

was no doctor, she could help him out with those two ailments. "Think you can stand?"

He pulled his legs up and gave a push with his arms, wincing as his left arm gave out and he landed on his backside. "Something's wrong with my shoulder."

Could be a trick, her wary mind warned, but she ignored it, following the demands of her compassionate heart. He couldn't fake the unmistakable look of ill health. Something had happened to this man, no matter what crimes had led him to this place, and the least she could do was get him somewhere warm and dry before feds came swarming into River's End.

She started to reach for him, planning to help him to his feet, when her last thought finally penetrated her brain.

She pulled back, staring at him with alarm.

"What's wrong?" he asked, slanting her a suspicious look.

"Nothing," she lied, even as her mind started scrambling for a solution to her unexpected dilemma. There was no way she could leave him to fend for himself out here in the sleet. There was supposed to be snow before midnight, and the temps were going to plunge into the midtwenties before morning. Dressed as he was, without even a coat to ward off the chill, he'd never survive the night.

But if she took him to the hospital in Bristol…

She couldn't. They'd call the FBI, who'd want to talk to her. There'd be a lot of terribly inconvenient questions and all her work for the past few months would be out the window.

Or worse.

But how to explain that to the hypothermic, battered

man sitting in the road in front of her? "Look, I tried calling 911—"

"No." His gaze snapped up sharply, catching her off guard.

"No?"

"I don't need medical help." His lips pressed to a thin line. "I'm okay. I just need to get warm."

Well, she thought, *that wasn't exactly a comforting reaction.*

"Are you sure?" Not that she wanted to contact authorities any more than he did, but his reluctance didn't exactly fit the picture of a man wrongly accused, did it?

Maybe that was good, though, considering the dangerous game she was playing herself. Dealing with bad guys was less complicated than dealing with good ones, she'd discovered. Their motives were easier to glean and usually involved one sin or another. Greed, gluttony, lust, hate—oh, yeah, she definitely knew how to deal with sinners.

Saints, on the other hand, were a cipher.

"Let's get you out of the cold, Dallas." She pushed aside questions of his particular motives. There'd be time to figure him out once she got him back to her cabin, where she could provide the basic comforts anyone in his condition needed, whether sinner or saint.

Avoiding his bad shoulder, she pulled his right arm around her shoulder and helped him to his feet. He stumbled a little as they made their way across the slickening blacktop to the Jeep, but she settled him in the passenger seat with little fuss and watched with bemusement as he fumbled the seat belt into place. Sinner or not, he apparently took seat belt safety seriously.

She circled around, slid behind the Jeep's steering

wheel and cranked the engine. Next to her, Dallas sighed audibly as heat blasted from the Jeep's vents.

"Good?" she asked, easing back onto the road.

"Heaven," he murmured through chattering teeth.

He couldn't have been out in the elements for long, she realized as his shivering began to ease before they'd gone more than a mile down the road. So where the hell had he come from?

"Should I be worrying about pursuit?" she asked.

His gaze slanted toward her. "Pursuit?"

"Anybody after you?"

He didn't answer at first. She didn't push, too busy dealing with the steady buildup of icy precipitation forming on the mountain road. Thank God she didn't have much farther to travel. The little cabin she called home was only a quarter mile down the road. They'd be there before the snow started.

"There might be," he answered finally as she slowed into the turn down the gravel road that ended at her cabin.

"Are they nearby?"

"Probably," he answered.

Great. Just great.

"What did you do?" She glanced his way.

His mouth crooked in the corner. "Because people in trouble usually got there under their own steam?"

She shrugged. "Usually."

"I broke a rule. I thought it was for a good reason, but as usual, the rules are there for a reason."

He was beginning to sound more like a saint than a sinner. "What kind of rule?"

"I skipped steps I should have taken," he said obliquely.

But she knew enough about his situation to know exactly what he was talking about, even if she didn't let on. "That's cryptic."

He smiled. "Yes."

So. He didn't trust her any more than she trusted him. Fair enough. She was in no position to quibble.

"Well, how about we don't worry about rules and secrets, and just get you somewhere warm and dry. Think you could handle something to eat?"

"Yes," he said with an eagerness that made her glance his way again. He met her gaze with a quick glance, his lips quirking again. "Sorry. I've missed a meal or three."

When he smiled, he was almost good-looking even with his sunken eyes and hollow cheeks, something she hadn't expected. The only photo she'd seen of him had been his driver's license photo. Nobody ever looked good in their driver's license photos.

Dallas Cole, she suspected, would clean up nicely.

Down, girl. He's not date material, and you've sworn off men, remember? Saints or sinners, they're nothing but trouble.

She pulled the Jeep under the carport connected to her cabin and cut the engine. "Sure you don't want me to call paramedics?"

His eyes were closed, his head resting against the back of the seat. When he turned his face toward her, his eyes opened slowly to meet hers in the gloom. "I just need to rest a little while. Then I'll get out of your hair."

The full impact of what she was doing hit her as she got out of the Jeep and locked the door behind her. Had she lost her mind, taking in a stranger wanted by the FBI? Even Alexander Quinn, a man who prided himself on his ability to read people, wasn't sure what side Dallas Cole had chosen. For all she knew, this might be a test of her loyalty to the Blue Ridge Infantry.

She had to tread carefully. Everything she'd worked for over the past few months was at stake.

Dallas stumbled on his way to the door, flashing her a grimace of a smile as she grabbed his arm and kept him from face-planting in the gravel between the Jeep and her kitchen door. "I'm usually steadier on my feet."

"How long has it been since you ate anything?"

"Not counting roots and berries?" he asked with a lop-sided smile, leaning against the side of her house while she unlocked the door.

"Yeah, not counting those." She opened the door and helped him up the two shallow steps into the kitchen.

Inside, the cabin was blessedly warm and familiar, driving away some of Nicki's tension. Dallas Cole didn't seem to be faking his weakness, and she was finally back in her own comfort zone. She knew where the knives were kept and where to find her Remington 870 pump-action shotgun and ammo.

And there was the satellite phone hidden under the mattress of her bed that would get Alexander Quinn on the line in a second. He might be two and a half hours away in Purgatory, Tennessee, but he had eyes and ears all over the hills. She knew from experience.

"How much snow do you think we'll get?" Dallas asked as she flicked the switch on the wall, flooding the kitchen with light. He squinted at her, as if it had been a while since his eyes had been accustomed to so much light.

"I guess you haven't heard a forecast in a few days?" She crossed to the stove and grabbed one of the saucepans hanging over the range. "We'll get an inch or two, maybe. It'll probably be melted off by tomorrow afternoon."

"Glad to be out of it." He nodded toward the small kitchen nook table. "May I?"

Polite, she thought. Though she'd met a few well-mannered devils in her day who'd give you the shaft and thank you for it. "Sit. I'll see what's in the pantry."

He groaned a little as he sat, and she wondered how many injuries he had hidden beneath his grimy clothes. "Thank you. I'm not sure how I'll be able to repay you for your kindness."

His accent was subtle but there, the hint of a mountain twang not unlike her own Tennessee accent. She'd done little more than glance over the information Quinn's mystery operative had left for her at the dead drop a few weeks earlier before she'd destroyed it, not exactly expecting Dallas Cole to show up in the middle of River's End. But there'd been something about a hometown in eastern Kentucky—

"No repayment necessary." She looked through the cans in her pantry. "Chicken and vegetable sound okay?"

"Sounds like heaven."

As she heated the soup, she searched her brain for any other details she could remember from the dossier on Dallas Cole. His job at the FBI wasn't exactly what she might have expected—that much she remembered. She wasn't dealing with a special agent or a forensic science whiz.

No, he was a graphic designer with the Bureau's public affairs office.

How on earth had an artist gotten himself crossways with the Blue Ridge Infantry?

HE HAD NO idea what to do next, so he did nothing. Nothing but sit and bask in the warmth of this tiny kitchen and watch a blue-eyed brunette with killer curves heating a can of chicken soup on an ancient gas range.

Nicki, she'd said. Short for Nicole?

"This is a nice place," he said, mostly to end the silence. Over the past three weeks, silence had become his enemy, an auditory void in which his deepest fears had held sway.

She glanced toward him. "Compared to what?"

Her blunt tone made his lips twitch with unaccustomed humor. He hadn't had a lot to laugh about recently. "I've been worse places."

"Haven't we all?" She pulled a couple of stoneware bowls from a nearby cabinet and put them on the counter by the stove. "You in the mood for a little or a lot?"

His stomach seemed to be turning eager flips, but his brain kicked in with a stern warning. The last thing he wanted to do in front of a pretty girl like Nicki was throw up. "Let's start with a little."

She slanted a curious look his way but put a bowl half-full of steaming soup on the table in front of him. "Careful. It's hot." She fetched a spoon and put it by the bowl.

He blew on a spoonful of the soup and took a sip. The savory broth tasted like heaven in a spoon.

Nicki took the seat across from him, not looking at him as she started eating her own bowl of soup.

Prickles of suspicion played at the back of his neck. Why wasn't she looking at him?

"Just you here?" he asked.

Her gaze snapped up to meet his, and he realized how shady the question probably seemed.

Her green-eyed gaze leveled with his. "Me and my Remington 870."

He smiled at that. "Message received."

"Sorry. That was a tad rude, wasn't it?" One corner of her lips tilted upward.

"Probably earned it with that badly phrased question." He fell silent and concentrated on eating his soup as slowly as his ravening hunger would allow. His stomach felt unsettled but the food was staying down, at least for the time being.

He needed food and rest, in that order. Because once he left this cabin, he wasn't sure when he'd get much of either again.

"How did you end up out there in the woods?"

The question he'd been waiting for ever since she'd stopped to help. "It's a long story."

"And you don't want to tell it?" In her voice, he heard a surprising thread of sympathy. He looked up and saw her sharp eyes watching him with understanding.

"Not at the present," he admitted.

"Okay." She turned her attention back to her soup.

That was easy.

Too easy.

He didn't know how to deal with someone who didn't seem to want—or need—one damn thing from him. Especially after the ordeal of the past few weeks. He didn't know how to relax anymore, how to sit quietly and eat a bowl of soup without waiting for the next blow, the next trick.

He knew his name was Dallas Logan Cole. He was thirty-three years old and had spent the first eighteen years of his life in Kentucky coal country, trying like hell to get out before he was stuck there for the rest of his sorry life. He was a good artist and an even better designer, and he'd spent the bulk of his college years trying to leave behind the last vestiges of his mountain upbringing so he could start a whole new life.

And here he was, back in the hills, running for his life again. How the hell had he let this happen?

"I guess those are the only clothes you have?"

He looked down at his grimy shirt and jeans. They weren't the clothes he'd been wearing when a group of men in pickup trucks had run his car off the road a few miles north of Ruckersville, Virginia. The wreck had left him a little woozy and helpless to fight the four burly mountain men who'd hauled him into one of the trucks and driven him into the hills. They'd stripped him out of his suit and made him dress in the middle of the woods in the frigid cold while they watched with hawk-sharp eyes for any sign of rebellion.

Rebellion, he'd later learned, was the quickest way to earn a little extra pain.

"It's all I have," he said, swallowing enough humiliating memories to last a lifetime. "Don't suppose you have anything my size?"

Her lips quirked again, triggering a pair of dimples in her cheeks. "Not on purpose. I can wash those for you, though."

"I'd appreciate that." He was finally warm, he realized with some surprise. Not a shiver in sight. He'd begun to wonder if he'd ever feel truly warm again.

She picked up his empty bowl and took it to the sink. "The bathroom's down the hall to the right. Leave your clothes in the hall and I'll put them on to wash."

"And then what?"

She turned as if surprised by the question. "And then we go to bed."

Chapter Two

Dallas gave Nicki an odd look. "To bed?"

She looked up quickly, realizing what she'd just said, and couldn't hold back a grin. "Not together, big guy."

He smiled back. "Yeah, I didn't figure you meant it that way. But this cabin's not very big. Do you even have a second bedroom?"

"No," she admitted. "But I have a sofa. And extra blankets. So go on and take a shower. Or a bath, if you like. The tub's pretty big." She bit back a smile at the thought of Dallas Cole folding his lanky body into her tub.

"Still the problem of clothes. Or the lack thereof."

"I probably have some sweats around here somewhere. I borrowed them from my cousin the last time I stayed at his place." Anson was only a couple of inches taller than Dallas, so surely his old sweatpants would fit him well enough. "Go get cleaned up. And let me know if you find any wounds you need treated."

The wary look he shot her way sent a prickle of unease racing up her neck. He was one more person who didn't quite trust her version of the truth.

And why should he? Why should anyone? She was lying through her teeth about what she was doing in River's End, wasn't she?

There'd been a time, not so long ago, when lying came as naturally to her as breathing. Life was one big story to be told the way she wanted it to happen, and inconvenient truths were discarded like yesterday's trash.

But she'd learned the hard way that the truth always came out, and usually at the worst possible time. She just hoped the truth about her assignment here in River's End didn't come out until she was somewhere safe and far, far away.

DALLAS LET THE SHOWER run as hot as he dared and stood under the needling spray until he couldn't stand on his trembling legs another minute.

Wrapping a towel around his hips, he sat on the closed commode and willed his strength to return. The last thing he wanted to do was face-plant in front of Nicki again. She pitied him enough already.

As the steamy heat of the bathroom dissipated, cooler air washed over his damp skin, raising goose bumps again. He grabbed a second towel from the nearby rack and dried off before he pushed to his feet.

Standing in front of the mirror over the sink, he wiped away the condensation to take his first good look at his physical condition after nearly three weeks of captivity.

He'd lost weight. At least fifteen pounds. Maybe more. The people who'd imprisoned him in the cellar of their mountain cabin had used deprivation to try to break him. Sleep, light, food—all had been withheld in an attempt to get him to tell everything he knew about a man named Cade Landry.

He wondered if Landry was still alive. From what little he'd learned from the men who'd held him captive, getting their hands on Landry was a big damn deal.

But they hadn't gotten any information from him.

Maybe they'd thought he was soft because he was nothing but a support staffer at the FBI, working a job that didn't require him to carry a weapon or stay in fighting shape.

They'd been wrong.

Not that he felt anywhere close to fighting shape at the moment. The mirror was merciless, revealing not only his prominent ribs but also the rainbow of bruises and scrapes he'd acquired during his time with the Blue Ridge Infantry.

He made himself turn away from his self-scrutiny and opened the bathroom door. Cold air from the hall assaulted him, and he wrapped the second towel around his shoulders.

"There are clothes on the end of the bed, across the hall." Nicki's voice drifted into the hall from the front room.

"Thanks." He entered the bedroom and found a small stack of clothes at the end of the bed. There was a pair of black sweatpants that wouldn't have fit him three weeks ago but now snugged over his hips as if they'd been made for him. She'd also laid out a couple of oversize football jerseys. He grabbed the darker of the two and shrugged it on. It fit only marginally better.

He dropped to the edge of the bed, tempted to lie down and sleep for a few days. But there was the matter of the pretty brunette down the hall. All the way through his shower, he couldn't stop thinking about what a stroke of fortune it had been to walk into the path of a woman who hadn't asked any inconvenient questions. Who hadn't insisted on calling the police when he asked her not to. What absolute luck.

Problem was, he'd never put much faith in the notion of luck.

Why hadn't she asked him more about who he was

and how he'd found himself facedown on a mountain road in the middle of a sleet storm?

He looked around until he found the scuffed oxfords he'd been wearing since he'd been run off the road somewhere north of Ruckersville. The dress shoes looked incongruous with the sweats and jersey, but he didn't like the vulnerability of bare feet at the moment.

Nicki looked up as he entered the living room. She offered a gentle smile that made her look like a goddess, her skin gleaming in the glow of the fire she'd just turned from stoking.

"Thanks for the clothes."

"They fit. Sort of." She stood and dusted her hands on her jeans. They hugged her curves like a lover, sending a rush of desire darting through his belly. He ignored his body's inconvenient reaction, determined to stay focused and on alert.

"I think I've lost weight," he said.

Her eyes narrowed slightly as she moved closer to him. "You seemed pretty hungry earlier."

"You haven't asked me how I got in this condition."

For a second, her faint smile faltered, and he realized he'd struck a nerve. But her smile recovered quickly and she gave an artful shrug. "I didn't want to pry until you were warm and fed. Maybe got some rest, you know? You've clearly been through a lot. I figured you might want to wait to tell me about it until you felt better."

He took a step closer to her, taking advantage of the difference in their height. "I could be a serial killer for all you know."

She didn't flinch, her smile expanding as his legs began to wobble under him. "I think I could take you. In this condition, anyway."

He reached for the nearest armchair and sat, his legs

trembling. The heat of the fire nearby was too tempting to resist; he turned toward the flames, stretching out his hands while slanting a look at his pretty hostess. "You're one of those women who's not afraid of anything?"

"Oh, you've never seen me with a spider," she answered lightly as she pulled her own armchair next to him.

One corner of his mouth lifted. "Now I know how to pay you back for your hospitality. Arachnicide is my specialty. Just give me a rolled-up piece of paper and stand back."

The smile she darted his way made his gut twist unexpectedly. Damn, but she was a good-looking woman, all wavy dark hair and eyes the color of a summer sky. And those jeans and that snug-fitting T-shirt showed off a slim but deliciously curvy body that he hoped would haunt his dreams tonight.

Anything to drive away the nightmares that had tormented him since the truck full of bearded thugs had run him off the road nearly a month ago.

"Is there someone I should call?" She stretched her own small hands toward the fire.

How could he answer that? The truth was, he wasn't sure what to do. The FBI employee he'd been for over a decade demanded that he call the authorities, turn himself in and tell his story. The truth would out.

But the boy from eastern Kentucky knew that sometimes, the truth wasn't enough to keep a man alive. Some of the most evil people in the world could hide behind a badge and the veil of authority. He knew that from experience, including his most recent brush with corruption in the guise of justice.

"I'm not sure," he said finally. "I think maybe sleeping on it is a good idea, if that's okay with you."

Her eyes narrowed slightly at his words, but she just gave a nod and laid her head back against the chair. They sat in silence for a while, tension sharpening the warm air wafting around them.

Did she think his hesitation meant he had something to hide from the authorities? Was she considering calling the cops herself as soon as he went to bed?

It was a chance he'd have to take, because he was almost asleep as it was. If he stayed here much longer, he wasn't sure he could drag himself out of this chair. And no matter how tough or strong she thought she was, he doubted she could haul his weary butt over to the sofa by herself.

"I'll take the sofa," he offered. "No need to run you out of your bed."

She shook her head. "Take the bed. You're the one in bad condition. The sofa sleeps fine, and I'm short enough not to be uncomfortable sleeping on it." She waved her hand toward the pillows and blankets piled up at the end of the sofa. "I'm set for the night."

He looked at her, taking in the guileless expression on her face. He wanted desperately to trust someone, especially someone as pretty as the woman who'd introduced herself as Nicki. But trust didn't come easily to someone like him on the best of days. And good days had been thin on the ground for him for a while now.

"You're remarkably easygoing for someone who just had a stranger crash her life," he said as he pushed to his feet.

She rose with him. "That'll probably change when you're stronger."

"Glad to know you plan to keep me on my toes."

"I've seen you flat on your face. On your toes is definitely the way to go." She nodded toward the hallway.

"Go to bed. I'll lock up and we'll see how you feel in the morning."

The walk to the bedroom felt as if he was hiking uphill all the way, but he finally made it to the edge of the bed and sank on the soft mattress, facedown. He would move in just a minute. Crawl under the covers and settle down like a real human being.

It was the last lucid thought he had for a long while.

WHEN SHE CHECKED on Dallas Cole, she found him lying facedown on the bed, angled diagonally across the mattress as if he'd fallen asleep as soon as his body hit the bed.

Good. She needed him to be dead to the world for a little while.

She had somewhere to go.

Bundling up against the dropping temperature outside, she headed east through the woods that butted up to her cabin, going uphill for almost a mile until she reached the small creek that snaked its way down the mountain to join with Bowden Fork south of River's End. At this particular curve of the stream, there was a small natural cave that was only a few feet deep and barely tall enough for Nicki to enter hunched over.

Just inside, a loose stone hid a cavity about eight inches deep into the cave wall. About the size of the mail cubbyhole at the motel where she'd worked a few years ago, the cavity was just big enough to hold a folded-up letter like the one tucked in the pocket of her jeans.

She took a deep breath and tucked the letter into the cavity, then replaced the stone.

Outside the cave, she scanned the woods around her to be certain she was alone. But there was nobody else out there. Only idiots and people with something to hide would be out in this weather.

Next to the cave was a fallen log. She turned the log onto its side until a broken limb about the length of her forearm revealed itself. She propped up the log with a stone to keep it from rolling back over and headed back down the mountain toward her cabin.

She didn't know how often the man she thought of as Agent X passed this way. Sometimes two or more days would go by before she'd see the log back in its original position, her signal that something was waiting for her inside the cave cubbyhole.

But she had a feeling he passed this way daily, just in case she needed his help. At least, she liked to think he did.

It made her feel a little less alone in this dangerous world in which she now operated.

The people she worked with at the diner in town called her a dinosaur because she eschewed so much of the technology they couldn't live without. She owned no computer, though she knew more about how to use them than any of her coworkers and customers would believe. She had a cell phone out of necessity, since power on the mountain could go down so easily, leaving her without phone service, as well. But she turned on the phone only when her landline wasn't working. She had no desire to be instantly reachable, especially when she was on what she'd come to think of as her secret missions.

How on earth had her life come to this? There'd been a time, not very long ago, when nobody who knew her would believe she'd take on a dangerous undercover mission on the side of the good guys.

Not Nicolette Jamison, the wild girl from the Smoky Mountains who'd never met a bad situation she couldn't make worse. Somehow, by the grace of God and a generous utilization of her good looks and native charm, she'd managed to skirt the edge of the law without quite crossing the point of no return, keeping her record clean enough to pass cursory scrutiny.

She'd never pretended to be a saint. Hell, she wasn't one now.

But she knew the difference between trouble and evil. Trouble could lose you a few nights of sleep. Evil would rob you of your life without blinking. And the men she was tangling with these days were about as evil as they came in these parts.

Snow had begun to fall by the time she reached the clearing where her cabin slumbered quietly in the dark. Fat, fluffy flakes started to pile up on her shoulders and dampen the ski cap she'd tugged down to cover her ears. She hurried up the porch steps as quickly as she dared, dodging the spot on the second step that creaked whenever it took any weight, and hurried to the front door, automatically checking the lock to make sure it was still secure.

Still locked up, nice and tight.

She slipped her key into the lock and turned it carefully. The door opened with only the faintest of creaks and closed behind her with an almost imperceptible snick. She engaged the lock and sat in the nearest chair to remove her hiking boots before she padded silently in socked feet down the hallway toward her bedroom.

The door was still open a crack, just as she'd left it. She could just make out Dallas Cole's lean form, still lying diagonally across the bed. She waited a moment until she could make out the steady rise and fall of his breathing before she tiptoed back to the living room and finished undressing for the night.

She slipped on a pair of flannel pajamas she'd found tucked in the bottom of her drawer, a gag gift from her cousin last Christmas inspired by her past visit, when he'd found her sleeping in his bed, dressed in his Atlanta Braves T-shirt and nothing else. The timing had been particularly bad, given that he'd promised his bed to the pretty blonde he had brought home for the night.

Flannel pajamas were about as far from her normal nighttime attire as it got, but she was trying out the straight and narrow these days. Well, straighter and narrower, anyway. No more wandering around in skimpy nighties when strange men were staying the night.

No more strange men staying the night anymore, for that matter. Some undesirable habits deserved to be broken, and her addiction to bad boys was one of them.

She wondered what kind of boy Dallas Cole was. If all she had to go on was the FBI record her boss, Alexander Quinn, had gotten his hands on, she'd say Dallas Cole was about as good a boy as they got. Hardworking, well liked by his colleagues, a go-getter who was looking to move up the ladder at the FBI even though he wasn't a special agent.

What had happened that night three weeks ago when he'd headed south out of Washington, DC, and disappeared without a trace until now?

Did he have a hidden bad-boy side nobody had ever seen?

She had to find out before he was strong enough to give her real trouble.

DALLAS EASED HIS eyes open when he heard Nicki's soft footfalls retreat down the hall. Damn. That had been close.

He'd barely made it back to the bedroom before he

heard her key in the front door lock, a tiny clink of metal on metal that he probably wouldn't have noticed if he hadn't been listening for it. If he'd still been asleep, he wouldn't have heard it at all.

But the sound of her leaving had roused him from a deep sleep, leaving his nerves jangling and his mind reeling. He'd dragged himself from bed in time to see her disappear into the woods on the right side of the house, bundled up against the cold.

He'd waited by the window until his legs had given out, then sat in the chair near the fire for almost an hour, going by the clock on the mantel that ticked away the minutes with sharp little clicks of the second hand.

Where the hell had she gone? Did she go to meet someone?

Had she told anyone where to find him?

It didn't matter, he realized as his vigil ticked over to a new hour. He was too tired and weak to make his escape. He had nowhere to go.

Her footsteps on the porch had jolted him from a light doze a few minutes ago. He'd peeked through the narrow gap in the curtains in time to see her easing her way up the wooden porch steps.

He'd made it back to the bed with only seconds to spare, forcing his respiration to a slow, even tempo even though his heart was racing like a rabbit chased by a fox.

He eased over to his back, wincing a little as the bed creaked. He held his breath, waiting for her to return, but after a few minutes, he realized she must have settled down for the night.

He stared at the dark ceiling over his head, his heart still pounding from the rush of adrenaline that had driven him back to bed.

Where had she gone tonight? Who had she seen? What had she said?

Would he live to regret stumbling into her path tonight?

Chapter Three

Frost painted the cabin windows with delicate fronds of ice, lit by the morning sunlight angling through the glass. Outside, snow blanketed the ground and glistened in the trees, catching every drop of dayglow and refracting it into diamond sparkles.

Nicki pressed her forehead against the icy glass, remembering her six-year-old self doing much the same thing on a snowy morning in the Smoky Mountains, before everything went so awfully, irrevocably wrong.

Footsteps behind her drew her back to jaded reality, and she turned to see Dallas Cole enter the kitchen. He moved with a painful hitch that made her own back ache in sympathy, and the night's sleep had done little to return color to his cheeks or vigor to his demeanor.

"You look like you could use another week's sleep," she murmured, reaching for the empty cup she'd set out for him earlier. "Coffee?"

"Please." He groped for the back of the nearest chair and settled down at the small table in the window nook.

"Creamer? Sugar?"

"Just black." He looked at the frosty window. "How much snow did we get?"

"Just a couple of inches."

His dark eyes narrowed as she set a cup of steaming coffee in front of him and took the chair across from him. "Did you sleep okay on the sofa?"

There was a strange tone to his voice that she couldn't quite read. "Yeah, it was fine."

"Thanks for letting me have the bed. Very comfortable." He took a sip of coffee, grimacing. She'd made it strong.

"Sure you don't want some creamer?"

"It's perfect." His gaze flicked up to meet hers. "Did I miss anything while I was dead to the world?"

There was that odd tone again. "Just the snow."

"Right." He looked down at the coffee in his cup.

"Is something wrong?"

He shook his head, not looking at her. "No."

Now she knew something was wrong. But he clearly didn't intend to tell her what it was, so she let it go for the moment. "That bump on your jaw went down overnight."

He lifted his fingers to the abraded spot where his face had grazed the pavement when he fell, wincing at the touch. "Should've seen the other guy."

"What other guy, exactly?"

His gaze flicked up to hers again. "Other guy? You know I got this when I hit the pavement."

"You didn't get in that condition by yourself." She had a pretty good idea how he'd ended up wandering in the woods, but she couldn't exactly reveal what she knew to Dallas Cole or anyone else.

Her life depended on folks in River's End believing she was an ordinary fry cook with some medical skills that might come in handy for a group of people who didn't want the authorities looking too closely at their activities.

"Doesn't matter now." He took a long drink of coffee.

"You still don't want to call the police?"

"No." He set the coffee cup on the table. "I should probably get out of your hair, though. If you can just point me toward the nearest town."

"Southeast," she said, keeping her tone light. "If you were in any condition to walk across the room, much less three miles over the mountain."

"I'm tougher than I look."

She couldn't stop a smile. "Right."

"You could say that with a little more conviction." With a sigh, he rose from his seat and turned to look out the frosty window.

Nicki sucked in a gasp at the sight of a streak of blood staining the back of the borrowed jersey. "You're bleeding."

He turned his head to look at her. "Where?"

"Your back." She got up and started to tug up the hem of the jersey.

He turned quickly, putting his hands out to stop her. "It's nothing."

"Let me look."

He closed his hands around her wrists, his grip unexpectedly strong. Tension rose swiftly between them, electrified by Nicki's sudden, sharp awareness that beneath the facade of weakness, Dallas Cole was a large, imposing male with chiseled features and deep, intense eyes that made her insides liquefy with appalling speed.

Desire flickered in her core, and she tugged her wrists free of his grasp. She took a step back, swallowing the lump that had risen in her throat. "I'm pretty good with a first-aid kit."

He probed behind his back with one hand, his fingers

returning bloodstained. He looked at the red wetness with dismay. "Damn it."

"I should treat that. Don't need you bleeding all over everything."

"No," he agreed, reaching for the back of the chair as if his legs were ready to give out beneath him. "Can you do it here?"

"Of course. I'll be right back."

When she returned with the first-aid kit she kept in the hall closet, she found him shirtless. He'd turned his chair around and sat hunched over the curved back, his arms folded under his head. An alarming Technicolor map of scrapes and bruises crisscrossed his back, including an oozing arch of abraded skin just across his left kidney.

She kept her horror to herself as she unpacked the supplies she needed to treat the wounds. "This is going to hurt."

"What's new?" he muttered against his arms.

She pulled up a chair and sat beside him. "I'm going to clean everything first, then put antiseptic in any open areas."

"Are you going to do a play-by-play of your torture?" he muttered.

"Only if you keep up the surly attitude," she retorted, pressing a disinfecting cleansing pad to his back.

He sucked in a sharp breath at the sting.

"Sorry," she murmured, wincing in sympathy. There'd been a time when she had considered a career in medicine. Well, of sorts. She'd been a licensed first responder when she was living in Nashville a few years back. But she'd found herself ill-suited for the job. Other people's pain bothered her too much, making it hard to stay objective and focused.

Even now, acutely aware that the battered man sitting before her might be a very bad man indeed, she couldn't help but feel twinges of empathetic pain as she cleaned the abrasions that marred the skin of his back.

"You seem to know what you're doing." He turned his head toward her, peering at her through one narrowed eye. "You a nurse?"

She shook her head. "Used to be an EMT, though."

"Used to be?"

"I gave it up for a career in the hospitality business." She smiled at his arched eyebrow. "I'm a fry cook at a place called Dugan's in town."

"I see."

"No you don't. Nobody ever does." She probed gently at his rib cage, feeling for any sign of a fracture.

He sucked in another sharp breath. "Couldn't stand the sight of blood?"

"Too many whiny patients," she said lightly. "Gave me headaches."

"And restaurant customers are a step up?"

"Fry cook, not waitress. I only deal with whiny servers." She blotted the oozing scrape over his kidney. "Any idea what made this wound?"

He didn't answer, and her imagination supplied a few answers she would have given anything not to visualize. But she'd already seen some of the brutality members of the Blue Ridge Infantry could mete out. Some of them enjoyed inflicting pain a little too much, as a matter of fact.

"You must've really pissed somebody off," she murmured as she covered the raw scrape with sterile pads and taped them into place.

His back arched in pain as she pressed another sterile pad into place. "I have a bad habit of doing that."

"What are you, a tax collector?" she joked.

Before he could respond, she heard the trill of the telephone coming down the hall. For a moment, she considered just letting it ring, but it might be the call she'd been waiting for.

"Wait right here," she said and headed to the bedroom.

It was Trevor Colley on the phone. He was the manager at Dugan's. "Can you work the morning shift?" he asked. "Bella's stuck over in Abingdon looking in on her mama because of the snow."

She paused, torn. Normally, she jumped at working as many hours at the diner as she could, both for the money and for the opportunity to rub elbows with the militia members and their wives and girlfriends who frequented the diner on a regular basis. She'd made friends with some of the women already, and an incident a few weeks ago had even earned her the respect of a couple of the men.

"Del McClintock is here."

She straightened. "Yeah?"

"He asked if you were coming in." Trevor kept his voice light, but she heard a hint of disapproval in his voice. The militia men might be good-paying customers, but the manager had never seemed particularly happy about their patronage. He took their money, of course. He'd be a fool not to, given that in this impoverished part of the county, paying customers could be hard to come by.

But he wasn't exactly happy about his best fry cook befriending members of the Blue Ridge Infantry.

Nicki did her best to straddle the line between her manager's feelings and her own need to make inroads into the BRI's inner circle. It could be a delicate dance at the best of times.

But even Trevor, as much as he disliked the hard-eyed

men who ate daily at the diner, wasn't above using her interest in them to get his way. "Should I tell him you're coming in?"

She pressed her lips together as she considered her options. Del McClintock's sexual interest in her presented a very tempting opportunity to get a little closer to her target.

But what was she going to do with Dallas Cole while she was working a shift at the diner? The last thing she wanted to do was leave him here on his own while she worked a few hours at the diner.

No telling what kind of trouble he could get into.

THE MURMUR OF Nicki's voice drifting down the hall was like a lure dangling in front of a hungry bass. Dallas couldn't have resisted the temptation to hear what she was saying any more than he'd have turned down a juicy steak after three weeks of near starvation.

Urging his aching body into motion, he moved as quietly as he could down the hallway until he could hear Nicki's end of the conversation.

"And Davey can't come in?" There was a brief silence, then she sighed. "No, I get it. Everybody else has family to see after, except me. I'll be there in a few."

She must be talking to someone at the diner where she worked, he realized. He eased away from the door and turned to go back to the kitchen. But his foot caught in the carpet runner in the hall, tripping him up. He landed against the wall with a thud, the impact eliciting a grunt.

Before he could tamp down the pain in his bruised ribs enough to breathe again, Nicki emerged from the bedroom, her blue eyes flashing.

"What the hell are you doing?" she challenged. "Eaves-dropping?"

His pain-fogged brain tried sluggishly to catch up. "Bathroom."

Her dark eyebrows arched. "You passed it to get here."

Damn.

"What did you expect to overhear?" she asked.

Ah, hell. Maybe he should just tell her the truth. "How about why you left the cabin for an hour last night in the middle of a snowstorm?"

Her eyes narrowing, she took a step away from him until her back flattened against the wall. "What are you talking about?"

"You left the cabin shortly before midnight and disappeared into the woods for over an hour. Then you snuck back in here, real quiet, and settled down for the night. Want to tell me where you went?"

"You were asleep at midnight. I checked on you."

"You thought I was asleep. I wasn't."

A scowl creased her forehead. "You were spying on me?"

"You woke me when you started to leave. I got curious. You're not the only one who spent the night with a stranger, you know."

"You're still alive, so I guess I'm not a serial killer." She folded her arms across her chest, angling her chin at him. In her defiance, she seemed to glow like a jewel, all glittering blue eyes and ruby-stained cheeks.

A flush of desire spread heat through his body, making his knees tremble. He flattened his back against the opposite wall of the hallway and struggled to stay upright beneath the electric intensity of her gaze.

She was dangerous to him, he realized.

In all sorts of unexpected ways.

He pushed himself upright, willing his legs to hold his weight. "You know, I think I should call someone."

Her suspicious gaze was as sharp as a blow. "Who're you going to call?"

"You've got a sheriff's department around here, right?"

Her scowl deepened. "They're probably a little busy today. With the snow and all."

"Not like it was a blizzard." His legs were starting to ache, from his hips to his toes. He fought the urge to slide down the wall to the floor.

"No, but in this part of the state, people aren't used to driving in snow."

"But you're going to, right?"

"What do you mean?"

"You're going in to work aren't you?" He nodded toward her bedroom. "That's who you were talking to on the phone."

"So you *were* eavesdropping."

No point in denying it. "You can drive me into town with you. I'll take it from there."

Alarm darkened her eyes. "No. I can't do that."

The first flicker of fear sparked through him. "Why not?"

"You don't want to go into River's End."

He urged his legs into motion, edging back from her. He hadn't seen any sort of weapon in his limited exploration of the cabin, but he hadn't exactly looked in every nook and cranny while she was gone last night. In fact, there were parts of the cabin that were still a complete mystery to him. She had already told him she had a shotgun. For all he knew, she could have a whole armory stashed somewhere in the back.

"Why don't I want to go into River's End?"

She moved with him as he stepped backward, maintaining the distance between them without letting him get out of reach. "Don't be coy, Dallas."

There it was again. He'd heard that same tone in her voice the night before, when she'd spoken his name while trying to help him into her Jeep. A flicker of knowing that hadn't really registered in the midst of his stress the previous evening came through loud and clear this morning.

"You know who I am," he said before he could stop himself.

Her expression shuttered. "Who you are?"

"Now who's being coy?" A surge of anger eclipsed his earlier fear. She was lying to his face. Had been lying this whole time. "If you know who I am, then you know there are people who are looking for me."

She dropped any pretense. "That's abundantly clear from the bruises and scrapes all over your body. Which is why I don't think you really want to go into River's End this morning."

His legs began to tremble again, aching with fatigue. "They're in town, aren't they?"

She didn't ask who he was talking about. Clearly, she already knew. "Yes. And not just in town. They're all over the place, Dallas. Everywhere you could possibly go."

Damn it. Fear returned in cold, sickening waves, but he fought not to let it show. Those bastards who took him captive had worked damn hard to break him, but they hadn't. He'd escaped before they could.

He wouldn't break in front of this woman, either.

"Then let me call someone to come get me."

The look she gave him was almost pitying. "I can't let you do that, either."

He forced a laugh, pretending a bravado he didn't feel. "And you're going to stop me how?"

Her response was a laugh in return. "You say that as if you think it would be difficult. I told you last night, in your condition, I'm pretty sure I can take you."

He didn't really want to test her theory, considering how shaky his limbs felt at the moment. "Okay, fine. I'll stay put."

Her eyes narrowed a notch. "I don't think you will."

Before he could move, she closed the space between them, grabbing both arms and shoving him face-first into the wall. Pain exploded where his bruised jaw hit the hard Sheetrock.

He struggled against her hold, but she was much stronger than he was at the moment, shoving him down the hall and into the kitchen. When he tried to turn around to fight back, she slammed her knee into the back of one of his, making his leg buckle under him. She released his arms just long enough to let him catch himself before he lunged face-first into the floor, but he still hit hard enough to drive the breath from his lungs.

The world went black around him for a moment, then started to return in flecks of light as he gasped for air. He felt movement, pressure and then a big gulp of sweet air filled his lungs. His vision cleared and all his aches and pains came into sharp, agonizing focus.

He was facedown on the floor, his hands twisted behind his back. He felt the weight of his captor settle over the backs of his thighs as she held him in place. The unmistakable sound of duct tape being ripped from its roll reached his ears a split second before he felt her wind the sticky tape around his wrists, binding his hands together behind him.

Nicki moved off his legs and grabbed him by his upper arms, her grip like steel. She might be small, he thought, but she was a lot stronger than she looked. "Sorry to do this, but you leave me no choice."

The fear returned, beating at the back of his throat like a wave of nausea. He swallowed it down, refused to give in. "And here you promised you weren't a serial killer."

"Believe it or not, this is all about keeping you alive." She got him to his feet and pushed him toward a door he hadn't noticed before. "Watch your step."

She opened the door and reached inside, flicking a switch. He saw he was standing at the top of a steep set of stairs descending into a dim basement. "You're not going to chain me to your dungeon wall, are you?" He tried to keep his voice light, make it into a joke. Anything to keep the fear at bay.

She helped him down the steps, grabbing the wood railing on one side of the descent when he stumbled and nearly pulled her down the stairs with him. "Sadly, I haven't had time to put in the shackles yet."

They reached the bottom of the steps and she gave him a little shove. He stumbled forward into the shadows, wincing in anticipation of the impact.

His upper body hit something soft. Opening his eyes, he saw he'd landed face-first on an old, overstuffed sofa braced against the cinder block wall of the basement.

Cellar, he amended mentally, his eyes beginning to adjust to the low light. There was a shelf against the opposite wall full of Mason jars full of home-canned fruits and vegetables.

"Stay put. I'll be back in a couple of hours." Nicki's voice drifted down toward him from the top of the stairs. He looked up at her, squinting at the bright daylight back-lighting her through the cellar door, rendering her little more than a curvy silhouette.

"Don't go," he called, fear hammering past his last defenses.

She paused in the doorway. When she spoke, she sounded genuinely distressed. "I'm so sorry. But I have to go."

Then the door closed behind her, shutting out the blessed daylight. He heard the soft thuds of her footfalls drift into a thick, deafening silence.

Once again, he was alone. Trapped and helpless, just like before, with nothing but darkness and fear to keep him company.

Chapter Four

What have I done?

The question rang in her head, over and over in rhythm with her pounding heart, as she muscled the Jeep down the mountain to the main road that led into town.

She'd tied a man up and locked him in her cellar. Had she lost her bloody mind?

The cell phone peeking out of her purse presented a powerful temptation. She had never felt this great a need to talk to another human being in her life. Calling Alexander Quinn was out of the question—he'd never answer a call from her cell phone and risk blowing her cover.

But her cousin Anson might answer. She could shoot the breeze with him, avoid anything incriminating. Just hearing a friendly, familiar voice might be enough to knock the edge off her nerves, right?

She dragged her gaze back to the road as her wheels slipped a little on the slick surface. No. No calling anyone from her past, no matter how freaked-out she felt at the moment.

She'd agreed to this job. She knew what was at stake.

Hell, that was why she'd just imprisoned a man in her cellar, wasn't it?

Despite the weather, the parking lot of Dugan's Diner was half-full when she pulled her Jeep into one of the employee parking spots and entered the kitchen through the employees' side door.

The only other person in the kitchen was Tollie Barber, one of the kitchen assistants who helped out with food prep and handled some of the easier cooking duties. She was busy at the counter, processing potatoes for hash browns, her frizzy blond curls tamed by a hairnet. She darted a quick gaze at Nicki. "So much for a snow day, huh?"

Nicki tucked her own dark hair under a protective cap and headed to the sink to wash her trembling hands. She kept her tone calm and light, hoping her agitation didn't show. "Gotta snow a lot more than this to keep people away from breakfast at Dugan's."

Trevor Colley entered the kitchen from the front area, moving at a quick pace for a man his size. His barrel chest and linebacker shoulders seemed to take up half the kitchen when he stopped next to where Nicki was preparing the griddle. "You're a good 'un to come in so fast, Nicki," he said in a gruff voice that rumbled like thunder. It was all the thanks he'd give her. Trevor wasn't one to gush.

"Quite a crowd for a snow day," she commented, cracking a couple of eggs for the first order clipped to the order wheel. Two eggs, sunny-side up, hash browns and bacon. "Something up?"

Trevor gave her an odd look. "You tell me. Del McClintock brought four of his boys with him. They brought their girls, too. Should I worry?"

Nicki supposed it was a good thing that Trevor believed she might know the answer to his question. It suggested that people were starting to connect her with the Blue Ridge Infantry. Which meant, hopefully, that the BRI members themselves were starting to think of her as one of them.

That was her goal, wasn't it?

"No, don't worry. If you have any trouble with them, come get me."

Trevor frowned at her but went back out to the front of the diner, leaving her and Tollie to get the orders filled.

As she laid out the strips of bacon on the griddle to fry, the image of Dallas Cole's rainbow-hued collection of scrapes and bruises filled her head. Her whole body went cold and numb, and for a second, she thought she was going to be sick.

Oh, God. She'd taped a sick, injured man's hands behind his back and locked him in her cellar without even feeding him breakfast first. She hadn't even left him a bucket if he needed to go to the bathroom. Which he couldn't do with his hands duct-taped, anyway.

What the hell had she been thinking? Had she lost her ever-lovin' mind?

But what else could she have done? Dallas had insisted on calling the FBI. Maybe it had been a trick—maybe the whole thing was a setup to prove she wasn't who she said she was. Maybe it had been a test. But if that was the case, she had no idea whether she'd passed or failed.

But what if he was legit? She certainly couldn't let him bring the FBI swarming into River's End at this point. Even if it didn't end up blowing her cover, every BRI member in town would crawl back in the holes where they'd come from, and it'd be months, even years, before she could get this close to the group's inner circle.

She was doing what she had to do. She was. She just had to get through this morning and she could hurry back home and let him out before anything bad happened.

Assuming something bad hadn't already happened.

THERE WASN'T AN inch of his body that didn't hurt in some way, including the new scrape on his inner wrist from the nail protruding from the wooden shelf where the beautiful but treacherous Nicki kept her canned goods. But Dallas was damned if he was going to be bound and locked in by the time she got back from her shift at the diner.

Who the hell was she? Was she connected to the militia members who'd taken him captive a few weeks earlier? If so, why had it taken her all night to decide he was safer behind a lock and key?

Everything had changed when he told her he wanted to call the authorities. That had been the catalyst. He'd seen fear in her eyes, not unlike his own reaction when she'd pinned him down and taped up his hands. His mention of the authorities had made her feel just as trapped as he felt now.

But why? What was she hiding?

The tape around his wrists snapped apart as the sharp edge of the nail head finally broke through the last of the fibers. He pulled his arms apart, groaning as the stretched muscles of his chest and shoulders put up a painful protest. He worked them slowly for a moment, taking care not to make his condition any worse than it already was.

He had to find the strength to get past that locked door and get the hell out of this crazy woman's cabin.

There were no windows in the cellar, no doors visible besides the one at the top of the stairs. As much as his wobbly legs protested the idea, he had to go upstairs and try to figure a way to get through the locked cellar door. Ramming it open was no option, given his weakened state.

But maybe he could pick the lock.

He'd already spent nearly an hour searching the cellar for something to cut himself free of the duct-tape bonds. He'd found a small, rickety cabinet in the corner that held a box of tools. He'd had no luck using the garden shears he'd found inside to cut himself free because he couldn't get the blades turned to the right angle behind his back to cut the tape. But there had been other tools in the box that might work to unlock the door, hadn't there?

He crossed to the box lying on the top of the rough-hewn cabinet and started to pick through the contents, looking for something—

There. A jumble of old paper clips, some of them hooked together, some twisted apart. If he was very lucky, the lock on the door at the top of the stairs would be a simple spring-driven lock, and he could use the paper clip to push it open.

But if it wasn't…

He grabbed a pair of pliers and twisted one of the bigger paper clips until he'd fashioned a crude tension wrench, then curled the tip of one of the smaller clips into a modified hook, hoping they'd work well enough to get the job done.

"Picking a lock isn't as hard as you'd think," an FBI special agent had told Dallas once, and then he'd proceeded to explain just how to beat a pin-and-tumbler lock. "It's all about the pins. That's how a key works—getting the pins in the right position to turn the cylinder."

He carried his tools up the steps and slid his makeshift tension wrench into the keyhole, turning it one way, then the other, until he was satisfied which way the cylinder had to turn to open. Applying a little pressure to move the cylinder just out of position, he inserted the second paper clip into the keyhole.

His hands shook and his legs began to ache, feeling as if they'd suddenly lost the ability to hold him upright, but he kept at his probing examination of the lock's internal workings. One by one, he painstakingly pushed the pins up until they caught on the ledge, clearing the cylinder. Finally, the last pin clicked into place, and he used the larger paper clip to turn the lock.

The dead bolt slid back into the door with a soft click, and he gave the door a push open.

He eased into the kitchen and looked around, squinting as bright daylight assaulted his eyes. Around him, the cabin was quiet and still.

He looked around the house to make sure he was still alone, then checked out the front door to assure himself Nicki and the Jeep were still gone. Then he went into the bedroom to find the phone.

But it was gone, no longer sitting on the bedside table where it had been the night before.

He checked the floor on either side of the table and even crouched to check under the bed. No phone.

A room-to-room search of the cabin revealed no sign of the missing phone. Nor did he find a computer or any sort of modem or router with which to access the internet if he wanted to reach the authorities that way instead.

He sank into one of the kitchen chairs and willed his wobbly legs to stop shaking. He clearly wasn't going to be able to call in the cavalry, so he was going to have to get the hell out of this cabin on his own somehow.

But first, he needed something to eat. Some of his unsteadiness might be from sheer hunger. He pushed himself to his feet and crossed to the refrigerator, bracing himself to find it as empty as the bedside table had been. But the refrigerator was well stocked, and he grabbed a couple of eggs from the carton for his breakfast.

She had plenty of cookware in her cabinets, too. Made sense, he supposed—she'd said she worked as a diner cook, hadn't she? As he heated a pat of butter in one of the pans on the stove, he grabbed a couple of slices of bread from the bread box and stuck them in the toaster.

The smell of toasting bread and frying eggs made him almost light-headed with hunger, but once he'd wolfed down his breakfast, he felt considerably better.

But did he feel well enough to walk out of these woods to seek help?

He left the pans for Nicki to wash—the least she could do, considering she'd locked him in her cellar—and took another look around the house, this time for some sign of who Nicki really was and what had compelled her to lock him up rather than let him call the authorities for help.

She'd admitted to knowing who he was. Which meant she had to know that he'd disappeared somewhere between Washington, DC, and wherever he was now. That foul play was suspected.

Or was it? Did people think he'd disappeared on his own? He'd been on the phone with a man named Cade Landry when those BRI thugs had run him off the road and dragged him out of his banged-up car. But Landry had been a fugitive. For all Dallas knew, he still was. He might not have had the opportunity to tell anyone what he'd heard over the phone.

So what, exactly, did Nicki think she knew about him?

There were no personal items anywhere around the cabin, he realized after another search of the place. She probably had her driver's license and other ID with her, since she'd taken the Jeep into town, but most people had other personal records scattered around the house, didn't they?

Back at his apartment in Georgetown, he had a whole four-drawer filing cabinet full of tax information, personal records, vehicle papers and more. He even had a box in his closet filled with things he'd kept from his high school and college days.

As far as he could tell from his search, Nicki had nothing like that stashed anywhere around the cabin.

He sat on the bed and looked around the small bedroom. Simple gray curtains on the window. Plain pine dresser that matched the bedside table. The bed was little more than a mattress and box set on a metal frame. No headboard or footboard. Plain gray sheets and pillowcases, plus a couple of matching waffle-weave blankets that acted as the bedspread.

A large woven rag rug stretched over the hardwood floor next to the bed, the hodgepodge of blues, grays, black and white offering only a little more color than the rest of the decor.

Drab surroundings for a woman as vibrantly beautiful as his hostess-turned-captor.

He pushed himself up from the bed and looked around, trying to make sense of all that had happened to him over the past twelve hours. And no matter which way he looked, it all came back to the same thing.

Nicki.

Who the hell was she? And what did she want from him?

BY NINE THIRTY, the breakfast crowd began to thin out, but Del McClintock and part of his posse lingered, nursing cups of coffee and chatting quietly in one corner of the diner. Nicki wasn't sure he was actually waiting for her to end her shift, but Trevor kept shooting troubled looks between her and the corner whenever he popped into the kitchen to check on things.

Nicki ignored her boss, taking advantage of the lull in customers to clean the griddle in preparation for the next crowd of hungry diners. She also tried hard not to think about the man locked in her cellar, without much luck.

People didn't starve to death in two hours. And if worse

came to worst on the bathroom end of things, she could run to the thrift store in Abingdon to pick up some clean clothes for him.

Everything would work out. She'd figure it out somehow.

Trevor stuck his head in the kitchen door. "Bella's here. Her mama's neighbor's takin' good care of her, looks like, so she told Bella to come on in for the lunch and dinner crowds. That is, if you're ready to leave." Trevor shot another look toward the dining room, where Del and his friends were still lingering at a couple of the tables near the window.

"Yeah, I'm ready. I know Bella wanted the hours, and I have some things to do today." Like release a man from her locked cellar and somehow figure out a way to convince him she wasn't some sort of psychopath.

But what about Del McClintock? The whole point of agreeing to come in for the morning shift was Trevor's comment about Del and some of the other guys from the BRI being there.

And now she was going to slip out the back and not even talk to him?

Damn you, Alexander Quinn.

One minute. She could take one minute to go say hi to Del.

She grabbed her purse and her coat, and headed out through the door leading to the front of the diner, ignoring Trevor's troubled look. Several of the people with Del had left while she was cleaning up, but he was still there, along with Ray Battle and Ray's girlfriend, Tonya. Ray sent Del a smirking look as Nicki approached.

"Hey there, Del." She pasted on a friendly smile. "Can't get enough of my cooking?"

"Never." Del smiled back at her, his straight white

teeth flashing. He was a good-looking man, tall and hard-muscled, which couldn't be said of all the BRI members she'd met over the past couple of months. He was also better educated than most, which made her wonder why he'd hooked up with a group like the Blue Ridge Infantry.

Then again, there were lots of people in the world blessed with good genes and good fortune who didn't have the moral fiber to make anything of themselves despite the raw material.

Del had been in the army, or so he claimed. Nicki had no reason to doubt him. But he had left the service as soon as he could manage, coming back home to join his father at Cortland Lumber in a town a few miles east of River's End, working in the sawmill.

As in, the business owned by Wayne Cortland, one of the most ruthless—and efficient—criminals to operate in southern Virginia until his death almost three years earlier.

According to the files Alexander Quinn had given Nicki to study, Wayne Cortland had pulled together a disparate group of black hat hackers, mountain meth cookers and members of the Blue Ridge Infantry to fill his organization. The hackers were the brains, the BRI served as the muscle and the meth cookers were the source of money.

But ever since Cortland's murder at the hands of his own son, those three groups had been struggling to take over the remains of the organization and keep it going on their own.

Nicki was pretty sure Del McClintock was part of the BRI's attempt to take over the drug business for themselves. And at least two or three of the guys in his entourage were hackers.

But what she hadn't yet discovered was who had taken over as head of the Virginia branch of the BRI. Quinn believed that the unknown leader might be the key to toppling the whole organization, from the group in Virginia to the branch in Tennessee.

What they needed was someone inside, close to the top man, who could funnel information to Quinn and, through him, to the authorities.

Nicki planned to be that someone. And thanks to a little tidbit Del had let drop a week ago, she had an idea how to make it happen.

"Were you serious about what you said last week?" she asked, lowering her voice so that only the people at Del's table could hear. "About me picking up some work for you? You know, medical work?"

Del's eyes narrowed, and she was afraid she'd overplayed her hand. But his expression cleared. "If you think you're up to it. It's not exactly legal."

"It's just me doing a little first aid as needed, right?" She flashed him a grin. "And if you and your friends want to show me a little gratitude with gifts of cash, who's to say there's anything wrong with that?"

"Exactly." Del's smile was deceptively attractive, making him look genial and harmless when she knew he was anything but.

Nicki hid a little shiver and brightened her smile. "So you'll let me know if you need anything, right?"

"Absolutely." He winked at her. "Can you stick around?"

"I wish," she lied. "But last night I picked up a stray cat, and I'm afraid he's making a mess on my floors as we speak."

"We shoot strays at our place," Ray said with a grin.

You would, she thought. She forced a laugh. "I guess I have a soft heart. Or a soft head. Whichever. See y'all later." She gave a little wave and headed out the front door, keeping a smile on her face until she was certain she was safely out of sight.

She blew out a pent-up breath and allowed herself a little tremble. She had to figure out a way to get over her revulsion, especially if Del required her to be a little more than just friendly and flirtatious in order to give her the breaks she was looking for.

But the thought made her sick. Which was silly, really—there'd been a time in her life when a guy like Del McClintock had been her particular brand of temptation. Dangerous, shady and handsome as sin.

Sort of like the injured man tied up in her cellar at home.

Damn it. What had she been thinking?

THE SOUND OF a vehicle engine drifted into the cabin, stirring Dallas from a light doze. He pushed himself up to a sitting position on the sofa, his nerves jangling, and tried to reorient himself as the engine noise grew closer. The nap on the sofa hadn't done much for his aches and pains, but he felt a little stronger than he had even this morning. Food and activity to work out the kinks from his weeks of captivity had gone a long way to restoring some of his earlier vigor.

But would it be enough to give him the edge over his feisty captor?

He glanced through the narrow gap between the curtains of the front window and spotted Nicki's Jeep pulling into the gravel driveway outside the cabin. She pulled to a stop and cut the engine, but she didn't get out right away.

What was she doing?

A minute ticked by. Then two. Dallas's legs began to ache again from the stillness of waiting.

When the Jeep door opened and she got out and turned

toward the cabin, he pulled back from the window and took up a position against the wall by the door. When she entered, the door would hide him until it was too late to prepare herself for his ambush.

At least, that's what he hoped.

Her footsteps ascended the wooden steps of the porch slowly. Deliberately. Inside Dallas's chest, his heart took a couple of hard leaps into a higher gear. He braced himself with a deep breath, preparing his limbs for action. He was still weaker than he liked, but his size and the factor of surprise would give him an edge.

He heard the rattle of keys in the door and pressed himself flat against the wall.

The door swung open with a creak of the hinges, and her boots hit the landing with a thud. He heard a soft huff of air escape her lungs as she stepped into the cabin and started to close the door behind her.

He hit her hard and fast, shoving her to the floor beneath him. Her soft cry of shock gave him the briefest moment of triumph, before his body landed flush against hers, his hips driving hers into the hard floor.

She started to struggle, her thighs opening as she kicked her legs toward him. The movement settled his hips more firmly into the cradle between her thighs, and, for a moment, he couldn't think. Couldn't come up with a single rational thought. All he could do was feel. The heat of her body under his. The softness of her curves, how perfectly they seemed to mold to his own lean hardness, welcoming him as if their bodies had been fashioned by a master craftsman to fit together in seamless perfection.

His heart rate soared, blood rushing south to where her sex cradled his. He exhaled, then sucked in another harsh breath as she stopped fighting and gazed up at him, her blue eyes dark and wide.

His hands tightened around her wrists, holding her captive on the floor beneath him, and she still didn't move.

When she spoke, her voice was a husky growl.

"Did you get anything to eat?"

Chapter Five

There was a roar in her ears, like a winter wind rushing through the pine boughs. Her blood pulsing in her ears, she realized, hard and fast. Maybe that's why she thought she'd heard herself ask if he'd gotten anything to eat.

Because surely she hadn't just blurted such a thing to the wild-eyed man who held her pinned beneath him on the cabin floor.

The grip of his hands on her wrists loosened. His hips shifted, pulled away from her body, as cold air rushed in to replace his heat. He rolled onto his back beside her, gazing up at the cabin ceiling.

"Who *are* you?" he asked the ceiling.

She looked up to see what had drawn his gaze, but all she saw was slightly dingy white Sheetrock. "Are you asking me or the cabin?"

He rolled his head until his gaze met hers. "I made myself some scrambled eggs and toast."

So she *had* asked if he'd gotten anything to eat.

"How'd you get free?"

He hesitated a moment, as if considering what he should tell her. Finally, he sighed. "There was a nail sticking out of the wooden shelves in the cellar. I used it to rip the duct tape."

He was still breathing hard, she realized. Taking her

down had winded him a little, which meant that, while he was clearly stronger than he had been the night before, he wasn't exactly in fighting form.

She pushed herself to a sitting position, trying to ignore the inconvenient—and highly inappropriate—tingling in her girl parts. She really had the worst taste in men. "That explains how you got your hands free. But how did you get out of the cellar? That's a good lock."

"Even good locks can be picked,"

"By a graphic designer?"

He sat up and looked at her. "You really do know who I am, don't you?"

"Did you think I was bluffing?"

His eyes narrowed. "No. But what I haven't figured out yet is who you are. And why you thought locking me up was a better option than calling the cops. What are you hiding?"

She couldn't exactly answer that question, could she? She started to get up, bracing herself for any move on his part to stop her. But he merely sat on the floor, gazing up at her with curious brown eyes. "What am *I* hiding? You're the fugitive from the FBI."

He tucked his legs up and started to stand, grimacing at the effort. She stuck her hand out to help.

He stared at her outstretched hand. "Yes. I'm the fugitive from the FBI. Which makes me wonder why you balked at my offer to call the authorities to take me off your hands."

She bit her lip and withdrew her hand. "Right."

He pushed to a standing position, his jaw tightly set. "'Right' doesn't exactly answer my question."

"I have my reasons for not wanting the police or anyone else sniffing around here. Can't we just leave it at that?"

The look he gave her made his answer superfluous. "I really don't think so."

She sighed and lied. "I'm a moonshiner."

His sudden bark of laughter caught her off guard. "No, you're not."

"How do you know I don't have a still hidden somewhere around here?"

"Because I searched this whole bloody cabin while I was waiting for your return, and there's nothing remotely like a still in this place. Nor, by the way, is there a phone, even though there was one in my room last night."

"It's broken."

He shook his head. "No, it's not."

Damn it. When had she become such a bad liar? She used to be really good at spinning tales, stories nobody could ever poke holes in because she made them sound so plausible.

Smack-dab in the middle of an undercover operation was a very bad time to lose her touch in the deception department.

"Let's go back to my first question," he said. "Who are you?"

"Nicki."

"Nicki what?"

"Nicki North."

His brows descended a notch. "Nicki North. Okay. We'll go with that."

"Someone named Dallas really has no room to question another person's name." She crossed to the door and locked it. "You picked the cellar lock? Really?"

"I'm out, aren't I?"

"What did you use?"

A faint smile touched the corners of his mouth, hinting at an unexpected set of dimples in his lean cheeks. "Trade secret."

"I don't have a tension wrench down there, so you must have improvised." She tried to remember what sort of tools were in the cellar. There was a box down there that had been here when she rented the cabin, apparently left behind by the last tenant. It had been a jumble of odds and ends, screws, nails, a hex key or two, some rubber bands, and a few brads and paper clips. She hazarded a guess. "Paper clips?"

"Should have known you were the lock-picking type."

"I like to think I defy easy categorization."

He laughed softly. "I bet you do."

She didn't like the way he'd turned this conversation into an exploration of her secrets, so she pushed back. "Where have you been for the past few weeks?"

"Don't you know that, too?" he challenged softly, taking a couple of steps toward her. "You seem to know so much already."

Though he was still too thin and too pale to look fully dangerous, her spine stiffened at his advance. He'd been strong enough to take her down by surprise, and she wasn't completely sure she'd have been able to fight him off if he hadn't rolled off and let her go.

Unfortunately, that hint of danger was doing all sorts of mortifying, tingly things to her insides. And she'd been doing so well with her "stay clear of bad boys" resolution to this point, damn it.

"Why don't we start from the beginning?" she suggested, taking a step back to maintain the distance between them. "I read an article about your disappearance a couple of weeks ago. Apparently your boss at the FBI reported you missing."

"Really?" He seemed surprised to hear it. "Which boss?"

"Some Japanese name, I think."

"Michelle."

She didn't like the way he said her name, with a touch of affection. Was she just his boss or something more?

She gave herself a mental kick. *What the hell, Nicki?* "Right. Michelle isn't a Japanese name."

"Matsumara is." There was a touch of humor in his voice. "What else did the article say?"

"Probably a lot less than you could tell me," she answered. "Since it happened to you."

He looked at her, his brow furrowed, and she thought he was about to refuse to answer her question. But after a moment, his expression cleared and he turned away from her and walked toward the fireplace. He'd started a fire, she saw, wondering why she hadn't noticed it when she walked into the cabin earlier.

Maybe because her mind was preoccupied with how she was going to explain her reckless actions once she let him out of the cellar?

"It was a Friday," he began. "I left the office, packed a bag and started south toward Kentucky."

"You're from there, right?"

He frowned. "The article was that thorough?"

"The articles," she corrected lightly. "There was speculation you might have been heading there for the weekend, maybe to visit family or something."

His expression shuttered. "No family left there anymore."

"So you weren't headed to Kentucky?"

"I didn't say that. It's still sort of home, I guess."

"But you didn't make it there."

"No. I didn't." He picked up the fire poker and she tensed. But he merely prodded one of the logs, stirring up embers before returning the iron to its holder. "I realized

I was being followed. And then, I was run off the road."
He shrugged one shoulder. "Don't remember much about
the accident, really. I think I might have hit my head."

"What *do* you remember?"

"Men. Six or seven of them. They were rough and
didn't really care if they were hurting me. In fact, if my
subsequent interactions with them are any indication,
they probably enjoyed hurting me." He turned to look at
her. "It doesn't matter. Yesterday morning, they left me
alone and didn't lock the door. Maybe they thought I was
too weak to do anything. I don't know."

"You got away?" She didn't mean to sound skeptical,
but even to her own ears, her doubt was obvious.

"I got away." A touch of defensiveness darkened his
voice. "I just started heading west. I knew I was somewhere on a mountain. I figured if I headed west, I'd reach
civilization sooner or later."

"So you were walking through mountains all day?"

"Not all day. Sometimes I was hiding from the people
looking for me."

Nicki tamped down a shudder. "You know they're
probably still looking for you."

He nodded. "That's why I'm still here in this cabin
instead of out there in the woods."

"The lesser of two evils?"

"Duct tape versus steel-toed boots in the ribs? Yeah,
definitely the lesser of two evils."

She shook her head, feeling sick. "I'm sorry. I didn't
know what else to do. If it makes you feel any better, I
couldn't even concentrate at work for thinking about you
in the cellar. I should have at least let you go to the bathroom before I locked you up."

He released a little huff of laughter. "And fed me, right?"

"You must think I'm a terrible person."

He shook his head, still smiling. "Where would I ever get that idea?"

This whole thing was just too much. Dealing with Del McClintock, who'd probably like to get in her pants, was bad enough. But dealing with this cipher of a man, whose pants were proving an unexpected temptation to *her*, had her feeling completely out of her element.

She'd worn a lot of hats in her short life, from go-go dancer at a Memphis club to an EMT in Nashville. Now she was a fry cook in little River's End, Virginia. What she wasn't, what she clearly had no talent for, was being an undercover operative for Alexander Quinn and The Gates.

She wondered if Agent X had left any word for her at the drop site. She hadn't even thought about stopping to check, so intent had she been on getting home to let her captive out of the dank cellar.

As a spy, she stank up the place.

"You can go. Whenever you want. Just do me a favor and wait until you're well clear of here to call your friends in the FBI, okay?" She waved toward the door. "You can take my Jeep. There's a train depot in River's End where you can even catch a train back to DC if you want. Leave the Jeep there. I can pick it up later with my spare key."

"How do you figure I'll be able to pay for my train ride out of here?"

Her heart sank. "I can probably come up with fifty in cash, but I don't know if that's enough for a ticket."

He nibbled at his lower lip, and she couldn't seem to stop wondering what those teeth might feel like worrying the tender flesh of her earlobe.

Damn it, Nicki!

"You know, I think I might prefer to stick around." Dallas's tone was low and thoughtful. "I'm not exactly in fighting shape at the moment, so I'm not sure I'm ready to face an FBI interrogation in my current state." His gaze flicked up to meet hers, a dangerous gleam in those dark eyes. "And I do enjoy solving puzzles."

She didn't miss his meaning, but she feigned ignorance. "I don't have any puzzles around here. I'm not very good at them, myself."

He smiled, his dark eyes crinkling at the corners. "Don't play stupid with me, Nicki North. I may not know who you are or what you're up to, exactly, but I'm not blind. I know you're smart and resourceful. And maybe, if I stick around here long enough, I just might figure out what sort of game you're playing."

"I don't play games."

"Of course you do. We all do." He moved toward her, his pace steady but unhurried, giving her time to retreat.

But she couldn't make her legs move. It was all she could do to hold his suddenly feral gaze as he closed the distance between them.

"I'm good at games." His voice was a low growl, barely more than a whisper. "And I play to win."

She lifted her chin, the challenge in his voice sparking through her like a jolt of electricity, firing up her own hidden resolve. "So do I."

If it was a game he wanted, it was a game he would get. Because he was right. Everybody played games.

But nobody played them quite as well as Nicolette Jamison.

HIS NAME WAS not Agent X, of course, but ever since Nicolette Jamison had referred to him by that moniker in one of her reports to Alexander Quinn, he'd found a certain humorous satisfaction in thinking of himself that way whenever he approached the drop site.

The name he was currently using was John Bartholomew, and he wasn't any sort of agent anymore. Hadn't been for nearly a decade, his nascent career with the CIA over almost before it began, thanks to his terrible timing during a black bloc protest in Athens not long after Greek police shot a teenager. He'd walked out of the hostel where he'd been staying and right into the path of a chunk of concrete that had caught him square in the temple.

At least, that's what he'd been told when he'd awakened nearly three weeks later in an Athens hospital with no memory of the previous two months of his life.

His notes on his surveillance operation were long gone by then. His hotel room had been thoroughly searched and sanitized within an hour of his injury, his station chief in Athens had told him with regret. His mission was compromised and the CIA didn't care that it hadn't been his fault. They had no further use for him.

After his recovery, he'd returned to the life he'd been planning before the agency had recruited him, working as a tax preparer in his father's accounting firm in Johnson City, Tennessee.

He'd hated every minute of it.

Thank God for Quinn. The old CIA hand had needed a man in southern Virginia, just across the border from Johnson City, for a mission his security agency had taken on.

Quinn had picked him.

The snow underfoot had turned slushy as the temperature rose above freezing shortly before noon. If the trees overhead weren't blocking the sunlight that had broken through the clouds after a gray morning, the snow would probably be gone altogether within an hour. But the canopy of shade would keep the crusty slush on the ground for a while longer, forcing him to walk carefully so he'd leave only a minimal trail of footprints in the snow.

He spotted the fallen log beside the drop site cave. The branch was sticking up, their signal.

She'd left him a message for Quinn.

He started toward the cave when the sound of voices carried through the cold air. Freezing in place, he scanned the woods for the source.

There. Two men in woodland camo topped the rise, barely giving him time to hunker down behind a clump of knotted vines. As long as he stayed still, he shouldn't be spotted.

He hoped.

The men were carrying .22 rimfire rifles propped on their shoulders. Dangling from their left hands were the limp carcasses of a couple of gray squirrels.

Hunters. Gray squirrel season in Virginia would be over at the end of the month, so these guys were probably trying to get in a few final hunts before March.

They passed the cave and the fallen log without so much as a glance, chatting quietly about where they should go after squirrels next. They walked perilously close to where he was hidden behind the twisted vines, but if they noticed him hunkering in hiding, neither of them gave any sign.

He waited until their voices drifted into silence before he moved, walking as rapidly as he dared to the cave to check the small stone cavity where Nicki Jamison left her missives for Quinn.

The message was there, as expected. He tucked the folded paper inside his shirt and melted back into the woods from where he'd come.

Only when he reached the privacy of his truck did he unfold the paper and read the message inside.

Eyebrows arching at the information, he started the truck and drove southeast.

Once he'd safely reached Abingdon, he pulled out his phone and dialed the number Quinn had given him. Quinn answered on the second ring. "Miller's Plumbing."

"Dallas Cole is alive. And guess who's nursing him back to health in a cabin in River's End, Virginia?"

Chapter Six

Nicki North was not her name. He didn't know what her name really was, but Nicki North sounded too much like an alias for Dallas to buy. But she really did seem to be a fry cook at a local diner, because he could still smell a delicious hint of hash browns and bacon lingering in her hair when she leaned close to check his wounds.

She touched his wrist just below the scratch he'd sustained while freeing himself from the duct-tape bindings. Her blue eyes rose to meet his. "This is new."

He nodded.

"You did it freeing yourself?"

"Yeah."

She dropped her gaze, looking troubled. "I'm sorry. I shouldn't have done that to you. I should have figured out something else."

"Taking men captive isn't your normal hobby?"

Her gaze flicked up. "No."

"That wasn't a serious question," he said, softening his tone.

"I wouldn't blame you if you thought I was a psychopath. Under the circumstances." She applied antiseptic to his new wound, wincing when he sucked in a sharp breath. "Sorry. Really, I'm sorry."

"You're afraid of something." He caught her hand as she started to pull away, holding her in place.

Her gaze met his and held. "I'm afraid for you. We both know you're in trouble. And River's End is full of people you do *not* want to run into."

"You've already delivered that message. Loud and clear. But what I can't figure out is why you still live in River's End if you're so afraid of the people around here."

"I'm not the one in danger." She said the words in an untroubled tone, but he didn't quite buy it. Beneath her calm, unhurried movements, he sensed a dark undercurrent of tension.

Maybe she was telling the truth. Maybe all her fear was for him.

But he didn't think so.

She finished bandaging his wrist and sat back. "That should keep you until I get back."

"You've got to go back to work?"

"No. I have to go check on a friend who's home sick." Her gaze shifted away, a sure sign of deception.

"A friend?"

"A woman I know. Long story that I don't have time to tell." Her expression shuttering, she packed up the first-aid kit and stood, pushing her chair back from the sofa. "You should take advantage of the peace and quiet to catch up on your sleep."

"Good idea," he agreed.

She slanted a look at him as she set the first-aid kit on the mantel, but if she suspected he was insincere, she didn't probe. "I shouldn't be more than a couple of hours. I'll bring back some groceries and fix us a proper dinner."

"Don't go to any trouble."

That time she stopped in the middle of unlocking the

door and turned to look at him. "You're being mighty accommodating."

"Where am I going to go?"

Her eyes narrowed a notch. "Where indeed?" She continued through the doorway and closed it behind her. He heard the rattle of her keys in the lock, shutting him safely inside.

He waited until he heard the Jeep's engine fade away before he began a slow circuit of the house, similar to the search he'd made before, after he'd freed himself from the cellar. But this time, instead of looking for incriminating evidence, he focused on trying to get a feel for the place in hopes of gaining a deeper understanding of the woman who lived there.

Like the simple bedroom, the rest of the cabin seemed sparsely furnished with anything that could be described as personal. Most of the furnishings were old and mismatched, but not in a particularly charming way. Instead, they seemed to be the products of a single day of shopping in a secondhand store, chosen more for utility than style.

Not at all what he expected from the woman who'd taken him down in her kitchen, taped his hands together and thrown him in her cellar.

He started a second turn around the cabin, this time looking in less obvious places. Drawers. Cubbyholes. Closets.

If the measure of the woman wasn't easily discerned from the surface of her life, then perhaps there were hidden places where all her deepest, darkest secrets lay.

After a second pass through the cabin without finding any obvious hiding places, he stopped in the middle of her bedroom and looked around, trying to figure out what hiding places there might be that were less than obvious. An alcove or a hidden trapdoor, something that he might not notice at a cursory glance.

The problem, he mused as he went from room to room, was that he was out of his element. Despite the artistic nature of his public relations career in the FBI, his world revolved around computers. Being stuck in this little mountain cabin without a computer or cell phone in sight was proving to be enough technological deprivation to drive him crazy.

He'd always been good with technology, even as a boy in the backwoods of Kentucky where computers were a luxury. He'd made friends at school with David Price, whose father was a computer programmer at the college up at the university in Lexington. David had spent all his summers with his dad, picking up everything there was to know about how computers worked.

He'd taught Dallas everything he knew, which hadn't been a lot. David hadn't been that interested in computers, preferring sports and, later on, girls.

Dallas had liked sports and girls, too, but he'd found himself utterly fascinated by the language of code, how the tiniest changes—a symbol here, a number there—could entirely change how a system functioned.

Unfortunately, when it came time to go to college, he'd lacked the skills to get into school on a technology scholarship. Instead, he'd gone on an art scholarship and focused on finding a job that would get him out of the backwoods for good.

That had been graphic design, first with an ad agency in the Virginia town where he'd attended college, then a few years later, working for the FBI in their public information office.

It had been the FBI and their focus on providing their employees with new educational opportunities that had

returned him to his first love. He'd struck up a friendship with some agents in the cybercrime division who
had talked him into a training track that might put him
in a position to make a career move.

He'd never considered himself special agent material,
but computers were something he understood. He hadn't
forgotten the things he'd learned as a boy, and college
had allowed him to pick up new information and skills
that he continued to expand and hone on his own time.

He was good with computers and even the cybercrime
guys had let him in to their inner circle once they saw
that what he lacked in training he made up for in raw talent and sheer desire.

But he wasn't an agent. And now, thanks to FBI Assistant Director Philip Crandall, he never would be.

He reached the small kitchen and looked around, losing hope. If she was hiding anything—and he knew she
must be, given the way she'd reacted to his desire to call
the cops—she'd hidden it well. If it was some secret she'd
ferreted away on her computer hard drive, he could have
found it without a lot of effort. Computers, he understood.

Low-tech backwoods women, however, were clearly a
mystery he didn't have a hope of deciphering. Never had.

Meanwhile, his back was aching, his legs felt like rubber and the start of a five-alarm headache was pounding a
path through his skull. Eschewing the chairs at the breakfast nook table nearby, he slumped to the floor where he
stood, leaning back against the oven. As he started to
let his eyelids drift shut, something in the narrow space
between the refrigerator and the cabinet caught his eye.

Pushing himself to his hands and knees, he crawled
across the kitchen floor and took a closer look. The space
was dark, but there was just enough light slanting into the
tiny aperture to reveal something tucked inside the niche.

His hand would never fit into the space, but surely there was something—

He eyed the utensil rack over the gas range and spotted a long-handled barbecue fork. Groaning, he pushed to his feet and grabbed the fork, carrying it back to the refrigerator.

It took a couple of tries to snag his elusive target, but finally the fork caught the edge of whatever lay within the niche and pulled it toward him.

It was a large manila envelope with a string tie fastening it shut. There was nothing written on either side of the envelope, but he could feel a thick stack of something enclosed inside. Papers, maybe. Documents.

Secrets.

Carrying it to the kitchen nook table, he pulled up a chair and set the envelope in front of him. "Okay, Nicki North, let's find out what you're hiding."

He untwisted the string clasp and opened the envelope, dumping the contents on the table. There were notes, some handwritten, some typed. At least three dozen notes, all told.

He picked up the nearest one and started to read, almost breathless with anticipation. But as he took in the words contained in the notes, his anticipation slowly turned to deeper confusion.

What lay inside the envelope answered some of his questions, but they didn't solve the mystery of Nicki North.

They only deepened it.

KAYLIE PICKETT'S EYES were wide with fear when she opened the cabin door to Nicki and hurried her inside. "Keith's gonna be back in an hour. I ain't got long."

The hair on the back of Nicki's neck rose but she pushed down the fear. Getting caught here with Kaylie wasn't anywhere near the worst thing that could happen to her. She could talk her way out of it.

Kaylie was the one who'd suffer most.

Kaylie and the baby she was carrying.

"You sure I'm okay to take these?" Kaylie looked at the bottles of prenatal vitamins Nicki pulled from her purse and set on the kitchen table.

"You need to take these," Nicki said firmly. "And you can't be drinkin' any 'shine or doin' drugs—"

"I don't do that stuff," Kaylie said quickly, peering at the vitamin bottles with a furrow between her eyebrows. She looked up when Nicki didn't speak. "I swear."

"I believe you," Nicki said, wishing she was more certain.

"I used to do a little weed, but I don't do that no more."

"Well, be sure you don't do weed or meth or any of that junk. You want a healthy baby, don't you?"

"'Course I do."

"Just take one of these a day. And you want to eat well, too. Plenty of green vegetables, carrots, lean meats—"

"Are squirrels lean meat?" Kaylie asked with a sudden grin.

Nicki smiled back. "Depends on the squirrel."

Kaylie laughed and gave her an impulsive hug. "Thank you for this. Keith won't even think about gettin' me anything like this. He thinks it's all some government conspiracy to suck money outta his pocket."

He would, Nicki thought. Or, at least, he used that excuse to get out of doing things he didn't want to do. "I'd better get out of here before Keith gets home. You got somewhere to stash those where he can't find them?"

"I do." Kaylie walked her to the door. "Thanks again."

"No problem. You call if you need anything." As she started to open the door, she remembered she still hadn't hooked her home phone up again after disconnecting it when she left for work. It was still in the floorboard of the Jeep. She'd have to put it back in case Kaylie needed to reach her. "Try not to worry, okay? As long as you eat right, take those vitamins and try to avoid too much stress, you and the baby should be fine."

Kaylie gave a soft huff of bleak laughter. "No stress, huh? I'll work on that."

Nicki tightened her jacket against the cold wind rolling down the mountain, ruffling her dark hair and sending little needles of cold drizzle into her face. She didn't think it was supposed to snow again, but she hadn't really checked the weather since this morning, had she?

She turned on the radio, flipping stations until she found a news break. After a couple of minutes, the announcer got around to a quick weather report. Sleet in places overnight, but no more snow expected.

That was a relief, at least. She hoped to get back to the dead drop later that night to see if Agent X had picked up her message. It would be faster and easier to get there without dealing with snow.

Come on, Nicki. You know the possibility of snow isn't what's got your nerves on edge.

No, it wasn't.

She had to worry about what she'd find when she got back to the cabin. Was Dallas Cole still going to be there? Was the fear of his former captors enough to make him stay put until she could get word from Alexander Quinn?

The front door of her cabin was still locked when she inserted her key in the dead bolt. Letting herself in, she stopped in the doorway and scanned the empty living room.

She locked up behind her and started into the hall, tempted to call out. But caution stopped her. If she wasn't alone, there was a distinct likelihood that who-ever else occupied the cabin might not be a friend. It was a possibility she'd had to live with every moment since taking the undercover job Quinn had offered her.

There was a light on in the kitchen. She took a brac-ing breath and entered the room.

Dallas sat in the kitchen nook, a cup of coffee cradled between his hands on the table in front of him. He looked up, his dark eyes serious.

A moment later, her gaze fell on the manila envelope sitting next to his elbow.

Blood rushed to her head, roaring in her ears. Her whole body went cold, then hot, then cold again, and for a moment, her knees felt as if they would buckle.

She fought the sudden weakness and forced herself to the table to take a seat in front of him, her gaze settling on the manila envelope. It was tied shut, the way she'd left it when she stuck it into the narrow space between the refrigerator and the cabinet.

She cleared her throat, feeling sick. "You've been busy."

He turned the cup around slowly between his hands. "Idle hands are the devil's workshop."

"Did you open it?" She looked up at him.

He gazed at her as if she'd said something terribly stu-pid. Which, she supposed, she had.

"Right." She nibbled her bottom lip. "Look, whatever you read, it's probably not what you think."

The left side of his mouth curved upward a notch, a dimple forming in his cheek. "It's not like it was en-crypted."

She sighed. "What do you think you know?"

He pushed his coffee cup away and looked at her.

"You're working with Alexander Quinn. Which means, you're probably working for The Gates. Right?"

She didn't answer him. She didn't see the point.

"That's why you know who I am, isn't it?" he prodded. "It's not like your story didn't make the news."

"But you don't even have a television here."

She looked down at her hands.

He sighed. "There's no photo of me in that envelope."

"No."

"But you've seen a photo of me." It wasn't a question.

"There are newspapers in town." She knew that she wasn't giving away much outwardly. She might be a little rusty at lying, since she'd turned over a new leaf, but she was still pretty good at a poker face.

"Okay." He pushed the envelope toward her. "Most of what's in here are messages from Quinn. At least, they're signed AQ. I'm assuming that's not short for al Qaeda."

She just looked at him, determined not to give anything away.

"These messages aren't encrypted. But they *are* cryptic. In case they fell into the wrong hands?"

She shrugged one shoulder. "This is your little theory. You tell me."

He shook his head. "Does Quinn think I've gone over to the dark side? Is that what Cade Landry told him?"

"Who?"

Dallas's lips flattened to a thin line. "Just tell me the truth, Nicki. Is that even your name?"

"Yes."

"Nicki North?"

She didn't answer.

"I don't believe that's your last name, but if you're undercover, I don't need to know. I just need to know what you're up to and whether or not I can help you."

"Help me?"

"Where did you go last night?"

She didn't answer.

"To pick up another message from Quinn? Or to leave one?"

He was too close to the truth. Everything she'd risked, everything she'd worked to set in place, could be destroyed with a single word to the wrong person. "I can get you out of here. Isn't that what you wanted?"

He looked at her a moment, a flicker of surprise in his dark eyes. "You're ready to let me go now?"

"I never wanted to keep you prisoner. I just—"

"You just didn't want anything to blow your cover." He reached across the table and put his hand over hers. His warm, callused fingers brushed across hers, sending an unexpected shiver up her spine. "I don't want that to happen, either. But I can help you."

"I don't know what you're talking about."

"Yes, you do. You're trying to get information on the Blue Ridge Infantry. Something about a guy high in the organization Quinn wants you to get closer to."

She tried not to flinch, but his words surprised her. Quinn's message about the unnamed leader of the BRI had been about as oblique as any message he'd ever sent.

So how had Dallas Cole figured out what Quinn was trying to say?

"That struck a nerve," he murmured.

She snapped her gaze up to clash with his and jerked her hand away from his. "What do you want?"

"Just what I said." There was an unexpected vibrancy to his sudden smile, as if someone had just turned on the electricity inside him. "I can help you, Nicki. I want in."

Chapter Seven

"You want in?"

Progress, Dallas thought. She'd clammed up once she spotted the envelope on the table, and he'd begun to wonder if she'd remain mute forever more. But apparently his offer of help had surprised her enough to overcome her caution.

"Those people kept me locked up for three weeks. They were rough on me, trying to get information out of me that I didn't have. And I think they've managed to find allies in the FBI who will be more than happy to make sure I don't make it back to DC to tell my story. So I want in. I can help you."

"I never said I needed help."

"You haven't said anything at all," he pointed out. "The silent treatment is starting to bug me."

"You're crazy. You don't know a damn thing about me. You've read my personal letters from a friend and somehow come up with some wild tale about me being some kind of spy."

"Undercover operative," he corrected.

"Whatever."

He rose to his feet and stood over her, wondering if she'd intimidate easily. He had a feeling she wouldn't.

"So, if AQ doesn't stand for Alexander Quinn, what does it stand for?"

"Alan Quincy," she answered without hesitation.

She was a pretty good liar, he had to admit. Quick and bold. And definitely not intimidated. "Boyfriend?"

"Old schoolmate."

"Really. What school?"

"Ridge County High School in Tennessee." She looked up at him, her expression placid. "He was a senior. I was a sophomore. We were both in the film club."

"Film club."

"We got credits for watching movies and writing about them. Total scam, but the school never called us on it." She flashed him a grin. "You should have read my essay on the symbolism in *Mean Girls*."

He couldn't stop a smile from crossing his lips in return. She was lying through her pretty white teeth—though he had a feeling she really had written one hell of an essay on *Mean Girls*—but he couldn't stay annoyed with her.

He was right, damn it. He knew she was working for Alexander Quinn. It was the only thing that made any sense of the past two days.

If she was really up to her elbows in the Blue Ridge Infantry, she'd have turned him over to the men he'd escaped. But she hadn't.

And clearly, she wasn't some normal person living in the woods, because she'd taped his hands together and left him locked in her cellar so he wouldn't leave while she was at work.

"Why did you lock me up?"

Her gaze, which had fallen to the manila folder he'd left on the table in front of her, lifted to meet his. "I told you why."

"To protect me."

She stared at him for a long moment. Then she put her face in her hands. "Damn it," she murmured, her voice muffled by her palms.

He eased himself into the chair across from her again, remaining silent while she muttered beneath her breath. Finally, she looked up at him, her eyes wide and scared. Fear radiated from her, infecting his own nerves until they hummed, deep and sonorous, with dread.

He'd told her he wanted in. And he'd meant it.

But the look in her eyes told him his declaration had been reckless.

"You're right, okay?" Her voice trembled. "You're right."

"Can you be more specific?"

She dropped her head in her hands. "I'm undercover. I'm trying to uncover the identity of the new leader of the Blue Ridge Infantry's Virginia branch."

"For Alexander Quinn."

She looked up. "For Quinn. For The Gates. For myself."

"For yourself?"

"Look, Quinn doesn't know this. And I don't want him to. Do you understand? I don't want him to know what I'm about to tell you."

The strangled tone of her voice sent alarm rattling down his bones. "I understand."

"Almost two years ago, I worked as a confidential informant for the Nashville Police Department."

He raised his eyebrows.

"It's a long story. I was in the wrong place at the right time." She shook her head. "Pretty much the story of my life. I had gone out a few times with a guy who, as it turned out, was one of the city's biggest fences. The cops all knew he had a shop somewhere but they hadn't been able to catch him at it. When they saw me with him, one of the cops approached me. He threatened to make sure I went down with Blake—that was the name of the guy, Blake Ridenour. But see, I really didn't know Blake was a criminal. I just thought he was cute and he treated me like a queen."

"Ouch."

"Well, when I found out who he really was, a lot of things started to make sense. Things I should have noticed before. I guess I just didn't let myself see the warning signs." She sighed. "Also the story of my life."

"Did you help the cops catch him?"

"Yeah. And he never knew it was me." There was a hint of pride in her voice. But that flicker of confidence faded quickly as she brushed her dark hair away from her face, revealing the graceful curve of her neck.

The urge to kiss a path down that long column of perfect skin hit him like a gut punch. He shoved the rush of desire deep inside him, clenching his hands together to keep from reaching out to touch her. "What does this have to do with the Blue Ridge Infantry?"

"After I proved myself with Blake, the Tennessee Bureau of Investigation approached me. They'd heard about me from the Nashville police and thought I was the perfect person for this particular job they had in mind."

"What kind of job?"

She met his gaze. "You're in the FBI. You know what a honey trap is, don't you?"

He nodded, feeling a little queasy.

"The TBI had been investigating reports of a militia group, originally from Virginia, that had begun to spread into eastern Tennessee."

"The Blue Ridge Infantry."

"Yes." She pushed up from her chair and paced to the

coffeemaker, pressing both hands on the counter and gazing at the half-full carafe. After a moment, she opened a cabinet and pulled out a mug. She remained quiet as she poured herself a cup of coffee and added cream and sugar.

Dallas stayed quiet, too, giving her time to gather her thoughts, though growing anxiety had begun to fray his patience. Whatever she'd been through seemed to have her thoroughly rattled, and he wasn't sure he wanted to know how bad a situation had to get to throw a woman like Nicki off her game.

She brought her cup of coffee to the table and sat again, cradling the warm mug between her palms. "It seemed an easy enough assignment. They hadn't had any luck getting anyone inside the militia, but there were people on the margins they thought could be exploited. One of those people was a farmer who lived in a tiny place called Thurlow Gap. He wasn't a member of the militia, but he had two brothers the TBI believed were members, and the farmer was known to be sympathetic to their cause."

"Your job was to get close to the farmer?"

She nodded. "He was recently widowed. His wife had died of breast cancer the previous winter, and he was left to take care of three kids. He needed a live-in housekeeper and nanny, I guess you'd call it. The TBI had done a lot of research on the guy, down to the kind of woman his wife had been. And they coached me how to be as much like her as possible."

"Oh." He was beginning to get an idea just how this story was going to end. No wonder she looked sick.

"It wasn't supposed to get personal. Not really. I wasn't sent there to seduce him. It wasn't supposed to cross any lines that way."

"But it did?"

"Kind of." Her grip on the coffee mug tightened,

though she still hadn't taken a drink. "He wasn't what I expected. He was nice. Decent. Still hurting from the loss of his wife. And those kids…"

He didn't miss the glitter of tears in her eyes. "What happened?"

"He wasn't as sympathetic to the militia as the TBI thought. He just loved his brothers. So he tried to protect them. And it ended up costing him everything."

"How?"

"I found out his brothers and their friends were planning an attack on some conservation officers who were doing license checks at a nearby reservoir. He'd been trying to talk them out of it, make them see the stupidity of doing something so destructive." She shook her head. "He sympathized with the idea of less governmental interference in the lives of its citizens. Hell, who doesn't? I know I do. But hurting or even killing people who are just doing their jobs—"

"You reported the plan to the TBI?"

"I did." She closed her eyes, tears squeezing through her eyelids and trickling down her cheeks. "But his brothers thought the information had come from him. So they made him pay."

"How?"

"They burned his fields. All his crops that would have paid the bills once it was time to harvest. But they didn't stop there." She dashed away the tears with quick, angry flicks of her fingertips. "Then they burned him out of his house. We almost didn't get the kids out in time."

"My God."

"He lost everything. His house. His living. Almost lost his children."

He reached across the table and took her hands. "You know it wasn't your fault."

"In my head I know it."

"You're not the one who set the fires. You're not the one who was planning murders."

"I told the TBI I was out. There wasn't anything more I could get for them, once that poor man's life was torn apart. And it wouldn't have done any good for them if I stuck around living a lie. So I said my goodbyes and I ran." She turned her hands palm up beneath his. "I ran home."

"Like I did."

She looked up at him. "Yeah. I guess exactly like that." Her grip on his hands tightened a notch. "Though I didn't get ambushed on the way."

"You sound as if you finally believe me."

"You didn't give yourself those scrapes and bruises." She dropped her gaze to their entwined hands. "There was always a question in Quinn's mind whether you were a good guy or a bad guy."

"You might want to ask a guy named Cade Landry his opinion." He tugged his hands, trying to pull them away from hers, but her grip tightened, holding him in place. "If he's even alive anymore."

"He's alive. And well."

Relief washed over him in a wave. He'd been almost certain Landry would be dead by now, thanks to his own stupidity. "Crandall didn't get to him?"

"Crandall?" She frowned at him. "Who's Crandall?"

She didn't know, he realized. But shortly before those thugs in trucks had ambushed him on the highway south, he'd talked to Cade Landry on the phone to warn him about Crandall.

Maybe Landry hadn't believed him.

"You're in contact with Quinn, right? You should ask him. Landry surely told Quinn what I told him about Philip Crandall."

"Maybe," she conceded, looking uneasy. "Quinn's pretty big on the whole concept of 'need to know.' But why don't you tell me what you told Landry? Because I think I need to know, and I don't think I can wait for Quinn to get around to agreeing with me."

"Philip Crandall is an assistant director at the FBI. And I'm pretty sure he's the one who sicced the BRI on me."

Nicki's eyes widened with alarm. "Assistant director at the FBI? The BRI has infiltrated the Bureau that high up?"

"I don't know," he admitted. "I just know that when I told AD Crandall what Cade Landry asked me to tell him, I got a very strong sense that I'd made a huge mistake."

"What did Landry ask you to tell him?"

"I think now it might have been a setup. Only problem is, I think I'm the one who got caught. And if I'm ever going to be able to get my life back, I have to prove that Crandall is dirty."

"How are you going to be able to do that?"

He met her worried gaze. "I have a few thoughts. But first, I'm going to need a few things. And I think maybe you can help me out with that."

ALMOST ALL THE SNOW had melted off during the afternoon hours, but the dead leaves underfoot had remained damp enough to form ice crystals when the temperatures dropped after nightfall. They crunched far too audibly beneath Nicki's feet as she hiked up the mountain, making her nerves rattle.

There's nobody watching, she told herself, even as she scanned the woods for any sign someone might be following her. She was coming up from the town side of the mountain this time, on her way home from an evening shift at the diner, leaving her Jeep parked behind the hardware store in hopes she'd escape notice.

She'd left Dallas behind in the cabin earlier with a warning to let her handle this part of the plan alone, but he hadn't exactly followed any of her orders to date, had he? What if he'd changed his mind about striking out on his own?

He wasn't what she'd expected. Quinn had described him as a worker bee, one of the nameless, faceless drones who kept the bureaucracy functioning. A graphic designer working in the public information office, putting out flyers and brochures describing the wonders of working for the FBI or touting their most recent successes.

But the Dallas Cole who'd picked the cellar lock and hunted down all her secrets was anything but a drone.

And while she wasn't exactly a technophile, she knew enough about computers to realize that the list of supplies he was requesting from Quinn suggested a computer savviness she hadn't expected.

By the time she reached the dead drop, she was shivering beneath her layers of warm clothing, but she knew it wasn't a reaction to the cold. Her life had been complicated enough before Dallas Cole stumbled in front of her Jeep in the middle of a winter storm.

Now it was becoming downright dangerous.

Her signal was gone, replaced by Agent X's downturned log. She had a message from Quinn waiting for her already.

What was she going to do if Quinn wanted her to abandon the case? There was a part of her that was scared senseless now that she was so close to getting the information she'd come here to find. If she continued to play her cards right, Del would introduce her to the head of the militia group, the man who was looking for someone to be his personal medic. And Nicki could make her own case for being that medic.

They'd have his identity. They'd have her on the inside where she could see and hear things another woman wouldn't get close enough to see or hear. And in the Blue Ridge Infantry's world, women weren't good for much of anything but sex, housekeeping and the occasional object of a man's anger. She'd be little more than a piece of furniture, ignored or forgotten most of the time, a fact she intended to use against the bastards.

But so much could go wrong so easily. One misstep could cost her everything she'd been working for.

And Dallas Cole was a misstep waiting to happen.

Nicki found a small packet of papers stashed in the small alcove inside the cave. She normally waited until she got back to the cabin to read the messages Quinn left her, but this time, curiosity got the better of her and she pulled a small penlight from her pocket and scanned the notes.

The first two papers contained a concise but thorough outline of what The Gates knew about Dallas Cole. To Nicki's relief, Quinn's assessment seemed to track precisely with what Dallas had told her himself.

Before she could check the rest of the notes, she heard the murmur of voices somewhere outside the cave.

Nerves jangling, she extinguished the penlight and pressed herself flat against the cold stone wall of the cave, holding her breath to listen.

The voices were male, but she couldn't make out words. They seemed to be some distance away but moving closer. She might have time to leave the cave and get out of sight before they could spot her.

But what if she was wrong? If someone saw her sneaking around this cave, they'd become curious. If word got to the wrong person—

She edged toward the cave mouth but stayed inside, straining to hear the voices of the men headed her way.

Definitely two of them, she decided as they came close enough for her to make out their words. From their conversation she quickly discerned they were night-hunting for opossum. And one of the voices belonged to Del McClintock.

"I don't know why he wants possum, but I've learned not to ask questions." That was Del, his drawl spreading like warm molasses.

"He still doin' poorly?" the other man asked. Nicki tried to place the voice but couldn't. Might be one of the crew she hadn't met yet.

"Yeah, but we're working on that. Seems like what he needs most is someone to monitor him, make sure he's gettin' his meds like he's supposed to. You know he doesn't want to involve a doctor, so we're trying to work out a different deal."

"You mean that girl, don't you? The cook at the diner?"

Nicki held her breath.

"Yeah, turns out she has some paramedic experience or somethin', but I don't think that's really why he's interested." Del laughed. "Can't really blame him for wanting a nice piece of scenery like Nicki around. I wouldn't mind exploring a little of that scenery myself."

Nicki grimaced. She might be laying a honey trap with Del, but she didn't have to like it. On the upside, Del seemed to think the mysterious head of the Virginia BRI was interested in her services as a caregiver. He'd played pretty coy and noncommittal with her so far, so this was good news.

Wasn't it?

She waited for the two of them to move on, but their footsteps stopped just a few yards away from the cave. The urge to take a peek to see if she could spot Del and his companion was almost more than she could resist, but she plastered herself to the cave wall and tried to calm her rapid respirations.

"Is that a cave?" That was Del's voice, terrifyingly close. Nicki swallowed a moan.

"Don't look like much of one," the other man drawled.

Del's footsteps crackled the frozen leaves underfoot as he moved closer to the cave. "Might be a possum nesting in there. Why don't we go take a look?"

Nicki's heart skipped a beat.

Chapter Eight

She'd been gone awhile, hadn't she?

Dallas glanced at the clock on the wall over the fireplace. Only nine thirty. She'd wanted to wait until after her shift at the diner to check the drop site, preferring the cover of darkness to make her trip through the woods. She'd told him the hike up the mountain would probably delay her by about thirty minutes, so she'd be home around ten.

Which meant there was still half an hour to wait before he could panic.

He had to do something to get his mind off Nicki's trip into the woods. Surely there was something constructive he could be doing while he waited? He could certainly use more sleep, but he didn't think his nerves would let him settle down for a nap. He'd already walked three circuits of the cabin's small interior, trying to build up his stamina, but the repetition was about to drive him crazy, as well.

He could always study the notes from Quinn. He'd had time to glance through them before Nicki returned home, but she'd stashed them back in the space between the refrigerator and the counter soon after.

But she hadn't actually told him not to touch them again, had she?

No, he decided. A glare was not an actual warning.

He pulled the envelope from the niche and started to untie the envelope closure when he heard the front door-knob rattle. The door creaked open slowly, and Dallas held his breath, waiting for the all clear signal Nicki had promised before she left on her hike.

But it didn't come.

The footfalls on the hardwood floors of the front room sounded heavy and, well, male. The door closed with a soft click, there was a brief rattle of keys and Dallas heard a male voice quietly ask, "The lights are on. You sure she's not here?"

With his pulse pounding like a whole drum line in his ears, Dallas gathered up the papers as quietly as he could and looked at the dead bolt lock on the back door. *Please be a quiet lock.* He edged over to the door and gave the dead bolt knob a slow twist. It glided open with only the tiniest of clicks.

"She's still at the diner, best I know. She never gets out of there early. You know how Trevor works those girls. We'll have to work fast, but we should have time."

Dallas waited, listening. Listening to the little voice in his head as his grandmother used to call it. "Trust that little voice. It knows what's what."

In the front room, a scraping noise gave him the open-ing he needed. He turned the knob and opened the door, the slight creak hidden by the sound of chair legs sliding across the floor. He slipped through the narrow opening and pushed the door closed, turning and running for the woods behind the cabin.

He didn't stop until he was several yards deep in the woods, his lungs aching from the cold air. He hadn't had time to grab his jacket, and the borrowed sweats felt inadequate to combat the frigid temperatures for long.

He tugged the papers tightly to his chest and looked

for anything he could use for shelter, but all he saw was trees, trees and more trees. He tamped down his dismay and just breathed, in and out, filling his aching lungs with clean mountain air until the rushing sound in his ears subsided.

Think, Dallas. You used to know the hills and woods like a friend.

He looked around again, this time without the rush of panic and despair. There were plenty of broken limbs on the ground, victims of past storms. Some of them were pine boughs—he could use them to construct a simple shelter to at least block out the wind.

He secured the papers back in the manila envelope and tucked them inside his sweatshirt for safekeeping while he went to work constructing his shelter.

Hunkering down in his cramped little pine bough fort a few minutes later, he finally had time to breathe and think about the intruders and what they might want. Nicki had told him she was trying to get on the inside of the BRI, so it made sense that they'd want to check her out a little more thoroughly. But entering her cabin to do a search when she was due home in under an hour suggested a brazenness that gave Dallas a very bad feeling about Nicki's infiltration plan.

What the hell was Alexander Quinn thinking, putting her into such a dangerous situation?

The cold was a living thing, with icy fingers that crept beneath his clothing and traced a shivery path down his spine. He tucked his knees up and curled into a ball, wishing he'd had time to grab a jacket. Not that it would have been much protection against the frigid night air. Nothing would protect him from the cold if he had to stay out here much longer.

He tried to calculate the time that had passed since

he'd checked the clock over Nicki's mantel. Ten minutes? Twenty? His watch had been one of the casualties of his abduction—his captors had stripped him of anything that could ground him in the world he'd left behind. He'd lost track of time, of day and night, even of who he was from time to time.

But he knew who he was now. He knew where he was. He knew it was night, it was cold and if Nicki came back to her cabin now, she'd walk in on an ambush.

He couldn't let that happen.

Pushing aside the pine boughs covering his makeshift fort, he rose to his feet and headed back toward Nicki's cabin. He wasn't sure what he was going to do when trouble came, but he'd do something even if it killed him.

He'd done all the cowering he planned to do for a lifetime.

"I DON'T THINK possums hide in caves." The voice of the unknown man carried into the cave.

Nicki flattened her back against the cave wall and tried to breathe quietly, despite the ache in her lungs. She couldn't risk drawing the attention of the men outside. There was nowhere to hide. Nowhere to run.

And if Del McClintock caught her in here and saw what she'd been hiding all these weeks, she'd never get out of River's End alive.

"I wonder if Craig and Ray are done at the cabin yet." Del sounded curious but not worried.

What cabin? Nicki wondered.

"You sure she's not there?" the other man asked.

"Her shift ended at nine, and you know Trevor keeps his crew workin' for another hour or so, spit-shinin' everything for the next day. She ain't gonna be home for another hour. They got plenty of time to take a good look around."

Oh, no. No, no, no.

Two of Del's boys were at her cabin, doing a search?

Dallas was as good as dead.

"There's a place down the mountain a ways where I think I saw a possum nest last spring. Want to take a look there?" Del asked.

"Sounds good."

Nicki kept her feet until she could no longer hear their footsteps crunching through the leaves. Then she slid down to the cave floor and took deep gulps of breath while her heart rate slowly returned to something close to normal.

Oh, God. That was so close.

She didn't let herself fall apart for long. She had to get to her cabin and find out what the hell was going on.

She hurried down the mountain to retrieve the Jeep, wishing like hell she had put the phone back on her bedside table. She just hadn't quite trusted Dallas enough to leave him alone with a line to the world outside, and that lack of trust had just come back to bite her.

She tried not to speed on her way home, well aware that in a town as small as River's End, even a traffic ticket managed to find its way into the town's grapevine sooner or later. Someone might wonder why she'd been on that particular road when it wasn't the most direct route home to her cabin. Or why she'd been so frazzled when she was pulled over.

Easing her foot off the accelerator, she took her time, concentrating on the one good thing that had come from the conversation she'd overheard. The head of the Virginia BRI was seriously considering taking her on as his personal caretaker. That meant she would find out who he was and would be uniquely positioned to find out what kind of trouble they were planning these days.

Unless Ray and Craig found something incriminating at her cabin. Like Dallas or that envelope full of messages from Quinn.

Stupid, stupid, stupid! Why had she held on to those messages?

Because they made you feel less alone.

Not a good enough reason. Not nearly good enough, especially now.

The gravel park in front of her cabin was unoccupied when she arrived. That meant nothing, however, she realized as she pulled the Jeep into its usual parking space. Ray and Craig didn't live that far away. They could have easily come here on foot to do their search of her cabin.

She should have been expecting something like this, she realized. She was a terrible excuse for a spy.

The front door was locked when she turned the knob. Which meant they had a copy of her keys. The thought made her skin crawl, and she made a mental note to change the dead bolt the next chance she got. And then make sure her keys were never out of her possession.

She unlocked the door and entered cautiously, in case they were still inside. There was a light on in the front room and also in the kitchen. Her cabin was isolated enough that she hadn't thought it necessary to warn Dallas to keep the lights turned off. Who would be passing by?

Craig Lafferty and Ray Battle, as it turned out, she thought grimly, some of her fear eclipsed by a rush of blazing anger. How untouchable did they think they were, that they could just break into her cabin at will and go through her things?

They're criminals, Nicki. What do you expect?

She clicked a button on the small black remote on her

key chain. Most people assumed it was a remote entry device for her Jeep. It wasn't. Instead, it was some contraption the security guys at The Gates had come up with to detect both trackers and listening devices. If there was a bug in her cabin, this little device would detect it.

Nothing. Whatever else Craig and Ray had done, they hadn't put a listening device in the cabin.

She pocketed her keys and made a slow exploration of the cabin, room to room, trying to hold back the acid panic eating a hole in her chest. She had to keep her head. Think clearly rather than react.

She had to give the boys credit—they had been careful not to leave a big footprint with their search, but she spotted subtle signs that someone had been inside the cabin. Her hairbrush wasn't on the same side of the bathroom sink where she normally put it. In the bedroom, the closet door was closed completely, where she left it open a crack during the winter so the heat from the bedroom could keep her clothes warm for those early morning drives to the diner.

And worst of all, there was no sign of Dallas anywhere in the house.

Had they found him here? Had they taken him captive once more, to inflict God only knew what kind of tortures on him? Or had they taken him into the woods out back and killed him?

Stop. Stop thinking the worst. Just keep looking.

She entered the kitchen and looked around. One of the chairs at the table was out of place, but there was no sign of a struggle here any more than there had been anywhere else in the house. That was a good sign, wasn't it? Dallas wasn't in top form, but he wouldn't have let those guys grab him without a fight.

So maybe they hadn't found Dallas after all. But had they found her messages from Quinn?

Holding her breath, she checked the niche between the refrigerator and the counter.

Her heart sank.

The envelope was gone.

That was that. Big break or no big break, she'd just worn out her welcome in River's End and it was time to pull up stakes and get her tail back to Tennessee while she still had time to get there alive.

She knew how to travel light, and this was clearly one of those moments where speed was more important than thoroughness. She grabbed a backpack from her closet and threw in a couple of changes of clothing and a few pairs of sturdy shoes. The strappy high-heeled sandals she'd bought in Abingdon last month would have to stay in the closet, along with the dress she'd splurged on because it went so well with the shoes.

There was a first-aid kit in the back of the Jeep, and a Leatherman tool in the glove compartment. There was a Swiss army knife in her purse. She grabbed a few snack bars from the cabinet and a six-pack of bottled water from the refrigerator.

That should be enough to get her safely to Purgatory, Tennessee, by sunup.

The sound of the back door opening made her nerves jerk, and she whirled around, ready to swing the six-pack of water like a bludgeon.

Dallas Cole stood in the doorway, looking haggard and pale. He was shivering but a slow smile spread across his face, digging dimples into his lean cheeks. "You look like you've seen a ghost."

"Are you all right?" The urge to throw herself in his arms almost overcame her good sense.

"I'm freezing to death and I just spent an hour trying to figure out how to take on two big mountain men with just my sparkling wit and winning personality. But other than that, I'm just dandy." He closed the distance between them, raising his hands to her face. His fingers were icy and she gave a little start, but when he started to pull his hands away, she put the water bottles down on the table beside her and put her own hands over his, holding them in place.

"You got out in time?"

"I did." His brow furrowed. "You already knew, didn't you?"

"That someone came in here while I was gone? Yeah." Was it her imagination or was his face suddenly a lot closer?

"Because I was missing?" His breath warmed her lips.

"That was one reason." Damn it. Her heart had just managed to get back to a halfway normal rate and he had to go all smoldery on her. She needed to get her scrambled brains back in order. She was forgetting something important—

"Lucky for me, I was back here in the kitchen when I heard them come in. Even then, I barely had time to get out."

He'd gotten out in time, but what about the messages from Quinn? That's what she'd been forgetting. "Please, please tell me you took the messages from Quinn with you. Because they're not where I left them."

He dropped his hands from her face and reached under his sweatshirt, pulling out the manila envelope. "I did. But you shouldn't have kept these, Nicki. Today should have made that very clear."

He was right. Hadn't she told herself the same thing on her drive home? "I know."

She took the manila envelope and headed down the hall toward the front room. Dallas followed, sticking close enough that she could feel his nervous energy behind her. She put the envelope on the mantel and bent to pick up the fireplace lighter.

"You're going to burn them?" he asked quietly.

"Should have done it a long time ago." She put the envelope on the logs still lying in the hearth and touched the lighter flame to the edge. It caught fire and she set the lighter on the mantel.

She turned to look at Dallas. He was watching her movements, his dark-eyed gaze intense. "Are you okay? You're still sort of shivering. Come sit in front of the fire and tell me everything that happened."

He pulled up one of the chairs and sat in front of the hearth. The logs beneath the burning envelope had caught fire, the warming blaze impossible to resist. Nicki pulled up a chair as well and sat close to him, holding her hands out in front of the flames.

Something about Dallas had changed while she was gone. It wasn't anything big or obvious, just a subtle difference in the way he held himself. The way he spoke.

The way he looked at her.

Focus, Nicki.

She cleared her throat. "The men who came in here used a key, didn't they?"

"I think so. I heard what sounded like keys in the lock. For a moment I thought it could be you, but it was too early."

"So they've made copies of my keys."

"Clearly."

She sighed. "Those sneaky bastards."

"You had to know it was a possibility. You're here as an undercover operative and you're trying to get inside their operation. They're going to give you a closer look, right? Maybe that's a good sign." The warmth of the fire seemed to be doing its job on Dallas. His earlier shivers had subsided, and his pale face had begun to take on a healthy color that she didn't think she could chalk up to the fire glow.

"It is a good sign," she agreed, remembering her own ordeal in the cave. "In fact, I think I know why they came here."

"You mean besides trying to see if you're up to something?"

"Well, that, obviously. What I mean is, there's a reason why they're doing it now."

"Something's changed, hasn't it?" He shot her a narrow-eyed look.

"Yeah. See, there's another reason I knew someone was here in my cabin. While I was picking up my message from the drop site, I heard people coming, so I hid. As it turned out, it was a good thing I did."

"Someone you knew?"

"Someone who may be key to getting me where I want to be on this assignment." She picked up the fire poker and gave the logs a nudge, igniting a shower of sparks. "His name is Del McClintock, and he's been my link to the people higher up in the BRI."

"Your link how?" The look Dallas slanted her way held an odd sort of vulnerability, as if her answer held a great deal of weight.

"Well, we're not sleeping together, if that's what you're asking."

"But you're seeing each other."

She sighed, leaning back in her chair. "It's complicated. We've been out a few times. Kissed a couple of times. I told him I was coming off a bad relationship and I didn't want to rush into anything."

"Kissed?"

Trust a man to latch on to that detail. "A couple of times. I think maybe it intrigues him—a woman who doesn't fall into his bed as soon as he looks her way."

"It can be very intriguing," Dallas agreed. "But how patient do you expect this guy to be?"

She sighed again. "Not very. But I'm not a little girl. I can handle myself with Del. And, apparently, what I'm doing is working better than I hoped."

He turned to look at her, his eyes narrowing. "Why do you say that?"

"Because when I was hiding from Del, I overheard him talking to another guy. And Del told that guy that his boss is very interested in me."

Dallas's brow creased. "What are you saying?"

"I'm saying, I think I'm finally going to get what I came here for. If I passed the test—I think that's what the search of my cabin must have been—they're going to hire me to be the man's medical caretaker." She smiled, torn between elation and sheer terror. "I'm about to find out who the head of the Virginia BRI really is."

Chapter Nine

Dallas took a step back, digesting Nicki's news with a sinking heart. Intellectually, he could acknowledge it was a significant turn of events in her investigation. He hadn't been on the front lines of the battle against the Blue Ridge Infantry and its attempt to build a complex and brutal crime syndicate in the guise of a homegrown militia, but anyone who worked at FBI headquarters knew what a coup it would be to position someone inside the group, feeding vital information to people with connections like Alexander Quinn had. He might be a civilian now, but Quinn still maintained a whole lot of ties to people inside the US justice system.

Nicki could be a real asset to the ongoing investigation.

She could also be embarking on a suicide mission.

"You might be getting into something you can't get out of," he said finally when the silence between them began to grow tense.

She sighed. "I know. But it's what I came here to do. I knew going in it wasn't going to be a trip to the beach."

"You don't know all they're capable of. I don't even know what they're capable of, and I was their unwilling guest for weeks."

She put her hand on his arm, her fingers warm. "I know. But I've come this far. I have to see it through."

He wanted to shake off her hand, wanted to put distance between them as if he could somehow forestall the anxiety already rising in his gut like a poison tide. He knew more about what people like the BRI were capable of than she did. It hadn't taken captivity in their mountain enclave to acquaint him with that level of ruthlessness.

As bad as they were, the BRI wasn't that different from any gang of backwoods thugs out there. Sure, they'd upped their game by co-opting groups like the black bloc anarchists they'd brought into their fold, but they were still small-minded punks, no better than the meth cookers they had strong-armed into submission.

All the talk of patriotism and sovereign citizenship didn't change that fact.

"What are you thinking?" Nicki's voice was as warm as her touch, seductive without trying. His resistance began to crumble under a swelling tide of desire.

He didn't dare tell her what he was really thinking. So he opted for what he'd been mulling before her touch had stoked a fire in his belly. "I was thinking the Blue Ridge Infantry isn't that different from people I grew up with back in Kentucky."

Her blue eyes narrowed slightly. "I suppose they're not. I've known a few like them myself. Back in Tennessee."

"They're mean. But they're also not nearly as smart as they think they are. I'm hoping we can use that against them."

She dropped her hand to her side. His arm felt cold where her hand had been, as if she'd taken all the warmth of the world with her. "I managed to leave the message for Quinn."

"How soon do you think your contact will show up?"

"I don't know," she admitted. Suddenly her eyes widened. "Oh. I forgot." She reached into the front pocket of her jeans and pulled out several folded sheets of paper. "Quinn had left me a message, but after I nearly ran into Del and his friend, I forgot all about it." She unfolded the papers and scanned them quickly, her brow furrowed.

"What is it?" Dallas asked.

"It's, um, just some notes." She darted a quick look at him.

"About me?"

She nodded. "Quinn isn't sure whose side you're on."

"And you're telling me that?"

Her gaze leveled with his. "I'm convinced you're on my side. If I weren't, I'd have told the boys from the BRI where to find you."

"Ruthless," he murmured, strangely unoffended.

"Would've earned me some points, don't you think?" She flashed him a quick smile that made his insides twist.

Maybe she was better prepared to deal with the BRI than he'd thought. "Anything else from Quinn?"

"He said to use my own judgment."

"He must trust you."

She gave a small shrug. "He knows my history. I take care of myself. I land on my feet."

"Your history?"

"It's a long story."

"One we have a little time for, since we're waiting on word from your boss about that computer equipment." He sat in the chair in front of the fire again and reached across to pat the empty chair beside him. "Come on. Story time. I'm too wired to sleep yet. How about you?"

Her lips quirked slightly as she gave him a side-eye

look and sat in the chair next to him. "Only if you spill a little of your story, too."

He waved his hand dismissively. "Mine is dull. We'd be asleep in no time. You tell me your story instead. Once upon a time, there was a little girl named Nicki North—"

"Jamison."

He slanted a look at her. "Jamison North?"

Her lips quirked. "Nicki Jamison. Nicolette, actually."

"Pretty."

"Thank you. I had nothing to do with choosing it."

"Who did?"

She leaned her head back against the chair. "My mother. Andrea Jamison. She was just seventeen when I was born. I never knew my father, and, to be honest, I don't really believe any of the stories she told me about him."

"Why not?"

She closed her eyes. "Because one eighteen-year-old boy from Ridge County, Tennessee, can't be an astronaut, a guitar player in a rock band and the next Bill Gates all at the same time."

"Your mother dreamed big."

"She did." Nicki turned her head and opened her eyes. "Too big, sometimes."

"What does she think about your new assignment?"

Nicki's slight smile faded. "She died when I was sixteen. Drunk driving accident. She killed herself and a family of four after a few too many at the Whiskey Road Tavern."

He winced. "I'm sorry."

"She just couldn't get it together." She sighed. "Hell, most of the time, she didn't really try."

"What happened to you after that?"

"Nothing. I got myself declared an emancipated minor. I was already working afternoons at a diner in Bitter-wood, and the owner, Maisey, let me live in a room over the diner until I graduated." Her smile was wistful, as if the memory was bittersweet. "Maisey offered to let me stay with her and her family, but I wanted out of Ridge County. So I left as soon as I could."

"Where'd you go?"

"Straight to hell in a handbasket." She laughed, but he didn't hear much amusement in her tone. "What about you? How'd you get from Kentucky to FBI headquarters?"

"By the skin of my teeth."

She nudged him with her elbow. "Are you trying to avoid my question, Mr. Cole?"

He was, a little. There was a lot in his past he'd rather not remember, including how close he'd come to destroying his life.

"You *are* avoiding it, aren't you?"

"I just don't like to dwell on the past." The directness of her gaze was making him feel restless. He pushed to his feet and walked over to the window near the door. He opened the curtains a notch, just enough to look out on the moonlit yard without showing his face. He saw no signs of movement outside, but the earlier home invasion had left him feeling wary and restless.

"What happened out there?" Nicki asked, her voice closer than he anticipated.

He turned to look at her. She stood a couple of feet away, her head cocked with curiosity. The glow of firelight brought out glints of red in her dark hair and burnished her skin to a warm gold. "Out there?" he asked.

She closed the distance between them until she was only a few inches away. Close enough that he smelled the lingering scent of lemon-basil shampoo in her hair. "You seem—different." Her voice lowered a notch. "Dangerous."

He almost smiled at that notion, a rueful, humorless sort of smile that came from knowing just how close to the mark she was. There had been a time in his life when he had been on the cusp of being very dangerous indeed. A few steps in the wrong direction and he could have ended up like his brothers, venal and ruthless, carving out a truly wicked sort of life in the harsh Kentucky hill country.

He'd lied when he said there was no family left in Kentucky. There were his brothers. But he hadn't seen them in years.

By design.

"I'm a teddy bear," he said aloud.

She laughed. "No. You're not." She placed her hand flat against his breastbone, as if feeling for his heartbeat. His pulse leaped in response to her intimate touch, and he couldn't stop himself from leaning toward her.

"You're right. I can be very dangerous if I want to." He pressed his hand over hers, pinning it in place over his heart. "I've just tried really hard for a lot of years not to want to."

"But you want to now?" Her voice deepened. Softened.

His pulse rushed in his ears. "I don't want to. But I can if I'm forced to. That's what I remembered today. Out there."

Apparently, he still had a little bit of those unforgiving hills left inside him after all. And that piece of Kentucky might be his best hope of getting out of River's End alive.

Nicki touched his face, her fingers sliding across the stubble of beard with a soft rasp. "Have I ever mentioned I have a soft spot for dangerous men?"

"No." He bent closer to her. "But I can't say I'm surprised."

She rose to her toes, her mouth soft against his. Sweet as mountain honey, darkened by the razor edge of raw desire. He wrapped his arms around her, pulling her closer, molding her body against his until he felt utterly enveloped by her soft heat. He explored the sleek contours of her body, drawing a mental map of the endless possibilities of pleasure.

With his fingers he traced the arch of her spine, sleeked along the dip of her waist and the sweeping curve of her hips. A soft hum of pleasure rumbled from her throat, and he kissed her there, along the taut tendon he found at the side of her neck, drowning in the scent of her, the silk of her.

She threaded her fingers through his hair and dragged his face away, looking up at him with passion-drunk eyes. "As much as I want this—and believe me, I do—I don't think we should."

He wanted to argue. Almost did. But the harsh crackle of the fire as a piece of burning log fell into the embers made his nerves jerk, a potent reminder that for all the trappings of security the cabin might offer, neither of them was truly safe. This night was, at best, a brief respite in the fight for their lives yet to come.

And letting desire sweep them into mindless oblivion, however tempting a proposition, was pure folly.

They couldn't afford folly.

"You take the bed tonight," he suggested, moving a safe distance from where she remained, temptation incarnate, her desire-dark eyes and kiss-stung lips promising pleasures beyond imagination.

"You're still weak."

"No," he assured her. "I'm not."

Her eyes flickered at the raspy tone of his voice. "Okay. Try to get some sleep." She turned quickly and disappeared down the hall.

He almost followed. He actually took a few steps toward the doorway before he stopped himself, turning instead toward the sofa. The pillow and blankets she'd used the night before were nowhere to be found, he realized. She must have put them up this morning when she rose.

He found the bedding in the hall closet.

One door down from the bedroom.

He stared for a moment at the closed bedroom door, pressing the pillow and blankets tightly against his chest. He heard a whisper of movement beyond the door and pictured her readying herself for bed. Stripping out of her sweater and jeans, unfastening her bra to reveal the ripe curves of her breasts. Berry tipped, he thought. As sweet and lush as her lips.

He forced his feet to move back to the front room, nearly stumbling in his haste. He made up the sofa, stripped out of his sweatshirt and lay on his back on the sofa, gazing up at the play of light and shadows on the exposed beams of the ceiling.

She needs your help, he reminded himself.

And you need hers.

DALLAS WAS AVOIDING HER. Not that he could really get very far away from her in the small cabin, but he somehow conspired to be in a different room as often as possible.

She aided his attempts at keeping his distance by taking double shifts at the diner for the next couple of days, partly to keep Trevor happy and partly in hopes of running into Del McClintock.

If the head of the Virginia BRI had really made the decision to take her on as a medical caretaker, shouldn't someone have approached her by now?

When her second shift ended without any sign of Del

or any of the BRI boys at the diner, she started to worry. Maybe they'd found something at the cabin to give them pause, though she couldn't think what it could have been. She'd taken all of Dallas's dirty clothes and discarded them in a Dumpster the next town over that first day when she'd gone into town to work the morning shift. The only other incriminating things Ray and Craig could have found were her notes from Quinn and Dallas Cole himself.

What was the holdup?

She parked behind the hardware store again after her evening shift and hiked up the mountain to the drop site, not really expecting a message this early. But the signal was in place. Agent X had left her a message.

She retrieved the bundle of notes from the niche in the cave and scanned Quinn's message with the penlight on her key chain. The message was a brief set of directions that led her to a fallen pine tree fifty yards to the north of the cave. Under a canopy of pine boughs, she found a large backpack stashed out of sight.

Inside the pack was a new laptop computer and several pieces of equipment that she couldn't readily identify.

But Dallas Cole could, she was sure. He was the one who'd requested them.

She trekked down the mountain with the pack on her back, careful once she was out in the open to make sure she wasn't being watched. She stashed the backpack in the passenger floorboard and headed for the cabin.

As she slowed for the stop at Miller's Crossroads, a loud horn blared behind her. Checking her rearview mirror, she saw Del McClintock's jacked-up Chevy Silverado idling behind her Jeep.

Damn it. If he saw the backpack and started asking questions—

The Silverado's driver's door opened and Del got out, heading for her Jeep.

She put the Jeep in Park and got out to meet him. "You scared the hell out of me, Del McClintock!" She softened her words with a smile.

He laughed. "I like to keep you on your toes, sugar!"

"Where've you been? I've been hoping to see you at the diner." She took another step closer to him, keeping him from getting too close to the Jeep. She touched the front of his jacket, fiddling with the zipper. "You don't like my cooking?"

"I love your cookin', sugar. You know that."

"You been out of town?"

"I had to go see somebody."

She flashed him a pouty look. "A girl?"

"No. It was business."

Her pulse quickened. "Anything good?"

"You might think so." He tugged at a lock of her hair. "How would you like to get away from that diner for a while? Work somewhere else?"

"Depends on where." She slid her hands teasingly up to his shoulders, swallowing her revulsion."

"I told you about my friend who's havin' trouble keepin' his diabetes under control, didn't I?"

"Right. You said he might need to go into the hospital for a while if he can't get his blood sugar regulated."

"He refuses to go to the hospital. His daddy went to the hospital a few years back with nothin' but a broken arm and died two days later. He won't go near a hospital."

"If he can't get his blood sugar under control, he'll end up there no matter what he wants," she warned, trying not to let her impatience show. Was he going to offer her the job or not?

"That's where you come in, sweetness." He stroked her

cheek with the back of his hand. She tried not to react, but a faint shudder rippled through her. She had gotten bad at this game. There'd been a time when she could play the role of dutiful girlfriend without even blinking.

A lot had changed over the past few years. Herself included.

"He needs a personal nurse, I'd guess you'd say."

"I'm not a nurse," she said, hoping it wouldn't change his mind.

"You're close enough. You know how to administer his medication, right? Monitor his condition. Cook the kinds of meals he needs to eat to keep his sugar under control. Right?"

"I can do that," she agreed, excitement and dread fighting for control over her emotions.

"He wants to meet you. If he likes you, you're hired." Del grinned at her. "He pays really good, baby. And if you do a good job, he's gonna remember I'm the one who recommended you."

"Is that important?"

"It is." He pulled her into his arms and pressed his lips against her ear. "Real important."

That almost sounded like a threat, she realized.

She pulled back to look at him. "Then I'll be sure to do a good job."

He kissed her lightly. "I knew you would, sugar." He nodded at her idling Jeep. "You in a hurry to get home?"

"I have the morning shift, and I've just worked a double shift today. I'm beat. Rain check?"

"I'll hold you to it."

"When do I interview with your friend?"

He laughed softly. "Interview?"

"It's a job, right?"

"Yeah, it's a job." His smile faded. "You doing a double shift tomorrow?"

"No, I'm off at noon."

"I'll see if I can set something up for later in the afternoon." He kissed her again, this time a longer, slower caress that made her skin crawl. "Call you tomorrow."

"I'll be expecting it." She pulled away from his embrace, flashed him a smile she hoped didn't look as sick as she felt and hurried back to the Jeep.

She hadn't stopped shaking by the time she reached the cabin, but she did her best to present a calm front when she carried the backpack of computer equipment inside where she found Dallas pacing by the fireplace.

He turned to look at her, his brow furrowed. "You're nearly an hour late."

She set the backpack on the coffee table and faced him. "I didn't know I was on a schedule," she snapped.

He shot her a disbelieving look. "You don't think I have a right to be concerned if you don't get back when I expect you to? Considering the kind of people you're rubbing elbows with?"

She wished elbows were all she'd rubbed with Del McClintock. She could still feel his hands on her back, his mouth on hers.

She felt dirty.

Dallas's expression shifted, his annoyance melting into concern as he crossed to her side. He put his hand on her cheek. "Are you okay?"

When he touched her, something inside her broke, and she flung herself into his arms, burying her hot face in the curve of his neck. He wrapped his arms tightly around her, holding her close and murmuring nonsense against her temple.

After a moment, he cradled her face between his hands and made her look at him. "Did something happen?"

In answer, she rose to her toes and pressed her mouth against his, silencing his questions.

Chapter Ten

She tastes like fear.

The thought entered his overloaded brain and dug in its heels, refusing to budge, even as his body responded wildly to the feel of her slim, curvy body pressed intimately against his.

Her tongue tangled with his and all he could taste was the acid bite of fear. Her hands tugged the hem of his sweatshirt upward and slid along the flat planes of his abdomen, and he felt only the tremble of dread in her fingers.

He caught her hands and pulled away, gazing down into her too-bright eyes. "What happened?"

Her gaze dropped to his chest. "So much."

He led her over to the crackling fire, sat her in one of the chairs and crouched in front of her. "Start at the beginning. Why are you so late getting home?"

"I checked the dead drop and found Agent X had left me directions to that." She waved her hand at the backpack she'd set on the coffee table.

"Agent X?" he asked as he crossed to the backpack.

She shot him a sheepish smile. "That's what I call him. I don't know his real name. I don't even know what he looks like."

He unzipped the main compartment. Inside, he found

a laptop computer and accessories that matched the inventory of items he'd requested to the letter. "Quinn got his hands on this stuff very fast."

"That's Quinn," she said faintly.

He left the computer equipment where it sat, ignoring the itch to set it up and get started. Computer equipment hadn't sent unflappable Nicki Jamison into an anxiety attack. He crouched in front of her once more, ignoring the aches in his knees and back. "Why do I get the feeling that's not all that happened?"

"Because it's not," she admitted. "After I got the equipment, Del McClintock flagged me down at Miller's Crossroads."

The unease wriggling in Dallas's gut intensified. "Did he see the backpack?"

She shook her head. "I got out to meet him so he wouldn't see it."

"Then what happened?"

"I may have an interview tomorrow."

"An interview?"

"For a new job. Medical caretaker for a man with uncontrolled diabetes." She managed a bleak smile. "It's what I've been waiting to hear."

He laid his hands on her knees. "Then why do you look terrified?"

"Because I am?" She pushed his hands away and got up, walking to the window, then back to the mantel. "I don't know why Quinn thought I was the person to do this. Or, hell, maybe I do. Once an accomplished liar, always an accomplished liar, right?"

He caught her hand, stopping her nervous pacing. "If you don't want to do this, tell Quinn to find someone else."

"And throw away three months of setup right when

it's about to pay off?" She shook her head firmly. "I've got a case of the nerves. That's all. It just came by surprise tonight and I wasn't prepared."

Just like that, her chin came up and her trembling subsided. A fierce light shone in her eyes, and he felt something turn flips in the center of his chest.

Damn, she was beautiful.

She nodded toward the backpack. "How quickly can you get that stuff set up?"

"Give me half an hour," he said, realizing he'd just been given marching orders. Tamping down the urge to argue her out of her plan of action, he gathered the items Quinn had provided for him to set up his own server and wireless connection, and got to work.

Within thirty minutes, the sea of gadgets and wires inside the pockets of the backpack combined with the high-powered smartphone Quinn supplied had transformed into a working internet system under his hands. He showed Nicki the search engine browser page with a smile of triumph. "We're in business."

"Yay?"

"Technophobe," he muttered with a laugh. "I don't know how you lived here three days without the internet, much less three months."

"You do know that Quinn has probably set up something that'll monitor whatever you do on that server, don't you?"

He looked up, surprised by her serious tone. "Is that how he does business?"

"Former CIA," she said, as if that explained everything.

Probably did, he conceded. "I'll check everything out." There were a few ways Quinn could have set up tracking software and a few other tricks that the average computer user would never find.

But Dallas wasn't the average computer user.

"I might be up a few more hours." He looked at her, noting the faint shadows of weariness beneath her eyes. "Go to bed. Get some sleep. Don't you have a morning shift?"

"I do," she agreed with a slight smile. "You sure you don't want to save this until morning?"

"Positive. Take the bed again. I'll bunk down here once I'm done."

She didn't move right away, her blue eyes holding his gaze for a long, heated moment. "Thank you."

"For what?"

"For making me feel less alone." She flashed him a twitch of a smile, then turned and left the room quickly.

He released a long, slow breath, quelling the powerful urge to put the computer aside and follow her back to the bedroom.

Focus, Cole.

He examined some of the more obvious places Quinn and his computer people might have hidden a keystroke logger in the system and found nothing. Digging deeper, however, he discovered a program he was pretty sure had been designed to track anything he did on the computer.

Removing it would be easy enough, but he'd never been one to do the easy thing.

Instead, he recoded the program slightly, ensuring that anything sent to Quinn would be gibberish.

Ought to make his point, he thought.

After another hour examining the ins and outs of the system, he'd found one more tracking program, quickly dispatched, then settled down to work.

Before leaving for work that afternoon, Nicki had given him a list of names she'd gleaned during her time in River's End. Del McClintock was the first on the list, and he began there.

A simple internet search came up with nothing of interest, but internet searches were child's play. Everybody had a footprint. The key was figuring out where to look. And one of the most useful things he'd learned in the cybersecurity classes he'd taken over the past couple of years with the FBI was exactly where to look.

GUILT TASTED LIKE ASHES, smoky and bitter. The flavor burned her nose and brought stinging tears to her eyes that spilled down her cheeks in hot streaks.

She'd done her job. The Tennessee Bureau of Investigation had acted on the tip she'd given them, the tip she'd gotten from Jeff Burwell.

Now she had to figure out how to say goodbye to Jeff and the kids without telling them the truth—she'd never been just their housekeeper.

She'd been a spy, taking advantage of the family's vulnerability to find out what the Blue Ridge Infantry was up to in the little town of Thurlow Gap, Tennessee.

"They're not going to know who gave us the information," her handler, Martin Friedman, had assured her earlier that day when they'd met at a truck stop out of town. "You can stick around the farm another two or three weeks, just so nobody gets suspicious, then turn in your notice."

"Then what?" she'd asked, feeling strangely empty.

"Then we'll find a new assignment for you. You've been a big asset. The higher-ups won't forget it."

She should have felt pleased with herself. The TBI certainly seemed to be pleased with her.

But all she'd felt was sick.

The farmhouse was quiet. Jeff was in town visiting

his mother, who'd been feeling poorly for the past few days. The kids were asleep upstairs in their bedrooms. Nicki had been trying to read for an hour, but her mind kept wandering back to the choices she'd made in the past few months.

She could almost smell the ashes of regret.

She sat up straighter, opening her eyes.

That wasn't regret.

That was fire.

The darkness outside had taken on an eerie glow. She hurried to the closest window and pushed aside the curtain, her heart skipping a beat as she saw flames edging close to the house, the edges blurred by a miasma of thick smoke.

The winter had been dry. Too dry.

As she started toward the stairs, the front door opened and Jeff Burwell rushed inside, his dark eyes wild and his face and clothes smudged with soot.

"The house is on fire!" he shouted, pushing past her up the stairs.

Her knees buckled beneath her, and she grabbed for the back of the rocker, her heart pounding with dread.

"Nicki!" Jeff called from the top of the stairs.

But flames rose up, surrounding her.

Scorching her.

It took a moment to realize the fire came from inside her own body.

"Nicki?"

Nicki woke with a cry, bolting upright in the bed, her galloping pulse thundering in her head.

The bed shifted beside her, and strong arms wrapped around her body, pulling her close. "It's okay," Dallas's voice rumbled in her ear. "It's just a dream."

She pressed her forehead in the curve of his neck,

gulping deep breaths until her heart rate settled down to a canter. "It wasn't a dream."

"Yes, it was. Everything's okay." He threaded his fingers through her hair, drawing her head back until she was gazing up at him in the dim half-light of the bedroom. Light filtered in from the front of the house, obscuring half of his face in shadow, but the determined look in his dark eyes was unmistakable.

Her knight in shining armor, she thought, swallowing a smile.

Who said they didn't exist?

"I'm okay," she assured him, but he didn't let her go, his thumbs drawing soothing circles on either side of her chin.

"You were moaning. I heard you all the way down the hall."

"Like you said, just a dream." His touch felt like a brand, burning all the way to her soul, the intensity of sensation reminding her strangely of her dream and the feeling that the fire that effectively destroyed Jeff Burwell's life had started somewhere inside her.

She pulled away, rising from the bed and crossing to the window. For a moment, the world outside seemed to be on fire, as if an afterimage of her dream lingered. But the mirage of hazy flames subsided, leaving behind only the moonlit winter woods.

"You said it wasn't a dream. What did you mean?"

She sighed. "Nothing. I guess I wasn't quite awake yet."

"Come on, Nicki. It wasn't nothing."

"I was just dreaming about the fire." She turned to look at him. "The one in Tennessee."

"When you were working for the TBI?"

She nodded. "I'd just met with my handler and he'd told me the job was done. They'd thwarted the plot against the conservation officers and I could leave the Burwell farm soon."

"You'd saved lives."

"I'd betrayed people who trusted me." She turned back to the window, remembering her encounter with Del McClintock. "It seems to be what I'm good at."

"Are you regretting your choice to come here?"

She shook her head. "No. Del McClintock isn't Jeff Burwell. He's a very bad guy with very bad intentions. All of those men I'm dealing with these days deserve everything they get."

"But there's something still troubling you."

She pressed her forehead against the cold windowpane. "They have families. Wives and women. Kids. Most of those women depend entirely on their men for their sustenance. Some of them can barely read and write. Not many of them have job skills that would give them a chance to get the hell out of this place and make a better life for themselves and their kids."

"So you're supposed to just let their men get away with murder?"

"Of course not." Her breath had made a foggy patch of condensation on the window. She lifted her fingers and wiped it away. "There just aren't any winners here."

She felt him walk up behind her, his body a comforting wall of heat against her back. He wrapped his arms around her and rested his cheek against her temple. "No, I guess there aren't."

She leaned back against him, taking comfort in his closeness. The sense of vulnerability should have scared her, but it didn't. It felt...right.

Now *that* scared her. But not enough to compel her to move away.

"How's Operation Computer Geek going out there?"

"All set up."

She glanced at her watch. It was only a little after midnight. She'd figure he'd be up for hours getting the system going. "That's fast."

"Not really. Want to see it at work?"

Part of her did. But the other part wanted to stay right where she was, safely wrapped in his warm embrace. She went with that part. "Maybe in the morning."

"Just so you know, I've set it up so that it's easily hidden in a matter of seconds. I can show you tomorrow, in case you ever have to stash it away quickly."

That was good thinking, she realized, considering their recent home invasion. "Are you sure it's something a techno-troglodyte like me can handle?"

He laughed in her ear. "Yes."

They fell silent as they gazed out the window at the woods, their breathing settling into harmony until she had the strangest feeling that she couldn't tell where her body ended and his began.

When a sharp pounding noise from the front of the house shattered the silent communion, it rattled her all the way to her bones.

Her heart instantly racing again, she jerked free of his grasp and turned to look at him. "That's someone at the door. You need to hide. Now."

"I've got to get the computer equipment."

Damn it. "Fine. Then you hide."

The banging noise continued as she led him into the front room. "Make it quick," she whispered, but he was already disengaging cords and packing equipment into the backpack from which it had come.

"Hide where?" he whispered as he zipped the bag.

"The cellar."

He shot her an odd look, drawing heat to her cheeks

as she remembered his last visit to her cellar. But he slung the backpack over his shoulder and disappeared down the hall.

The pounding on the door grew louder. "Nicki!" The voice on the other side belonged to Keith Pickett. He sounded drunk and scared.

"Coming!" she called, listening for the sound of the cellar door shutting. When she heard the soft click, she hurried to the door and turned the key in the lock.

Keith stood outside, looking pale and sick. His eyes were bloodshot and there was blood on his jeans.

A lot of blood.

"I think I've killed her," he said, his voice slurred and pitiful.

Nicki's heart skipped a beat. "Kaylie?"

"She's bleedin' all over the place. I didn't even hit her that hard."

"Where is she?" Her sluggish brain tried to catch up, tried to gather up all the scattered pieces of her thoughts into something coherent. She needed supplies, to start with. The first-aid kit in her bathroom would have to do.

"She's out in the truck!"

She stared at him in horror. "You drove her here?"

"She's dyin' and she kept sayin' you'd know what to do."

It was a miracle they'd made it up the mountain road alive, as drunk as Keith was. "Stay right here—let me get my kit."

She hurried back to the bathroom, taking a quick look around as she went to make sure she and Dallas hadn't left anything incriminating in the den. Her heart skipped a beat when she realized the extra pillow and blankets were out on the sofa, but she shoved the worry aside. He was drunk and probably wouldn't remember much of this night at all by morning.

She grabbed her kit and followed Keith's weaving path out to his battered Chevy Tahoe. The passenger door was open and Kaylie was bent forward, vomiting on the gravel.

Keith hadn't been lying. There was a lot of blood, staining the lap of her cotton housedress and spilling down her legs onto the truck's running board.

Her face was bruised, her lip bloodied. The son of a bitch had been hitting her.

"Did you hit her in the stomach?" she growled at Keith.

"No, I swear I didn't."

"He didn't," Kaylie growled between heaves. Nothing was coming out now but she couldn't seem to stop retching.

There was no choice. She pulled out her phone and dialed 911.

Keith grabbed her arm, trying to pull the phone away. "What the hell are you doin'?"

She jerked her arm free. "Saving her life. And keeping your ass off death row." She heard the dispatcher answer and quickly gave her address. "I have an injured, pregnant woman in trouble," she said, her gaze drawn to the puddle of blood pooling on the gravel beneath Kaylie's feet. Her heart sank to the pit of her stomach as she opened her kit and pulled out a pair of surgical gloves. "Get an ambulance here, stat!"

Chapter Eleven

The sirens had come and gone, and above Dallas's hiding place in the cellar, the house had grown silent. Without a watch or any way to gauge the passage of time, he was beginning to grow restless and panicked.

The frantic sound of a man's voice had carried all the way down to the cellar, but whoever had been banging on the front door had retreated moments later, and all had been silent for a long while.

Then came the sirens. They'd died away for a few minutes, then fired up again and began to fade into the distance.

And still, he waited.

He was certain more than an hour had passed before he finally heard the sound of footsteps on the floorboards overhead. Slow, deliberate steps moving closer until he heard the cellar door rattle open.

"You can come up." Nicki's voice sounded hoarse and tired.

He climbed the steps, meeting her at the top. She leaned against the wall across from him, purple shadows bruising the skin under her eyes. There was blood streaked on her jeans and the hem of her sweater, and her arms from the wrists up were similarly stained.

He looked her over, trying to find the source of the

blood, but she didn't seem to be injured. "Are you okay?" he asked, his heart thumping painfully against his sternum.

She looked down at her red-stained arms. "I need a shower."

"Whose blood is that?"

"A woman I know. She was pregnant."

"Was?"

"I don't know if she still is. I don't see how she could be." She walked down the hall to the bathroom and entered, leaving the door open.

He followed, standing in the doorway as she turned on the tap and washed her arms in the sink. "Miscarriage?"

"Of a sort."

"What does that mean?"

She soaped her skin up to her elbows liberally, the suds turning pink as they dripped into the sink. "Her man hits her. He didn't admit it, but I think he hit her in the abdomen tonight."

"Bastard."

She nodded solemnly. "That's the sheriff's problem now."

"I heard sirens."

"That was the ambulance. The deputies came in lights on but siren off." She rinsed off the soap and examined her arms closely, frowning. She grabbed the soap and lathered up again.

"The last thing you needed, huh? The cops nosing around?"

She rinsed off the soap again. "I'm hoping they won't hold it against me. It's not like I asked to be involved in this mess."

"Why'd they come to you?"

"I told you, I took pains to build myself a reputation as the go-to person when someone in the BRI had a medical issue."

He frowned at her bleak tone. "Were you able to do something for her?"

"I kept her from going into shock. I kept her calm. But a uterine hemorrhage is beyond my ability to stop outside of a hospital." She examined her arms again and apparently found them satisfactory. She wiped them dry on a hand towel hanging nearby and turned to look at him. "This isn't about me or this case. That son of a bitch knew she was pregnant. He got her that way, and then he took it from her." Her lips were trembling, and her jaw was tight with rage.

"I take it this isn't your first time dealing with them?"

"I've been trying to help some of the women." She pushed past him into the hall, then through to her bedroom. "Sometimes I think it's a lost cause. Nobody respects them as valuable human beings. Not even themselves." She opened one of her dresser drawers and pulled out a change of clothes. "Some of them barely know how to read or write. Some are hooked on meth or heroin. They have babies who are born with drug habits."

"Poverty is brutal."

"It's not just poverty. It's these people. These sick, violent, power-hungry bastards called the Blue Ridge Infantry." She slammed the dresser drawer shut, making the mirror rattle against the wall. "I've known people in militias before. Some of them honestly wanted to be prepared to defend themselves in the case of some sort of foreign invasion. Some were just idiots with guns looking for a reason to play soldier. But the BRI is different. They're criminals who try to excuse their crimes under the guise of patriotism. They make me sick."

"Tell me what I can do," he said quietly.

She stopped in the middle of picking up her clothes and looked at him, as if startled by his tone. "There's nothing you can do."

"I'm not talking about the BRI. I'm talking about you. What can I do for you?"

Her lips trembled, and she shook her head. "I'm okay."

He didn't believe her. When she reached for the clothes again, he caught her hand and tugged her to him, wrapping his arms around her.

She resisted a moment. "You'll get blood on your clothes."

He didn't let her go. "It'll wash out."

She relaxed against him, resting her temple against his chin. Her breath was warm on his collarbone. "I don't know if this will affect their plans for me. I hope it won't, but I may have to work at this a little longer, regain some of their trust."

"Because you tried to help one of their women?"

"Because I called paramedics for help. They really don't want to get any sort of authorities involved. And the paramedics called the sheriff's department."

"Which means the big bad bully has to answer to the law?"

"Also not a good thing."

"Did you lie to the deputies?"

Her voice came out low and tight. "No. I told them everything I knew about the things that bastard has done to Kaylie since I've been in River's End. Maybe I shouldn't have played it that way, but—"

"Good for you. Being undercover shouldn't have to mean selling your soul." He cradled her face between his hands. "Go take a shower. I'll make sure everything's secure for the night."

He took his time, making sure the cabin was locked up

tight while she showered off the rest of the blood. As he was looking around, he scouted a new place to keep his computer equipment, since tonight's surprise visit had made it clear that the front room was far too exposed to be a good choice.

Besides the front room, the small cabin had four other rooms—the bathroom, the kitchen, Nicki's bedroom and a tiny room that she seemed to use as a storage area. He was still looking around the small room, gauging its utility as a computer room, when Nicki came out of the shower and found him there.

She'd changed into a pair of slim-fitting yoga pants and a long-sleeved T-shirt, her feet encased in a thick pair of socks and her wet hair turbaned in a towel. "What are you looking for?"

He told her. "I think we could stack a few boxes in the corner there and make room for some sort of desk here near the window. It should allow for decent cell phone reception, which I'll need for the internet."

"Del said he'd try to set up an interview for me later in the afternoon. He'll call to let me know. But I think that'll give me time to pick up a desk at the thrift store in Abingdon before the interview." She looked him over with a bemused half smile. "I could pick up some clothing for you, too."

He looked down at his mismatched, borrowed clothes. "That would be welcome," he admitted. "But are you sure you'll have time?"

"I'll make time," she said firmly. "I'll need you to feed me information once I get deeper into the operation, so it's in my best interest to get your computer set up and working."

"Are they going to expect you to give up your cabin?"

"I'm sure I'll be moving in with the patient to give him twenty-four-hour care."

"So people will expect the place to be empty." He frowned.

"It's so far off the beaten track, I'm not sure there'd be anyone around to notice if it's occupied," she said. "Not that it matters. I rent the place, anyway, so if I leave, they'll just figure someone else rented it."

"What about your landlord? Won't he or she ask questions?"

She smiled. "My landlord is Alexander Quinn, actually. Though this place can't be traced back to him easily. So you can remain here to do your computer magic while I'm gone."

His gut twisted a little. Gone seemed such a final word. "Are you sure this is a good idea?"

Her brow furrowed. "Your staying here?"

"No. Your going there."

"Oh." Her smile faded. "I don't know if I'd call it a good idea, no. But it's necessary. And I'm in the best position to do it."

"Assuming what happened tonight doesn't change their plans."

She nodded. "Assuming that."

"You look tired. You should get some sleep. I'll go fetch the computer stuff I left in the cellar. I think there might be an old table down there I can use until you have a chance to pick up a desk at the thrift store." He started past her, then stopped, touching her cheek with his fingertips. "I hope your friend is okay. When will you find out?"

"I don't know. Probably when I get to work in the morning. Small town. News travels fast." She touched his hand where it lay against her cheek, giving it a light squeeze. "Thank you. I'm not sure what I'd have done if you hadn't been here tonight."

"You'd have done exactly what you did," he said with certainty. There was a reason a man like Alexander Quinn chose Nicki Jamison to take on the job of getting inside the Blue Ridge Infantry when none of his male operatives had been able to pull it off.

And it wasn't just her pretty face or killer curves.

Impulsively, he kissed her forehead, his lips smoothing over the furrows he felt forming there. "Good night." He left the room while he still could and headed down to the cellar to gather his computer equipment.

By the time he'd carried everything up to the spare room, including the battered wood worktable he planned to use as a desk, Nicki had disappeared into her bedroom and closed the door. Taking care not to make a lot of noise that might wake her, Dallas set up the equipment again and got to work making a to-do list of things he wanted to accomplish with his newly regained access to the internet.

He had started a cursory search for information about Del McClintock before Nicki's nightmare had interrupted him. He hadn't gotten very far, though he'd found a promising entry in a list of Virginia National Guard members involved in a counterdrug program. A Delbert McClintock had been part of the program in southwestern Virginia.

He made a note to look deeper the next day. But he had another priority at the moment.

His own access to the FBI's network would have been cut off by now, but he knew where the back doors were in the system. If he played his cards right, took care not to leave a footprint, there was a chance he could sneak all the way to the top of the food chain.

Well, almost the top. Assistant Director Philip Crandall hadn't made it to the top spot yet.

But taking down an assistant director would take more than the word of a disgraced FBI support staffer.

Dallas needed proof. Hard evidence that Crandall had an agenda that had nothing to do with bringing the Blue Ridge Infantry to justice.

And time was running out.

DEL MCCLINTOCK HADN'T called Nicki by the time she finished her morning shift at the diner. In fact, none of the BRI boys showed up at the diner at all, a fact that made Nicki more nervous than she liked to admit.

But news of Kaylie Pickett's misfortune was already making the rounds on the River's End grapevine. Descriptions of her condition varied from critical to stable, but everyone agreed that Keith Pickett had caused her injury and Nicki had saved her life.

"You're a hero," Bella told her in a hushed tone, her eyes wide with admiration that made Nicki feel a little uncomfortable. "I heard she was bleeding to death and you stopped it."

"I just called an ambulance and kept her warm and as calm as I could," Nicki said, trying to cut off any further discussion. The last thing she wanted to be was the center of attention. It was a sure way to put a target on her back. "It's too bad about the baby."

"Oh. You didn't hear?" Bella lowered her voice. "She didn't lose the baby."

Nicki stared at her. "That's not possible."

"I heard the doctor said the same thing. But that little fella was still hanging in there last I heard."

Bella must have heard wrong, Nicki thought. She'd

seen the amount of blood, the condition Kaylie had been in by the time the ambulance arrived. The grapevine must have this part wrong.

But, as it turned out, Nicki was wrong. The diner phone rang shortly before eleven, as she was helping Bella and Trevor clean up after most of the breakfast crowd had cleared out but before the lunch crowd started to wander in. Trevor went to answer it and came back with a frown on his face. He looked pointedly at Nicki. "Del McClintock. Wants to talk to you."

She went very still, her pulse suddenly pounding in her ears. Forcing her feet into motion, she walked back to the break room and picked up the phone. "Hi, Del."

"I hear tell you're a hero."

She glanced at Trevor, who had followed her down the hall and stood in the doorway, watching her with a troubled expression. Turning her back, she lowered her voice. "I think that's a bit of an exaggeration."

"You saved Kaylie Pickett and her baby. That's pretty big, I'd say."

"So the baby really did make it."

"He did."

"It's a boy?"

"That's what Kaylie said the doctor told her. Says she's going to name him Nick. After you."

To her surprise and mortification, hot tears welled in her eyes. She pushed them away with her knuckles. "Tough little fellow. I never would've thought he'd make it."

"Kaylie's gotta be real careful for the next couple of months. But the doctor thinks she's got a real good chance of that baby comin' out just fine."

"Amazing."

"That's what I said when I told my friend about what you'd done." Del sounded satisfied. "He was very impressed. In fact, I think the word he used for you was 'gutsy.'"

"I'm surprised you and your buddies aren't slamming me for telling the law what Keith did to Kaylie."

Del's tone was dismissive. "Keith's an idiot. And a brute. Not everybody thinks women are punchin' bags, you know."

"Enough do."

"We're workin' on that," Del said.

Nicki knew better than to believe him. She'd heard the way he talked to—and about—women when he didn't know she was listening. He was putting on an act for her because he needed her as much as she needed him.

She was as much his "in" with the top guy as he was hers, she suspected.

"He wants to meet you, but he can't do it today. How about tomorrow?"

She suppressed a sigh of frustration. Waiting another day wouldn't kill her, but patience wasn't one of her virtues. "Okay. Tomorrow's great. Any particular time?"

"What's your work schedule?"

"I'm off Fridays."

"Great. I'll pick you up around eleven and we'll go meet your new employer."

"Don't jump the gun," she said, trying not to sound as nervous as she felt. "He may hate me."

"Impossible, sugar."

"Listen, why don't we just meet at the diner so you don't have to come all the way out to my place?" The last thing she could afford was Del finding out she had Dallas Cole stashed at her cabin.

"If you want." Del lowered his voice, as if he didn't

want to be heard on his end of the line. "I have tonight free. Want to drive into Abingdon with me for dinner?"

She frowned. Del had never asked her out on a formal date before. "I've let my cabin get in terrible shape this week, so I really need to stay home and clean. Maybe tomorrow after we talk to your friend? Maybe we can make it a celebration."

"It will be."

"It's a date," she said with as much warmth as she could muster. She hung up and turned around to see Trevor still watching her.

"What?" she asked Trevor.

"Del McClintock isn't a nice guy."

"Maybe I'm not lookin' for a nice guy."

"Nicki—"

"I know what I'm doing, Trevor." She met his gaze without flinching. "I know exactly what I'm doing." She untied her apron and tossed it in the laundry bin near the break room door. "I'll come in early Saturday, but I'm leavin' for today." She walked out past him, her head held high.

Outside, the day was mild, with plenty of warm sunshine to drive away the slight morning chill. Spring would be here soon. She had a feeling it would be a pretty season in this part of the Blue Ridge Mountains. It always had been one of her favorite times of year back home in the Tennessee Smokies.

She slid behind the wheel of the Jeep and pulled out her cell phone. Calling information, she got the number of the hospital in Abingdon and called to see if Kaylie was still a patient there. To Nicki's surprise, she'd already been released.

She'd drop by later to check on her, she decided. But first, she needed to make a run to the thrift store in Abingdon.

An hour later, she had a bag full of used clothes for Dallas, but she'd had no luck finding a desk. The work-table would have to do a little while longer, she supposed.

Before she'd left that morning, she and Dallas had worked out a knock signal. Three sharp raps meant everything was okay. If she entered without knocking, he was to bug out as fast as he could.

She parked in front of the cabin and climbed the stairs, giving three sharp raps on the door before she entered. She half expected to hear the clatter of the laptop keyboard coming from down the hall, so the silent stillness that greeted her caught her off guard.

The storage room was empty, though Dallas's computer setup was still there, out in the open. She continued to the kitchen, where she found him sitting at the table, reading what looked like a letter.

He looked up when she entered, waving for her to sit at the table with him.

She put the bag of clothes in the empty chair next to him. "Got you a few clothes, but I didn't find a desk yet."

"Thanks." He flashed her a strained smile that quickly faded. "How was your shift?"

"The usual," she said. "Del called before I left."

"Is the meeting with your potential patient still on?"

"Tomorrow afternoon." She nodded at the letter. "What's that?"

"A message from your boss. I found it on the hard drive when I got in there and started looking around. He was kind enough to include a small printer in the setup, so I printed it out." He handed it to her.

She scanned the note quickly, recognizing Quinn's terse tone. She reached the end and read it again, her gut tightening. "This is crazy."

Dallas nodded, looking grim. "I know."

"This Michelle Matsumara—she was your boss at the FBI, right?"

"Right." His voice came out low and strangled.

"And now they think you killed her?"

He looked up, tears in his eyes. "Maybe I did."

Chapter Twelve

"You didn't kill her."

Dallas looked up at Nicki as she rose from her chair, flattened her palms against the table and leaned over him, her expression fierce. Not for the first time, she reminded him of some sort of fabled warrior princess, her eyes flashing blue fire and her jaw squared with determination.

He was lucky she was an ally, not an enemy.

"I didn't mean it literally." He slumped back against the chair and regarded her, acutely aware that by coming here, he may have put her in Philip Crandall's crosshairs, as well. "But she was killed because of me. Because of the choices I made."

"You don't know that."

"Don't I?"

"Have you even looked for the story online? Or did you read that note from Quinn and immediately start beating yourself up?"

He glared at her. "I looked it up."

"What happened to her?"

"The police have been tight-lipped, but the speculation is that she surprised an intruder."

"Maybe that's really what happened."

"There's a reason the police are looking for me for questioning. Don't you think?" He pushed up from his chair and paced to the window, gazing out past the curtains at the small backyard. Sunlight dappled the ground, filtering through evergreens that towered over the small cabin. The day looked mild, the first mild day in a week.

He suddenly felt trapped, a prisoner to his own choices.

"I should turn myself in," he said aloud.

Behind him, Nicki remained silent. But he felt her tension.

"I'm putting you in danger by being here," he added, turning to look at her. "I'm certainly not making your assignment any easier."

"If you turn yourself in, you'll be a sitting duck," she warned. "A man like Philip Crandall can make things happen, even in the jailhouse."

"At least he wouldn't be trying to get to me through other people."

"So you let him win? You fall on your own sword and make it easier for him to keep doing whatever it is he's doing?" She shook her head. "That's cowardice. And I don't think you're a coward."

Anger welled inside him. Anger and a gnawing, grating pain that seemed to be shredding his insides, inch by inch. "I don't understand why he went after Michelle. Why her? She was so decent. Funny and good-natured and so very, very decent." Tears burned his eyes, but he fought them. Fought the weakness they represented.

He could mourn later. Right now, Michelle needed his vengeance, not his grief.

Nicki pulled the chair up next to him and took his hands in hers. "Tell me about her."

He shook his head. "I don't need to talk it out."

"Tell me about her, anyway. I want her to be real to me."

He looked up and found her eyes blazing at him again. "Why?"

Her grip on his hands tightened. "Because I want her in my head when I help take those sons of bitches down."

He lifted her hands to his lips and kissed her knuckles. "You'd have liked her."

"So tell me about her," she said again. "Was she married?"

"Divorced. Married young, right out of college. She never talked badly of him, but I got the feeling he wasn't exactly the faithful sort."

"Any children?"

"No. She had two cats she treated like they were her children." He frowned. "I wonder what'll happen to them."

"I'm sure someone will take them. Did she have family around?"

"No. They lived in San Francisco. All the way across the country." It was stupid, he thought, that of all the things he should be worrying about, all he could think about was those two silly cats of hers. "You don't think they'll take those cats to a shelter, do you?"

"I don't know. I could get a message to Quinn, see what he could do. He probably knows people who could make sure they get a good home."

He squeezed her hands. "You think I'm being foolish."

"No, I don't. I think you're grieving a friend. And however you need to do that is okay."

"I wish—" He broke off, not sure what he wished. That Michelle was still alive? Of course he wished that. He wished he'd never gotten that second call from Cade Landry. He'd be at his office in DC right now, putting together a brochure or creating new graphics for the next recruiting pamphlet.

He wouldn't be sitting in a cabin in the Blue Ridge Mountains, holding hands with an undercover operative and missing the hell out of a woman who hadn't deserved to die so young.

"Did she have any reason to suspect Philip Crandall was behind your disappearance?" Nicki asked a few minutes later.

"I don't know. She was smart. But she didn't know I went to Crandall about Cade Landry. I didn't suspect anything about Crandall myself until I spoke to him directly."

"Did he say something to make you suspicious?"

"Just that he wanted me to keep silent about it. Not tell anyone else that Cade Landry had called me."

Her eyes narrowed. "That doesn't sound unreasonable."

"It wasn't, I suppose."

"But it made you suspicious, anyway."

"You ever had that little voice in the back of your head that says 'something's not right here'?"

She nodded.

"That's what I heard. Something wasn't right." He brushed his thumb over the back of her hand, knowing he should let go. Put more distance between them rather than cling to her as if she was his only lifeline.

But he couldn't seem to do it. It felt as if there was a part of him that would shatter if he let go. And as much as that notion should scare him, it didn't. It made him feel steadier somehow. Needing another person—needing her—wasn't a sign of weakness.

It was a show of strength.

"You're sure it was Crandall who sicced those guys on you? The ones who ran you off the road?"

"I didn't tell anyone else my suspicions about Crandall. Nobody but Cade Landry and Olivia Sharp. You know Olivia, right? I mean, since she also works for The Gates."

"I know her."

"Anyway, by that time, I was already being followed."

"Could someone have intercepted the call from Landry?"

"Maybe. But I'm not exactly someone they'd have thought to put under surveillance, especially after the last time."

"The last time?"

He looked down at their entwined hands. "You know Cade Landry disappeared almost a year ago, don't you? Long before he resurfaced again earlier this year."

"Right. The FBI suspected him of being involved in a plot to kill one of their undercover operatives."

"He knew he was a suspect, and he had some information to share with Assistant Director Crandall, but he didn't want to go through normal channels. So he called me."

"Why you? You're not an agent."

"I think that's probably why," he answered with a smile. "I'm nobody. Who'd suspect that I'd get a call from a rogue agent?"

"How did Landry even know you?"

"He went through a cybersecurity course the same time I did a little over a year ago. He was being moved to an RA—Resident Agency—down in Tennessee and they wanted him to be their point man on cybersecurity. I guess he remembered me when he needed help."

"You didn't suspect Crandall the first time you went to him?"

"I didn't go to him," Dallas answered quietly, letting go of her hands and sitting back.

"But you said Landry asked you to bypass channels."

"I didn't listen to him. I thought he was being paranoid. The rules were there for a reason. The chain of command isn't just some arbitrary set of standards."

"And that's when things went wrong for Landry."

"From what I've heard, he disappeared overnight. All his stuff was gone from his apartment and a lot of people thought he'd just run off."

"But he hadn't."

"No. I never thought he had. I knew from the scuttlebutt at the Bureau that the brass thought Landry had been corrupted by the Blue Ridge Infantry and their criminal cohort. Do you remember hearing about those two bombers who blew up a warehouse in Virginia a few years ago?"

She nodded. "I was doing some work for the Nashville police then. Everybody was on edge, wondering if we were about to see a bunch of those small-scale terror attacks from the likes of the Blue Ridge Infantry or maybe some low-level copycats. Everyone was on high alert."

"Landry was on the FBI SWAT team that went after those guys. He and his team went in early, against orders, although he swears he got an order to go in. Two of the men on his team were killed. It basically ruined his career."

"The FBI thought he botched the raid on purpose?"

"They weren't sure. They couldn't prove anything obviously, or they'd have charged him."

"So when he suddenly went missing in the middle of an investigation of the Blue Ridge Infantry—"

"A lot people figured he'd gone over to the dark side for good," he finished for her.

"What about you? What did you think?"

"I thought he was dead." He stood up. "But clearly he

wasn't. And when I heard from him again, I decided to do things his way."

"Which still didn't work the way he hoped?" She stood, as well.

"You tell me. I thought he was dead until you told me he's not." He nodded toward the hallway. "Sitting here wallowing in regret isn't going to stop Crandall. I need to figure out more about what's going on with the BRI. Especially if you're about to come face-to-face with their top man."

She followed him to the spare room and stood in the door, watching while he pulled up a chair to the worktable holding his computer. "Do you really think you can get that kind of information on the internet? I'm pretty sure there are loads of people, civilians and lawmen alike, trying to get that kind of information. And nobody's had any luck so far."

"That's because they're looking in the wrong places," he said.

"And you think you know the right places to look?" She sounded skeptical.

He shot her a cocky look, taking masculine satisfaction in the rush of color that stained her cheeks in response. "I guess we're about to find out."

"Sir, you asked me to inform you of anything that might be an attempted intrusion."

Assistant Director Philip Crandall looked up from his paperwork and found Hopkins from the cybersecurity section. He waved the woman in. "You've found something?"

"I believe so," she answered, a frown etching thin lines in her pale forehead. Jessica Hopkins was a tall, slim woman in her late twenties who looked a decade younger, thanks to good skin and her apparent disdain for makeup. She dressed professionally enough, but her trim suit made her look like a teenager playing dress-up in her mother's clothes. And being a tall girl, she wore a utilitarian pair of flats that seemed to symbolize her obvious discomfort with her own gangly body.

But the bright green eyes staring back at him through a pair of wire-rimmed glasses were as sharp as diamonds.

"Do tell me what you've discovered, Hopkins," he prodded when she didn't continue right away.

"Well, there was a query of sorts. In the system. It's complicated." She waved her hand as if the hows and whys weren't important. Crandall supposed they weren't, as long as she could tell him what those complicated things meant.

"Was it an intrusion or not?"

"I think it was."

"Can you tell where it came from?"

"That's the strange thing. It was pretty well masked, as if whoever was poking around in the system knew how to cover her tracks."

"Her tracks?"

"Or his. It's just—before the intruder could duck back into his or her shell, I discovered how they entered the system." She leaned toward him, lowering her voice. Her eyes were wide and troubled. "I think—I'm sure the intruder got in using the log-on and password of Michelle Matsumara."

Crandall went very still for a moment, trying not to react. Then he realized that he should be reacting. It was surely what the woman would expect of him upon hearing that a dead FBI employee's computer log-on had been utilized two days after her murder.

"Is there any way to track the intrusion back to the intruder?" he asked, wishing he'd been less cavalier about upgrading his rudimentary computer skills. He'd figured he'd reached a level at the FBI where understanding advanced technology could be safely left to underlings. It was his job to put the connections together, not root out the connections in the first place.

He made a note to talk to some of his associates about remedying the gaps in his technological education. Computers were clearly here to stay, and, as he had no intentions of retiring to his Virginia farm anytime soon, it would behoove him to update his skills.

Especially if he wanted to maintain absolute secrecy.

He looked across the desk at Jessica Hopkins and realized a time might come, not too distant from this moment, when he would have to have her dispatched. He hoped that time would never come. He hoped she didn't ask the wrong questions—or, he supposed, the right ones.

He wasn't one of those people who lusted for power for its own sake. He took no pleasure in some of the things he had to do in order to achieve his goals.

But he'd come to the conclusion long ago that the nation he'd pledged his life to protect was incapable of freely governing itself. Sooner or later, without the intervention of practical men such as himself, the nation would collapse beneath the weight of its own excesses.

Sadly, a country's salvation made for some very strange bedfellows indeed.

He dismissed Hopkins, asked her to keep him apprised of anything else she discovered and walked with her as far as the elevators. But once she entered and the doors swished shut behind her, he continued on to the stairs.

The walk from the J. Edgar Hoover FBI Building to the Federal Triangle Metro station took him past grand alabaster buildings that never let a person forget he was in the grandest city in the grandest nation in the world.

At least, that was the story told by the grandeur of those facades. The reality, as always in this mercurial universe, was far more debatable.

The Metro Silver Line took him to a small café in Arlington, where he sat at the counter and ordered black coffee and an apple crisp. His order arrived promptly, delivered by a quiet, clean-shaven young man who poured coffee with a smile. His dark eyes settled on Crandall's face for a moment. "Haven't seen you in here in a while."

"Haven't had occasion to be in this part of town," Crandall answered with a brief smile. He pulled his wallet from his jacket pocket and handed the server a twenty, folded around a note he'd composed on the train. "I hope to be back soon."

"I'll have your coffee and apple crisp waiting, sir." The young man took the money with a smile and carried it to the cash register. He opened the register drawer, unfolded the bill and laid it in the tray with one hand, while he pocketed the note with his other.

He nodded at Crandall and disappeared into the back of the diner.

Crandall relaxed against the stool back, enjoying a sip of the hot, strong coffee. He might lack the knowledge to make sense of what Jessica Hopkins had told him earlier in his office, but he knew plenty of people who could.

All he had to do was wait.

WHEN NICKI WAS a little girl and her world had been as changeable as the Tennessee weather, she'd found solace in cooking. It wasn't the food itself that gave her a sense of normalcy, although she'd enjoyed the results of her culinary efforts as much as anyone. It was the act of cooking, the alchemical magic of food meeting flame, that had given her a sense of calm purpose when the world around her went insane.

Her mother's emotional ups and downs had made life unpredictable, but as long as she had a stove and a pan, Nicki could control at least one part of her world. She'd taught herself to cook using an old, tattered cookbook that had belonged to her grandmother, sometimes with wretched results. But kitchen disasters had become fewer and farther between by the time she reached her teens, and her first real job in high school had been tending the grill at Maisey Ledbetter's diner. That's where she'd learned that cooking wasn't a skill but an art.

Funny how her life always seemed to cycle back to cooking, sooner or later.

Tonight, her pans were providing her a much needed distraction from Dallas's focus on his keyboard and the mysteries of the internet. She hadn't tried whipping up anything ambitious since taking up residence in this tiny little mountain town, but she'd found some nice fillets of trout at the grocery store in Abington a couple of weeks ago and had been waiting for an occasion to take them out of the freezer and do something interesting with them.

She whipped up a lemon butter sauce for the trout and tossed some fresh mixed greens and spinach into a side salad, humming tunelessly as she worked. The day's tension seemed to melt away as quickly as the butter she used in the sauce, and by the time Dallas wandered into the kitchen, sniffing the air, she was feeling relaxed and nearly optimistic again, despite the stressful news that had marred their day.

"What on earth is that amazing smell?" he murmured, bending close to look over her shoulder at the trout fillets browning on the stove.

"Trout with lemon butter sauce and a side of mixed greens in a honey vinaigrette." She struggled against the urge to lean back into his body, to wrap herself in the heat of him, though she found it harder and harder to come up with a good reason why she shouldn't.

She'd been alone for a while now. By choice.

So what if she chose something else now? Whatever was happening with Dallas Cole didn't feel rushed or reckless, despite their short time together. In some ways, she felt as if she knew him better than anyone she'd ever known.

And perhaps more to the point, she felt as if she'd shared more of herself—her true self—with him than she'd ever shared with anyone else.

She'd let him see who she was and he hadn't run away as fast as he could.

Of course, he wasn't exactly in any position to run away, was he?

"I think you're about to burn the trout," he murmured in her ear.

She removed the pan from the heat. "Sorry. I'm not used to distractions in the kitchen."

He brushed his hand down her cheek, making her shiver. "Am I a distraction?"

She turned to face him, pressing her hand flat against his chest. "By now, you have to know you are."

He gazed at her for a breathless moment. Then he bent to kiss her.

Heart pounding, she met him halfway.

Chapter Thirteen

Dallas fought the urge to scoop her up and carry her straight back to the bedroom, though the temptation was almost beyond his ability to resist. She was warm and soft, the scent of her a heady combination of sweet and tangy, stoking a level of sexual hunger he hadn't felt in ages.

And maybe if sex was all he wanted from her, he wouldn't have tried to slow things down.

But he needed more than just two bodies coming together to scratch an itch. She was his lifeline, and he had a feeling that, in a lot of ways, he was hers. That level of trust, of need, was a fragile thing.

He couldn't break it, no matter how much he wanted her.

Still, the urge to kiss her was beyond his ability to resist, especially when she rose to her toes and wrapped her arms around his neck, drawing him down to her. Her lips glided against his, lightly at first, nipping and teasing him until his head began to spin.

Then she ran the tip of her tongue against the seam of his lips, urging them apart. He deepened the kiss, relishing the sweet heat of her tongue against his, the intimacy of her hands exploring the contours of his chest.

Only when she dipped her hands under the hem of his

shirt and started to push it upward did he catch her hands and hold her away from him, taking a few deep, harsh breaths to get himself back under control.

She gazed at him with desire-drunk eyes. "You're not like any man I've ever tried to seduce, Dallas Cole."

"Is that good or bad?" he asked.

She cocked her head, a smile flirting with her kiss-stung lips. "Both."

"In case it's not clear, I do want you."

She stepped closer until the soft curve of her belly pressed against his sex. "I know."

She was damn near impossible to resist, but he made himself ease her away. "We have to trust each other."

"Yes," she agreed.

"And sex complicates things."

She nodded. "It does."

"I've just found out someone I've worked with for years is dead, and it might be connected to the trouble I've gotten myself into." He took another step back, turning away from her soft gaze before he lost sight of his good sense. "It would be easy to let myself get caught up in you, as a way of forgetting my grief for my friend."

"Comfort sex."

"Yes." He stole a look at her. "I don't want there to be any doubts between us. I don't want you to ever feel used."

"A little late for that," she said in a wry tone, and he realized she was revealing more about her past than perhaps she meant to.

"I don't want you to feel used by me," he clarified firmly.

An odd light shone in her eyes. "I wouldn't. But I get it."

"And I'm not saying no forever."

"Good." Smiling, she crossed back to the stove and picked up a slotted spatula. "You still up for dinner?"

"Yeah." He smiled back at her. "Can I do anything to help?"

"There are glasses over the sink and a pitcher of iced tea in the fridge." She gave an apologetic shrug. "I don't keep wine or beer in the house. Alcoholism runs in the family, so I've learned to just steer clear."

"Tea is great. Sweet, I hope?"

She shot him a look. "Is there any other kind?"

He found the glasses and filled them with ice from the freezer before pouring the tea. "Lemon?"

"Please." She pointed to the half a lemon lying on the cutting board near the stove.

He sliced the lemon into wedges and added one to each of their drinks. By the time he found the flatware drawer, she'd plated up the trout fillets and the green salad and placed them on the table.

They ate for a few minutes in comfortable silence. The trout was delicious, cooked to a delicate flakiness that rivaled anything Dallas had eaten in any of the fancier restaurants in Washington. "How long have you been cooking?" he asked a few minutes later.

"Since I was a kid." A smile played at her lips. "When I was younger, my life was pure chaos. I had to fend for myself a lot, and cooking was something I could control. If we had food in the house, I could make my own meal. I found comfort in being able to feed myself that way. It made me feel less vulnerable, not having to depend on my mother to put food on the table. Because when she was drunk or high, she'd forget to eat for days at a time, and she certainly wasn't thinking about me."

"I'm sorry."

"It's not a good life for a kid, but it made me tough. I don't regret those life lessons. I've survived because of them."

He reached across the table. "Survival isn't enough."

"Sometimes it has to be."

"I want more than survival." He held on to her hand, brushed his thumb across her knuckles. "I want more for you."

When she looked up at him, her eyes were damp. "Thank you."

He knew he should stop while he was ahead, but the anxiety eating away at his insides wouldn't allow him to remain silent. "Nicki, I know you've worked hard to get in a position to go inside the BRI. But what you're about to do could get you killed."

She dropped her fork and put her other hand over his. "Walking out the door can get you killed. Pulling your car onto the road can get you killed."

"Don't be flippant."

"I'm not. I'm just being realistic. Life is a risk. All of it. I could play it safe and still die in a senseless accident on any given day. Then what good would my life have been?"

"So this is your way of living a life of meaning?"

"I guess it is."

He wanted to argue, but he understood her feelings. One of the reasons he'd decided to train for a position in the FBI's cybersecurity division was to do something more significant with his life than putting together recruiting packets and public relations pamphlets.

"I'm going into this with my eyes wide-open," she said when he didn't respond. "I am. I know the danger I'm getting into. But I'm the right person to do this job. You know I am."

As much as he'd like to deny it, she was right. She'd managed to put herself in the right place at the right time to get closer to the top of the Blue Ridge Infantry than anyone had managed before. "How did you manage it? How did Quinn know you'd be the right person?"

"I don't know," she admitted. "I think it helps that I come from the hills, just like they do. I know what life here can be like, and I understand the struggles and frustrations that make them feel so powerless that they think the only way to control their lives is to take drastic steps like joining a militia. I get them, way more than I like to admit." Her voice lowered to a raspy half whisper. "I *was* them, in a lot of ways for a lot of years."

He'd gotten out of Harlan County young enough to escape the worst of that sort of desperation, in large part thanks to a high school teacher who'd seen his potential. He knew he was very fortunate.

It hurt to think of Nicki having to fight her way out of the poverty and desperation on her own, but it was a powerful testament to her inner decency that she'd managed to find her way back to a sense of purpose.

Even if that purpose was about to put her life in grave danger.

"Did you leave a message for Quinn about your breakthrough?" He poked at the remainder of his trout, his appetite long gone.

"Yes. I'm hoping he'll be able to get a message back to me before my meeting tomorrow." She nodded at his food. "You don't like it?"

"It's delicious. I'm just not as hungry as I thought."

She smiled, her expression sympathetic. "Worried about me?"

"Yeah. Is that allowed?"

"It's appreciated." She reached across the table and brushed her fingers over his. "Want to get out of here later tonight?"

He arched an eyebrow. "Out in the open?"

"Up the mountain." She nodded her head toward the hill rising behind the cabin. "I thought I'd check the drop site before bedtime. I know it might be too early, but I can use the exercise. How about you?"

He realized what she was offering, the level of trust in him to which she was admitting. "You're going to let me see your dead drop?"

"This is about your life now, as much as it's about mine." She drew her hand back and rose, picking up her plate. "I'll put the leftovers up so you'll have something to eat tomorrow while I'm at my meeting."

He followed her with his own plate. "Do you think they'll want you to go right away? If you end up getting hired to be this guy's caretaker."

"I'd have to come back and pack."

He felt a flicker of relief. He'd get one more chance to talk her out of it, then. Not that he thought he'd be successful.

She was a headstrong woman. It was one of her charms.

"How's the computer magic coming?" she asked as she put the leftover food into containers for the refrigerator.

"Slowly," he admitted. "I'm trying not to leave any traces of my intrusions."

"Have you been successful?"

"I don't know. I think so, mostly. It's not really possible to intrude on a secure network without leaving some traces, but you try to leave them in places where most people wouldn't think to look. And it's not like the networks I'm looking through are going to be monitored carefully for a breach in the areas I'm targeting."

"What if they are?"

"They'll still have to be smart and lucky to catch it."

He didn't tell her where he was looking for clues. Breaching the FBI's network was dangerous as hell, and she'd probably be about as happy about the risks he was taking as he was about her meeting tomorrow with Del McClintock and his boss.

But he needed to know Crandall's secret connections. He needed a way to prove the AD was crooked if he was ever going to be able to clear his good name. If it meant taking big risks, well, Nicki wasn't the only person who was willing to put her neck on the line for a life of meaning.

JOHN BARTHOLOMEW HAD lived in a modest but comfortable apartment in Abingdon, Virginia, for the past few months while he worked as a security consultant by day and glorified errand boy by night. The money wasn't great, but if he wanted a job that paid well, he'd have stuck to accounting.

He'd wanted a job that had meaning. The kind of job he'd had once, the kind of job he'd been forced to leave behind.

He'd been a good spy, while it lasted. He had the sort of face people didn't seem to remember once he'd passed from their field of sight. Average height, average build, hair that was neither black nor blond but somewhere in between, darker in the winter and lighter in the summer. He was neither fair-skinned nor olive-skinned, his eyes neither blue nor brown but a sort of murky hazel that shifted with his mood.

If he had possessed a criminal bent, he probably could have gotten away with any number of crimes, because nobody would have remembered what he looked like when all was said and done.

Only his speech drew people's attention, the mountain twang of his eastern Tennessee roots he'd never quite been able to lose. Here in the foothills of the Blue Ridge

Mountains, he fit in almost like a native. Being nondescript was an asset in his business.

Nobody seemed to notice when he left his apartment shortly after sunset and drove to a scenic overlook on Bellwether Road, where he left his truck and started hiking up the mountainside to the drop site.

He left the note from Alexander Quinn with a minimum of fuss before hurrying down the mountain as quickly as he'd climbed it. On his way back to Abingdon, he stopped at a convenience store for a six-pack of beer and was back in his apartment, sock-clad feet propped on his coffee table, before nine o'clock. If anyone had noticed him leave or arrive, they weren't likely to be curious about it. Who didn't go for a beer run now and then?

Window shades down, TV turned up, he pulled the note Nicki had left him earlier that day from his pocket and read the scrawled message again.

She had finally set up a meeting with their mark, which meant that the scrappy girl from Ridge County, Tennessee, had managed to disarm the notoriously suspicious Blue Ridge Infantry crew where dozens of men before her had failed.

Or had she? Was her planned meeting with Del McClintock and his mysterious boss really just another test of her trustworthiness?

The most dangerous test of all?

She would check the drop site before tomorrow, which meant she'd find Alexander Quinn's instructions before her meeting. Like Agent X, Quinn seemed wary of trusting this stroke of fortune, as well.

He opened one of the beers and took a sip, reminding himself there was only so much of this operation that he could control. It was a fact that he sometimes found very hard to take. For a man who craved action, who longed for an occupation with real meaning, the hardest part of his job was what he was currently doing.

Sitting and waiting.

THE NIGHT AIR was cold and sharp, but it felt ridiculously good as it filled Dallas's lungs. The trek up the mountain left him winded and tired, but he made it without collapsing, something he wouldn't have been able to accomplish only a few days earlier. The physical remnants of his ordeal with the Blue Ridge Infantry had mostly faded from his body over the past few days. Only the psychic scars remained.

Those, he suspected, might take a while to disappear.

But reaching the small cave near the top of the mountain ridge felt like a victory, so he enjoyed it as well as he could while gasping for breath.

"You still hanging in there?" Nicki asked as he leaned against the cold stone wall of the cave's exterior.

He nodded, too winded to reply.

She brushed her hand down his arm as she passed him and entered the dark cave, disappearing from his sight. She emerged a moment later and nodded at him. "You need to rest a little longer?"

He wanted to say no, but the truth was, he needed to sit for a moment, let his flagging body catch up with his stubborn will. He nodded at the fallen log nearby, which she'd turned onto its side before entering the cave. "I take it that log means something?"

"It's our signal. He turns it up. I turn it down. Sit there if you need to."

He sat on the fallen tree trunk. "Did you read the note?"

Nodding, she sat next to him, keeping her voice low. "Quinn is worried this might be another test. He said I shouldn't assume I'm in yet."

"He's right."

"I know." She scooted over until their bodies touched, leaning her head against his shoulder. He put his arm around her, keeping her close.

"It's not too late to back out if you want to."

She sighed, her breath condensing in the cold night air, rising in whorls of vapor. "I can't back out. Not when we're so close."

"What if he wants you to move in with him?"

"I'm assuming that's exactly what he'll want." She sat up, looking at him. "It's what we want, too. To get that close, to be right there on the inside, gathering information—it's why I came here."

"How am I going to know if you're okay?"

"You won't. Not right away." She took his hand and held it. Her fingers were cold but the warmth of her enveloped him, anyway, driving away the chill of the night. "Maybe we should arrange for Quinn to extract you. He can put you in one of our safe houses in Tennessee."

"I don't know Quinn. I don't trust him." He met her gaze, his heart throbbing heavily in his chest. "I trust you."

"Then stay in my cabin, the way we planned." She rose to her feet, tugging him up from the log. "Ready to go home?"

Home, he thought bleakly as he fell in step with her as they headed back down the mountain.

The cabin wouldn't feel like home once she was gone.

THE KNOCK ON the front door came late in the evening, as Philip Crandall was preparing for bed. His wife, Melinda, preferred life on their horse farm in Fairfax County, so he kept an apartment in the city during the week and commuted on weekends.

He rarely had visitors at the apartment, and never from people at the Bureau, which meant one of two things. Either the person at his door had the wrong apartment—or his trip to the diner in Arlington had produced results sooner than he'd anticipated.

When he opened the door to a young man dressed in a bright red polo shirt emblazoned with a pizza chain logo, he first assumed it was the former, a pizza delivery to the wrong apartment.

But when he looked into the familiar blue eyes of the diner barista who'd taken his note with the twenty that afternoon, he realized his error.

"Pizza delivery," the young man said. "That'll be fifteen dollars."

"I only have a twenty," Crandall said.

The young man smiled. "I can make change."

Crandall pulled out his wallet and handed over the twenty. The man returned a folded five to him and gave him the pizza box. "Enjoy, sir."

Crandall closed the door and locked it, then carried the pizza box to the coffee table. He sat and looked at the closed pizza box, his heart suddenly pounding.

Surely the man wouldn't have come all the way out here if the news wasn't significant. Would he?

Remembering the way he'd delivered his request earlier that day at the diner, Crandall unfolded the five-dollar bill. Inside, he found a small square of paper with four words written on it: *check under the pizza.*

He stared down at the pizza box, suddenly tense. He hadn't yet experienced any difficulties in dealing with the men he had chosen to be his unlikely comrades, but he'd always known that aligning himself with them held inherent risks. There could come a time, at any moment, when they decided he was no longer of any use to them.

And it would be so very easy to dispatch him with a simple shrapnel bomb hidden inside a pizza box, would it not?

"Life is a gamble, Phil." His father's gravelly voice rang in his head. *"You can't win if you don't play, so suck it up and roll the dice."*

Crandall took a deep breath and opened the pizza box.

Nothing exploded. The contents were just eight slices of pepperoni and mushroom pizza. He released a gusty sigh and picked up one of the pieces to look beneath it.

There was a clear plastic bag lying flat beneath the pizza. He tugged it free, wiped off the dusting of semolina flour and looked at the note inside.

"We've tracked the intrusion to a cell phone signal bouncing off a tower in Dudley County, Virginia," the note said. Beneath that terse announcement were several details, including the coordinates of the cell tower in question.

Dudley County, Virginia, Crandall thought. *Why does that sound familiar?*

He dug in his pocket for the burner phone he used for his more secretive pursuits and dialed a number. The person on the other end of the line answered on the second ring. "What do you want?"

"Information," he answered. Then he outlined what he needed to know. "By morning?"

"It'll cost you."

"It always does." He hung up the phone and reached for the slice of pizza he'd moved aside, suddenly starving.

Chapter Fourteen

Friday turned out to be a beautiful day, sunny and mild. Nicki wanted to believe the fine weather was a good omen, that her meeting this afternoon would go well and she'd finally get this undercover operation running on all cylinders.

There was just one problem. She didn't believe in good omens. And once this operation really got underway, she'd be in the gravest danger of her life, far away from anyone who gave a damn about her or her safety.

"You don't have to go through with this." Dallas's voice was a warm rumble behind her. The heat of his body washed over hers as he crossed to stand behind her at the kitchen window.

"Yes, I do." Of its own volition, her body swayed backward until she rested against his chest.

He wrapped his arms around her waist, holding her loosely. "No, you don't. Quinn shouldn't have put you in this position to begin with. You're not a trained agent, are you?"

"I've had experience working with agencies—"

"As an informant, not an undercover operative."

"I'd be essentially an informant in this situation, too. Besides, I was sort of undercover at the farm." Although, given how badly things had ended for Jeff Burwell, maybe that wasn't such a good example to bring up.

Dallas felt so solid behind her, so steady, she wished there was a way she could take him with her, stash him away in her luggage so that when she was alone and scared on this upcoming mission, she could pull him out, wrap his arms around her like a warm sweater and feel this safe again.

"It's not the same thing." He tightened his hold on her, pressing his cheek against her temple. The rough bristles of his morning beard pricked her skin, sending a light shiver down her spine.

"I've got three more hours before I have to go meet Del. Can't we talk about something else?" She turned in his arms to face him, flattening her hands against his chest. "Tell me something I don't know about you."

His lips curved in a brief smile. "This game will bore you to death."

"I'll be the judge of that." She tugged the lapel of his shirt. "I never did find you that desk. I need to do that before I leave for my new job."

"What if he wants you to leave right away?"

"I'll tell him I need to give notice at work and talk to my landlord. They can't expect me to drop everything and go to work today." She shook her head. "If I agreed to that, I'd come across as entirely too eager. I'll make them meet some of my terms before I'll meet some of theirs."

He tugged her closer. "You're a tough negotiator, huh?"

"I can be."

"Good to know."

She moved closer to him, pressing her cheek against his collarbone. "I wish I had a way to stay in touch with you while I'm gone."

"How are you going to stay in touch with Quinn?"

"There's a tracking device on my key chain. Quinn can find me wherever I am." She could tell by the sudden tension in Dallas's body that he didn't like the sound of that solution. "I have to trust Quinn. He's taken care of me this far."

"Do you know the coordinates of your tracker? For today? I could track you myself—"

She drew back to look at him. "I told you, this is just a meeting. I'm not going anywhere yet."

His brow creased. "It would make me feel better if I could keep an eye on you." He flashed a quick, sheepish smile. "That sounds kind of pathetic, doesn't it?"

"It sounds really sweet, actually." She rose to press her lips against his. With effort, she kept the kiss light, even though the need to draw him even closer, kiss him even more deeply, welled inside her like floodwaters seeking to breach a weakening dam.

He threaded his fingers through her hair, holding her still while he returned her kiss with more desperation, crumbling her defenses until she wrapped herself around him, drinking in every bit of passion he offered.

The sound of a phone ringing down the hall made her groan. Dallas released a deep sigh against her lips. "That's going to be Del, isn't it?"

She nodded.

"Don't answer," he whispered, bending to kiss her again.

The temptation to give in was nearly overwhelming, but she pulled free of his grasp and went down the hall to answer the phone on her bedside table. "Hello?"

"Hey there, Nicki. Just wanted to make sure you were up and getting ready for our meeting today."

"Of course. I'm looking forward to it." She sat on the

bed and looked up as Dallas came to stand in the doorway, watching her. "Is there anything I need to know before the meeting?"

"I've talked you up to him, so I think he really just wants to talk to you about what your duties would be. He wants to get his health back under control without having to deal with doctors and hospitals."

"He's going to have to have a doctor to prescribe medication," she warned. "There's a limit to what I can do for him."

"He knows that. Trust me, sugar. He's going to love you."

Maybe it was a case of the nerves, but something about Del's cheerful tone was starting to make her second-guess her decision to let him drive her to the meeting. "Listen, I know we planned to meet at the diner so you could drive me to the meeting, but can't I just meet you wherever your friend is going to be? If I'm going to work with him, I'm going to need to know how to get there, anyway, right?"

There was a taut pause on the other end of the line. "All in good time," he said finally, his tone a little sharper than it had been before. "He's been clear about how he wants this to take place, and I don't think we should make him feel uncomfortable right out of the gate, do you?"

"Of course not," she said quickly, not wanting to give him any reason to back out. "I'll meet you at the diner as planned."

"You'll knock his socks off," Del said. "Trust me."

"I do," she lied. "Thank you so much for setting this up. I'll see you around eleven?"

"See you then, sugar. Bye now."

She hung up the phone and looked at Dallas. "Am I crazy to do this?"

"Yes," he answered flatly.

"I can't back out now."

His jaw tightened and his eyes flashed with anger as he gazed back at her, but he didn't speak. He didn't have to. He'd already told her his opinion of the job Quinn was asking her to do. But she was too close to her goal to stop now.

She had to see it through.

Starting with today's meeting.

Technically, John Bartholomew didn't work for Alexander Quinn. Instead, he worked for a limited liability corporation called Citadel Properties, a security consulting firm with which Quinn had signed a contract. But the truth was, Citadel had only one employee. And Quinn kept that one employee pretty damned busy.

On the desk beside him sat a folder containing several job applications Quinn had faxed over earlier in the week. After experiencing some troubling issues with his in-house vetting procedures the previous year, Quinn had decided to contract out the background checks for his company.

Before the end of the week, John would have to make his way through those resumes and make sure that Quinn didn't make any hiring decisions that would come back to bite him.

But first, he had a meeting to attend.

The drive from Abingdon to River's End took almost thirty minutes, most of that time spent on winding two-lane roads that wound around the mountains and dipped into shady hollows deep in the backwoods of the Blue Ridge Mountains.

Dugan's Diner wasn't much to look at from the outside, just a boxy glass-front eatery on the main road into town. At a quarter to eleven, the parking lot was just starting to fill up for the midday crowd. John parked to one side, near the road, to give him a decent view of any cars entering or exiting the area.

Quinn hadn't told him specifically to tail Nicki and Del McClintock to the secondary meeting place, but he hadn't told him not to, either. John was still considering his options when he saw Nicki's Jeep pull into the lot and park a row away from the front.

He picked up the small pair of binoculars lying on the seat beside him and took a quick look at her through the driver's side window. She looked tense. Understandable. He was tense on her behalf. But he hoped she'd get her nerves under control before McClintock arrived. The success of this operation might well depend on her being able to keep a cool head.

His cell phone trilled in his pocket, giving him a start. He checked the display and found the number was blocked.

Quinn, of course. His boss didn't bother with the niceties. "You have her in sight?"

John lowered his binoculars. "I do."

"Don't interfere. I don't know how well trained McClintock might be, but you can't risk his catching you tailing him."

John swallowed a sigh.

"Are we clear?" Quinn asked, steel in his voice.

"Perfectly."

"Is the tracker working?"

John picked up the tablet lying on the passenger seat and brushed his fingertip across the screen. The GPS tracking software popped into view, a flashing green light indicating Nicki Jamison's current position on the map. "Working fine."

"Let's hope she keeps that key chain on her at all times."

John spotted a blue Chevy Silverado pulling into the parking lot. It stopped behind Nicki's Jeep, engine revving.

"McClintock's here," John told Quinn.

"Is he alone?"

"Seems to be." He lifted the binoculars and took a good look at the truck. McClintock sat alone in the cab. "Just him."

As he watched, Nicki exited the Jeep and walked toward the passenger door of the Silverado. She opened the door and climbed into the cab, gracing McClintock with a nervous smile.

The door closed and the Silverado pulled out of the parking lot into the light stream of traffic on the main road. They disappeared around the curve.

"She's gone off with McClintock," he told Quinn.

"Tracker still working?"

John checked the GPS tracker. On the move with the truck. "Yes."

"Keep an eye on the tracker. I'll be in touch." Quinn hung up.

John put his phone in his pocket and cranked his engine. The urge to ignore Quinn's orders and follow the Silverado set John's nerves on edge, but he forced himself to turn the wheel and head down the highway in the opposite direction. Nicki Jamison was a resourceful woman who'd smashed through barriers to the Blue Ridge Infantry's inner circle that experienced agents hadn't been able to get beyond.

He had to trust her to do her job, just like he had to do his.

He had almost reached the road back to Abingdon

when his phone rang again. He pushed the speaker button and answered. "Yeah?"

It was Quinn. "We have a situation."

THERE WAS NO KNOCK, just the rattle of keys in the door and the creak as it opened. Dallas quickly closed the laptop and picked up the baseball bat Nicki had given him that morning before she left for the diner.

Pushing to his feet, he headed for the door to the makeshift office, easing a quick look down the hallway. His heart skipped a beat as a man stepped into the hall, his gaze locking with Dallas's.

"Get out of here or I'll call the cops," Dallas growled, pulling himself up to his full height and swinging the bat in front of him.

The other man's eyebrows rose, but he didn't look overly worried. "You're not going to call the cops, Mr. Cole, because they're already looking for you." He held up his hands, showing they were empty. Dallas didn't see any sign of a weapon on him. "My name is John Bartholomew. I work with Alexander Quinn. I've got to get you out of here."

Dallas tightened his grip on the bat, caught off guard by the man's terse announcement. "Alexander who?"

"Don't insult my intelligence, Cole. I'm the man who picked up Nicki's messages on the mountain, including the information about your unexpected intrusion into her undercover operation. She calls me Agent X."

How would he know what Nicki called her contact? Unless—

No. Maybe this man had intercepted something. Or worse—what if he'd gotten his hands on Nicki herself?

"I'm who I say I am," the man who'd introduced himself as John Bartholomew said brusquely. "But I don't have time to prove that to your satisfaction. So I really, really need you to take a leap of faith here."

"Why don't you have time?" Dallas asked, his grip on the bat so tight that his fingers had begun to feel numb from the pressure.

"Because there are FBI agents heading this way right now, with plans to take you into custody. They could arrive at any moment, so it would be in your best interests to get the hell out of here while we still can."

"And I'm supposed to take your word for it?"

The other man sighed deeply, as if he was growing exasperated with Dallas's stalling. "How about Cade Landry's word?" He lowered one of his hands and reached for his pocket.

Dallas took an instinctive step back toward the storage room, putting the door frame between him and the other man. "Put your hands back up."

The man withdrew his hand from his pocket, a cell phone clutched between his fingers and thumb. "Quinn texted me a video link. He thought you might need persuasion." He turned the phone toward Dallas. "You'll need to come closer."

Dallas shook his head. "Put the phone on the floor and slide it to me."

One of the man's eyebrows lifted, but he did as Dallas said. Dallas stopped the sliding phone with his foot.

"Turn your back and put your hands up on the walls."

John turned around and lifted his hands, pressing his palms flat against the walls on either side of him.

Dallas crouched and picked up the phone, keeping his eyes on John until he had the phone in his hand. He glanced at the screen. There was a video link cued up. Pressing his lips to a thin line, he hit the play button.

A familiar face filled the screen. "Cole, it's Landry.

Quinn seems to think you're going to be your typical pain-in-the-ass self, so listen quick. John Bartholomew is telling you the truth. Get out of the cabin now."

"How do I know this wasn't filmed under duress?" Dallas asked aloud.

"By the way, nobody's forcing me to record this," Landry continued on the video, as if anticipating his question. The man actually smiled a little, as if he knew he'd predicted Dallas's reaction correctly. "Olivia says hello. Now please get the hell out of there."

The video ended, and Dallas looked up at John. Before he could speak, John's cell phone rang, nearly scaring Dallas out of his skin.

John looked at Dallas over his shoulder. "That's Quinn. He's the only person who has that number. I need to answer it. He may have new information."

Dallas pushed the Talk button. "Quinn?"

There was a pause on the other end of the line before the man spoke. "Dallas Cole, I presume?"

"Why did you send your errand boy to come get me?"

"He didn't tell you?"

"I'd like to hear it from you," Dallas said tightly.

"There's no time." Quinn sounded impatient.

"Make time."

"I have contacts in the FBI who informed me that certain intrusions into their computer system have led them to believe you are trying to hack the FBI's network." Dallas could hear the irritation in Quinn's voice over the phone. "They've somehow traced the intrusion to a system working off a cell phone operating in Dudley County, Virginia. They're sending agents from the Bristol resident agency. They should be there within the next twenty minutes. I suggest you get out now."

Dallas glared at John, who was watching him with wary eyes.

Quinn's voice sharpened. "By the way, once you leave, I suggest you ask John to show you the GPS system he has tracking Nicki's whereabouts."

John spoke up, his expression alarmed. "Why's that?"

"Because," Quinn answered in a voice as sharp as shattered glass, "the Blue Ridge Infantry has somehow figured out Nicki is an undercover operative."

Chapter Fifteen

The radio in Del's Silverado was cranked up high, tuned to a satellite station playing headbanging metal so loudly that Nicki couldn't think. She stole a look at Del, who was drumming the frenetic bass line on the steering wheel as he drove about twenty miles an hour over the speed limit.

She supposed once a man decided to get involved with domestic terrorism, speed laws posed no particular impediment to his whims.

"How much farther?" she asked, having to raise her voice over the radio. They'd been driving for nearly twenty minutes, moving deeper into the mountains as they left River's End behind. She hadn't ventured this far into the mountains in her time in River's End, so she wasn't really sure exactly where they were going.

"Not far," he answered, flashing her a smile that made the skin on the back of her neck prickle.

Something wasn't right. She couldn't point to any one thing that raised her suspicions, but all of her instincts were telling her that she needed to proceed with extreme caution.

She couldn't demand that Del turn the truck around and head back to River's End, not without throwing away everything she'd worked for. But she intended to move forward on high alert. The first minute anything started to go sideways, she had to have a plan of escape.

She wasn't armed. She'd grown up with an aversion to firearms, given her mother's steady stream of well-armed boyfriends who thought nothing of scaring the hell out of a little girl who got in their way. Alexander Quinn had insisted on training her how to use a weapon in case she ever had to, but she always hoped like hell she'd never have to.

She was beginning to rethink her position on guns, however, the deeper into the woods Del drove her.

"Is this where your friend lives?" she asked, peering through the windshield at the thickening woods. In this part of the mountains, what houses and buildings existed sparsely dotted a landscape of untamed acres of dense woodlands where evergreens outnumbered hardwoods.

It would be easy to get lost in these woods, she thought, her skin prickling madly. Lost and gone forever.

A dirt road crossed the road ahead, and finally the Silverado slowed, preparing to turn. Nicki eyed the narrow dirt road with apprehension. Just how far back in the woods did Del's boss live?

Once on the dirt road, Del was forced to drive with considerably more care, the ruts and bumps putting the truck's shocks to a grueling test. The jouncing and bucking didn't do much to calm Nicki's suddenly jangling nerves, but she tried to remain steady, at least outwardly.

Del was taking her to meet the man she'd been trying to meet since she first showed up in River's End. It was happening faster than anybody had hoped. That was good news, right?

So why didn't it feel like good news?

"Almost there," Del said, his mouth curving in a broad smile.

Something about that smile set Nicki's teeth on edge. Maybe because it looked feral and hungry.

Like a predator with his eyes on the prize.

"THEY'VE STOPPED." Dallas darted a quick look at John Bartholomew. The other man drove with an enviable combination of skill and speed, eating up the distance between their location and the blinking red dot on the GPS locator map.

"Address?" John asked.

"It's not really an address. It's not even a road, as far as I can tell." Dallas peered at the tablet, trying to zoom in for a better look. "The last road they were on seems to be Partlow Road. Heading east in the general direction of Saltville."

John released a quiet sigh. "I should have anticipated this."

"Yeah," Dallas agreed in a tight growl. "You should've."

"She wanted to do this work," John added, glancing toward Dallas. "She asked Quinn for the chance. Did you know that?"

"I know she was involved in an incident where the BRI attacked someone she was working for."

"Someone she was informing on," John corrected. "Burned him out of house and home. Nearly killed his kids."

"She said that guy wasn't really involved with the BRI."

"He wasn't. But she didn't know that when she signed up to inform on him."

Dallas glared at the other man. "Your point?"

"My point is, this ain't her first rodeo." John's tone flattened into a drawl. "She knew what she agreed to when she took this job. No point in arguing about whether she should have been undercover in the first place. She chose to do it and now she's in serious trouble. Quinn can't get backup here for another few hours, so it's up to the two of us to get her out of there alive. Are you with me or not?"

"Of course, I'm with you." He turned his attention to the GPS tracking program on the tablet. "My guess is, they turned off on a drive or road that's not marked on the GPS map."

John waved his hand toward the GPS navigation system built into the dashboard of his truck. "Can you feed the last four coordinates into that?"

"Sure." Dallas entered the coordinates. "Once we get to number three, we need to start looking for a turnoff on the left."

They fell silent as the GPS intoned the directions for the first set of coordinates. After a few moments, John asked, "What sort of physical condition are you in?"

Dallas looked up, surprised. "Not top form, but I'm in a hell of a lot better shape than I was a few days ago."

"You were their captive." It wasn't a question.

"For about three weeks."

"Any idea where?"

Dallas gave it some thought. "Couldn't have been too far from here, actually. As soon as I escaped, I headed west. I ended up falling flat on my face somewhere in the mountains."

"On Bellwether Road," John murmured, his tone thoughtful.

Dallas looked down at the tablet, scanning the GPS tracker map. Looking a little closer, he located Bellwether Road.

Due west of the spot where the red dot indicated Nicki's current position.

Panic tightened his gut. "Do you think they've taken her to the place where they were holding me?"

"Not sure," John admitted. "It's just interesting. Don't you think?"

Interesting wasn't the word Dallas would have used. *Terrifying* seemed more appropriate. "We can't just drive in there, you know. If that really is the place where they were keeping me, there are armed thugs everywhere."

"We'll have to go on foot. Figure something out when we get closer and have some idea what we're up against."

As Dallas started to respond, the GPS navigation program announced their arrival at their first set of coordinates and gave directions to the next spot on the map.

"What can you remember about the place where you were held captive?" John asked.

"It's in the woods. Up in the hills. There was a cabin, but that's not where they kept me. Not far from the cabin, they had a root cellar built into the ground. They stuck me down there. They had shackles screwed into the cinder block walls. Like a damn dungeon." He shuddered at the memory. "I wonder how many men they've kept in that place over the years."

"They have other places like that," John said. "Not just here in Virginia."

"I know. Nicki told me Cade Landry spent some time chained up in a basement in some cabin down in Tennessee."

"That's what I hear," John said quietly. "Is this going to be too much for you? If we get there and it's the same place?"

It was a fair question, Dallas had to admit. Even now, his gut ached with apprehension at the thought of being back in that place. He could still feel the dank chill, the smell of mold and sweat and fear. The darkness, at times, had been a living thing, every bit as threatening as the gun-toting men with beards who'd enforced his captivity.

No, he didn't want to go back there ever again. He didn't want to relive a single one of those memories.

But if that's where they were taking Nicki, he'd do it. Because the only thing that scared him more than what he'd already been through was the thought of never seeing her again.

ONCE UPON A TIME, in what seemed a lifetime ago, Nicolette Destiny Jamison had thought the world was a place full of infinite possibilities. She'd always had a flair for the dramatic, and at the age of seven, the inescapable facts of a foolish, alcoholic mother who made bad choices and the total absence of a father in her life had seemed little more than the melodramatic trappings of her life story.

She was going to be somebody. Someone important. Someone beautiful and elegant, a secret princess who would emerge from her chrysalis—a word she'd learned that very day at school—and wow the world with her shiny, rainbow-colored wings.

Then she'd stumbled on the body in the woods. It was a man, or at least, she thought it must have been, from the grimy, tattered remains of his clothing. There were hands, bloated and discolored. Shoes that could barely contain the gas-swollen girth of his feet. And his face— what the insects and wildlife had done to his face had fueled nightmares for months.

And in those nightmares, she'd come to the grim realization that princesses didn't come from the hills and hollows of Ridge County, Tennessee. Drug addicts and alcoholics did. People who killed other people over women or money or just a bad mood and left them to rot in the woods.

Nothing she could do, or dream, or scheme, was ever going to change that fact.

Nicki Jamison had given up her dreams for a long, long time. Until she met Jeff Burwell and his three little kids.

It wasn't that she'd fallen in love with him. She hadn't. Not in any romantic way. But in Jeff she'd found someone who'd come from the hills, just as she had. Someone who'd made the life he loved, tilling the soil, tending it with the same sort of love and patience with which he reared his three motherless children. He wasn't a storybook prince, but he was living a life of meaning and joy, even in the face of his lingering grief.

She'd started to believe again that she could have that kind of life for herself. Maybe she wouldn't be a princess with iridescent wings. Maybe she wouldn't charm a prince into undying love and devotion.

But her life could mean something. It didn't have to be an endless series of misadventures and mistakes. She could be happy if she could just find something she loved as much as Jeff loved his family and his farm.

When the Blue Ridge Infantry had burned his dream to the ground, she had taken it personally. She'd grieved his loss deeply because in a way, it had been her loss, as well.

The loss of hope for that future of happiness.

She hadn't heard from Jeff since the Tennessee Bureau of Investigation had hurried her out of Thurlow Gap, safely away from the men who'd taken their devastating revenge on the man they considered a traitor. The TBI wouldn't give her any updates, even when she'd asked. Her TBI handler, Martin, had stopped taking her calls finally, leaving an underling to tell her to stop calling and move on with her life.

She just hadn't known how to do that. Not until she'd met Alexander Quinn and talked him into giving her a job.

A purpose.

Beside her in the Silverado, Del McClintock had begun humming off-key along with the radio, but his lips were still curled in a half smile that gave her the creeps.

Wait it out, she told herself, even as she started taking furtive looks around the truck cab for something she could turn into a weapon if she started to lose control of the situation.

But the cab was clutter-free. There wasn't even an ice scraper in sight.

Through the trees ahead, she saw what looked like the corner edge of a cabin. Thirty yards later, the entire cabin came into view.

Four men stood in front of the cabin, armed with rifles. They weren't aiming at the approaching truck, at least, Nicki thought, swallowing a nervous giggle. That was a good sign, wasn't it?

"Expecting trouble?" she asked Del, turning to look at him.

Her gaze never made it to his face, locking instead on the barrel of the big black pistol he held pointed at her heart. "Sugar, you've got trouble written all over your pretty face."

"I don't understand." Nicki stared at the pistol and tried not to let her brain get too far ahead of her fear. If she was the innocent woman she was pretending to be, she'd be freaking out entirely.

Sort of exactly the way she *was* freaking out.

"Did you think we wouldn't figure it out, Nicki?" Del's

predatory smile widened. "Do you think you're dealing with a bunch of stupid hicks?"

"Figure out what?" She couldn't even make a run for it, surrounded as they were by men with rifles. And it wasn't as if she could get out of the truck before Del shot her dead, anyway. He was too close to miss.

"You're working for the cops, aren't you?"

She stared at him, genuinely dumbfounded. He thought she was working for the cops? What the hell? "What are you talking about?"

"One of our guys dropped by the diner the other day during your shift. He kept thinking he recognized you, and it finally came to him. You were Nicki Geralds, the woman who worked for his cousin down in Thurlow Gap, Tennessee."

Nicki Geralds had been the pseudonym she'd used when she was working for Jeff Burwell. "Are you talking about Jeff?"

Del looked surprised. "You're admitting it?"

"I worked as a housekeeper and nanny for a guy named Jeff Burwell after his wife died. I wasn't there long—there was a fire—"

"Nicki *Geralds*?"

"My married name," she lied. "I was still using it then, even though the divorce was almost final."

For a moment, Del looked uncertain. "You were married before?"

"Yes."

"You never mentioned that."

She frowned. "It wasn't a happy marriage. He was a serial cheater. And he treated me like garbage. I don't like talking about that time in my life. It's embarrassing and painful." She frowned at the pistol still pointing at her chest. "Please put that down. You're really st-starting to scare me."

He didn't lower the pistol, but he shifted it to his left, the barrel now pointing toward the dashboard instead. "Darby said the boys in Tennessee were all sure you were just playing Jeff. Trying to get him to turn his back on his kin and inform on them to the FBI."

She tried not to react, but this was the first she'd heard that anyone had even suspected her time with Jeff Burwell had been anything but aboveboard. "That's crazy. My God, Del, the FBI? Do you know what kind of thugs work for the FBI? We've talked about this, haven't we?"

"Was it just talk?" His look of uncertainty shifted to suspicion, and she realized she was starting to lose him again. "What did you and your FBI buddies do, profile me? One of those militia nuts, right? Bitch about the government, flash him a pretty smile, wear a tight-cut blouse and painted-on jeans, and the stupid backwoods hick'll buy anything you're tryin' to sell." His voice rose to a roar. "Right?"

The pistol barrel whipped back toward her heart.

"No! God, Del!" She shrank back, not pretending the rush of paralyzing fear. He was furious with her now. His rage blazed in his eyes, reminding her of the inferno that had whipped across the fields that night in Thurlow Gap, whipped by the night wind. It had spread wildly, eating up everything in its path.

The door behind her opened, and she would have tumbled out if not for the seat belt holding her in place. A pair of arms caught her as her torso pitched backward when the door behind her back fell away.

Del's eyes widened, and he lowered the pistol.

Whoever held her from behind smelled like…bacon and toast.

She pulled away from the arms grasping her and turned to see who had caught her.

Trevor Colley stood in the open door, a faint smile curving his lips. "Surprised to see me?"

She stared at him, her mind reeling. What was the diner manager doing out here in the middle of this mess? "I don't understand."

He shook his head. "Your problem, Nicki, is that you think you know how to read people. You're not bad at it, really. I mean, you read Del here in a heartbeat. Saw he was the one you'd have to deal with if you wanted to get anywhere around these parts, right? 'Cause he's a little bit smarter, a little more powerful than the others. A born leader, right?"

Her pulse thundered in her head as she stared at the man she'd worked with for months now without ever suspecting a thing. "You hate the BRI."

"Do I?" His smile widened. "Or is that just what I wanted you to believe?"

"Why?" she asked. "Were you trying to set me up or something? Why would you do that? What do you want from me?" She looked from Trevor back to Del. "Is there even a friend of yours who needs medical help?"

"There is," Trevor answered, drawing her attention back to him. "But it's not the leader of the BRI, sweetheart."

"Then who?"

Trevor nodded toward the cabin. Following his gaze, Nicki saw the front door open and a woman exit, holding the hand of a small boy of four or five. The child was pale and thin, too thin for his gangly height, and dark circles shadowed the skin beneath his eyes.

The woman eyed the men with rifles as she led the child to the edge of the porch. She was a tall, thin woman in her early thirties, but she looked nearly as pale and haggard as her little boy. Her red-rimmed eyes rose and locked with Nicki's, wide with desperation.

"Oh, Trevor," Nicki murmured, her heart squeezing. "Your son?"

"My son," he answered quietly. "So you see, I really don't care who you're working for. Or why. Because now, you're working for me. And you're going to stay here and do whatever you can to get my little boy well."

Chapter Sixteen

The day was unseasonably mild for mid-February in the Blue Ridge Mountains, only a faint breeze adding a hint of chill to the midday sunshine. This deep in the mountains, however, the canopy of evergreen boughs blocked out most of the warming sun, forcing Dallas to hunch more deeply beneath his borrowed camouflage jacket to ward off the cold.

He'd been fortunate that John Bartholomew carried an extra jacket in his truck, and more fortunate still that his feet were only a half size smaller than his benefactor's, the difference in size between his feet and the sturdy dirt-colored hiking boots easily minimized by wearing a second pair of socks. The shirt and pants Nicki had purchased at the thrift store were a little too short in the legs and sleeves, but they fit well enough and kept him reasonably warm as they trekked as silently as possible through the dry underbrush toward the blinking red light that denoted Nicki's position on the GPS map.

The borrowed Smith & Wesson M&P .40 tucked into a holster behind his back felt heavy against his spine, as well. The good kind of heavy, the kind that said he wasn't going into this fight unarmed.

John drew up and held out his arm to block Dallas from walking past him. He turned to look at Dallas, his hazel eyes blending in remarkably with the woodland camouflage face paint he'd smeared over his face before they left the truck and headed into the woods. He nodded his head toward a point directly ahead of them before turning around again.

Dallas peered through the shadowy gloom and spotted what John had seen—the edge of a clearing about seventy yards due east. Movement caught Dallas's eye, but he couldn't make out what he was seeing.

Beside him, John lifted a small pair of binoculars to his eyes and took a look. He held up three fingers.

Three what? Three little pigs? The Three Stooges? What the hell did three fingers mean?

John must have sensed his confusion, for he turned a quick glance his way and murmured, "Three men. Near a cabin. We need to get closer, but you're going to have to move slowly and carefully. And silently. Understood?"

Dallas nodded.

John started picking his way carefully ahead, moving with deliberation and stealth. Dallas fell into his wake, drawing on his own long-forgotten skills in the woods. He'd learned to hunt at a young age, sent out with his brother to bring in food to supplement what his father could steal or purchase with the money his drug sales brought in. He and his brother Clanton had seen themselves as modern-day Daniel Boones, blazing new trails through the mountains of Harlan County, Kentucky.

Of course, those trails had all been blazed long before, by good men and evil men, and his childhood dreams of adventure and discovery had soon given way to the reality of his dead-end existence.

He'd gotten himself out of Kentucky, used his wits and his brains to create a new life for himself. Yet here he was again, creeping through the woods in search of prey.

The human kind, this time.

They closed the distance to just under twenty yards from the sunlit cabin now visible through the thinning trees. John pulled to a halt and crouched behind a scrubby huckleberry bush. Dallas squatted beside him and gazed toward the cabin. The three men John had seen before were still visible, standing near the low-slung front porch. A fourth was now visible, leaning against the railings of the porch steps. Sunlight gleamed on the barrels of the rifles they carried.

John spoke quietly, his voice barely more than a hiss of air in the wind rustling the pine needles overhead. "Remington 798. Browning X-Bolt. Marlin XS7. Another Remington. Model Five, I think."

He was telling Dallas what kind of guns they were up against, as if he felt certain Dallas would know what those guns were and what they could do.

Which suggested John knew a little more about Dallas than most people did. Enough to know that he was more than just some civilian graphic designer working for the FBI. That he might know a little something about rifles.

And, if the trust John had shown so far meant anything, he also believed Dallas knew a little something about moving with stealth through the woods, as well.

Just how much did Alexander Quinn and his people know about him and his past, anyway?

John edged a few yards forward, toward another bush. Dallas followed, wincing as his foot hit a dry twig, making it snap.

For a moment, the nearest man jerked to attention, his brow furrowed. He glanced toward the trees, and Dallas and John both froze in place. Camouflaged as they were, it would be movement that would give them away. Dallas breathed shallowly, keeping his eyes half-closed as he peered toward the alerted rifleman. The man finally appeared to relax and wandered away from the corner of the porch.

After a long pause, John led them forward another few yards and finally hunkered down again. From their new vantage point, they had a decent view of the whole yard in front of the trees.

There was a large blue Chevy pickup truck parked at the edge of the yard. John turned to look at Dallas, a grim smile twisting the corners of his mouth. "Del McClintock," he said quietly.

Dallas took another look at the truck. The cab was empty, so Del and Nicki were apparently inside the cabin.

The very well-guarded cabin.

What were they going to do now?

"I CAN'T SEEM to fix things for Jason. Much as I try." Lynette Colley's pale eyes met Nicki's with wary hope. "Trevor says you can help him."

"I can help with some things," Nicki said as gently as she could manage. Whatever she might think of Trevor and his merry band of thugs, Lynette Colley's love and fear for her child were unmistakable and genuine.

"I know he needs insulin, and Trevor takes care of that, no worries, but ain't there more he needs?" Lynette touched Jason's pale cheek, her expression teeming with concern that made Nicki's heart ache.

"Jason needs a doctor," she said quietly but firmly.

Lynette slanted a look at her. "Trevor ain't gonna have it. You know he ain't. That's why you're here."

"He loves his son, doesn't he?"

"Yes." Lynette's chin came up in a show of angry defiance. "Don't you dare suggest he don't."

"I wouldn't," Nicki said quickly. And she wasn't suggesting any such thing. Clearly, whatever his sins and faults, Trevor Colley loved his son enough to take a woman hostage in order for his son to have the care he needed.

But Nicki wasn't a doctor, and while she'd had some experience helping people with diabetes, her experiences had been more with adults suffering from type 2 diabetes. Type 1 diabetes, the kind that had once been called childhood diabetes, was a whole different animal.

Still, Jason Colley was clearly ill, and there were things she knew how to do to get his blood sugar levels back to a better place on a continuing basis. "We need his glucometer."

Lynette nodded. "You want to test him now?"

At the strangled tone of his mother's voice, Jason looked up with dismay. "No tests, Mama. Okay? No tests."

Nicki crouched next to where the boy sat on the sofa. "Jason, has your mama told you what diabetes is?"

"It's what makes me sick." He sounded more irritated than afraid. "I can't have candy except sometimes."

"It's because things like candy and mashed potatoes and cookies—all those things are full of carbohydrates. Do you know what carbohydrates are?"

He shook his head no.

"They're part of the things that make foods good for you. But in your case, too many of them can make food very bad for you."

He stared at her, clearly not understanding.

"Ever been stung by a bee?"

His eyes widened. "I hate bees."

"Me, too," she said, glancing at Lynette with a smile. "But did you know bees can be good things?"

He looked skeptical.

"They help plants grow," she said, keeping it simple. "When they do that, they're good."

"But not when they sting you," he insisted.

"Definitely not when they sting you." She looked at Lynette with a little nod. Lynette rose and left the room for a moment.

Jason followed his mother's exit with worried eyes, but he looked back at Nicki when she spoke. "Carbohydrates are like bees. When they work the way they're supposed to, they help your body grow like bees help plants grow."

"Until they sting you," he groused.

"Yup, until they sting you."

"Tests sting."

"They do," she agreed. "But they help us know whether or not we need to give you medicine to make you feel better."

Lynette came back in the room with a small pouch. She set the pouch on the coffee table in front of the sofa where Jason sat and looked at Nicki.

Nicki pulled the glucometer from the pouch. It was a medium-sized monitor, not really ideal for the continual level of glucose testing Jason needed if he was going to keep his blood sugar well regulated. Nicki looked up at Lynette. "Where'd you get this?"

The woman looked panic-stricken. "Is it wrong?"

"No," Nicki assured her. "It can do what you need to do. Did a doctor prescribe this?"

Lynette shook her head. "I told you—"

"How'd you get a diagnosis?"

"I got a friend to take us to Bristol a few months ago. I knew somethin' was wrong—"

Nicki pressed her mouth to a thin line. "And Trevor wouldn't let you take him to a doctor?"

Lynette shot her a defensive look. "He has his reasons."

Fear and stupidity, apparently. "The doctor diagnosed him?"

"Yeah. He wanted me to come back, let him see Jason again in a few days, but—"

"But Trevor wouldn't let you." She looked at Jason, who was staring with apprehension at the lancing device sitting next to the glucometer. She looked in one of the inner pockets of the pouch and found a sealed packet containing a few alcohol wipes. She'd already washed her hands before entering the room, but to be safe, she opened an alcohol wipe and gave her hands a quick cleaning before she picked up the lancing device. "How often do you test his blood?" she asked as she cocked the device.

In front of her, Jason made a soft moaning sound.

"He hates it so much, I try not to do it more than twice a day."

"That's not often enough." Nicki shot Lynette an apologetic look. "I know you both don't want to hear that, but regular testing is necessary to keep his blood sugar from reaching dangerous levels."

Tears welled in Lynette's eyes as she gazed at her son. "He hates it so much."

"I bet you hate feeling sick even more, don't you, Jason?"

His gaze snapped up from the lancing device and met hers. "I just want to play with the other kids."

His plaintive reply made her heart hurt. No matter how she'd come to be here, or how much danger she might be in, she was going to help this little boy if she could.

Maybe that was as close to a princess with rainbow-colored wings as she'd ever get, but that would be pretty damn good, wouldn't it?

"Let's see if we can do something about that," she

said, turning on the glucometer and holding out her hand to him.

Tentatively, he reached over and laid his hand, palm up, in hers.

She wielded the lancet as gently as she could, but she couldn't make it painless. Jason whimpered a little as the lancet pierced his skin, but he didn't cry. Tough little kid.

She touched the droplet of blood from his finger to the test strip in the glucometer. A few seconds later, the reading came up on the meter. "It's too high," she told Lynette. "When did he last eat?"

"A few hours ago."

"When did you last administer insulin?"

Lynette's face creased with distress. "Last night."

"We need to give him another shot. Now."

Jason started crying. Lynette moved to comfort him, but Nicki caught her arm. "Get the insulin now."

Lynette changed course, and Nicki reached out to put her arms around Jason. He resisted at first, but then he laid his head against her shoulder and started to relax.

The door to the room slammed open and Trevor entered, his usually friendly expression hard as granite. "What are you doing to him?"

She met Trevor's gaze without flinching. "What you brought me here to do. I'm trying to make him feel better."

"You sayin' I want something different?"

She was growing sick of these belligerently ignorant men and their ceaseless bullying. "I'm saying you're too afraid of hospitals and doctors to get your son the help he needs, so I'm all you've got. You need me more than I need you, so stop throwing your weight around as if you can scare me into doing what you want. Because you can't."

His nostrils flared with anger, but he didn't speak.

She'd take that as a win.

Trevor backed out of the room, slamming the door shut behind him. A moment later, the door opened again and Lynette returned, bringing with her a bag of supplies.

"Did he yell at you?" she asked quietly as she handed the bag to Nicki.

"Not much," she answered with a smile of reassurance as she retrieved the insulin and syringes from the bag. "Did the doctor you saw in Bristol prescribe the dosage written on this package?"

"Yes, but we're nearly out."

Of course they were. She kept her mouth firmly shut and opened one of the syringes, earning another soft whimper from Jason. She tamped down the rush of sympathy, knowing what the little boy needed from her now was competence, not sentiment.

"You've been giving him the shots in the soft part of his belly, right?"

"Yes."

"Think you can help me out, Jason?" she asked, turning to the boy. He gazed back at her, wide-eyed. "Do you know how to pinch someone?"

His eyes widened even more. "Mama says I'm not s'posed to pinch."

"Well, sometimes it's okay. Like now." She held out her arm. "Pinch me. Right here on my arm."

He hesitated for a moment, glancing at his mother. She gave a nod, and he turned back to Nicki, reached out and pinched her arm.

"Ow!" she cried, making him jerk back from her. Then she grinned. "Just kidding. That barely hurt at all."

Slowly, he grinned, showing his teeth for the first time. "You tricked me."

"I did," she agreed. "Now, can you pinch your tummy just like you pinched my arm?"

Frowning, he looked down at his T-shirt. "Why?"

"Because if you're pinching your belly when I give you the shot, you might not even feel the shot. Want to give it a try?"

He hesitated a moment, then tugged his shirt up, baring his belly. She saw a couple of little bruises that had probably come from previous injections. He pinched a little bit of the flesh just below his navel.

"Can you feel the pinch?" she asked.

He nodded, squeezing a little harder.

"Close your eyes now and just pinch."

He did as she asked, and she quickly injected the insulin into the pinched skin. "All done."

He opened his eyes and looked at her. "You're tricking me again."

"Nope, all done."

Behind her, Lynette started to cry.

THE MEN WITH the rifles left, one at a time, until by just before nightfall, only the Silverado remained parked in front of the cabin. Hours of stillness had begun to make Dallas's legs and arms ache, reminding him that however improved he might be since his escape from captivity, he was still recuperating.

This wasn't the place where he'd been held captive. He was certain of that. But he was pretty sure it had been somewhere close by. The terrain was right. The lay of the land. And after a few minutes of surveillance, he was certain that at least one of the armed men guarding the cabin had been among those who'd kept guard over him while he was in the BRI's custody.

The fact that he'd managed to realize that bit of information without giving in to emotional paralysis was a victory of sorts. He was still plagued with nightmares, and probably would be for a while yet, but in the cold light of day, he wasn't going to be held hostage by those memories.

"Closest side window," John murmured, the first words he'd spoken in well over an hour.

Dallas followed his gaze and saw the curtains shift in the window closest to the corner of the cabin. A face appeared there briefly, lit by the setting rays of the sun.

Nicki's face.

So she was in there. The GPS signal had suggested as much, of course, but now they had visual confirmation.

Was she a prisoner? Or was she still playing her part?

"How sure is Quinn that they know she's undercover?" he asked John.

"He wouldn't have sent us after her if he wasn't sure."

Dallas looked at the window again. She'd disappeared from the space between the curtains, replaced by a tall, broad-shouldered man who peered out at the woods with a frown on his face.

"Del McClintock," John said.

Dallas took another look at the man before, like Nicki, he'd backed away from the window and disappeared from view. "If they know she's an undercover operative, why haven't they finished her off?" Merely saying the words aloud made his stomach ache. "They don't even seem to be keeping her prisoner, do they?"

"If you mean she's not shackled in a cellar somewhere, no they don't." John's voice softened. "But there are many ways to be kept captive."

Dallas looked at the cabin, his gaze settling on the window where he'd last seen Nicki's face.

"I know," he said.

That's what scared him.

Chapter Seventeen

"I didn't know they were going to do this to you."

Lynette Colley's soft voice roused Nicki from a half doze. She sat up straight and looked up to find the other woman now sitting in the rocking chair across from her, holding her sleeping child.

Jason's blood sugar had finally reached a normal level and was so far maintaining, even after a light dinner. He'd fallen asleep soon after, exhausted from the illness and the trauma of the day.

Nicki knew just how he felt.

"How long have you been here?" she asked, stifling a yawn.

"Just a few minutes. The men just finished eating."

Nicki glanced around the room, making certain they were alone. She lowered her voice a notch. "Who's here now?"

"Del and Trevor. The others left before I made dinner. I don't think they're coming back until morning."

Nicki got up and looked out the window. Outside, night had fallen, only the faintest of indigo still touching the sky to the west. "Is this cabin usually guarded like this?"

"No," Lynette answered, sounding as tired as she looked. "When I married him, Trevor was just a short-order cook.

We were poor, I suppose, but happy. And then I found out I was pregnant. Things got more complicated."

"Poor and happy wasn't enough?"

"I guess not." She sighed. "You take shortcuts. Then it works and you start to get some of the things you never had, and you end up wanting more and more. No matter how much you get, it just ain't enough. I swear these hills are hell on earth. And I guess that means Trevor's become the devil himself now. 'Cause he's the king around these parts."

"I'm from the hills," Nicki murmured, turning back to look at Lynette. "Sometimes, I look at places like this, with all the wildness and the beauty, and I wonder how anything bad could ever come from a place this grand."

"You think I'm a terrible mama, don't you?"

"I think you love your son. And you're scared. And you don't know how to give him what he needs." She crossed to the rocking chair and crouched in front of Lynette, thinking about Kaylie Pickett and that little baby still holding on inside her despite all the odds against him. These hills could be harsh and unforgiving, but grace could still be found. Courage.

Miracles.

What she was about to say could get her killed, she knew. But it could also save three lives.

"Lynette, if I could get you and Jason out of here, I could help you get everything you need to give him as normal a life as possible. I see that's what you want for him."

Tears welled in Lynette's eyes. "Trevor wouldn't let me take him out of here."

"If that's true, then we have to take him out of here without Trevor knowing."

The thought caused Lynette real pain, Nicki saw.

Whatever his flaws and his sins, Trevor meant something strong and binding to his wife. Leaving him would break her heart.

But if she didn't leave him, she might lose her son.

Damn Trevor. Damn him for putting this woman in the position to have to choose.

"You helped him before. Can't you keep helping him?" Lynette gazed at her sleeping son, tears dripping from her eyes and landing on his cheek. He stirred in his sleep, lifting one hand to wipe away his mother's tears.

"Not long-term. He needs close monitoring and frequent doctor's visits."

"I can't afford that. You know I can't."

"There are programs that can help you. People who would help you."

Lynette looked up. "Like you, I suppose?"

"I would."

She shook her head. "If we get out of here, you're gonna press charges against Trevor."

"If we escape, I don't know that anyone will be able to track down Trevor for a long, long time." She knew he wouldn't stick around to face the law. One thing the members of the Blue Ridge Infantry had gotten very good at was disappearing when the heat was on.

Lynette's face crumpled. "I know you can't understand this, but I do love him."

Nicki put her hand over Lynette's. "I do understand. I know what it's like to love someone difficult."

"Are you in love with Del?" Lynette asked.

Nicki's gaze snapped up to meet hers. "No."

"But you have a man, don't you?" Lynette's mouth curved a little, the expression driving away some of the haggard lines from her facing, hinting at the pretty young woman she must have been when Trevor Colley made her his bride. "A woman as pretty as you are. Is he difficult, too?"

An image of Dallas's face flashed through her mind, and she felt the keen ache of longing. What must he be thinking right now? She should have been home ages ago. Was he starting to panic? Had he already used her phone to call for help?

What if he tried to find her? It would be just like him to put his neck on the line for her that way, wouldn't it?

But he would be outnumbered. Even if he was in top fighting form—and she knew he wasn't, despite his remarkable improvement over the past few days—he was still at a severe disadvantage. It would be one unarmed man fighting at least two armed men just to get anywhere near this cabin.

"He's very difficult," she admitted aloud. "Stubborn and impossible."

But, somehow, she loved him, anyway.

Oh, God, she thought. *I love him?*

She almost laughed at the sheer absurdity of her bad timing.

"Could you leave him?"

"I left him to come here." She looked at Jason's sleep-softened features and felt her heart squeeze into a knot. "I knew I might never see him again if I took this job. But it was the right thing to do." She looked up at Lynette. "Jason will never have a normal life here. Trevor will never do what it takes to make that happen. You know that, don't you?"

Lynette's lip trembled, but finally she nodded.

"Is there a way out of here without going past Del and Trevor?"

Lynette stared at her a long moment. "We don't have to worry about Del and Trevor."

Nicki met her gaze, confused. "Why not?"

Lynette kissed the top of her son's head and smiled a faint smile. "Because I put enough diazepam in the beef stew I served for dinner to keep them asleep at least a couple of hours."

THERE WAS NO way of knowing how many people were inside the cabin, though over the past hour, Dallas had seen a second man looking out one of the front windows and what had looked like the silhouette of a woman in the same window where he'd earlier seen Nicki. "It's not Nicki," he'd told John confidently. Nicki was taller and curvier than the slim woman whose shadow had passed by the window.

"I think the second man we saw may be Trevor Colley," John murmured. "Nicki's boss at the diner."

Dallas frowned. "She never mentioned he was connected to the BRI."

"Maybe she didn't know."

"Did Quinn?"

John's face turned toward him, his eyes glinting in the dark. "If Quinn had known, he'd have told her."

"Come on. Quinn was a former spook. You think you can trust a former spook to tell you everything you need to know?"

For a second, John's teeth gleamed in the low light.

Well, hell, Dallas thought. "You're a former spook, too, aren't you?"

"Not for nearly as long as Quinn," John answered, still grinning.

Dallas supposed it was probably a good thing that John knew a few sneaky spy tricks, but on the whole, he'd have preferred to have a few extra men on his team.

Well-armed men who knew how to take and hold ground in a fight.

He had to believe Nicki was still all right. Any other option was unthinkable.

Unbearable.

She was the most remarkable woman he'd ever met, a combination of sweetness and fire. Strength and gentleness. Compassion and steel. He had no idea if he deserved a chance to make her his woman, no idea if he was worthy of being her man, but he damned well intended to find out.

Which meant he had to figure out a way to get her out of that cabin to safety.

"I think we're down to just two men, a woman and Nicki," he said quietly. "They're armed, but so are we."

"They probably have multiple weapons at their disposal," John warned.

Dallas nodded. "But we have surprise."

John slanted another curious look his way. "You have something in mind, don't you?"

"This isn't the place where they kept me when I was their prisoner before. But it's a lot like it."

"So?"

"So, maybe this cabin also has an underground cellar where they keep prisoners now and then."

"You think that's where Nicki's being kept?"

"Maybe. Or maybe, if it's like the one where they had me chained up before, it has both an outside and an inside access point."

"You mean if we could find the outside door to the cellar, it might give us a way to get inside the house."

Dallas nodded. "Exactly."

"They'll hear the door opening."

"Unless they're busy doing something else. Like, say, checking out the distraction going on at the front of the cabin."

John's eyes narrowed. "I'm guessing I'd be the distraction?"

Dallas shrugged one shoulder. "Nicki knows what I look like. She doesn't know you. She might not trust you at first, and that would slow everything up too much."

The other man's lips flattened, but he nodded for Dallas to follow him toward the back of the cabin. "So let's find out if that cellar exists."

The grass was high behind the cabin, dry from the winter but overgrown, as if they'd not bothered to mow it down after the summer growth. With spring just around the corner, the danger of stirring up hibernating snakes in that overgrowth hovered at the back of Dallas's mind as he edged out into the open, staying low to the ground and moving slowly through the grass in search of—

He almost tripped over the door set into the ground near the back edge of the clearing. Dead leaves hid most of the wood-slat door from view, but the hasp that held it closed glinted in the wisps of moonlight visible through the clouds scudding across the night sky.

There was a padlock looped through the hasp closure, which would keep it from opening easily from inside. But the lock itself wasn't engaged. As quietly as he could, Dallas unthreaded the padlock from the hasp and laid it aside in the high grass.

He looked up to find John Bartholomew watching him from a few yards away, his eyes barely visible over the waist-high grass. Dallas gave a nod, flashing a brief smile of triumph.

John's nostrils flared for a moment, then he edged over to where Dallas crouched. "Get in there, make sure the cellar is clear and see if there's a door to the inside. Then come back and report."

Dallas stared at the other man for a long moment, realizing how easy it would be for John to double-cross him if that was his intention. Once Dallas was inside the cellar, John could simply put the lock in the hasp and shut it. Or jab a sturdy stick in the hasp to keep it closed for that matter.

Of course, if John had wanted to double-cross him, he could have shot him dead at any point on this crazy search for Nicki, couldn't he?

He had to trust someone. Nicki's life was at stake, and no matter how much he might wish things were different, this was one rescue mission he couldn't pull off by himself.

Taking a deep breath, he opened the cellar door, wincing as the hinges creaked a little. Hopefully, the sound hadn't carried inside the cabin.

"Cover my back," he whispered and eased himself onto the stairs barely visible through the open doorway.

"Take this," John said, holding something out to him. It was a key chain, Dallas saw, with a small flashlight attached. He closed his hands around the keys to keep them from rattling and nodded his thanks, then headed down the steps.

The cellar was pitch-black and musty smelling once he got to the bottom. He listened a minute for any sound of habitation. There was the faint scuttle of something small and probably rodent somewhere within the cellar's dank confines. He turned on the flashlight, hoping whatever he'd heard had already scurried out of sight.

The cellar was smaller than he'd anticipated. He felt the first smothering sensation of claustrophobia, a sensation that only intensified when the flashlight beam swept over a set of shackles bolted to the wall.

A flood of dark memories nearly paralyzed him, but he forced himself to breathe deeply and slowly, concentrating on keeping his pulse steady. After a moment, the dizzying slideshow in his mind faded away and he moved forward into the cellar.

There was a steep set of steps at the other end of the room, leading up to a door at the top. He tested the first step carefully. It was sturdier than he'd anticipated, not even creaking beneath his weight.

He eased up the stairs until he reached the top. With great care, he tried the door handle. It turned in his hand, unlocked.

Okay. Okay, then.

He backed down the steps and crossed to the outdoor hatch, gazing up at John's face peering over the edge. "The inside door is unlocked. Give me a diversion in two minutes and I'll get in there and get Nicki out."

John gave a short nod and moved out of sight.

Dallas retraced his steps to the top of the other set of stairs, willing himself to remain calm.

LYNETTE CAME BACK into the room, her eyes bright with a blend of fear and excitement. "They're both asleep. But we gotta be real quiet. They're not unconscious. Just sedated."

Nicki nodded, tucking Jason more snugly in her arms. "Is there a back door?"

"Yeah, but it creaks real loud when you open it. That could wake one of 'em."

Damn it. "We can't go out past them, can we?"

"There's the cellar," Lynette suggested, nodding for Nicki to follow her. "It has an outside exit."

Praying the movement wouldn't wake the sleeping little boy, Nicki shifted his weight to one hip as she followed Lynette into the darkened hallway. To the left, she saw dim lamplight filtering into the hall from the front room where Del and Trevor were dozing. To the right, there was a closed door.

They reached the door and Lynette started to reach for the knob when there were two sharp cracks of noise coming from the front of the house. Lynette's body jerked, bumping into Nicki and jostling Jason awake.

"Mama?" he cried.

Down the hall, Nicki heard the sound of stumbling footsteps.

"Go!" she growled, pushing Lynette toward the door.

But before either of them could touch the knob, the door swung open, nearly hitting them. Lynette fell back, bumping Nicki into the wall as a man's broad shoulders filled the narrow opening.

Dark, familiar eyes locked with hers. Her heart skipped a beat.

Then Dallas grabbed her. "Let's get out of here."

THE VOLLEY OF FIRE coming from the front porch might have seemed as if it was coming from a small army, but there appeared to be only two armed men defending the cabin.

John pinned them down with a couple of shots from his own pistol, observing them carefully enough to notice they were moving sluggishly, their reactions slow and largely inaccurate.

But even bad marksmen got lucky now and then. One of the wildly aimed shots pinged off the tailgate of the Silverado parked in the yard and sliced a deep furrow through the top of John's shoulder. The fiery pain that quickly followed seemed accompanied by an odd numbness in the arm below it. Not his weapon hand, thank God, but for all intents and purposes, his left arm was currently useless.

He fired more shots and shifted to a new position before they could fire back, trying to angle his way toward the back of the house, where he hoped Dallas and Nicki would be emerging from the cellar at any moment.

Then shots fired from the woods behind him threw his plan into utter disarray.

"WHO ARE YOU?" The slender woman standing between him and Nicki stared at him in shock, flinching each time a gunshot sounded behind her.

"He's a friend," Nicki said, pushing Lynette forward with one hand while holding the crying little boy tightly despite his frantic squirming. "Lynette, take him." She pushed the child into the other woman's arms and looked at Dallas. "Are you okay?"

As the woman she'd called Lynette gathered the crying child into her arms, Dallas caught Nicki's hand, the warm solidity of her skin pressed to his nothing less than a lifeline. He didn't know who this woman and child were, but it was enough that Nicki was trying to help them. That made them his responsibility, as well.

While the sound of gunfire at the front of the cabin seemed to have Lynette's nerves stretched to the breaking point, Dallas took heart from it. It meant John was keeping the other men occupied, at least for the time being. He went up the steps first, then reached back down to help Lynette and the boy climb out of the cellar. Nicki brought up the rear, gazing at him with eyes that looked as shiny and pale as the peekaboo moon.

"Who's doing the shooting?" she asked in a low tone as she let go of his hand.

"You know him as Agent X."

A rattling noise in the dry grass nearby startled Dallas into a crouch. He grabbed the pistol from the holster at his back, looking for the source of the sound. Suddenly John Bartholomew's head rose over the top of the grass, his gaze meeting Dallas's.

"More men coming. I'm going to lead them away. Get them out of here. Use the truck. Don't wait for me."

There was something odd about the way John was holding himself, as if one half of his torso was sagging lower than the other, but Dallas didn't have time to make out any more details before John turned and scurried toward the woods on the other side of the house.

Dallas heard gunfire erupt on that side of the house and realized he had to be on the move.

Now.

He grabbed Nicki's elbow and pushed her toward the woods in the opposite direction, away from where John seemed to be leading their pursuers.

Ahead of them, Lynette was running with more speed than he'd expected a thin, fragile-looking woman her size would be able to muster up, especially burdened with a child on her hip. Dallas glanced at Nicki as they started to race after her. "Watch our backs," he said, picking up speed to catch up with Lynette.

"Always," Nicki called softly after him, her words carried on the cool night breeze.

"Follow me," Dallas murmured to Lynette as he passed her, leading the way through the woods to where John had parked the truck. He knew there would be no time, no chance to wait for John to reach them. He'd told them not to wait, and as much as it went against Dallas's instincts to leave the man behind, he knew he had no choice.

The truck was where they'd left it, just far enough off the shoulder to be hidden from easy view from the road. Dallas unlocked the back door of the extended cab and helped Lynette onto the narrow bench seat. "Buckle him in and try to stay low," he told her as he unlocked the door for Nicki.

By the time he'd reached the driver's door, Nicki had already unlocked it for him, holding out her hand to help him climb in. Not bothering with seat belts for the moment, he started the truck and pulled out onto the empty road, bracing for the worst.

But no gunfire followed them. No armed trucks pulled out in pursuit to run them off the road the way Dallas had been run off the road the last time he'd met up with the BRI.

In fact, for four or five miles, they saw no sign of any other vehicles at all. The emptiness of the road ahead, illuminated by the truck's headlights, evoked an eerie feeling of isolation in the pit of Dallas's stomach, as if the four of them had escaped an apocalyptic disaster only to find themselves the last people left on a desolated earth.

When he first heard the engine noise, it was almost a relief. Until he realized it was moving closer—and louder—at an impossible rate of speed. As it neared, the sound became more distinct, the heavy *whump-whump* of spinning rotor blades unmistakable.

The noise became deafening and then the helicopter came into view, impossibly close to the ground, and settled about three hundred yards down the highway in front of them.

Dallas just had time to bring the truck to a stop short

of the whipping rotors. He turned to look at Nicki. She met his gaze, her eyes wide and afraid.

The sudden appearance of the helicopter had at least stunned the crying child into silence, Dallas thought as he glanced back to see both mother and child staring at the spectacle through the windshield with slack mouths and startled eyes.

Movement in the periphery of his vision caught his attention, and he peered through the windshield to see a man illuminated in the truck's headlights. He was bent low, beneath the downdraft of the spinning helicopter rotors, but Dallas could make out a head full of sandy brown hair and the faint shadow of a goatee covering the man's chin.

Beside him, Nicki started to laugh. He looked at her, wondering if the stress of the day had finally gotten to her.

She grinned at him, nodding toward the man approaching the truck.

"That," she said, "is how Alexander Quinn makes an entrance."

Epilogue

"We haven't located John Bartholomew yet."

Nicki opened her gritty eyes and saw Alexander Quinn standing in front of her, holding out a steaming cup of coffee.

"Which means you haven't found his body, either," she said, wishing she felt as optimistic as her words would suggest. But she'd seen enough battles in the war between the Blue Ridge Infantry and their enemies to know that the lack of a body didn't always mean a death hadn't occurred.

"If he's alive, he'll find a way to get in touch." Quinn sat on the edge of his desk in front of her, nodding toward the door to the hallway. "I think they're nearly done with Cole."

"They" were a small group of US congressmen who'd agreed to meet with Dallas on neutral ground, which was how Quinn described the conference room at The Gates. The security firm's offices were located in a slightly shabby old Victorian house in the heart of Purgatory, Tennessee, as unlikely a setting for a high-powered security firm as Nicki could imagine.

Nicki herself had undergone questioning by the FBI soon after she arrived in Purgatory, but somehow Quinn had managed to keep the feds away from Dallas until he could set up the meeting with the congressmen who were looking into the troubling suicide of an FBI assistant director named Philip Crandall.

"They're not sure it's suicide," Quinn had confided to Nicki when he told her about Crandall's death.

"What do you think?"

He'd shrugged. "It could go either way."

She pushed up from the chair, stretching her legs. She slept the past two nights at the office, in one of the six dormitory rooms housed in what used to be the mansion's basement. She had no idea where Dallas had spent those nights, as Quinn had separated them the minute the helicopter touched down on the helipad they'd constructed atop the hardware store down the street, much to the chagrin of Nicki's cousin Anson and his wife Ginny, who lived in the loft apartment just below the new helipad.

Anson and Ginny had greeted her warmly, reminding her that no matter how alone she sometimes felt, she wasn't without people who cared about her. She had Anson and Ginny.

She hoped she had Dallas as well, but it would be nice to finally get to talk to him.

"I know you can't tell me where Lynette and Jason are, but have you heard anything from them? Is Jason okay?"

Quinn's features softened, just a notch. "They're both fine. The doctors treating Jason believe he will respond well to regular treatment, and they're making sure Lynette knows how to help provide it."

"And Trevor can't get to them?"

A strange look came over Quinn's face.

"What is it?" Nicki asked.

"Trevor is dead."

Nicki sat again, the news catching her by surprise. "How?"

"The investigators believe Del McClintock shot him, then fled."

She pressed her hand to her lips, remembering the man she'd worked with for a couple of months. The man whose secret life had caught her completely flat-footed.

"Does Lynette know?"

"Yes."

The door to the office opened. Nicki looked up and saw Dallas standing in the doorway, looking thinner than she remembered. Older.

But alive. Gloriously alive and gazing back at her with fire in his dark eyes.

"I'll go speak with the congressmen," Quinn said as Nicki rose to her feet, her gaze following Dallas all the way in as he crossed to where they stood. Quinn nodded and left his office, closing the door behind him.

For a moment, Dallas just looked at her, his gaze seeming to drink her in. She let her own gaze roam over him, taking stock of the small changes their brief time apart had wrought. He hadn't shaved, his beard dark on his jaw and chin. Her first assessment was right—he looked thinner, giving his features a lean, almost feral appearance.

But his eyes were clear and bright, full of an emotion she was afraid to believe. "Are you okay?" he asked.

She almost laughed. "I'm fine. How are you?"

"Tired," he admitted. "Wrung out."

She couldn't stop herself from reaching out to touch him, her fingers rasping on his beard stubble and settling against the side of his neck. "What happens next?" At his slightly puzzled look, she added, "With the congressmen. Do you have to deal with the FBI next?"

"No," he answered quickly. "The FBI is satisfied with my story. Apparently your boss has a great deal of influence within certain agencies of the government. But I'm not going to be able to resume my job with the Bureau."

She hadn't thought he would. "So you're a free agent, then."

"An unemployed free agent."

"Quinn's always looking for smart people. You're smart."

"I'm a graphic designer."

"Who was studying to be a cybersecurity expert."

"Who wasn't finished studying yet."

"We can work on that," she said firmly, stroking his collarbone with her thumb.

His lips curved in a smile. "We?"

She took a step closer, shivering a little when his hands settled over the curve of her hips. "I thought we made a pretty good team. Didn't you?"

He lowered his head until his forehead touched hers. "I did, actually."

"You don't just break up a good team if you don't have to."

He nuzzled his nose against hers, sparking another delicious shiver down her spine. "No, you really don't."

"So we're agreed?"

He drew his head back, looking down at her through slightly narrowed eyes. "Agreed?"

A flutter of alarm darted through her belly. "That we're a team."

"Depends."

"Depends?"

He bent closer again, his lips brushing against the curve of her earlobe. "Do teammates get to kiss?" he whispered.

She turned her head to whisper back. "Among other things."

He pulled back just enough to grin at her. "Never let it be said I'm not a team player." Then he bent and pressed his lips to hers.

She tugged him closer, relishing the feel of his heartbeat thudding a lively cadence against her breast as his kiss deepened, his tongue sliding over hers, claiming her. Cherishing her.

Damned if she didn't suddenly feel like a princess.

Rainbow wings and all.

* * * * *

MILLS & BOON®

INTRIGUE
Romantic Suspense

A SEDUCTIVE COMBINATION OF DANGER AND DESIRE

A sneak peek at next month's titles...

In stores from 11th February 2016:

- **Navy SEAL Survival** – Elle James *and*
  Stranger in Cold Creek – Paula Graves
- **Gunning for the Groom** – Debra Webb &
  Regan Black *and* **Shotgun Justice** – Angi Morgan
- **Texas Hunt** – Barb Han *and*
  Private Bodyguard – Tyler Anne Snell

Romantic Suspense

- **Cowboy at Arms** – Carla Cassidy
- **Colton Baby Homecoming** – Lara Lacombe

Available at WHSmith, Tesco, Asda, Eason, Amazon and Apple

Just can't wait?
Buy our books online a month before they hit the shops!
visit www.millsandboon.co.uk

These books are also available in eBook format!

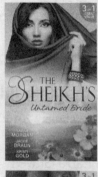

MILLS & BOON®

Let us take you back in time with our Medieval Brides...

The Novice Bride – Carol Townend

The Dumont Bride – Terri Brisbin

The Lord's Forced Bride – Anne Herries

The Warrior's Princess Bride – Meriel Fuller

The Overlord's Bride – Margaret Moore

Templar Knight, Forbidden Bride – Lynna Banning

Order yours at
www.millsandboon.co.uk/medievalbrides

MILLS & BOON®

Why shop at millsandboon.co.uk?

Each year, thousands of romance readers find their perfect read at millsandboon.co.uk. That's because we're passionate about bringing you the very best romantic fiction. Here are some of the advantages of shopping at www.millsandboon.co.uk:

* **Get new books first**—you'll be able to buy your favourite books one month before they hit the shops

* **Get exclusive discounts**—you'll also be able to buy our specially created monthly collections, with up to 50% off the RRP

* **Find your favourite authors**—latest news, interviews and new releases for all your favourite authors and series on our website, plus ideas for what to try next

* **Join in**—once you've bought your favourite books, don't forget to register with us to rate, review and join in the discussions

Visit **www.millsandboon.co.uk**
for all this and more today!